Praise for *The Highlander's Sword*:

"A masterful storyteller, Amanda Forester brings new excitement to Scottish medieval romance!"

—Gerri Russell, award-winning author of *To Tempt a Knight*

"Against the backdrop of fourteenth-century Scotland, the talented Forester has constructed a highly entertaining debut romantic comedy of miscommunications and misunderstandings... entertaining secondary characters and plenty of intrigue keep the reader cheering all the way."

—*Publishers Weekly*

"A radiant gem... If you love stories of Highlanders then you will most certainly love this... such a wonderful story that it invaded my dreams, making me long for a Highlander of my own."

—*Yankee Romance Reviews*

"I loved the richness of [Ms. Forester's] work... the lush and vividly created scenes added to the realism of the story... The narrative is fantastic."

—*Long and Short Reviews*

"Moody, atmospheric Scottish fiction at its best! Amanda Forester makes fourteenth-century Scotland jump off the page and into your imagination with her strong attention to detail and great characterization."

—*Queen of Happy Endings*

THE HIGHLANDER'S HEART

Amanda Forester

sourcebooks
casablanca

Published by Sourcebooks Casablanca, an imprint of Sourcebooks,
Inc.
P.O. Box 4410, Naperville, Illinois 60567-4410
(630) 961-3900
FAX: (630) 961-2168
www.sourcebooks.com

Printed and bound in the United States of America
RRD 20 19 18 17 16 15 14 13 12 11

To my husband, who encouraged me to write, and gave me the time to make it possible. You are my real hero. And for Grandma, who taught me to follow my dreams.

Prologue

Tynsdale Castle, England
Late spring, 1355

THE EARL OF TYNSDALE HOVERED NEAR DEATH, AND not a soul wished him to linger. Simon lounged in a chair by the bedside of his dying father, his long legs stretched out before him. The old man moaned and gasped for breath. Simon was hopeful for a moment, but the earl continued his rattled breathing. Hellfire but this was dull.

Simon had been waiting for his father's death for weeks now. He'd helped himself to his father's wine, his father's wenches; he was running out of things to do. He was not a man who enjoyed being idle.

Lord Tynsdale's eyes were sunk deep into bony sockets, his dried, sallow flesh hung loose from his face. Simon turned away with disgust. His father couldn't do anything right. He had been a hard man in life, greedy and capricious with his affections. Simon was his bastard son, and his father never let him forget it. The earl would acknowledge Simon when it suited him, deny him when it didn't. The earl wanted to sire a legitimate son, but Simon made sure that never happened. It was just a game they played. The earl denied much to Simon, and Simon returned the favor.

Simon shifted in his chair and took another long draft of ale. Five years ago his father, always the optimist, had taken another young wife with the hopes of yet siring an heir. Simon was forced to take measures into his own hands before his father could get the wench breeding. As a result, the young Lady Tynsdale had fled back to her home at Alnsworth, and his father had been at war with Alnsworth ever since.

But now the lady's uncle had died, leaving Alnsworth Castle to her, and thus to her husband. Since Tynsdale would soon be departing this earth, Alnsworth would revert to Lady Tynsdale. If she were to learn of Tynsdale's death and marry another, Alnsworth Castle and its surrounding lands would be given to some other lucky bastard.

Simon stood and took another deep swig. No, he would not allow that to happen. His father's lands and holdings, including Alnsworth, would be his. Whatever his father had denied Simon in life, Simon would steal from him in death.

"Page!"

A young lad burst into the room and stood at lock-kneed attention.

"Send a messenger to Alnsworth Castle to summon the Lady Tynsdale to present herself. Her lord demands her presence at once."

The lad bowed and scurried from the room. Simon fell back into his chair, the wood squeaking under his weight. He would take care of the problem of Lady Tynsdale.

The earl moaned and gasped again. Simon rolled his eyes. How long could it possibly take for this bag of bones to die? Simon fingered a pillow by his father's side. Perhaps it was time to hasten things along...

One

Northumbria, England
Late spring, 1355

ONE THING WAS PERFECTLY CLEAR; IT WAS TIME TO get rid of her husband. Isabelle, Countess of Tynsdale, tightened her grasp on the saddle and continued to plot ways to end her marriage, for if she ever was returned to her husband, she would die.

Unfortunately for her train of thought, her tall mount moved with a swaying motion Isabelle found disconcerting. She had imagined riding a horse would be delightful, but now, perched on top of the stiff, boxlike saddle, Isabelle was reevaluating her opinion of horses.

"You must not let him take you back," said Marjorie, Isabelle's former nursemaid and companion who rode next to Isabelle on the dusty road. It was an unnecessary reminder. Other than trying not to fall off her horse, Isabelle could think of little else but escaping her husband, the Lord Tynsdale.

"I am not going to sit idly by whilst that husband of yours murders you," continued Marjorie. "I have raised you since you were naught but a bundle of swaddling clothes, and I will not be having that old worm take you with him to perdition."

"I have no intention of being my husband's fourth deceased wife. I had hoped to be a widow," said Isabelle with a wistful sigh.

"It would be most considerate of him if he was to keel over dead, but I warrant we cannot expect kindness from the likes of him."

"No, not him," replied Isabelle in a soft voice. She had been married five years ago when she was sixteen, and Tynsdale carried more years than anyone cared to count. She spent one violent night with him before fleeing back to her uncle at Alnsworth Castle. Isabelle rubbed the scar on her temple, the one visible reminder of that dreadful night.

"'Tis a shame having a rat bastard for a husband is not grounds for divorce," Marjorie sniffed.

Isabelle smiled at Marjorie. "Indeed, quite so."

"I hesitate to suggest it, but maybe you could do something to cause your husband to divorce you, like take up with another man?"

Isabelle laughed but shook her head. "I could present Lord Tynsdale with a dozen illegitimate babes and he would never dissolve the marriage. Not when he stands to gain all of Alnsworth. The castle is too great a prize."

"I wish your uncle could have clung to life a little longer."

"I wish I had not inherited Alnsworth." Isabelle shuddered to think of what would happen if Tynsdale ever became lord of Alnsworth. Her uncle had protected her from Tynsdale for the past five years, which had sparked a bloody feud between the two barons. If Tynsdale took control of Alnsworth, his revenge would be felt by all. A heavy mantle of fear wrapped around her shoulders, but Isabelle resisted giving in to the seductive draw of despair.

"I must convince King Edward to dissolve this union," Isabelle said brightly, shaking off her fear. They had left Alnsworth that morning to travel to the court of the king of England. Isabelle smiled at the prospect of going to court and meeting King Edward II. For five years Alnsworth Castle had been a safe refuge, but Isabelle longed for freedom.

Isabelle took a deep breath of fresh air, untainted by the smells of castle life. Granted, the smell of horses figured prominently, but the aroma was at least different, if not completely fresh.

The procession of horses was unexpectedly called to halt. On the road ahead, her entourage had been stopped by a group of soldiers riding toward them. It was a bright, sunny day and the hard-packed dirt road bordered a grassy field to her right and a tall forest to her left.

Her captain of the guard rode forward to meet with the lead rider. After a short exchange, both men dismounted and continued to speak with each other. Small in stature, the stranger was as wide as he was tall, a contrast to Captain Corbett, a tall, broad-shouldered man with a thick mustache.

"What is this about?" asked Marjorie.

"I have no idea," answered Isabelle. Captain Corbett turned toward her with a grim expression. "But I fear it is not in my favor."

Rounding the bend, the rest of the approaching party came into view. Mounted guards were followed by a small troop of foot soldiers. Their banner waved bright blue and gold in the sun. Isabelle's stomach churned. They were Tynsdale's men.

"Isabelle!" Marjorie's eyes went wide. Isabelle knew what she was thinking. If she was given to those soldiers she would never get another chance to escape. The small man and her captain walked toward her. She needed to do something—fast.

"Tell them I had the sudden need for privacy. I'll go yonder across the field. Tell Captain Corbett I'll meet him later at the church at Bewcastle. Only..." Isabelle's eyes met Marjorie's. "I do not wish to make trouble for you."

"Nonsense, Isabelle, if they catch you it could mean all our lives." Marjorie leaned toward her, speaking in a fierce whisper. "You are a clever girl, keep your wits and you will do well. Now make haste!"

Marjorie slapped the rump of Isabelle's horse. Isabelle swung the reins and dug in her heels, something she had never before attempted. Her horse jumped and skittered sideways, then bolted into the field. Isabelle hung on for dear life, thrilling in the speed and her newfound freedom. She risked a backward glance. The guards were speaking heatedly with Marjorie and Captain Corbett but had not yet given chase. She had a head start. Isabelle bounced across the field relishing her swift mount, the sun on her face and her last-minute reprieve.

Without breaking his stride, her horse bolted into the thick forest on the other side of the field. Isabelle shrieked and ducked to avoid a low-hanging branch. She abandoned the reins in favor of holding onto the saddle with both hands.

"Ease up!" she called to her errant mount. Despite her desire to put distance between herself and Tynsdale's men, she did not care for being splattered against a tree. "Stop, oh stop, you vile creature."

The vile creature in question did not stop and, being a sturdy mount with fresh legs, continued to run. Isabelle grabbed at the horse's mane and screamed at the horse to no avail. If anything, her mount gained speed. Isabelle closed her eyes and gripped the pommel, hoping the horse would not stumble or collide with a tree.

After what seemed like an eternity, her well-conditioned horse began to break his stride and settled into a jarring trot. Isabelle gritted her teeth, sure the wretched beast had chosen this pace to cause her the most discomfort.

Thick foliage brushed against her, scratching her face, arms, and legs. The road where she had last seen Tynsdale's men was now miles behind her. Her reins were caught on the bridle, and she leaned forward to reclaim them. The horse, sensing her movement, broke into a run, heading straight for a stream. Galloping closer, Isabelle realized the stream was a wide river, swollen from the spring rains.

"Stop! Oh, why will you not stop? Can you not see there's a—" Isabelle's words were stolen with her breath as the horse plunged into the icy water. She clung with desperation to the saddle. The horse splashed forward into the swiftly moving waters. When the horse began to swim, Isabelle feared for her life. It would be so disappointing to escape certain death, only to be killed later that same day by one's own horse. Isabelle clung tighter with icy fingers and fiery determination.

They were swept downstream a good ways before the horse struggled to the far shore and fought its way up the bank. Isabelle hugged the neck of her horse as her mount continued to trot along. Afraid to reach again for the reins, Isabelle contented herself to watch the scenery until her mount finally stopped and put down his head for a bite of grass.

"Oh, finally," Isabelle muttered and slid down the side of the horse, landing in an undignified heap. Isabelle collapsed in the grass, reveling in the wondrous feeling of being on solid ground again. Taking a deep breath, she regained her feet. Tugging at the ties of her wet, wool cloak, she pulled it off and tossed it over the saddle.

"You are a very ill-mannered beast," she reprimanded her mount. "When we get to wherever we are going, I shall ask their cook to serve me some horseflesh stew for supper." The bay horse looked up from his meal. "I shall have your tail made into a flyswatter and your hooves carved into ink wells." The horse turned his head and looked at her with big, brown eyes framed with long, black lashes. Too late, Isabelle noted a flash of intelligence.

"Nooooo!" Isabelle shouted as the horse trotted away. "I didn't mean it. I would never do anything like that." Isabelle ran after her mount. "Come back, oh, please don't leave me. I lost my temper, but it has been a trying day. Oh, please do come back!"

Isabelle ran until every gulp of air burned and her sides stung. Unable to continue, Isabelle doubled over panting, her hands on her hips, watching her horse's disappearing backside. She collapsed on a large rock and evaluated her situation. She was lost somewhere along the border between England and Scotland. Her horse was gone. She had no provisions, not even her cloak, and she was still damp from the river. Not good.

On the bright side, she had escaped her husband's guards, and if she could survive this minor mishap she would no doubt live a long, happy, and prosperous life. She smiled to herself and decided not to let a little thing like being lost, alone, wet, and hungry bother her in the slightest.

Isabelle stood tall, shoulders back, chin high, to march back to the river and from there to the nearest town. From there she could arrange transport to Bewcastle... with her coin purse that was in the pocket of her cloak. She twisted her signet rings, trying to think of what to do. Her rings were her only material possessions now, one on each hand. Tynsdale was on her left and Alnsworth on her right. Her two worlds at war. Twisting off her rings she deposited them safely in the pocket of her gown. It would not do to lose them.

Isabelle marched forward in the direction she thought was the river, ignoring the unpleasant way her wet chemise clung and chaffed her legs. After two hours walking and no river in sight, even she had to admit she was lost. All the trees looked exactly the same. A buzzing sensation in her stomach told her that either she was hungry or starting to panic. She gulped down fear, chose a new direction and strode boldly, telling herself that this was surely the correct path.

Isabelle marched on through the day, trying to find any sort of human habitation. Clinging to the hope that help was near, she pushed her way through thick brush and bramble until shafts of sunlight were no longer filtering down through the trees, a sure sign the sun was low in the sky. Through the fading light she kept moving, hoping that somehow her luck would take a dramatic shift in her favor.

Isabelle's feet were sore and blistered, her gown ripped and tattered, and her long, black hair hung loose, having long since lost her headdress. Her thin veneer of optimism had been scraped away by a thousand clutching branches, and even she had to admit her situation was growing dire. She wanted nothing more than to stop and rest, but feared if she lay down she may never again get up, so she forced her legs to keep moving.

She tore through one more bush and stumbled out onto a wide, empty path. Exhausted, it took her a moment to recognize what she had found—a road. She collapsed to her knees and ran her hands along the hard-packed dirt. The road was rutted and narrow, dense forest on either side, but Isabelle was overjoyed for such a lovely sight. On impulse, she leaned down and kissed the ground.

"There now, what do we have 'ere?"

Isabelle whirled around and stood up so fast her head spun and she stumbled on shaky legs. Three raggedy men were walking down the road toward her.

"Why 'tis naught but a dirty wench," said a thin man in a red cap.

"Looks an ill-used whore at that. Must have been dropped by her last sport," said a portly man with the remnants of his porridge still in evidence on his shirt.

"Been too long for me," said a third man with large forearms and no front teeth. "I dinna care how used she is. I thinks I'll have me a tickle."

Isabelle gasped. Her heart pounded in her chest and she glanced around for her guard to put a swift end to these insolent men. All she saw was uncaring trees. She considered fleeing, but the brush was thick, and her legs were barely holding her up. She straightened her shoulders and tried to appear severe and forbidding.

"You will come no farther if you please. My guard surrounds you. I command you to leave at once."

The three men stopped short, looking around her suspiciously.

"She be English," whispered Red Cap, loud enough for all to hear.

"Yes, English," said Isabelle, hoping that would be a deterrent. Were these ruffians Scots? What were they doing on English soil? "My patience is not without end. If you value your lives you will leave without delay."

The men stopped walking toward her, but they did not leave. Suddenly, No Teeth pushed Red Cap forward, knocking him into her. She struggled to keep upright, and he jumped back from her immediately. The men drew their knives and watched the bushes, waiting for attack. When nothing happened, Isabelle knew her bluff had been called.

"Well now, lassie," smiled No Teeth, "looks to me no one will mind if we enjoy yer company a bit."

"Leave me alone," said Isabelle, wishing her voice had not wavered when she said it.

No Teeth, Red Cap, and Porridge Shirt crept toward her, their knives still drawn. She backed down the road away from her assailants.

"I am not a... a whore," said Isabelle, hating the way the word sounded on her tongue, but not knowing how else to convey the meaning.

"Aye, ye'd only be a whore if we paid ye," snarled No Teeth, "and we dinna plan to pay."

Isabelle faced her attackers and screamed for all her worth. No Teeth leapt for her and she turned and ran with another ear-piercing screech. She was pushed to the ground with such force it knocked the scream from her lungs. Hands grabbed all over her. She spun on the ground and kicked with ferocity, gaining some satisfaction on hitting something solid and seeing Porridge Shirt doubled over in pain.

"There now, hold her lads, while I gets me turn."

Isabelle shut her eyes and screamed again. Her voice sounded much louder and more ferocious than she expected. Surprised, she opened her eyes to find her three assailants had vanished. She closed her mouth, but the horrible noise continued. A cloaked figure rushed past her, nothing but a blur of fury, his battle cry blasting through the trees.

He disappeared into the brush after her assailants and the forest sank into an unnatural silence. Isabelle sat on the dirt road, unable to scream, unable to move. She strained to hear what was happening, yet all was still. Suddenly, a barbarian emerged from the forest before her like some fey creature. Isabelle gasped and covered her mouth with her hands. He was a monstrous beast holding a long sword with both hands, his face obscured in shadow.

And he was half-naked.

Two

ISABELLE STARED AT THE BARBARIAN BEFORE HER. THESE would surely be her final moments on Earth. She tried to think of something worthy of her last thoughts. *I can see his knees.* Isabelle groaned and squeezed her eyes shut. This would never do. Thoughts like that would send her straight to purgatory. She put her hands over her eyes and tried to think of something pious. Nothing but a mental vision of his thighs came to mind.

"No, no, no." She looked up pleading. "Do not kill me yet, I am not ready."

"Sassenach," said the shadowy figure with disgust. "Get up, English, I will no' be killing ye."

He lifted his sword over his head. Isabelle cringed, but the man only sheathed it in the harness he wore on his back. The action should have been comforting, but she could not overcome the shock of his appearance.

He was a tall man with a muscular body, around which he wore some kind of woven blanket. It was belted around his waist and thrown over one shoulder, pinned to a thick shirt. He wore large, black leather

boots, but between the top of his boots and the edge
of his blanket he was naked. She stared at his bare legs.
Strong, hairy, man legs. She had never seen the like.
She swallowed hard.

"I... you... perhaps you require time to finish
dressing?" She cringed at her inane babbling.

The stranger sighed and glanced toward the heavens. "I
am fully dressed." It was more of a growl than a statement.

"But I can see your legs," she blurted, wishing she
had held her tongue.

"And I can see yers," he retorted.

"Oh, merciful heavens!" Isabelle realized her gown
had been rucked up to her thighs. She pushed down
her skirts and struggled to stand. Her face burned from
being caught in such a compromising position and
from the memory of what had almost happened.

"I should thank you," Isabelle stammered, focusing
on smoothing her ruined gown.

The stranger shook his head. "I kenned ye were a
Douglas lass or I woud'na troubled myself. Well, good
day to ye, English."

"Wait! If you please, where am I?"

"You are in Ettrick Forest and the land of Sir
William Douglas."

"The Douglas?" Isabelle gasped. She had been
raised in fear of the Black Douglas. She could still hear
the hushed voice of her nurse threatening the Black
Douglas would come for her if she did not go to sleep
or eat her porridge.

"Aye." The man frowned at her, his eyes piercing
into hers until his face softened. He looked away and
shook his head. Muttering something to himself, he

turned and walked down the road from where he had emerged.

"Wait!" called Isabelle, hobbling after him on sore feet. She did not wish to be left alone again. "I am a bit lost. I... please, sir, could you help me?"

Struggling around the bend in the road, Isabelle saw that the man had reached his horse, which, unlike her own, was standing still, placidly waiting for his master to return.

"Go back to your menfolk, English. And tell them to get off Douglas land. I have no time for trouble today but if I come across them, they shall no' be spared my blade."

Isabelle stammered, trying to find the right words, unsure what to do. He was a Scot. Worse yet, she strongly suspected him of being one of those Highlanders, a wild race of barbarian warriors. Yet he was also the only human being she had seen all day who was not trying to return her to her husband or molest her. She was hungry, lost, and the sun was low on the horizon.

"I have become separated from my party and have walked all day. I would greatly appreciate your assistance."

He pointed toward the dark forest. "England is that way."

"Would you consent to escorting me home?"

"Ye would have me set foot on English soil?" He snorted. "Nay, I winna be throwing away my life just because ye got yerself lost." He sighed and rubbed his forehead. "Och, come on then. I'll see ye to the next burgh."

"But, please, sir, I wish to be returned home. I assure you that you will be well compensated for your time and effort if you would but consent to see me safely home to… um, that is to Bewcastle."

"Have ye a husband in Bewcastle?"

"No!" It was spoken with a bit too much emphasis, but she certainly hoped she would not find her husband there.

"Yer father, then?"

"No."

The man sighed as if trying to maintain his patience. "Where is yer father?"

"Resting with the Lord."

"Have you any man to care for ye?"

It was a question she had never been asked. Standing lost in a strange forest before a strange man, she realized how alone she truly was. She shook her head. "My uncle recently passed away and…" Her voice broke and she pressed her lips together, trying to get control of her emotions.

The man's face softened. He stepped toward her, assessing her person. His gaze traveled down her body and back up, lingering on her face, his eyes catching hers and holding them. He stepped closer until he stood directly before her. Isabelle's mouth went dry.

He was a large, solid man, with a sword as long as she was tall. He reached out to touch her shoulder, stroking his hand down the length of her arm, her skin burning at his touch. "Let me hazard a guess. Ye were distraught. Ye had no one to care for ye. Some ne'er-do-well came along, made a lot of promises, gave ye this old gown, and ye took up wi' him, but it dinna go well."

"No!" Isabelle recoiled with indignation. "I am not... I would never..." *I am the Countess of Tynsdale!*

Isabelle held her tongue to consider the outcome of her confession. First, he would probably not believe it, considering her state. Second, if he did believe her, he would most likely do what any Scot would do, hold her for ransom and return her to her... *husband.*

"I did not..." Isabelle struggled to find some explanation for her being in the woods alone that did not make her a countess or a woman of ill repute. "Whilst I was traveling, my horse bolted, and I got lost."

"Where is yer horse?" He folded his arms in front of him, clearly not believing her.

Isabelle focused on smoothing her ruined velvet riding gown once more. It had been a beautiful deep wine red; it wasn't anymore. "I lost that too."

She dared to glance up at the stranger once more and found him staring at her intently.

"I want the truth. Who waits for ye in Bewcastle?"

Isabelle tried to think of a suitable answer. "I... my... er..."

"Stop wi' yer lies, Sassenach."

"I have an aunt in Bewcastle! I am going to see my aunt!" exclaimed Isabelle, relieved to have blurted out something sensible.

He leaned closer, forcing her to crane her neck to look up at him. "Tell me the truth for I will ken if ye speak to me false."

Isabelle nodded, her heart thumping hard. What was he going to do?

"Ye dinna have an aunt in Bewcastle, do ye?"

Isabelle hesitated for a moment and shook her head, fearful of what he might do if he knew she was lying.

"Ye are here because of the wrongdoing o' some man."

Isabelle nodded furiously. "'Tis all his fault!"

"I am sure it is. Come wi' me then, I will drop ye at the next burgh. Mayhap they can find a suitable arrangement for ye."

Isabelle was not sure what kind of "arrangement" he had in mind, but she was certain she did not wish to discover it for herself. "No! Please, I must get to Bewcastle. Someone awaits me there."

"Going from one man to another?" The man shook his head, his lips pressed into a thin line of disapproval "I can take ye to the next burgh, but I winna stand here all night. Ye can come wi' me or take yer chances on the road, English."

"I must return to England!"

"Sorry, but I dinna care to have my neck stretched."

"But it is imperative I get to Bewcastle!"

The man shrugged. "Good luck to ye, then. I'm sure yer next conquest will enjoy ye."

Isabelle put her hands on her hips, a hot wave of righteous indignation washing over her. Did he not know that a knight should always help a damsel in distress? He was devoid of all proper feeling. This is what she got for asking a barbarian for help.

"I thank thee for your kind offer to find me an arrangement—is that the word you used?" Her tone was hardly polite but she gave herself some latitude considering the circumstances. "But I prefer to walk back on my own." With as much dignity and poise as she could possibly muster, she walked past him into the forest.

"England is the other way."

Isabelle stopped short. She balled her hands into fists and slowly turned around. Her tall, not-so-heroic Highlander had the audacity to look amused. She *hated* this man. Clenching her jaw, she walked with false confidence to the other side of the road. She held her head high, her back straight, but feared her cheeks burned in evidence to her embarrassment.

"'Tis getting dark, lassie. Night will be upon ye soon."

Without looking back, Isabelle walked with determined defiance into the forest. She had made it this far, she could make it back.

"There be all sorts of beasties in this forest at night," he called after her.

Now that did make her pause, but the thought of being taken farther into Scotland to be settled in an "arrangement" got her feet moving again. She had wished to escape her husband, not the whole of England. True, she had evaded her husband's guards, but being dragged into Scotland by a half-dressed barbarian was little improvement. Even if he did have striking green eyes and long eyelashes. Not, of course, that she'd noticed.

A rustling sound in the brush ahead of her gained her attention. She froze, hoping whatever it was would go away, but luck had utterly abandoned her this day. Concealed by the dense foliage, something snorted and pawed the ground. With a high-pitched squeal, a wild boar emerged from the brush.

Isabelle gaped at the beast, her heart pounding in her chest. The beast was covered with coarse, black bristles and had two sharp tusks curving out of its pointy snout. Prior to this unfortunate day, the only boar she had ever seen had been as God intended, dead and roasted with an apple in its mouth.

Isabelle swallowed hard, as if some of those sharp bristles were lodged in her throat. This angry pig was far from being supper. The beast pawed the ground and snorted, steam rising from its warm breath in the cool dusk. Isabelle stood as still as a statue, hoping it would not notice her. Those sharp tusks could tear a person to shreds. The boar grunted again, lifting its snout to the wind.

Suddenly the beast squealed, lowered his head, and charged.

Three

ISABELLE SCREAMED.

She spun, lifted her skirts in both hands, and ran with all her might. A large shape passed her and she screamed again, her lungs bursting. She tripped and fell hard. Behind her the boar shrieked. She grasped at dirt and tree roots trying to stand, panic coursing through her veins.

When at last she regained her feet she swirled around, but all was silent. Trembling, she put a hand on a nearby tree trunk to steady herself and cautiously scanned the surrounding forest. Cloaked in the shadows, was the Highlander. He stepped toward her. His sword was in his hand, its blade dark red. She put her hand on her chest and tried to take a step forward but swayed, light-headed. Her legs would not seem to hold her and a gray fog circled her vision. Bright lights danced before her eyes.

Warmth engulfed her and she struggled to remain conscious.

"Are ye injured?"

Isabelle opened her eyes, wondering when she had

closed them. She looked up into the Highlander's face, so very close to her own. She tried to step back, but her feet were not touching the ground. He was holding her close, his strong arms pressing her to his warm body. She opened her mouth to speak, but for once, nothing emerged. Her skin tingled and she was dizzy again. She must tell him to put her down. She leaned her head on his shoulder instead.

"Where are ye hurt?" He spoke softly and Isabelle's traitorous body melted into his. She relaxed until he started moving his hand down her side to her hip, searching for injuries.

"Oh, stop. I am uninjured. I just tripped and fell," she stammered, the blush spreading like fire across her face.

"Can ye stand?" he asked gently, putting her feet back on the ground.

"Yes, I believe so. Thank you kindly. Most inconvenient time to feel faint."

He lowered her to the ground, but kept a hand around her waist, holding her securely against his solid frame. His eyes searched hers, until she could no longer hold his gaze.

"It must be the shock of it, of seeing the boar, that is," Isabelle rambled, her eyes flickering around, looking at anything but him. "I never knew they were quite so big, nor quite so bristly. They look much nicer roasted, do you not agree? Maybe I am just suffering from lack of nourishment, for I have not eaten since porridge this morning. And I do not think porridge was sufficient for the exercise I have had today."

She put her hand to his warm chest, trying to steady herself. Despite her bold words, a wave of fear passed over her. She was lost and surrounded by monsters. What was she to do now? A single tear rolled down her face.

He dropped his sword and covered her trembling hand with his. "Hush now, 'tis over. The beast is dead."

Isabelle stifled a sob and clung to her protector, wrapping her arms around his neck, her body still shaking from the fright. She took a deep breath and tried to compose herself. "'Tis not only the beast. It has been a horrid day. Ghastly, wretched day." She pressed her face into his shoulder, trying to keep from crying like a small child. He smelled nice for a barbarian.

"I understand." The big man sighed. "My day has no' been going so well either."

"And yet you stopped to save me—twice. I should thank you."

"Indeed ye should."

"I wish I had something to give you to show my appreciation, but I have nothing, I fear."

The man wrapped both arms around her waist. "I woud'na say that."

Isabelle swallowed hard on a throat that had instantly gone dry. "I... I have no..." It occurred to her, somewhat belatedly, that she was in the middle of a forest with a man she did not know holding her close, and the only thing she wanted was for him to be closer.

"Would you accept a kiss as a boon?" she asked, surprising herself with her own boldness. She had been lost in the woods, attacked by highwaymen, and nearly gored by a wild boar, all valid justifications for this shocking lapse in propriety.

"Aye." His green eyes smoldered.

With some hesitation, she gently pecked his cheek with her lips. He frowned.

"You do not appear to like my kiss," said Isabelle, frowning herself.

"I dinna ken ye would kiss like my Aunt Edna, God rest her soul. She used to pinch my cheeks to keep me from running and give me a peck like that. I warrant if I saved good ol' Edna from a boar, even she might find a wee more passion."

Isabelle could not suppress a smile. "I do apologize for kissing like Aunt Edna. How dreadful."

"We'll ne'er speak o' it again. And to show ye how forgiving I can be, I'll give ye another chance."

Heat crawled up the back of her neck. She was acutely aware of all the parts of her that were touching all the parts of him. Very wrong. Very nice. She went up on her toes and lightly gave him a peck on his lips.

"Thank ye, Edna."

She scrunched her nose. "I am not your sainted aunt."

"Then stop acting like it."

She grabbed either side of his head and smashed her mouth to his. She came away breathless. It was the single boldest thing she had ever done with a man. "There! Not Edna."

He looked up at the sky, considering. "Better, I grant ye. But still with an Edna quality."

"Oh! You are a wretched man to say so! Pray tell, how would you give a kiss?"

He smiled at her, his eyes gleaming. "Since ye have asked, I will give ye some instruction." He leaned down and brushed his lips across hers, soft and tempting. He kissed her sweetly on her lips, while massaging his hands up her back to her neck. It was achingly good. She arched back into his touch and a small *ahhhh*, escaped from her lips. He kissed her again, caressing her open mouth with lips and, shockingly, tongue. She had not known such a thing was possible and leaned into the kiss, the rest of the world slipping away.

When their lips finally parted, she took several short breaths, trying to remember who she was and what she was doing.

"Not Edna," she said, stepping back from him, trying to regain some composure.

"God rest her soul." He made the sign of the cross.

"Sainted woman she was." She also made the sign of the cross. He raised an eyebrow. "To tolerate you, she must have been."

He picked up his sword with one hand and held out his other to her, leading her back to the road. "Ye're no' much o' a lightskirt, though ye look like one."

Isabelle tried in vain to smooth the wrinkles from her gown. "It has been a trying day, but I can hardly look as bad as that."

"Yer hair is loose."

Isabelle winced. No decent woman traveled unaccompanied with loose hair. Little wonder everyone thought she was public property. "A tree got my veil."

"Ye ought to have fought harder for it. Ne'er let yerself be bullied by a sapling."

"It was a large tree and I was on horseback and I could not make the dreadful beast turn around and..." She noticed he was laughing at her. "You are making a jest of me."

"Aye, lassie."

She stopped and put her hands on her hips. "I warrant you have younger siblings."

"Aye, verra good."

"I pity them."

"I will send them yer regards. Come wi' me, lassie. I'll set ye at the next burgh." He pushed through some thick brush to reach the road.

Isabelle hobbled after him, deciding she would do better to stay with him, at least for the night. Tomorrow she could try again to return to England. No more forest beasties for her this night.

Loud shouting got her attention and she hustled through the brush to find her Highlander standing in the middle of the road yelling at the disappearing figure of the man with the red cap riding the Highlander's horse down the road. Though he spoke a foreign tongue, Isabelle had no need for translation to have a basic understanding of what the warrior was shouting at the horse thief.

The large man stood in silence, watching the dusty cloud left by his stolen horse waft into the light of the setting sun. Isabelle fingered her dress, wondering what sort of expression he might be wearing. She doubted she wanted to know. Surely he would not blame her for the incident... would he?

"How many attacked ye?" the Highlander asked, without turning.

Isabelle gulped at being addressed. "There were three, No Teeth, Porridge Shirt, and Red Cap."

The hulking shape in front of her cursed again in some foreign tongue. Well, she guessed it was cursing; it sounded very angry.

"I only got two of them and now yer Red Cap has stolen my horse," shouted the barbarian, still not turning around.

Isabelle glanced at the forest, wondering if she might do better to take her chances with the beasties. The Highlander turned slowly and Isabelle clenched her velvet gown. His eyes blazed. Any trace of gentleness or compassion was gone. He strode toward her, shouting more in his unknown language. Isabelle stood her ground, more because she was frozen in fear than due to any abundance of courage.

Isabelle made an unfortunate shriek when he reached for his sword. The man stomped past her to the brush by the side of the road and attacked the foliage with abandon. Isabelle was flooded with a mixture of horror and awe as he hacked at the brush with enraged vengeance, bits of twig and branch flying every which way. When the leaves finally settled, the square-shouldered man stood panting for a moment, then sheathed his sword and turned to her. She was startled by his calm appearance.

"We'll rest here for the night," he said in a mild tone, but Isabelle could still see the veins bulging in his forehead. Isabelle followed him into the clearing he had just made, walking slowly and giving him a wide berth. She did not wish to disrupt the perilous calm.

Isabelle sighed contentedly. She took another bite of roast pork, though her belly was already full. She had not quite realized how hungry she was until her Highlander rigged up a spit and started roasting part of the boar. Despite her irritation at this Scot's presumption regarding her morals, she had to admit he was a fine camp cook. He had a large fire roaring, a fine roast of wild pork, water from a small stream, and he had even fashioned a comfortable bower for her bed with the brush he had so aggressively hacked.

He had spoken very little to her, focusing on his work. Occasionally he had barked out orders, but since they were mainly commands like, "Sit by the fire," and "Here, eat this," she was inclined to overlook his tone and comply. She stretched out on her bower, warmed from the heat of the fire and her full belly.

Niggling in the back of her mind was the objection that sleeping alone with a barbarian was hardly an acceptable situation for an English lady such as herself, especially since the barbarian in question believed she was of loose moral character. To be fair, she could not blame him for that assumption, considering her appearance and unfortunate situation. Her behavior toward him after he rescued her from the boar certainly did nothing to dissuade the impression. She wanted to correct his misunderstanding, yet feared if he knew the truth it would only make things worse for her. She focused back on her meal. It would do her no harm to eat and rest before setting out toward England on the morrow.

Worry of what happened between her guard and

Tynsdale's men after she left also frequented her thoughts. Had they fought? What would Captain Corbett do when she did not appear in Bewcastle tonight? She shoved aside those thoughts too. She must regain her strength, for she had a long walk ahead of her.

In the flickering light of the campfire, the Highlander ate his meal in silence, though often she found his eyes on her, causing her temperature to rise. At first she was afraid he would take out his frustration on her, but he was clearly not that sort of man. Then she feared he may take liberties with her person, considering his low opinion of her. But it appeared he was not that sort of man either.

He produced a flask from a small pouch he wore around his waist and took a healthy swig. In the orange glow of the fire he looked rather handsome, for a barbarian, that is. It must have been a trick of the firelight, but his features seemed not quite as harsh as they did in the sunlight.

The man had piercing green eyes with remarkable lashes. His nose was straight, his jaw was square, and when he frowned, which was often, deep worry lines appeared on his forehead. She was surprised that this barbarian was clean shaven and had short, neatly trimmed, brown hair. Who was this man?

The Scot finished his meal and turned his attention to his hip. He pulled up his garment, uncovering a dark line trailing down his outer thigh.

"You are injured!" Isabelle was up and walking around the fire toward him before she could consider the wisdom of the action.

"'Tis naught but a scratch."

Isabelle knelt beside him and examined the cut. "I cannot quite see the extent of it with all this dried blood. Why did you not tell me you were hurt?" Isabelle grabbed the flask from his hand and poured it onto his thigh, washing away the blood and revealing a three-inch gash on his outer thigh.

"Arrghh!"

"Did I hurt you?"

"That was good whiskey, and the only flask I have left o' what Douglas gave me, thanks to ye."

"I am sorry about your horse. I seem to have bad luck with beasts today." Isabelle ripped away part of her chemise, which was not difficult since it was already quite torn, and fashioned a bandage to wrap around the wound.

"In the future, I will take pains to keep ye from my cattle." The Highlander spoke gruffly but made no effort to push her away.

Isabelle bent at her work, covering the wound and beginning to wrap it around his thigh. Halfway around, she realized she would need to move her hands around to his inner thigh to wrap the cloth and paused, unsure of how to proceed. "I've found wounds heal faster and are less likely to fester if they are cleaned and wrapped," she explained.

His green eyes flickered, reflecting the dancing firelight. "A healer, are ye?" His voice was soft.

Isabelle swallowed hard. Heat licked the back of her neck. "Y-yes, at least I was trained to treat common complaints. If the wound was still bleeding, there is a plant to help it to stop. There are herbs for almost any complaint, some to help you sleep, some to ease pain, some if you are bilious…"

The Highlander raised one eyebrow at this, a slow smile creeping on his lips. Isabelle blushed, remembering too late her tendency to ramble when flustered, yet still was unable to curb her tongue. "I've been called to stitch and bind many a wound. The menfolk are always getting themselves hurt one way or another."

He leaned closer, a small movement. "Wi' ye around I dinna doubt it."

Isabelle's mouth went dry. She focused back on her work, slowly wrapping the strip of cloth around his thigh, her hands trembling and uncharacteristically awkward. She accidentally brushed her hand across his inner thigh and he caught his breath. Tying the ends of the bandage, she raised her head, finding his face close to her own. His expressive eyes mirrored her surprise.

"You should be well now," she whispered.

"I thank thee." He leaned closer and kissed her chastely on the cheek. "A boon for ye."

"Thank you, Edna." The words escaped her lips without thought.

The man brushed back her hair from her eyes and kissed her sweetly. She leaned closer into him and he deepened the kiss. She could taste the whiskey on his lips, and wondered if that was the cause of the intoxicating sensation coursing through her.

Behind her the fire popped, casting flaming sparks. He jerked back and reached around her, beating out the burning embers that had fallen on the hem of her gown.

He took her hand and helped her to her feet. "Ye are too close to the fire."

Her head spun. She was much too close indeed. She should not speak to him again. "I am sorry... that is... too close, I understand... dreadful losing the horse." She inwardly groaned. She was babbling again.

He gave her a faint smile of amusement. "Not yer fault about the horse. I shoud'na have lost my temper, but I am due in Glasgow for a meeting, and it will be verra bad if I should miss it."

"Am I to know your name?" She blurted the question that had been on her lips all night.

He was silent for a moment, his gaze fixed on her. "I am Sir David Campbell."

"You are a knight, then?"

"Aye. And what shall I call ye?"

"I am the... Isabelle."

"*The* Isabelle?"

"How came you by the honor of knighthood?" Isabelle asked, trying to cover her blunder.

"I was knighted by Sir William Douglas for service rendered to Scotland for ridding Ettrick Forest o' the English."

A slight tingle on the back of her neck gave her a twinge of warning. He said the word English as if it was a curse. Campbell dropped her hand and folded his arms across his chest.

"For the same act," Campbell continued, "yer king declared me a criminal and put a price on my head."

Isabelle sucked in a gasp of air. This Highlander was a wanted man, a criminal. He was her enemy and she would do best to remember it. Isabelle hastened back to her bower. She laid down with her back to him, closed her eyes, and said no more. At first light she would slip away, back to England. She would not be going anywhere with this man.

Four

ISABELLE WOKE EARLY IN THE DIM LIGHT OF DAWN. THE barbarian was sleeping sitting up, his back against a tree, an unsheathed knife in his hands. Even asleep he emanated power. She froze, fearing he would wake at any moment, yet he continued to sleep, snoring slightly. He was not so fearsome without his customary frown. Memories of his kisses warmed her even in the morning chill. In the gray light of dawn, she concluded Sir David Campbell was the most attractive man she had ever seen. How she could have thought otherwise was a mystery.

It was a shame to have to leave him, but she must return to her people. She moved very slowly, taking care to be silent with each movement. With considerable stealth born of fear, she crept from the camp. She was not sure if he would stop her, but waking him posed too great a risk.

Several yards from camp she paused, trying to decide which way to go. She could follow the road, but Campbell had indicated it did not lead to England. On the other side of the road was a small hill. She decided to climb it to see if there was another road that might lead her back toward England. At the top of the rise she could still not see beyond the thick foliage. If only she was taller, she might be able to see above the bushes and small trees.

A large boulder caught her eye and a moment later she was scrambling up it, ignoring the painful sound of ripping velvet. She had been a tree climber in her youth, before someone decided she was old enough to leave the nursery and become a lady, thus ending her amusements in life.

Standing on the boulder was better, but still her view was obstructed. A low-hanging branch provided a tempting option and she took it, hoisting herself up into a tree. Now she had a clear view of the surrounding area. Below her was the road she had found yesterday, and beyond that was another road, which might suit her purpose of returning to her country.

She was engaged with trying to find a path to this road when she noticed something else. A line of men leading horses were tracking through the forest in her general direction. At first her hopes soared, thinking it must be her captain, come to rescue her. She was disabused of this happy notion when the men stepped into a clearing, and their livery became clearly visible. They were Tynsdale's men.

Isabelle gasped and leaned forward, hoping that perhaps she had been mistaken. She was not. Careful scrutiny confirmed they were indeed her husband's guard come looking for her.

At once she felt the deprivation of her genteel

education, which did not afford her with such language as she now felt necessary to convey her true feelings. She envied Campbell, for in his darkest moment he had not appeared to suffer from a loss of words.

What with leaning forward to see her tormentors drawing nearer, and her idle musings on her lack of vulgar vocabulary, she lost hold of the branch and slipped forward with a shriek onto another one a few feet below. She swung forward, her feet dangling in the air. The branch was not sufficient for her weight and it bent down at such an angle that she lost her grip, and fell to the ground, a mere few feet away. She landed in a heap, panting and shaken, but unhurt.

"Bother!" she exclaimed, and knew it to be a woefully inadequate expression of her current wretched situation. Throwing off all propriety she lifted her skirts in both hands and raced down the hill, ignoring the sting and scrape of branches as she ran. She must fly or risk being taken prisoner.

Her only hope now was in throwing herself on the mercy of a barbarian Scot. Truly, not even one proficiently schooled in the art of foul language could have the words to describe this sad circumstance.

But... what if he was gone?

❧

David Campbell regained his mount after a brief but decisive altercation with the knave who had stolen his horse. He had heard Isabelle leave early that morning, and considered trying to stop her, but let her go. He had offered his help. If she chose not to accept it, the better it was for him. He was already behind schedule and taking up a female would only slow him further.

After she left, he followed the trail left by the horse thief. Fortunately, he found the thief had made his own camp about a mile away. Unfortunately, the thief had helped himself to the whiskey Douglas had given him. If stealing his horse had not already inflamed Campbell's anger, drinking his whiskey sealed the thief's fate.

Astride his mount, Campbell turned toward Glasgow. The dark road stretched out before him, still cast in the shadows of early dawn. He ought to move fast, for he was already late. He turned back to where he had made camp with the little English vixen. He had offered his help. She had refused it. He had no obligation to help her. And yet he was plagued by memories of her kiss, warm yet innocent. He could not shake the impression that there was more to her story than had been revealed. She was in trouble, that much was clear. Good thing it was none of his concern.

Campbell had enough female trouble of his own. His visit to Douglas, his former foster father, had been brief. He had ducked some rather pointed questions from Lady Douglas as to the timing of his nuptials with her daughter, replying that he still mourned the loss of his father. His sire had died last fall, and this being spring, the excuse was growing a bit lame. Campbell cited urgent business at one of his holdings and left the castle with some haste.

It was not that he had anything against Eileen Douglas, except that she was a shrew with a shrill voice and a haughty laugh, but that was hardly a consideration. An alliance with Douglas would be a highly desirable thing, but other alliances and loyalties must be taken into account. Rumblings of discord were in the air, whispers of treason and preparation for war. It was a dangerous, lawless time in Scotland.

A man waited for him in Glasgow. Campbell dreaded the meeting, but it must be done. He needed the information to make a difficult decision. Though Campbell had traveled with his brothers for most of his journey, he had separated from them for this last task. For this meeting, he must go alone.

Campbell rubbed the linen bandage around his thigh. It was not his fault Isabelle was alone in Ettrick Forest. He had no responsibility for her. He had already saved her twice, what more could he be expected to do?

Campbell rubbed his head that was beginning to ache. English. They brought nothing but ruination. And poverty. England had held Scotland's King David captive for the past nine years. England demanded a crushing ransom for his release. As laird, Campbell was expected to make large annual contributions, money that could be better used to support his own clan. He had every reason to leave that English piece of baggage on the road where he found her. And yet…

With an audible sigh Campbell spurred his mount and galloped down the road. He pulled up when he reached the point in the road where he had made camp with Isabelle. She was not there. He paused for a moment, listening to the birds singing in the morning. He frowned at his own stupidity. He had wasted his time by returning. He must hasten to make up for lost time.

He turned his horse to leave but stopped short at the sound of a familiar shriek. With a loud rustling Isabelle skittered onto the lane in front of him. She looked up at him, wide-eyed. Her long, silky, black hair was disheveled, and her red cast-off gown was torn, revealing more of her lush décolletage than was the dressmaker's original intent. Her appearance was even dirtier and more tattered than the day before, if such a thing was possible.

Isabelle was a wild thing, a fey wood nymph, decorated with twigs and bits of shrubbery. He had never beheld a more beautiful creature. Her dark eyes were large and alluring, her red, full lips matched what her scarlet velvet gown might once have been, and her body was curved in all the right places. He was not a man to take up dalliances easily, especially with a disgraced English miss, but he was sorely tempted.

"Good day to you, sir," she said with a graceful curtsy as if they had met in a ballroom. In a fruitless gesture she tried to smooth her hair and gown.

"Good day." He smiled in spite of himself. She amused him, and precious little in this world did.

"You have recovered your horse!" she exclaimed with sudden recognition.

"Aye."

"That was very clever of you! What did you do with Red Cap?"

"He stole my horse," said Campbell. Further explanation could not be needed.

"Oh. Yes. Well." Isabelle scanned the forest, her brows knit together in apprehension.

"Looking for someone?" asked Campbell, scanning the forest himself.

Isabelle's eyes opened wide. "N-no. I was… lovely day. Where do you go today, sir?"

"I am to Glasgow."

"Glasgow!" Isabelle clapped her hands together as if enraptured with the idea. "I would dearly love to visit that town. It is a town—yes?"

Campbell was suspicious. "Yesterday ye said 'twas imperative ye returned to England and now ye wish to visit Glasgow?"

"Yes! Only I do not wish to keep you. I recollect you said you needed to make haste."

"Why this sudden change in plans? When ye left this morn I believed ye had decided to walk back to England yerself."

"I… yes." She looked into the forest again with growing anxiety. "But I saw something in the forest that made me change my mind."

"These woods are not safe for a woman traveling alone."

"No, indeed they are not. Please let us leave here."

He was a little irked by her concern. What did she imagine would come through the trees that he could not handle? "Dinna fear. I winna let any harm come to ye."

She looked up at him not moving, her large eyes filling with tears.

"Isabelle?"

She wiped away the tears with a quick swipe of the back of her hand. "I beg your pardon. My uncle had the occasion to say the very same words to me many

THE HIGHLANDER'S HEART   43

years ago, but now he is gone." Her voice became quite soft and Campbell's own attitude toward her softened as well. Poor thing. He guessed her uncle's death had left her quite defenseless. If only she was not quite so English.

"Take my hand," he said gently, reaching out to her. She put her hand in his and he drew her up behind him.

"My, it is high up here. What a large horse!" She clung to him tightly enough to squeeze the breath from his lungs.

"Aye," he choked, but did not ask her to loosen her grip. Nor did he ask her to remove her legs, which brushed against his thighs in a most suggestive way. He spurred his horse and galloped away faster than he would have normally done, causing her to press herself to him even tighter.

He decided to let the horse run awhile, shamelessly enjoying the way her body moved against his. He was a veritable knave, but he smiled and spurred his mount faster.

Five

DAVID CAMPBELL SET OUT AT A BRUISING SPEED, causing Isabelle to hold on tight and hope she would not fall to her death. After a while, he slowed to a brisk trot and Isabelle was able to loosen her grip. By afternoon, a new fear had settled upon her.

"When shall we make Glasgow?"

"If we make good speed I hope to be there by tomorrow before the gates close."

"Tomorrow! Oh my, I had thought Glasgow closer than that."

"Ye dinna ken whether it was a town, a loch, or a person. Ye want to tell me why this sudden desire to see Scotland?"

"I did not wish to be left alone in the forest." It was true, if vague.

Isabelle pondered her limited options. She always prided herself in being able to find solutions to problems, though she had been told often enough that being clever was not an endearing quality in a wife. Still, she was going to need whatever wits she had to save herself from her husband's men and return to her own guard, a particularly difficult challenge since she was traveling farther from England with every passing minute.

If only she could convince the Highlander to return her to England. She considered what little she knew of him, searching for weakness. Unlikely as it was for a barbarian, he did feel compelled to rescue her—twice, and even returned after regaining his horse. The first time he may have mistaken her for a Scot, but the other times were sheer chivalry. Perhaps he would be moved by sympathy.

Isabelle bit her lip. What she needed were some tears. She filled her mind with thoughts of doom, imagining what horrors Tynsdale may inflict on her people if she should fail in her efforts to prevent him from taking Alnsworth. That thought alone was enough to make her bottom lip quiver.

The Scot reined in his mount and came to a stop by a small creek. "Time to give the horse a rest." He dismounted with ease and handed Isabelle down. Isabelle seized the opportunity to put her hands on his shoulders.

"Please, sir," she managed a convincing half sob, "please do not take me away, so far from my home." She was pleased when tears spilled from her eyes. "I cannot bear to be separated from my family. Could you find it in your heart to return me to England?" She sniffed and wiped away a tear. She actually had no family left her, but a whimpering homesick lady sounded more pathetic. "Please, will you not show some mercy?" She rested her head on his chest and cried with abandon.

"Ye are verra good, I'll admit, my lady. But I've

seven sisters to me and I've learned to tell the real tears from the fake."

"What!" Isabelle jerked her head up, annoyed. Their eyes met and he gave her a sly smile. "Oh, fine then," she snapped, stepping back from him. "You are a most dreadful man. I hope you know that."

"Aye, so my sisters have said on many occasions."

"How am I to return to England?" she asked, more to herself than anyone.

The Scottish knight shrugged and pointed toward the horizon. "England is that way."

"Do you think I could make it walking by myself?"

"Nay," he replied with brutal honesty.

Isabelle sat on a rock by the creek, trying to work out how she would escape. She accepted the leftover meat and some water with thanks, but still no obvious solution presented itself.

"Is Glasgow a large town?" she asked hopefully after considering and discarding many poor plans.

"Aye."

"Do they trade with England?"

"Aye."

"Mayhap I could go with a trading party back to England?" asked Isabelle, brightening.

"Mayhap," said the taciturn Scot.

"Then that is precisely what I shall do."

Campbell said nothing, but caught her eye and held his appraising look. Isabelle looked away, flushed and confused.

"What is it, sir? Why do you stare at me so?"

"I was wondering when ye are going to tell me the truth."

"I… have told you…" Isabelle stammered, her cheeks burning.

"Nay. Another thing seven sisters taught me is how to tell the truth from a falsehood. Ye may be a bonnie lass, but ye are no' telling me the whole truth."

"I…" Isabelle swallowed hard and thought fast. "The honest truth is I must get to Bewcastle."

"I believe it. I also believe ye would say anything if ye thought it would get ye there."

Isabelle straightened her shoulders and looked him directly in the eye. She would not allow him to shame her. Despite her appearance as an unlucky harlot, Isabelle knew who she was. "You are correct," she acknowledged. "I would do much to return to Bewcastle, though perhaps not as much as you think. There are people who are depending on me. People I care about. Children even. I must get to Bewcastle safely."

"Ye have many children?" he asked, turning away to prepare the horse for travel.

"Oh no! Not my children. Others whose welfare I must consider."

He stopped his work and his eyes met hers with a critical frown. "Who are ye?"

The wind rustled through the tall grass, the birds chattered merrily, but Isabelle held her tongue. Campbell waited for an answer.

"I must get to Bewcastle," Isabelle finally said. She could not tell him the truth. It was too dangerous.

"That is the only thing about ye I ken is true." The Highlander shook his head. "Come on wi' ye. I plan to change horses up the road a ways. Mayhap ye can

pay for passage back to England there. They trade wi'
the borders."

"Thank ye, but I have no coin."

"Aye, I reckoned ye woud'na, but I do."

"Thank you." Relief flowed down her tense
shoulders and Isabelle viewed Campbell from a fresh
perspective. Maybe he was her knight in shining
armor after all.

David Campbell mounted his horse and reached
down to help her up. This time he lifted her up in
front of him. She gasped at the forced intimacy of it.
His arm was around her, and she was sitting mostly in
his lap, her legs over one of his thighs.

"I can ride behind ye," she gasped.

"I am tired o' ye squeezing the life from me."

"I—" Isabelle tried to move away from him, but
it was quite impossible. "I do apologize for squeezing
you, but this must be unnecessary."

"Only if I wish to keep ye from cracking a rib."
Campbell's eyes glinted with mischief and he clicked
to get the horse moving.

"Surely not, sir!" exclaimed Isabelle, resisting the
urge to grab for him when the horse began to saunter.
"Oh, you are jesting with me again."

A faint smile graced Campbell's lips and he held her
securely.

Isabelle attempted to shift into a more respectable
position, holding herself bolt upright and determined
to keep herself aloof. It was not long before the muscles
in her back were cramping from the uncomfortable
position and she was fidgety from trying to hold her
tongue. Silence was not a natural state for her.

With a resigned sigh she leaned her shoulder against him. His chest was very solid and very warm. His arm wrapped around her comfortably and she relaxed into him. She seemed made to fit there. The sun shone bright with promise on the lush green landscape before her. If not for her desperate need to return to England, it would be an enjoyable ride.

"Seven sisters is a lot of sisters," she said.

"Aye, I have always thought so."

"You have brothers too or just the sisters?"

"There are fifteen of us together, seven sisters, and eight brothers."

"My gracious, what a large family you have." Isabelle swallowed down the taste of envy. "I had a sister once, and two older brothers. They are dead now, along with my parents. The plague, you understand, many years ago when I was young. I went to live with my uncle, but he is gone now too." She opened her mouth to say more but instead coughed a bit to cover her mistake of saying more than she ought. At what point had riding through the countryside become a confessional?

"I am sorry for the loss of yer family." He must have noticed the contradiction in her words, first crying for her family, then admitting them to be gone, but he was charitable and let it pass.

"My family was spared the ravages of the plague," Campbell continued, "maybe because we were living far in the Highlands at the time. I was in Glasgow on an errand when it broke out. I chose to stay rather than risk bringing the pestilence home wi' me."

"You were fortunate not to be afflicted."

"Indeed, I was afflicted. I thought I would die, I was sure of it. But then one morn I awoke and the fever had passed." Isabelle felt the muscles in his shoulders stiffen, the worry lines on his forehead creased deeper. "'Tis all forgot now."

Isabelle suspected it was far from forgotten. "Were you the only one afflicted?"

"Nay. I was staying wi' my uncle and cousins. None in the family survived. The whole house was ill and no one was left to call the priest for last rites, not that he would come. That was the worst part, thinking I would go to my grave unconfessed. Then the fever took me and I dinna ken what happened after that. One morning I woke up. I dinna ken how long I had been there. All I can remember was the thirst. It was a powerful thirst. It drove me out of bed and searching for water. I found my kin had all perished but me. Eventually, I made it back home. It was so many years ago now, but I still wonder why I was the only one spared."

She reached up and laid her hand on his shoulder. "What horrors you must have faced."

His eyes slid down to hers. Their eyes held together longer than they should. Ever so slightly he pressed her closer. It was a small movement, the faintest of movements, but her heart beat faster. She should look away, but she did not, could not.

"Forgive me, I never speak of it. I dinna ken what has come over me," said Campbell softly.

"The plague was something terrible. Now it seems no one wants to talk about it. They want to pretend it never happened and get back to life." It was quiet for a moment before Isabelle added, "I still sometimes miss my mother."

Campbell slowly took her hand in his. "Both my parents died last winter. An inflammation of the lungs. First one, then the other. It was… no' what I expected. My father, Laird Campbell, had been poorly for years, and as eldest I had taken over many responsibilities for him. I was no' shocked when he took ill, but my mother was always verra hale. I was surprised at her death."

"I am sorry for your loss."

"I am sorry for speaking of such sad events."

"I do not mind." Isabelle placed her other hand on his chest.

"Sometimes 'tis easier to speak to a stranger than to family," Campbell's eyes met hers.

"You can tell me anything."

He leaned closer and touched his forehead to hers. "What am I to do wi' ye?" he whispered.

"Take me to Bewcastle," Isabelle whispered in return.

Campbell jerked back as if the spell had been broken and focused on the road ahead. "I hope this man in Bewcastle will take better care o' ye than yer previous beau."

Isabelle did not know what to say in response. She played with the idea of telling him the truth, but could not see how it would improve her situation. Men had a habit of thinking women should return to their husbands, no matter what the situation. Isabelle sighed. She believed Campbell to be an honorable man, but she could not risk trusting him.

They continued in awkward silence until a few houses appeared in the distance.

"Is that the town? The place where I may find passage back to England?"

"Aye."

Isabelle leaned forward in anticipation. Campbell was a good man, but perhaps too good at seeing through her lies. She needed to return to England before he discovered who she truly was.

The little hamlet was a small but cozy place. The thatched roof houses were well kept, many with little kitchen gardens planted in neat rows beside the house. Children played happily, and people appeared to be congenially talking with one another or going about their business, at least until Campbell rode into town.

As their presence was noticed, conversations stopped, people stared, and then the roar of fierce whispering began.

"Wish ye had no' lost yer veil," muttered Campbell. He stopped by a small inn with a stable beside it. He dismounted and helped her down. His eyes raked over her and focused on her bosom. "Wish ye had a cloak too."

Isabelle raised a protective hand to her chest and felt skin where there should have been material. A quick glance down confirmed there was much more of her natural assets on display than she would wish. She gave her gown a fierce tug up and was rewarded with the sound of the garment ripping further.

Walking into the inn, they met two people with opposite expressions. The innkeeper was all smiles, welcoming Campbell and Isabelle's breasts, for he never once looked at her face. The woman next to him, whom Isabelle guessed must be his wife, wrung her hands on her apron and regarded Isabelle with narrow eyes.

"She can stay in the stable wi' the other animals," said the woman, pointing a red, pudgy finger at Isabelle.

"Wheesht!" hushed her husband. "Any friend of Campbell's is welcome here." He gave Campbell a licentious wink.

Campbell sighed and rubbed his forehead, the worry lines appearing deeper than ever. "I require a hearty repast and a fresh horse. This young miss has become lost and separated from her escort. She requires safe passage back to England."

"She be *English*?" the woman innkeeper shrieked. Even her husband raised an eyebrow before hustling his wife back to the kitchens. Isabelle swallowed hard, and her stomach took an unhappy roll. She followed Campbell blindly to a table in the corner, keeping her eyes down so as not to see the looks of the other patrons.

The innkeeper returned, spoke quietly to Campbell and provided food and drink to the table. Isabelle ate, but the food was tasteless in her mouth. From the way Campbell shoveled food into his mouth it was clear he was either very hungry or had no desire to linger either.

"I am a God-fearing woman and I'll no' have that English tart served!" The loud rant of the innkeeper's wife in the kitchen could be clearly heard in the main room.

"Hush yerself, woman. If Campbell wants to keep a lightskirt he is welcome to it."

"But he is no' welcome to bring her here. This is a decent inn, Nigel. See her gone!"

The Nigel in question came hustling back to the table, a tight smile on his face. "Is everything well here? Aye? I can see this young thing to the borders myself." He looked down the front of her gown. "Indeed I can."

Isabelle covered her exposed cleavage with a hand and flashed her eyes at Campbell. She wanted to get to Bewcastle, but she feared she would get no farther than the hayloft of the barn with this man.

"We will be traveling on, thank ye for yer hospitality. I require a cloak for the lady."

"Ye go on together? No need. No need. I will care for her, aye, I will."

"She will no' stay. A cloak is what we need."

"Cloak?" The man frowned. "Nay, I have none." He folded his arms across his chest in a gesture reminiscent of a spoiled child not getting what he wanted.

Campbell stood up, towering over the man. "A horse and a cloak." His voice was low and there was an edge to it.

"Y-yes, sir," the man stammered and ran away.

Isabelle stood and put her hand on Campbell's sleeve. "Thank you."

Within minutes Isabelle was clothed in a wool cloak, old but serviceable. Campbell chose a fresh horse to replace the one he left with the inn, and they were on their way. Despite the angry frowns of both the innkeeper and his lady, Campbell lifted Isabelle up into his lap. It was not decent, and Isabelle flushed at being handled such, but it was also a sign of acceptance and she was glad for it.

"Thank you for not leaving me there," breathed Isabelle.

"English. Naught but trouble." His words were hardly comforting, but his tone was soft and his arm around her waist was warm and secure.

The sun was low on the horizon as they continued down the road on their journey. Campbell gently rested her head against his chest. "Get some sleep as ye can. We ride all night."

Isabelle considered protesting but leaned against him instead. The gentle sway of the horse lulled her to close her eyes and wish Sir David Campbell was not quite so much a Scot, and she was not quite so much married.

Six

Dundaff Castle, Scotland

"ROUSE YERSELF, SWEETLING. YE'VE BEEN SUMMONED by Laird Graham."

Gavin Patrick yawned and opened one eye at his mother. "Why?"

"I dinna ken, but it must be important. Lady Graham is wi' him."

"Lady Graham?" Gavin sat up in bed. "What does that auld battle-ax want wi' me?"

"Wheesht now! I've no' taught ye to speak so. We are much indebted to the Grahams and well ye ken it."

"Aye, Mother," said Gavin sheepishly.

Mary gave Gavin one of her no-nonsense, get-your-arse-out-of-bed looks and swept from the room. Gavin grumbled in response, but moved quickly and dressed in some of his finest for such an audience. His mother, Lady Mary, and his stepfather, Sir Chaumont, met him at the entrance to the great hall.

"Ye look verra braw," his mother beamed up at him. "Happy nineteenth birthday, my dearest."

"Thank ye, Mother."

Chaumont clapped him on the back with a smile. "Ready to find out what the old battle-ax has planned for you?" he asked in his faint French accent.

"Chaumont!" protested his wife.

Chaumont gave her a winning smile and a cocky wink and led them into the great hall. The great hall of Dundaff Castle was as impressive as the castle itself. Brightly colored tapestries lined the walls showing vibrant scenes of battles and hunts. On the raised dais, Laird Graham sat in a high-backed chair next to his wife. He was a large man, his round face tanned and wrinkled. He had been a renowned fighter in his day. Many years ago Chaumont, then a landless French knight, had saved Graham's life. In appreciation, Graham adopted Chaumont as a foster son.

"Come, come, my son," boomed the loud voice of Laird Graham. "Many returns o' the day, Gavin my lad."

"Thank ye," replied Gavin and gave a bow to the stout laird of Dundaff Castle.

"Many returns o' the day, Master Gavin," said Lady Graham. She sat beside her husband, drenched in fur.

Gavin was careful to provide his lowest and most dignified bow to avoid Lady Graham's quick temper should she consider herself slighted.

"Well now, Gavin, seems ye've grown to be a man and I'm sure ye've been thinking on taking a wife," said Laird Graham in a jovial tone.

Gavin's breath caught in his throat. He had been thinking no such thing.

"Ye need no' concern yerself anymore, we have made you a most eligible match," continued Graham.

"One of Laird Campbell's own sisters," Lady Graham purred with delight.

"Lady Caitrina Campbell to be exact. She'll be coming soon for the wedding. Are ye no' surprised?"

Gavin stared at Laird and Lady Graham. Surprise could not do justice to his feelings. Married? Now? Campbell and a few of his brothers had visited Dundaff a few weeks ago, but no one had spoken to Gavin of marriage. Had his mother and Chaumont been part of this plot? One glance at their startled faces told him they had not.

Chaumont was the first to recover. "You have surprised us beyond measure."

"Indeed, we have taken great pains to see to yer comfort. Let me assure ye that Lady Campbell comes wi' a generous dowry. I saw to the negotiations myself," said Lady Graham with pride.

Graham gave his wife a broad smile. "Poor Campbell ne'er had a chance against my lady wife."

Gavin knew how he felt. His gaze flitted from Lord Graham to Lady Graham to the tips of his leather boots. It wasn't that he did not wish to be married... eventually. It was just that he had planned to have some adventures first, maybe even choose his own bride.

Lady Graham's smile faded and she gave Gavin a hard look. "Why is the lad silent?" she asked Laird Graham in a loud voice. "Why is he no' thanking us?"

Gavin shot a pleading look to Chaumont. One that hopefully conveyed the message, *Help, save me!*

Chaumont caught Gavin's eye and put his hand on his shoulder. "Thank you for your generosity. But Gavin here is of the MacLaren clan. I warrant we should consult with Laird MacLaren before we settle on the lad's nuptials."

"I have already spoken with my daughter and MacLaren about the matter," said Lady Graham in an arch tone as if they should be grateful she was condescending enough to explain the matter. "She assured me they had made no previous arrangements for Gavin's bride."

"MacLaren told me I need no' trouble myself," said Graham. "But it was no trouble at all for ye, my good lad. He gave permission for ye to wed where'er ye please."

"Yer bride should be arriving in a few days. I wanted to have some time to train her before ye wed," said Lady Graham with a self-satisfied grin.

Gavin gave Lady Graham a shrewd look. It was all becoming clear. Lady Graham was not as interested in a wife for Gavin as in a chatelaine and personal servant for herself. Gavin was determined to get out of this, but how?

"I thank ye both for this most unexpected surprise, but I... but I..." Gavin struggled to find the words he wanted to say without seeming terribly offensive. Despite his reticence, he was not unaware that a marriage into the Campbell family, to one of the laird's own sisters, was quite an eligible match. Gavin had no title and only a modest farm on MacLaren land to call his own. Marrying a Campbell would indeed be an advantageous connection.

"I wish to prove myself, to earn my spurs before I take a wife," finished Gavin. There now, that didn't sound half bad.

"And so ye shall, my lad," said Graham in his booming voice, the smile returning to his face. "And right ye should."

Lady Graham was mollified. "Ye may take a few years if ye like. Lady Campbell will arrive soon. As yer fiancée, she is most welcome to make this her home until ye are prepared to take yer vows."

I warrant ye would. Gavin had evaded an immediate marriage, but a fiancée was just as bad, just as binding. He would have to think of something to get out of it, and to save poor Cait Campbell from the horrible fate of serving Lady Graham.

❧

David Campbell watched the sun rise across fields of swaying heather, bathing the countryside in a warm, orange glow. He held the sleeping Isabelle in his arms and rode on, though his muscles ached and cramped.

Ever since he saved Isabelle on the road, his journey had gone poorly. No, that was not entirely true. Things had gone bad from the moment he saw Laird Douglas and began to dodge questions regarding his nuptials with Douglas's daughter. Campbell still had a difficult meeting ahead of him in Glasgow, so his day had the strong possibility of getting worse. At least he had been able to arrange a good match for his sister, Cait, so his journey was not a complete loss.

Isabelle moved slightly, made a soft mewling sound, and slept on. At least one of them was comfortable. Despite the cramp in his back, Isabelle was warm and soft and smelled like only a woman could smell. Her straight black hair spilled over her sleeping form. She had tried to braid it back, but without a tie it fought for its freedom and flowed free once more. He had been unable to resist the urge to touch it and had stroked its silky length in the dark of night. Though her deep red velvet gown was quite ruined, the fabric was still soft to the touch. His hand rested on her waist and burned with the desire to caress the soft fabric and the woman beneath it.

Who was this Isabelle and how had she come to be alone and ruined on the road to Glasgow? He suspected he had not gotten the full story. Despite some lack of clarity as to her past, one thing was perfectly clear, she was undeniably English. Her regrettable lineage should have put an end to the direction his thoughts had taken. Unfortunately, his body responded to hers in a manner beyond all rational control.

Isabelle stirred again and stretched. Campbell had to hold on tight to prevent her from slipping to the ground. Her eyes flew open. "Where am I?" Isabelle's wide eyes met his. "Oh!"

"Good morn to ye."

"Yes, well. Good morn—is it morning already? Did we not have a brown horse? Have I slept all night?"

"Aye, we had a brown horse; we changed hours ago. And aye, ye did sleep through the night."

"I did? Well, I do apologize. It has been a trying time, I must have been quite exhausted. I hope I did not cause you any trouble carrying me."

"No burden at all," Campbell lied.

Isabelle sat up straight, which should have relieved his aching arm, but instead left him missing her warmth. "How beautiful. The morning sun makes the grasses shine like gold."

Campbell looked out over the fields and indeed they glistened. Isabelle's eyes also shone warm and brown. Her dark eyes were intriguing, enticing him to gaze into them longer than he should. He forced himself to keep his eyes on the road ahead of him. She could never be his.

Even if he was not promised in marriage, he was still the laird to the large and powerful Campbell clan. It was expected, no required, that he form an alliance with a Scot clan. And she would never be anything other than English. Odd that he had to remind himself of this fact. Generally he was reserved with women. As laird, he could not risk having a bastard son to grow up and challenge his rightful heirs. He had to be discreet.

Holding this infernal English bundle on his lap reminded him of just how discreet he had been. It had been long, much too long, since he had allowed himself the comforts of a bedmate. His body screamed with need.

He needed to direct his thoughts to more pressing matters. His sister Cait would be wed soon. And he too must marry. But whom? Somehow he needed to choose a bride... without sparking the clans into war.

"I'm to be married." He had not the slightest idea why he said that.

She turned to face him, her brown eyes warm. "Congratulations. Is that who you were visiting?"

"Aye. The daughter o' Douglas." Campbell frowned, the words feeling rough and awkward in his mouth. And not quite true.

He pulled up short and handed her down to the road. He needed to get her off of his lap before she noticed he was growing friendlier than he ought. She landed hard and turned back to him, her eyes flashing. He was not about to explain the problem.

"Walk, we need to give the horse a rest." Campbell set his jaw and trudged forward. She had addled his brain, it was the only explanation. He needed to be rid of her, but there was no way to return her to England without being drawn and quartered, and no way to set her free in Scotland that would not end most unpleasantly for her.

"Well!" Isabelle spun away from him and glided down the road ahead of him, her back straight, her head high, her ridiculous velvet train following her like a bedraggled puppy.

Seven

CAMPBELL LEANED DOWN FROM HIS HORSE AND
reached for Isabelle. "We need to move quickly if we
are to make it into Glasgow before the gates close."

Isabelle was too tired to answer. They had traveled
hard all day, alternating between riding and walking,
though Campbell's walking stride required Isabelle to
hustle to keep pace. Her feet hurt, her legs hurt, her
back hurt, and she was greatly tired of this journey.
Campbell offered his hand and she allowed herself
to be hauled back onto the horse, and onto the
Highlander's lap. She collapsed against his chest and he
spurred his mount toward Glasgow.

Having spent most of her life in a castle, Isabelle
thought herself immune to whatever splendor the
Scots may have created, but as they approached
Glasgow, she realized she had misjudged. They
plodded over a wooden bridge crossing the River
Clyde, and she stared at the large wooden ships.
Several were tied along the banks, looking impressive
with their single, tall mast in the middle. Never had
she seen such a wonder. At Briggait Port Gate her

Highlander had a few words with the guard, and they proceeded into the burgh.

Isabelle was immersed in the sights and sounds and smells of the Glasgow market. The streets were lined with small shops and carts of people selling wares. People crowded the streets, brushing by her as they passed. Vegetables, fish, and game were proudly displayed, along with cloth, ribbons, and spices. Each little, crowded shop sold goods from their particular guild: tanners, skinners, weavers, and fishmongers. Carts of fresh produce lined the street. The pungent aroma of dead fish, cinnamon, roasting meat, and many bodies assailed her like a restorative.

She sat up tall, soaking in the new sights and sounds. Never had she seen so many people, so many wares, such brilliant colors. She was accustomed to traders who came once a moon to Alnsworth Castle, but this was extraordinary. Her uncle had never allowed her to leave the castle, so she had never been to a fair or market. Apparently she had missed much.

"Ye've ne'er seen a market before?" Campbell raised one eyebrow.

Isabelle shut her gaping mouth. "No, never."

"Saltmarket, this is. The weekly market at Glasgow Cross."

"Cross?" Isabelle looked for some sort of sculpture.

"The cross streets of Saltmarket, High Street, Trongate, and Gallowgate; 'tis market day, almost its close. The time when the best deals can be made." The corners of Campbell's mouth twitched up.

Isabelle glanced at him sideways. "I've heard tell the Scots are a frugal folk."

Campbell smiled, "With seven sisters I've had to be. Here, maybe ye can be of service to me." He dismounted and helped Isabelle down. "If I dinna return wi' cloth, my sisters will have my head. Perhaps ye can help me choose?"

Isabelle smiled at the chance and put up the hood of her cloak to appear more respectable. She walked to a storefront of a cloth merchant in one of the thatch-roofed houses crowding the streets. Cloth was arranged in organized piles, and hung on rungs of short ladders leaned up against the walls. Isabelle ran her hand over several selections, smiling. There was a nice variety, some rough, some fine.

Isabelle brushed her hand over gray wool, russet brown damask, and saffron yellow linen. The shop clerk eyed her and Campbell with interest and disappeared back into his shop, emerging a moment later with an armful of silk. Isabelle's pulse quickened.

The silks were high quality, smooth and soft, with vibrant colors of dark red, sage green, and bright blue. She glanced up at Campbell, but his face was unreadable. The silks must be quite costly. Time for a little revenge for her blisters.

"I'll take this wool here, no, not that one, it smells of mold, this one here. I'll take the russet damask, the green silk, and the blue." Isabelle spoke with confidence. She had been bartering for goods for years, though admittedly never in an open market.

The shopkeeper stared at her, then at Campbell. "She is English?"

"Aye," said Campbell. "Is that a problem?"

"Nay, nay." The shopkeeper smiled broadly.

Isabelle could almost see the coin being counted in his head. "'Tis fine, good quality cloth, I will give ye a good price."

Campbell said something to the shopkeeper in his own Gaelic tongue, and the burgher answered in kind. Though she could not understand their words, it was not difficult to comprehend they were negotiating for price.

The burgher gave them a wide smile, reverently stroking the blue silk, showing its fine quality. Campbell fingered the silk as if it was rough and displeasing, probably saying something about an inferior weave.

"I am sure we could get a better price at the borders." Isabelle could not help but get into the act. Campbell nodded in agreement. "I think this cloth has been stored too long, it has a damp smell to it. Not up to English standards, I say."

"My lady!" cried the burgher, much grieved. "This is the finest silk ye would find anywhere. It arrived last week from France. Finer silk ye'll ne'er see."

The two men continued to barter until Campbell made his purchase of the cloth Isabelle chose, along with a handful of ribbons. He tied the bundles to his saddle and steered her through the rest of the market, his arm around her shoulder.

"Ye barter well, my lady. My sisters will be well pleased, though ye beggar me wi' yer choices. Still, Cait is getting married and I promised her something special for her dowry."

Campbell bought two meat pastries and gave one to Isabelle. She breathed in the savory smell. The crust was buttery and the tender meat melted in her mouth. She smiled and took another bite of flavorful pastry, the meal reviving her spirits.

They walked slowly through the waning crowd, Isabelle trying not to be happy and failing at it. She felt not at all like a lost English lady, but more a friend or relative, or something else to this man Campbell.

She had to admit that while still a barbarian, Campbell was a considerate man and a kind brother... and not at all difficult to look upon. His arm was warm around her shoulders and her side touched his as they strolled down High Street, their backs to the setting sun.

"The Black Friars are o'er there." Campbell had taken on the role of tour guide.

"Black?" asked Isabelle.

"Dominican. So-named because of the color o' their robes." The lane turned to the right, revealing an impressive cathedral high on a hill, surrounded by fields on one side and a forest on the other. The setting sun caught the glass and stone of the cathedral, giving it a rosy orange hue. Isabelle paused at the impressive sight.

"Glasgow Cathedral. Beautiful is she no'?"

Isabelle nodded. The arm around her shoulder dropped and Campbell took her hand. "We'll be here for the night." He led her to a large stone inn and retrieved his packages, handing off his mount to a lad. The hazy common room of the inn was filled with people and smoke, but the conversation was friendly and the atmosphere was relaxed.

Campbell spoke with the owner and led her upstairs to a bedroom.

"Stay here, get some sleep." Campbell's eyes were kind. "Ye've had a long journey and bore it better than some o' my sisters might." He pulled out a red ribbon from the bundle he carried. "This is for ye, to replace the one ye lost."

"Thank you." Isabelle received his gift with surprise and pleasure. "'Tis kind of you to think of me."

"Ye must be tired, I'll let ye rest." Campbell lingered for a few moments, then left the room, shutting the door behind him.

Isabelle smiled and reclined on her bed, a pallet stuffed with straw, but it smelled clean and it was a heavenly relief to lie down. Despite her fatigue, a basin of water on a side table was tempting enough to get her back on her feet. She washed her face and hands in the cool water, appalled at how the clear water turned brown and muddy.

Isabelle traced her finger along the smooth edge of the ribbon lying next to the basin. It was a kind gesture. Perhaps being dragged halfway through Scotland was not so bad after all.

A new thought crept into her head. David Campbell was often kind and had not mistreated her during their journey, though he'd certainly had the opportunity. She would be safer under his protection than under that of her husband, of that she felt sure. Perhaps if she told him the truth of the matter, he would protect her from her murderous husband and help her return to her king.

It would mean telling him who she was and risking him sending her back to her husband. And yet... without his help she would not have made it this far.

How was she to travel back to England by herself? Even with her brightest optimism, she had to admit her chances of success were poor. She weighed the odds of successfully traveling back to England by herself, versus the odds that Campbell would return her to Lord Tynsdale.

The strains of music floated up from below, and the crowd laughed and sang. Campbell was a good man. Perhaps it was worth taking a risk to trust him. Isabelle put her hand in her pocket to make sure her two signet rings were still with her. These would help her prove her words were true.

Refreshed with purpose and eager to hear the music, Isabelle combed her fingers through her straight black hair and braided it down her back, entwining the red ribbon and tying it securely. It was hardly modest enough for a married woman, but it would have to suffice. Her gown was a mess, but she was only going to find Campbell.

The common room hummed with the excitement of a boisterous crowd talking and laughing. A man in a brightly colored tunic played a lively tune on the lyre. Isabelle tapped her toe to the music and longed to join a few lads who were dancing, mugs of ale in hand.

"Excuse me," Isabelle asked a serving lass. "Could you tell me where I can find Laird Campbell?"

The wench frowned at her. "Where ye from? I dinna ken ye."

"I'm looking for Campbell." Isabelle emphasized the name, wishing he would appear.

"Weel, now. 'Arry, this lass says she's looking fer the Campbell."

Harry turned around. A larger, more gruesome man Isabelle could not imagine. Harry was covered in pockmarks, had a bent nose, was missing most of his teeth, and smelled of rot. Her heart beat a bit faster and the hair on the back of her neck rose.

"I'm looking for Campbell." She tried to speak with confidence but was afraid it sounded more like a squeaking mouse.

"What are ye? English?" Harry growled, his gruff voice booming through the room. People paused their conversations to see what was happening.

"If you please tell me where I could find him." Isabelle took a step back.

"Sassenach!" Harry spit on the ground. The minstrel stopped playing, the room hushed. Isabelle took another step back and wished she had simply gone to bed. More angry men who resembled Harry's unfortunate visage joined him.

"What's an English doing here?"

"What does she want from Campbell?"

"There's a price on his head, the wench must be a spy."

"Whatever ye want o' Campbell I can give ye, English."

Isabelle stepped back until she was out of the room. The red-faced men followed her. Her heart pounded in her ears. "I am with Campbell and I will not be spoken to such."

Harry's uglier mate sneered. "Ye lie, English. Campbell would ne'er be caught wi' a Sassenach. He hates them bastards more than we do."

"Leave me be."

"She looks like a lightskirt, and an ill-used one at that. How much for a roll?"

"I'll be damned if I pay a Sassenach!" The man grabbed Isabelle by the arm and pushed her hard against the wall. He wrapped a huge hand around her throat and crushed her mouth with his. Isabelle clutched at his hand, trying to free herself.

"Gentlemen, please. Join me back in the hall. I have some ballads I know you will enjoy." Somehow the minstrel pushed his way between Isabelle and the man. Isabelle gasped for air when her neck was released, and leaned against the wall for support.

"Stand aside, lad. Ye've got no business here."

"We'll let ye have a poke when we're done wi' her, but fer now get back to the hall."

"Come now, my fine lads." The minstrel's voice was calm and cheery. "Let us speak to Campbell before we molest his prize."

That gave the Harrys pause, allowing the minstrel to back up a bit. He kept her behind him but turned so that she now had access to the front door.

"She's naught but lying English," one man shouted to the affirmative growls of the men. The minstrel held his ground, but with a lyre as his only weapon he would be short work for the Harrys.

"Run!" the minstrel hissed to her.

Isabelle spun and ran for the door, hitting Campbell smack in the chest.

Eight

ISABELLE GASPED, HER HANDS FLYING UP TO THE SOLID wall of Campbell's chest. David Campbell did not spare her a glance, but glared past her, past the minstrel, straight at the group of men who had gathered in the small hall. Campbell was by no means the largest brute in the hall, but the air around him was charged.

Campbell's face was chiseled stone, his expression murderous. He said nothing, but rage crackled the air around him. Isabelle backed to the wall, pressing herself into it. She noted the minstrel had likewise moved out of Campbell's way. She had not known how dangerous he was. It would not be forgotten.

"She's mine." Campbell's voice was low and threaded with warning. Isabelle felt a quiver of excitement at having been so claimed and waited for the bloodbath to begin.

Harry opened his mouth to speak, but showed a remarkable instinct for self-preservation, and stomped back to the common room without a word. His compatriots likewise had the insight to avoid certain annihilation and slinked after him.

Campbell motioned for the minstrel to go upstairs and the lad complied with alacrity. Indeed, it would be a very brave or utterly foolish man who would cross Sir David Campbell when death was in his eye. Campbell placed a hand on her shoulder, not hard, not grasping, but firm, and in control. He led her up the stairs to the room he had given her and entered with the minstrel, closing the door behind him.

"What happened here?" His eyes were hard on Isabelle.

Isabelle tried to swallow the lump that had formed in her throat. "I went down to the common room to find you and I was accosted by those brutes you saw."

"What did ye do to arouse their anger?"

"Nothing. I asked for you and they called me English and things turned ugly."

Campbell nodded. "Ye're English. 'Tis enough." He turned his attention to the minstrel who was casually leaning against the wall. The minstrel had long limbs that seemed loosely attached to his body. Campbell, in contrast, reminded her of a snake coiled and ready to strike. "And how did ye get involved in this?"

"He stepped in between me and them after one of them forced himself on me." Isabelle spoke up for her would-be rescuer. "Very gallant. I must thank you, sir."

Campbell never took his eyes off the minstrel, but she noticed his shoulder muscles tensed even tighter.

"The lady did not appear to be enjoying his attentions." The minstrel spoke with a lazy nonchalance, laced with a French accent. "Never leads to any good. Once a brawl starts, I'll get no more tips for the night."

"Ye have my thanks. Ye be French?" asked Campbell.

"*Oui*. I am Jacques le Chanteur a traveling minstrel and your humble servant, my lord." The minstrel gave Campbell a well-practiced bow.

"If ever ye find yerself on Campbell land, ye will be welcome."

"A gracious offer. My lord. My lady." The minstrel gave another elegant bow and quit the room, leaving Isabelle alone with Campbell.

Campbell turned slowly back to her. The man who leveled a penetrating glare at her shared no resemblance to the friendly Campbell whose company she had enjoyed earlier. His face was cold, expressionless, his eyes accusing. Silence filled the room, a void of sound that spoke much.

"Ye wished to find another protector?" Campbell's voice was hard.

"No! I was looking for you."

"I saw ye kissing that man."

"He attacked me!"

"I told ye to stay here. I grow weary of constantly rescuing ye from yer remarkable penchant for finding trouble. How much more will ye ask o' me?"

"I never meant—"

Campbell waved a hand at her, cutting her off. "Ye wished to see me. Here I am. What did ye want?"

"I… I…" Isabelle had wanted to confide in this man, to tell him of her fears, to ask for his help. She had been so naïve. "'Tis nothing. I apologize for causing trouble."

Campbell stepped forward and gently touched her neck where the man had grabbed her. She flinched instinctively, fearful he would take over where Harry left off. *Campbell would ne'er be caught wi' a Sassenach. He hates them bastards more than we do.* Harry's mocking words flooded her mind. She knew nothing of this man. Nothing.

Campbell dropped his hand. "Now I need to deal with yer friends downstairs."

"What will you do?" asked Isabelle.

"They have insulted me. It will no' go unanswered."

Isabelle crossed her arms in front of her. The men had insulted *him*? "I rather thought it was me they were insulting."

"Ye should never have left yer room. I should have known ye would be trouble. I'll find ye a suitable situation on the morrow, but for now stay here."

"A suitable situation? What do you mean?" Isabelle's heart pounded. His intentions sounded ominous.

"I canna take ye farther and ye clearly canna take care o' yerself."

"I need to return to Bewcastle."

"How? Ye canna walk into a common room wi'out finding trouble. I think it is time ye realize Scotland is yer new home. I'll find ye a place for lasses like ye tomorrow. For now, when I tell ye to stay in yer room, I expect ye to obey, ye ken."

Isabelle folded her arms across her chest, fighting the tears that pooled in her eyes. It was all going so horribly wrong.

Campbell stalked out of the room and closed the door behind him. A loud click of the door being locked made her flinch. She was trapped.

Isabelle was exhausted. She wanted to cry, but decided it would take more effort than she had for the task. She gazed longingly at the bed. It had bright linens and the straw mattress smelled fresh and inviting. The goose down comforter and pillow beckoned her to take her rest. Her muscles ached, her bones screamed for sleep. She refused.

Isabelle must escape. She did not know what Campbell had planned for her tomorrow, but she could not risk finding out. Did he mean to give her to a house of ill repute? Isabelle trembled at the memory of the man's face on hers, his fingers around her neck. It all reminded her of that horrible night, her wedding night. No, she could not let herself be taken captive. More than just her life was at risk. What must her guard and Marjorie be thinking now?

She must return at once to England, find her people, and petition the king. Who knew what sort of "situation" Campbell was going to find for her? She must escape now or it would be too late.

Fearing if she succumbed to rest even for a moment she would sleep all night, Isabelle remained on her feet. The inn was of sturdy construction, stone walls, solid and secure, which in her current predicament provided no comfort.

Isabelle pulled back the heavy curtains to reveal a window opening in the stone covered by an animal skin screen. Carefully removing the screen she was invigorated by a rush of cool night air. She needed it. She was ready to sleep on her feet. Yet fear was a powerful motivator, and enough to endure sleep deprivation.

The vantage from the window was not encouraging.

Fortunately, her room was in the back of the inn, where no one would see her try to escape. Unfortunately, she was three stories up, with a sheer drop to the kitchen garden below. It was a cool night, cloudless, with a bright moon. A good night to travel. She ignored her body, which screamed in protest. Clothes hung on the line below, a few gowns, and several pairs of tunics and trews.

Isabelle scanned her surroundings. What she needed was a plan. She could not tramp across the country dressed as she was, but in a lad's clothes she may raise less attention. Trouble was if she spoke, she'd be known as English before she finished her sentence. Perhaps she could pretend to be mute? Or wrap a strip of white cloth from her chemise around her neck and pretend to be injured. Isabelle smiled; that might work. All she needed to do now was get out of the room.

The plunge from her window was sobering. This was not going to be easy. She needed a ladder or a rope. She glanced around the room for inspiration. No rope. No ladders. The sheets! She smiled. One sheet rope and she would leave this place behind. She worked quickly, stripping the bed and tying the linens together to form a rope. By the time Campbell or Harry or anyone else realized she was gone, she would be far away.

She tied one side to the bed and threw the rest out the window. Looking down, the smile faded from her face. Her brilliant sheet rope fell woefully short. The end of her rope only reached midway down the building. She wondered if she could climb down and hold on to the end to drop to the ground.

Isabelle frowned. It was a long way down. She had never been particularly bothered by heights, but snapping her ankle in a fall wouldn't serve at all. Along the wall, some of the stones protruded more than others, and sometimes there were small indentations, remnants of the building process.

A new idea flashed through her mind. Tying the sheet rope around her waist, Isabelle eased herself out of the window, searching for toeholds through her soft leather boots. Outside the window, she held onto the windowsill and paused to reconsider her sanity. What on Earth was she doing?

She reviewed her current situation. Escape was necessary to prevent being given to a whorehouse and leaving her people at the mercy of her husband. How long would Captain Corbett and Marjorie live before Tynsdale took out his revenge on them?

Bolstered by these encouraging thoughts, Isabelle searched for handholds and eased herself completely out of the window, clinging to the stone wall. Slowly she climbed across the side of the inn. Her voluminous gown proved a significant hindrance to her progress, and several times she was required to release the wall with one of her hands to pull up her skirts in order to get a toehold. She wished she had the foresight to remove the gown and throw it to the ground, but she had not and it was too late to undress now.

Isabelle was almost to the next window. She reached out with her left foot, found a toehold and released her left hand to find her next hold. Suddenly, the rock beneath her left foot began to wobble. She lurched to the right to grab the wall with both hands as the stone gave way beneath her and fell with a crash to the garden below. Shaken, Isabelle grasped the wall, her muscles quivering with fatigue. She was going to fall if she didn't get to the ledge soon.

She clung, frozen, her hands starting to sweat. Her arms shaking, she forced herself to reach out again and continue edging along the wall. She was almost to the window. One more stretch and she would have it. She reached out for the ledge, but the sheet rope held her fast. It was too short!

Her fingers trembling, she struggled to untie the knot. The sheet rope slithered away, leaving her alone, clutching the wall without her safety line. Her muscles shook, pushed beyond the point of endurance. She was inches from the ledge and seconds from slipping from the wall. Forcing her arms to move, she shifted along the wall and grabbed on to the ledge. With her last ounce of strength, Isabelle pulled her body onto the window ledge.

Her breath came in gasps, her heart pounded loud in her ears. She closed her eyes and leaned back on the small stone ledge, waiting for her body to stop shaking. She did not look down. The moon shone down on her, a silent witness to her desperate plan. She rested on the ledge until her breathing slowed, and her heart stopped hammering out its pounding complaint.

The inn was quiet, the perfect time to escape. All she needed to do now was climb into the room, get into the hall, and slip down the stairs to freedom while the others slept. What she required was a bit of luck… and for this room to be empty.

Isabelle began to work at removing the screen.

It was hooked on the inside, making the operation awkward. She tried to be as quiet as possible, not knowing what inhabitant may be sleeping inside. She heard no noise from the room and hoped for the best. She managed to lift and push the screen until it started to move. Slipping from her fingers, the screen fell from the window to the floor of the room with a loud crash. Isabelle froze. There was nowhere for her to hide.

She held her breath and listened for movement, still concealed by the heavy brocade curtains that hung over the window. Presently, as she heard nothing from the room, she dared to open the curtain just a crack to peek into the room. The room was dark, nothing to see. Gathering her courage, she opened the curtains a little more, the moon illuminating the small room. It was empty. Isabelle released her breath in relief.

She stepped down into the room and propped the screen back against the wall. The click of the door latch froze her to her core. The door creaked.

Someone was coming.

Nine

"YE MUST KEN HOW IMPORTANT THIS IS, DAVID. I need to know ye will stand wi' us," said a man, speaking in a low voice. Isabelle gathered her skirts and crouched back into the window ledge, concealing herself with the curtain.

"Ye are my mother's kin. We have always supported the Stewarts, I see little need to prove our loyalty now." That voice! Isabelle's heart sank. It was Campbell.

"There is mischief about, lad. I have heard that our king wearies of his captivity wi' the English, enough to make a treacherous deal wi' the Sassenach devils. I have information that our king plots wi' the Douglas to overthrow me from the stewardship of Scotland in return for his release from captivity. Our useless king will also agree to give over the succession of the Scottish throne to one of King Edward's own sons."

A chill ran through Isabelle that had little to do with the cold night air. Was Campbell talking to Stewart, the man acting as the steward and ruler of Scotland? If she was discovered, she was dead.

"Nay, I canna believe Douglas would be a party in that."

"Aye but he would, lad. For he will be getting all the lands he was forced to forfeit to England returned, plus some additional lands. It is said that Tynsdale has fallen out of favor wi' the king and his lands will be forfeited to Douglas in this unholy deal."

Isabelle put her hand over her mouth to prevent herself from making a sound. Could this be true?

"Douglas has always fought for Scottish independence," said Campbell, but his voice was less than sure.

"Douglas will serve his own interests. That much land would make his the most powerful clan in all o' Scotland. His power would be greater than mine or yours or even our wretched king himself. I need ye to stand wi' me, lad, if we are to prevent this."

"Ye have my word I will support ye in the council. I winna allow England to claim our throne."

"Verra good, lad. Years ago yer mother and I negotiated a marriage between ye and my daughter. She's passed now, but I have a granddaughter who will serve ye as yer wife. I understand yer good mother told ye o' this after yer father passed."

"Aye."

"Come now, let us set a date for yer nuptials. It will send a much needed message to Douglas that ye will stand wi' us against him."

The room was silent. Isabelle held her breath, waiting to hear what Campbell would say. Had he not told her that he would marry Douglas's daughter?

"I understand yer sense of urgency in this matter, yet I feel we should proceed wi' caution. I will fight wi' ye against the English, but I am slow to raise arms against my brother. Too often, we Scots have been divided and weakened by fighting amongst ourselves. I have no love for war against my neighbor and kin. Recall my father's dame was a Douglas."

"Ye have good feeling, lad. I respect yer reticence to battle against the Douglas. This course gives me no pleasure either. But this is no time for hesitancy. We must act and quickly if we are to foil this plan."

"And in doing so, I am plotting against my king. Nay, give me leave to consider what must be done. I fostered wi' Douglas; he is like a second father to me. Let me talk wi' him and see if I can reason wi' him from this course."

"And what if he draws ye to his side? I need to know yer loyalties, lad."

"I give ye my word I will take up my sword before I will accept an Englishman as the king o' Scots."

Another silence permeated the room.

"I will take my leave then," said Stewart. "Remember, Scotland may once again call for her true sons to defend her."

"Always."

❦

Campbell shut the door with a sigh. He was exhausted. The clans may soon be at war. And he was engaged to two women. Another sigh escaped his lips. His head throbbed, his shoulder blades were clenched together so tight he might never get them to relax. This was his parents' legacy to him. Two brides.

He sat down hard on the bed, the weight of his

decision heavy on his shoulders. His parents, with rival loyalties of their own, had both engaged in secret negotiations for his bride. Never able to agree during their lifetime, he remained unwed, even at the age of thirty-three. Now that they were both gone, Stewart and Douglas were both calling for him to choose a bride, each assured that the choice would be his own maiden.

Yet to choose one of these powerful clans over the other was to risk inciting the conflict that loomed, waiting for a single spark to ignite the clans in battle. It was impossible to choose a bride and equally impossible for him to remain unwed. Yet how could he choose without sending his clan to war?

He needed sleep. It had been days. It felt like years. He stripped off his clothes and brushed back the goose down comforter. He blew out the candle and sunk down into the soft, straw mattress. It was pure heaven.

Squeeeeak.

Campbell sat bolt upright. He did not know how long he had been asleep, but someone was trying to sneak into his room.

He grabbed his knife.

Ten

A DEAFENING ROAR STRUCK ISABELLE A SPLIT SECOND before she was knocked on her back.

"Who are ye, speak!"

Isabelle shrieked as she was lifted up by her hair. She was dragged back to the window where Campbell slashed aside the curtains. Moonlight glinted off the blade in his hand, and his naked body.

"Saints alive—Isabelle?" Campbell let her go, his arms falling to his sides. His eyes were wide, his mouth open. Even he could not hide his astonishment.

Isabelle gaped at him. She had been rattled by the view of his knees. Now she was staring at the real David Campbell in all his naked glory. She should turn away. She should blush. Instead, she gawked, openmouthed.

Campbell said something harsh in Gaelic and reached for his plaid, wrapping it hastily around some of his more interesting parts.

"What are ye... how did ye...?" Campbell wasn't quite himself.

The vision of the glorious David Campbell was still

too fresh in her mind to allow comprehensible speech, so she mutely pointed at the window.

Campbell braced himself with a hand on the wall and edged carefully to the window. He glanced down briefly, then back at her. Perspiration beaded on his forehead, the confusion was clear in his eyes.

"I climbed across," Isabelle managed.

Campbell's jaw dropped. "Outside? On the wall?"

Isabelle nodded.

"Ye could have killed yerself. By the saints, what were ye thinking?" He grabbed her shoulders and gave her a little shake. "If ye had fallen, ye'd be dead for sure."

"I had a rope." Her voice was faint in the face of an outraged David Campbell. She leaned out the window and pointed at the sheet rope, still dangling from her window.

Campbell grabbed her arm and pulled her back to the room. "Have a care. Ye'll kill yerself." He braced himself on the wall once more, and took a cautious peek at her dangling sheet rope. He pulled back, replaced the screen, whipped the heavy curtains shut, and wiped the sweat from his brow. Crossing himself, he murmured something that was either a prayer or a curse.

"Stay here, dinna move." He grabbed a key from the table and left the room. She could hear him enter her room next door. Briefly she considered making a run for it, but she would have to pass him in the hall to escape. Before she could conclude that her chances were slim, Campbell returned.

"I dinna ken what ye are about, but ye made a mess o' yer bed. Were ye trying to meet another man, Isabelle?"

"No! Men are what I was trying to avoid."

"Then why do ye sneak into my room?"

"I did not know it was your room." Isabelle was indignant. "You locked me in my room and I needed to find a way to escape, so I climbed over to the next room to leave that way."

"Escape? Escape what?"

"You said I would never get back to England. You said you were going to find me a-a situation. I do not know who you think I am, but I will not, I cannot go to a house of..." Isabelle turned away, clenching her jaw to hold back the emotion.

"Where did ye ken I was taking ye?"

Isabelle took a shaky breath and shrugged.

"My aunt lives about an hour's ride from here. I thought ye could be a companion to her."

Isabelle spun back to stare at Campbell. "You were going to take me to your aunt?"

"Aye."

"Oh." Isabelle shook her head, she was too tired to think.

"Tell me the truth for once. What were ye trying to do?"

"I need to get to Bewcastle."

"And how did ye expect to make it back to England?"

"Oh, I had a plan." Isabelle warmed to her confession. She was proud of this part of her scheme. "I was going to borrow a lad's clothing from outside on the line and walk back. I'm sure I could do it."

"I'm sure ye're daft."

"That's hardly kind."

"Ye're lucky I dinna run ye through when I kenned

ye to be a thief. Ye're no' safe to look after yerself. I
begin to understand why someone abandoned ye on
the road."

Isabelle gave him what she hoped was a withering
glance. All she wanted, all she needed, was to get back
to England, yet the chances of making it home soon
were slim.

Campbell rubbed the worry lines on his forehead, his
eyelids drooped. He looked every bit as exhausted as she
felt. "What am I going to do wi' ye?" he asked more to
himself than to her. "I canna leave ye alone in yer room
wi'out ye jumping out the window. I'm too tired to
watch ye." David Campbell shook his head, the deep
creases in his forehead plainly evident in the moonlight.

"Please let me back in my room. All I desire now
is sleep."

"And ye promise no' to try to escape?"

Isabelle paused, considering her answer.

"Nay, I'm responsible for ye, I winna have yer
death on my head. Ye need to stay wi' me tonight.
Take off yer gown, I want to get some sleep."

Isabelle gasped. Take off her gown?

"Dinna fear for yer virtue, I'm too tired to do
anything to ye even if I…" Campbell sighed and
rubbed his eyes. "I dinna have a rope so I'll just have
to hold ye through the night. 'Tis the only way to
make sure ye dinna kill yerself."

Isabelle's heart pounded against her ribs. Sleep with
this man? No, it was impossible. She reached back to
her braid and untied it, pulling the scarlet ribbon free.

"Ye could tie me wi' this." She handed him the
ribbon.

Campbell stared at the ribbon in his hand and gave another audible sigh. "That is not what I bought it for." He laid it on a bundle of cloth on the small table by the bed. "I bought this for ye too. A gown to replace the one that was ruined."

"You bought me clothes?"

He shrugged. "Ye canna wear that gown wi'out people thinking the worst o' ye."

"Thank you. But I cannot sleep with you."

He shook his head. "I dinna buy it to woo ye, I bought it so I could stop having to beat some manners into every man ye meet. See here, I'd be no kind o' man if I took my rest wi' a lady tied to a chair." His voice was weary. "Nay, we are both greatly tired. Let us sleep together this night. No harm will come to ye, I swear it." He slowly crossed the room toward her until he was standing before her.

Gently, he loosened the stays of her gown. Her breath came short and rapid as his fingers skimmed the soft skin of her chest at the top of her ripped bodice. Slowly, as if not to spook her, he reached down and gradually pulled up the velvet fabric of the gown. She should tell him to stop but was stunned into silence.

Warmth emanated from his naked chest, and she had a sudden compulsion to touch it. The desire was impeded by a velvet barrier as Campbell pulled her gown up over her head. Shocked, she found herself standing before him in nothing but her chemise.

She opened her mouth to protest but glanced at her gown in his hands. It was torn and filthy. How long had she worn that bundle of rags?

"Go lie down."

Isabelle looked at the bed, white and clean. It beckoned her louder than any other voice she heard.

"I protest this scandalous treatment of my person." Her complaint may have carried more weight had she not already been walking eagerly toward the bed.

"Noted. Yer virtue is secure."

What a shame.

She climbed into bed and sank into the fresh mattress, curling up on her side. It was heavenly. She might have even groaned in a most unladylike fashion. Behind her Campbell chuckled. Her eyes flew open as she was enveloped into Campbell's arms. His body curled next to hers, his arm wrapped around her securely.

She gasped at the shock of his heat. She could feel the length of him down her back. The blanket he wore was clearly tossed aside and now all that separated her from him was her chemise. She never thought her virtue would depend on nothing but a thin piece of linen.

Unlike hers, Campbell's breathing was steady and slow, which quickly turned to soft snoring. She fought the impulse to elbow him in the ribs. How could he fall asleep so fast? She wanted to defend her virtue as much as the next lady, but this disregard was downright insulting.

Did it not bother him at all that they were in bed together almost naked? She was feeling hot and sweaty in all sorts of odd places—how dare he just go to sleep! She was sure she would lie awake all night.

She closed her eyes and snuggled back into his arms.

Despite everything, she felt safe.

◦✦◦

Sometime in the wee hours of the morning, Isabelle awoke to the strangest sensation. She was warm and tingling all over. She stretched happily and David Campbell pulled her closer, wrapping his arm around her. His thumb brushed lazily over her breast as he continued his caress. His slow massage had woken her.

Isabelle opened her mouth to protest, but the sensations he was building were so relaxing, so pleasant, she sighed instead and surrendered to the experience. Perhaps she was dreaming. It must be a dream. No mere mortal man could inspire such budding joy. Never had she been touched this way. She closed her eyes and drifted somewhere between waking and sleeping until arousal got the best of her.

She shifted from her side to her back so she could see Campbell, but his eyes were closed. Was he even awake? By rolling onto her back, she had given access to new parts of her body and Campbell's hand wandered slowly down to her thigh, brushing up her chemise. She should really say something now to stop him. His hand moved higher up her thigh to that long-neglected part of her body now throbbing with the desire. She would stop him. She must. She…

A soft sigh escaped her lips as his hand caressed her. What wonders was he doing? She would not stop him for anything now. Excitement and tension built up within her and she pressed herself into his magic hand, wanting more. Heat surged through her and she panted for breath, chasing something, wanting desperately for something she had never known but now needed more than her next breath. Something inside her clenched and exploded. She cried out clutching Campbell's shoulder, afraid she would shatter, and not truly caring if she did.

"Isabelle." Campbell smiled at her, opening his eyes. "I thought I was dreaming. I am not accustomed to finding a beautiful woman in my bed."

"Wha-what was that?" Isabelle trembled with aftershocks of pleasure.

"I would have thought ye would know. It is the pleasure one finds between a man and a woman. Have ye ne'er experienced it?"

Isabelle shook her head, unable to yet form words.

"Yer English lover has no' done right by ye."

"Indeed!" Isabelle squeezed her eyes shut, trying to chase away unhappy memories. That she had been denied this pleasure was yet one more reason to despise her husband.

Campbell drew her closer and nuzzled her neck. "Do ye want more?"

Isabelle's eyes flew open. "There is more?"

He chuckled soft and low. "Aye, there be much more. Och, but nay, I promised ye I would defend yer virtue this night."

"I release you from that promise." Isabelle's bold words surprised herself. But *more*? Oh yes, she wanted more.

Campbell laughed but released her, saying, "I gave ye my word, and I canna break it. Tomorrow though, I can promise ye more tomorrow." He held her close, and she rested her head on his shoulder. "I have a better idea than taking ye to my aunt. What if ye came home wi' me?"

"I wish I could but I…"

"I know, ye need to get to Bewcastle. Does a lover wait for ye there?"

"There is no lover. There never has been any lover in my life—except you."

"But I thought ye—"

"I know what you thought, but the man who ruined my life was not of my choosing."

Campbell held her tighter and she snuggled into his arms. "Come away wi' me, Isabelle. I shall protect ye. Ye shall want for nothing as long as I live."

"I thought you were to be married."

"Aye, I must, though I would rather avoid it. I never thought to take a leman—"

"What is that? You mean ye wish me to be your mistress?" Isabelle was shocked. She had never, ever considered anyone would make such an indecent offer to her.

"Aye. I have been wondering what to do wi' ye, and now I know exactly what I wish. Ye could, do naught but relax all day and play all night. How does that sound?"

Sinful it might be, but it sounded heavenly. He was offering protection, safety, and carnal delights she had only just become aware existed. Her husband would never be able to find her. Her people… Well, they would survive without her, wouldn't they?

"Dinna answer me now, think on it. 'Tis still dark; let us sleep a little more." Campbell kissed her on her forehead and rolled over.

Isabelle lay next to his warm back until his breathing was slow and steady. It was a tempting offer. She could simply walk away from being an heiress and a countess. With a word she could leave it all behind and escape to a life of relaxation and pleasure. Did she dare?

Maybe it was time to forget being responsible, look how much trouble it brought her already. She had little hope to make it back to England alive anyway, and even if she did, she would still need to evade her husband's guards and somehow convince King Edward to nullify her marriage and support her annulment with the Church.

It was safer to stay. Her chances of a happy life were greater with Campbell than with any other option.

Maybe it was time to think of herself. She snuggled closer to Campbell's warm back. For the first time in her life she knew exactly what she wanted. She wanted to stay with David Campbell.

Eleven

THE COLD LIGHT OF DAY BROUGHT WITH IT A LOATH-some reality. Her people would die without her. Isabelle must leave the one good thing she had ever found in her life. She considered waking Campbell and explaining it all, but she dared not risk it. If he asked her one more time, she would say yes. She wanted to say yes, for she knew she would very likely die if she returned. But she must go, and though she knew it was cowardly, she could only do it while he was asleep.

Slowly, Isabelle slipped out of the bed. David Campbell continued to snore softly. Dawn had broken, and dim light filtered through the curtains. She would need to move fast. She glanced at her ruined velvet gown on the floor, then at the tempting package by the side of the bed. She ought not to take from this man. But what was he going to do with a lady's gown?

Isabelle tiptoed around the bed to the side table and untied the bundle. Inside was a clean, linen chemise, a faded green gown, and decent linen head covering.

They were used garments, but better than her ruined gown and well suited for traveling. She quickly slipped into the gown, struggling with the ties in the back and on the sleeves.

Campbell coughed and rolled over. Isabelle froze, her heart pounding. *Please, please do not wake up.* The snoring resumed and Isabelle headed for the door. Her rings! Isabelle turned back to the velvet heap on the floor and retrieved them without a sound.

Remembering last night, she opened the door slowly, only as wide as she needed to slip through. She softly closed the door behind her, and slipped into what had been her room to retrieve her wool cloak.

Now to find the lad's clothes she saw hanging on the line. While she appreciated the gown, she knew she could travel easier alone if people thought her a man. Ladies who traveled alone attracted a different kind of attention than what Isabelle wished to garner.

Isabelle walked quietly out of the inn, her heart beating faster as she passed the common room, but there was no one there to cause trouble. She slipped around the back, only to find a stout woman taking down the wash.

"G'morn to ye, dearie," said the washerwoman with a smile. She took Isabelle's coveted trews from the line, folded them quickly and dropped them in a basket.

Isabelle's smile in return was not nearly as sincere. With a sigh she walked back to the front of the inn. She needed to figure out how to get back to England, dressed as a woman, traveling alone, and without any money. Her stomach growled. Or food.

"Good morn to you." Jacques the minstrel walked

out of the inn, a long loaf of bread in his hand. He was dressed in a bright yellow tunic and vivid blue trews.

Isabelle jumped at the sight of him. Would he return her to Campbell? "Good morning," she responded hesitantly.

"Up early, are you? Good morning for it," Jacques said with a smile, but he looked her over carefully. Isabelle doubted there was much that escaped his notice.

"Yes, a beautiful day." The sun had just peeked above the horizon casting a warm glow on the stonework of the large inn. The cloudless sky was bright blue with promise. It would be a good day to travel, if she ever got that far. Isabelle tried to think of some explanation to give the minstrel for her presence outside the inn, but instead her stomach rumbled.

"Me, I think this bread is a little stale," said the minstrel, his soft French accent pleasant to her ears. "What do you think?" He handed her the loaf and she obligingly ripped off a piece and took a bite.

"It tastes good to me." Isabelle offered the loaf back to him, but he waved it off.

"No, you keep it, I care not for it. Have a safe journey, m'lady." He gave her a wink and brushed past her to the door of the inn.

"Thank you!" she called and walked quickly down the road toward the center of Glasgow. She had to come up with a plan, and fast. Campbell would be awake soon. Would he look for her? She did not know, and contrary to what she knew she needed to do, she almost wished he would. She took a bite of the loaf the minstrel had given her. His kindness gave her hope. But how was she going to get back to England?

Isabelle strolled through the market street. Shop owners were opening the windows to the houses that served as their store and their dwelling. In many a shop she could see the family sitting around the table for the morning meal.

Isabelle took another bite of the loaf, then stuffed it into the pocket of her cloak. She had a long journey ahead of her, and needed to conserve her food. Inside the pocket she felt a strange round object. Pulling it out, she found a heavy gold coin. She stopped short and nearly tripped on her own feet. Clutching the coin to her breast, she wondered who could have put it there. Would Campbell have given it to her? It seemed unlikely. The minstrel! He had brushed past her and must have slipped her the coin. His kindness brought tears to her eyes.

Isabelle got her feet moving again before she made a spectacle of herself. Now she had hope. Surely this would help her get home. But no, she remembered, Alnsworth was not safe for her now. She must travel to Bewcastle, find her guard, seek an audience with the king and get him to dissolve her marriage. The enormity of the task threatened to crush her with despair. Resolute, she pushed aside those unhappy thoughts. She must consider things one step at a time. First she needed to escape Campbell's tempting offer, for if she saw him again she doubted she would have the strength to leave.

The conversation she had overheard on the ledge had been shocking, but now she turned it around in her mind, trying to use her husband's fall from favor in the English court to her advantage. Initially she considered this to be good news. If the king disliked Tynsdale, he would be more likely to support her request for a divorce. However, if the king was considering Alnsworth to be part of Tynsdale's holdings, could he be considering giving Alnsworth to Douglas too? If her warm reception in Scotland was any basis for judgment, she doubted her people would fare better with Douglas than with Tynsdale.

The road she was on led her back the way she and Campbell had walked last night to the River Clyde. Tall masts peeked over the clustered thatched roofs. Isabelle drummed her fingers together, a new plan forming. A boat, yes, a boat would be just the thing. She had funds now to pay for safe passage... if she could find an honest captain who would sail to England.

Along the edge of the River Clyde, several boats were lashed to a rickety wooden dock. Some boats were small, some large. Many had a single tall mast. Some had nothing more than oars. One looked suspiciously like a Viking ship. Men on the boats were waking up, performing their morning routines, and beginning to ready their craft. But how to find an honest sailor?

It was an impossible choice, and the consequences if she got this wrong could be dire. She slowly turned around searching for some answer. In the distance shone the steeples of the cathedral, haloed in the light of the rising sun. Isabelle never spared much thought for God, other than trying to avoid being an object of His wrath. After losing her family to the plague, and being given in marriage to an abusive old man, she figured God did not care for her much. But perhaps, given her desperate need, she should try asking for assistance.

Isabelle closed her eyes and made an attempt at piety. *Please, God, help me find my way home so I can save my people. Yours sincerely, Isabelle, the Countess of Tynsdale. Though I would truly prefer not to be if you could help me—*

"Ow!" Something slammed hard into her left shoulder. Her eyes flew open and she found herself face-to-face with a sweaty man carrying a large crate on his shoulders.

"Watch yerself, lassie!" he snarled and continued along his way.

Isabelle rubbed her aching shoulder. That's what she got for attempting prayer. It was up to her now. Isabelle eyed the sailors, mentally rejecting crafts whose crew looked like they were suffering the ill effects of drink. One crew was dressed in the Highlander's kilts. She mentally crossed them off her list too. The men on the craft next to them, however, were respectably dressed and were already hard at work. Yes, this was a good candidate.

She walked boldly up to the craft, wondering how to get this accomplished. She took a deep breath and gathered her courage. "Excuse me!" she called to the men on the boat. "May I speak with your captain?"

The men came to the side of the boat and looked down at her with suspicion. One man with a dark, neatly trimmed beard stepped forward. "I am Captain Erskine. State yer business."

"May I speak with you?" She wanted to avoid calling out her business like a fishmonger.

Captain Erskine jumped down to the river walk. He regarded her with a mixture of curiosity and reserve. His men on the boat made no pretense of doing anything but hanging over the side of the boat and listening.

"I wish to return to England. Might you be traveling that direction?" Isabelle asked.

"I might."

"Could I pay for safe passage back to England? I have become separated from my guard and I must return."

"Who would be traveling?" he asked.

"Just myself."

"Ye only? None other?" The captain raised an eyebrow.

"Yes."

The captain crossed his arms across his chest. "How much ye willing to pay?"

Isabelle paused, considering her actions. If she revealed the coin she could simply be robbed. And yet, in order to get back to England she needed to take a risk. "Would this buy passage?" Isabelle held up the coin.

Captain Erskine reached for the coin, but a loud howl behind her startled Isabelle, causing her to jerk back her hand. One of the kilted men was yelling loudly, attracting the attention of not only Isabelle but everyone else on the neighboring boats and shore.

"What are ye howling about, Hamish?" asked one of the Highlanders as they all ran to the injured man's side.

"My finger! I slipped and fell and now my finger, och look at it!" The lad held up his hand, showing one of his fingers was bent up at an awkward angle. "Do something, Dain, it hurts like hell."

Isabelle realized that the injured man was little more than a lad, and his finger indeed looked quite painful.

"The coin, mistress," said Captain Erskine, holding out his hand.

Isabelle glanced at the captain and back at the injured lad, distracted.

"Naught I can do for ye," said Dain to the whimpering lad. "We'll need to get ye back to Mairi."

"But that winna be till tonight or the next morn," wailed the lad.

"Here, we can wrap it for ye," said another man. Whatever he did to the lad's finger caused the young man to scream in pain.

"Mistress!" demanded Captain Erskine.

"Please, wait a moment. I believe I can help this injured man." Isabelle stepped up to the boat of the injured lad. The ministrations of his shipmates caused him to scream again. "No, please stop whatever you are doing and let me look at it."

Two of the Highlanders looked at each other and shrugged, then helped her on board the craft.

Hamish, the injured lad, sat on the deck, holding his hand protectively, while the man he had called Dain kneeled beside him.

"Who are ye?" Hamish asked, his eyes narrow, his mouth surly.

"I am here to help. Let me see your hand," replied Isabelle.

"Ye're English! I hate English," snarled the lad.

Dain cuffed him softly on the head. "Mind yer manners. He's just a hurt lad, mistress. Please dinna bear him no mind. Can ye help us?"

"If he will let me."

Dain nodded to Hamish and the hurt lad held out his finger, his bottom lip trembling. Isabelle gave him a bracing smile, and gently examined the finger. The ring finger extended at an awkward angle from the middle joint.

"I don't think it's broken. This may hurt a bit." Before Hamish could respond, Isabelle grabbed the finger and popped the dislocated joint back into place. Hamish screamed, and everyone leaned in to examine the finger. Hamish tentatively tried moving it and found that it once again worked properly.

"Well now, Hamish," said one man. "Looks like ye're in the service o' an English woman." He laughed and gave Isabelle a bow. "I'm Finnáin and this is my twin brother Gill Crist, my older brother Dain, and our young, accident-prone Hamish."

The four men were all various forms of tall, broad-shouldered, and handsome. "Good morn to you," said Isabelle.

"Good morn to ye, mistress," said Gill. He motioned to his twin. "Ye can call us Finn and Gill. Like fish, ye ken?" Finn and Gill resembled each other so closely Isabelle gave up all hope of ever telling them apart. They both beamed at her, their eyes dancing.

"I thank ye, mistress," said Dain, his gray eyes more serious. "Ye have been a great service to us. Pray tell me how we can be a service to ye."

"I am looking for passage back to England."

"We dinna travel in that direction, but I will find ye someone who will."

Isabelle smiled and sighed in relief. "That would be a great help, sir. I was speaking to the Captain Erskine next to you about passage."

"Dain, Gill, Finn, Hamish," called a familiar voice. Isabelle cringed at the sound, while the four Highlanders stood at attention, blocking her from the man on the shore. "Make haste, I need ye men."

David Campbell leapt onto the boat. "I've lost a lass and I need yer help to find her."

"Ye've lost a lass?" asked Dain.

Isabelle stood behind the four men, effectively hidden from Campbell's view.

"Aye," barked Campbell. "She is an Englishwoman who was separated from her traveling companions. We need to spread out, search the city. I have already asked at the gates, but no one has seen her leave. Och, who knows what trouble she might be in."

"What does she look like?" asked Hamish.

"She's young, excellent figure, wearing a green gown and a brown traveling cloak. She has long black hair and is too beautiful for her own good."

Beautiful? Did he say beautiful?

"She's English, did ye say?" asked Finn.

"Aye."

"Green gown, black hair, good healer?" asked Gill.

"Aye, dinna stand there, get moving. We need to… Wait, how did ye know she was a healer?"

Dain, Gill, Finn, and Hamish turned to look at her, then stood aside, revealing her to Campbell.

"Isabelle!" Campbell's jaw dropped.

Gill and Finn began to laugh, making it difficult for Isabelle to take the situation seriously. How could she possibly end up back with David Campbell? Served her right for attempting prayer as a course of action. Clearly she was not on the favored list. No doubt even the angels took amusement in her predicament.

"Good morn to you," she said, smiling in spite of herself. Perhaps it was fate. She was destined to be Campbell's lover. But no. It could never be. Now she had to tell Campbell she was leaving to his face. The smile faded from her face.

"How did ye find my brothers?" asked Campbell.

"Brothers?" It was in keeping with her perpetually rotten luck. "I did not know they were your brothers. Master Hamish was injured so I stopped to help."

"I see." Campbell was silent, his face growing grave. Campbell's brothers also said nothing, looking back and forth between Isabelle and Campbell. "Ye left," Campbell finally said.

"I must return to England. I have no other choice."

"Ye had a choice." Campbell looked out over the river, his face a frozen mask.

"Please let me explain."

Campbell raised a hand to stop her and shook his head. "No explanation is necessary. We need to be on our way for we have a long day of travel ahead of us. If I can no longer be o' service to ye, I will bid ye farewell."

Isabelle opened her mouth to try to say something, but what could she say? Perhaps it was best to simply leave. "I never meant for any of this to happen."

Campbell nodded and continued to look away.

"I thank you very much for all your help."

Campbell nodded again.

"Farewell, Sir Campbell."

"Good day to ye. Ready the boat, men. We leave immediately."

Dain helped her back to the shore. "Good luck, mistress," he whispered.

"Thank you," Isabelle answered in a small voice.

"Be wary o' Captain Erskine. He cares to make a profit and naught else."

Isabelle nodded an acknowledgment. Back on the river walk she looked up for Campbell, but he was fast preparing to sail and was much too busy to look back at her. If she did not know better, she would say she had hurt him.

Captain Erskine was waiting for her, accompanied by another man. The stranger was tall and thin with a slight slump to his shoulders. He looked her up and down in a manner she could not like. He spoke something to Erskine and handed him a bag that jingled like coins.

Isabelle flushed, though she did not know why. She stood tall; she would not allow their rudeness to intimidate her, yet she could not help but glance back at Campbell's boat. Good to his word, the brothers were pushing off from the dock. He was leaving her. She told herself it was for the best. It was a lie not even she could believe.

"I can pay for safe passage, Captain Erskine," said Isabelle, getting back to the task at hand. "The coin I showed you and two more once I am safely to Bewcastle."

"Bewcastle is a long way from here, but this man can take you where you need to go."

Something was not right about this. Prickling warnings slithered up her spine. "I do not understand you, Captain. Will you be able to take me to England or shall I find another captain?"

Captain Erskine merely smiled and gave her a mock salute before returning to his boat.

"Come along wi' ye," said the skinny man. He smiled, revealing several rotting teeth, and grabbed her hand like a vice.

"No! Let go of me!" demanded Isabelle, but found the man was surprisingly strong. "Where are you taking me?"

"Somewhere ye can work for a living."

"Work? Whatever do you mean? Unhand me!"

The man began to walk forward dragging her behind him. Despite twisting and pulling she could not get him to release her.

"Ye're a bonnie lass. Ye'll bring in a fair fortune, I wager." The man turned to stare lewdly at her breasts.

"Let me go!"

"Or what? Ye have any man to come for ye? Nay? Dinna worry, I'll help ye find a man willing to pay the right price."

"You mean to… to *sell* me?"

"Aye, that's it. Ye're a smart lass, now dinna kick up no trouble." He continued to pull her along the river walk.

"Stop! Unhand me!" Isabelle screamed as loud as she could.

The man spun around to strike her, but Isabelle managed to twist herself free.

"I am the Countess of Tynsdale," she declared. "You will leave me be."

"I dinna care who ye are, Duchess," the man snarled. "I paid for ye and ye're coming with me." He lunged at her, but a blur of a man jumped from a passing boat and knocked the man to the ground.

The man scrambled up, blood dropping from his bent nose. "She is mine!" he screamed.

"Nay," said Campbell in a cold, low tone. "She belongs to me."

Campbell did not spare her a glance, but grabbed her hand and ran down the walk, Isabelle racing to keep pace. He came astride his boat that was slowly moving down the river.

"Dain, catch!" Campbell lifted her up and before she could protest, tossed her over to the boat, and was caught neatly by Dain, who appeared almost as shocked as she.

"Have a care, man!" exclaimed Dain.

Campbell jumped onto the boat himself and glared at Isabelle. Dain wisely stepped away, and Isabelle too wished she could go elsewhere, with Campbell regarding her with such menace.

"I will ask this once, and I want an honest answer." Campbell's calm voice was in stark contrast to the murder in his eyes. "Who are ye?"

He had heard her. Isabelle had hoped if she revealed who she was to the evil man at least she would be spared being sold into slavery, if only because other parties would pay more for her. Should she lie now to Campbell?

"I am the Countess of Tynsdale," said Isabelle in a small voice.

"Ye're *married*?" Campbell exclaimed.

Isabelle nodded slowly, the poisonous truth creeping between them like a specter. Too late she realized keeping this a secret had been a horrible mistake. Campbell's jaw clenched, in his eyes she saw betrayal. No one spoke, the only noise the lapping of the waves against the hull.

"Explain yerself." Campbell cleared his throat. He would not speak until he had a full command of his voice. "Why did I find ye on the road alone?"

"My horse bolted and I became separated from my guard and was lost."

"How can I believe ye? Ye've done naught but speak falsehoods."

Isabelle took her signet rings from her pocket and showed them to him. He studied one, then the other, his face turning gray and frozen, like chiseled stone.

"Why did ye not tell me immediately who ye were?" Campbell spoke in French. A test, she realized, and one she was not sure she wanted to pass.

"I feared you would return me back to my husband," she responded also in French, the language of court in both England and Scotland.

"Ye are running away from him." Campbell spoke English once more, his face a stone mask of disapproval. "Why did ye no' tell me ye were married when I asked?"

"You asked if I had a husband in Bewcastle and I do not."

"Nay, only the lover ye are running to."

"No, it is not—"

"Save yer breath, my lady. I understand now, but

I winna be part of yer wicked schemes, though ye tried to tempt me wi' yer charms last night. Ye shall go back to yer husband where ye belong, and I do believe I will ask a hefty ransom to pay for all the trouble ye caused." Campbell stormed off to another part of the boat.

Isabelle collapsed in the stern, her shaky legs unable to hold her as the boat softly swayed. Despite the sun on her face, she was cold. She wrapped her arms around herself and sat numb and still, unable even to cry. She was going to be returned to her husband, who would use her to gain control of Alnsworth, then kill her and terrorize her people.

But the worst part, the absolute worst, was that she had lost favor with David Campbell. He had asked her to be part of his life last night. Now, he could not stand to look at her. She had not realized he had touched her heart, but she knew now that it had broken.

Twelve

IT TOOK SEVERAL HOURS OF ROWING DOWN THE RIVER Clyde before the banks widened and they could sail. Isabelle remained in the stern enumerating all the things wrong with her life until she was too depressed to continue. Yet the day was sunny with a cool, brisk wind, making for excellent sailing conditions. Isabelle had never before been on a boat and, despite her situation, found herself enjoying the gentle, rocking motion and the views of the bright green hills as they passed.

After several hours, Campbell moved back toward her. Isabelle's pulse jumped, yet she could not tell by his hard expression what he was thinking. His brothers noticed his movement too, and while all hands remained busy, Isabelle knew she was being watched.

"I hear I am to thank ye for yer service to Hamish." Campbell towered above her, glancing at her ever so slightly before looking beyond her to the green hills she had been admiring.

Isabelle stood to speak with him. "I did not do much."

"Aye, ye did. And I appreciate it. I will see ye safely reunited wi' yer husband."

If Campbell was trying to comfort her, his effort fell well wide of the mark. "Actually, I'd rather not," said Isabelle.

"It is where ye belong. Ye must return." Campbell spoke with finality.

"But I—" A large swell rocked the boat and Isabelle, unaccustomed to life at sea, stumbled forward. Campbell caught her and pulled her close to him.

"Careful, my lady." Campbell's face was still an emotionless mask, but his green eyes shone bright in the sun.

"Hmmmmm." The twins made teasing, humming noises, smiling at Campbell with wide grins. Campbell scowled and released her. Isabelle sank back into the stern of the boat, and Campbell spent the rest of the day looking important and much too busy to notice her.

They spent most of the day on the water, traveling down the River Clyde, then out into the Firth of Clyde where the water became choppy, and Isabelle found she had no natural talent for life at sea. After heaving a few times over the side, she was more than content to be ignored by Campbell, and continued to feel ill until they put into the more protected waters of Loch Fyne. Her only comfort was that Dain suffered the same malady, and kept her company leaning over the side of the boat.

They traveled up Loch Fyne, the brothers Campbell all taking a turn at the oars. At least her stomach was mollified, and they had not asked her to grab an oar. Isabelle leaned her head against the wooden railing, worn smooth, and warm in the sun. What was she to do? She needed to plead her case before her king, yet with every stroke of the oar she slid farther from home.

At midday, they put in at a sheltered inlet where they met more of Campbell's men. They had brought horses and provisions. After a quick meal, they mounted the horses and continued the journey. Campbell gave directions for Isabelle to have her own mount, but kept her reins himself, leading her along the road. With Campbell himself leading the way and his men behind her, trying to make a run for it was pointless.

The sun was setting in the west when they crested yet another hill (it seemed to Isabelle that Scotland was comprised mostly of hills), and Campbell's castle came into view.

Campbell turned to look back at her for the first time during the ride. "Welcome to Innis Chonnel, my lady."

Isabelle said nothing. Innis Chonnel was built on a small island surrounded by the dark waters of Loch Awe. The main castle itself was at least five or six stories high and of square construction, with two square towers on either side of the main entrance. Around the castle was a stone wall forming the inner courtyard, then another stone wall forming the outer ward, and an impressive gatehouse. There was not even access to the island from the shore. Instead, a large barge was used to ferry people, cattle, and supplies from the mainland to the small island.

There was no denying it was picturesque. The setting sun gleamed on the stonework, casting an orange glow and long shadows. Brightly colored flags flapped proudly from the towers. On the shore across from the island castle, small timber houses with thatched roofs dotted the shoreline, forming a quaint village. It was beautiful. It was impressive.

It was a prison.

Isabelle searched for possible escape routes. All she saw were tall buildings, surrounded by guarded walls on a secluded island. All it needed was a *Welcome, Lady Tynsdale, to Your Prison* banner hanging across the portcullis. Isabelle twisted a lock of hair around her finger. How was she going to escape this time?

Isabelle walked up to the castle gate from the ferry dock with mixed emotions. Campbell slid his arm around her shoulders. Perhaps he meant to prevent her from running away, but instead it was comforting and warm. As they strolled through the main gate, his arm slipped around her waist, and that felt even better. Isabelle closed her eyes and smelled the wood smoke from the kitchens, the briny smell of fresh fish, and the musky scent of the man standing next to her. She breathed deeply and had the odd sensation that she was coming home.

Despite these comforts, Isabelle noted that the castle wall was at least eight feet thick. The main gate was even larger, with not one iron portcullis, but two, one at the entrance, one at the end. In between, Isabelle glanced up at the murder holes, from which defenders would shoot at invading armies. The castle was well fortified: a comfort for those seeking protection, a distress for those seeking escape.

Inside the castle walls, Isabelle was confronted by a multitude of sights and sounds. The courtyard was large and housed several wooden structures. People were busy at work of various kinds: a blacksmith, washer-women, soldiers training in a far corner of the ward. Things seemed orderly and familiar to Isabelle, accustomed as she was to castle life, except that none of the men were properly attired according to her standards.

"David!" A woman ran to him from the tower house. She gave Campbell a warm embrace, which he returned in kind.

Isabelle felt ridiculously abandoned by him, removing his arm from her waist.

"David!" said another woman's voice. "Look, it is him." Five more women poured out of the tower house and embraced the returning laird.

Isabelle crossed her arms in front of her, irritated by the public display. She was about to say something caustic until she realized her own jealousy for what it was. Why should she begrudge the man for keeping a flock of beautiful women? Even if some were shockingly young, it was no concern of hers. Isabelle diverted her attention to admiring the stonework, and waited for the reunion to be done.

The first lady to exit the tower, a tall, sharp woman, looked Isabelle over and whispered to Campbell.

Campbell shook his head saying, "Nay, this is Lady Tynsdale. I am holding her until she is ransomed by her husband."

The tall lady looked down her considerable nose at her, and Isabelle had the sudden compulsion to apologize for any inconvenience her kidnapping might have caused.

"Lady Tynsdale," said Campbell, "these are my sisters, Mairi, Caitrina, Effie, Elyne, Gwyneth, and Jyne."

Sisters!

Isabelle was flooded with relief, though she knew she should feel nothing at all. More people streamed through the doors to greet them. His cousins came out with their wives and children, followed by more relations of every sort. There were a lot of Campbells. There was still only one of her.

Berating herself for feeling envious, Isabelle stepped out of the way and focused once again on the fascinating stonework. After a lot of greeting and telling of news, Isabelle followed the clan into the tower house. She was put in the care of Mairi, Campbell's eldest sister, a shrewd woman who welcomed her like a plague-ridden boil.

Isabelle was led to the women's solar, a pleasantly appointed room, comfortable and lit on two sides by windows. More women and girls were in the solar, chatting and laughing. Everyone stopped when Isabelle entered.

"This is Lady Tynsdale," announced Mairi. "An English lady Campbell is holding until her ransom can be paid."

Isabelle shut her eyes to prevent them from rolling back into her head. Mairi made it sound like she was delinquent on a debt she owed. Isabelle curtsied to the ladies, who were now eyeing her with suspicion. With a tight smile plastered on her face, Isabelle walked through the silent room to a bench in the far corner. When she sat, the whispering began. Nice to bring some excitement into these ladies' lives.

"So ye're from England?" asked a blond-headed Campbell sister.

"Yes."

The young lady moved over to sit next to Isabelle, despite some ferocious frowns from some of the elder ladies in the room. "I have ne'er been there, nor am I likely to, since there's a price on David's head. What is it like?"

Isabelle smiled at the forthright nature of this young Campbell. "I have lived in my castle at Alnsworth, and I like it very much. Though Innis Chonnel appears quite pleasant too."

"Thank ye. David is expanding it. It was getting a wee bit crowded."

"You have a large family."

The girl laughed, "Aye, we are a large family to be sure. Have ye met all o' us? David's the eldest and he's no' married, though I dinna ken why. Then there's Malcom, he married Innes, and he is holding one o' our fortresses to the north. Then Tomas, he wed Janet and holds a castle to the south. Mairi is next; she was married but her husband died. She serves as chatelaine here until David marries."

The blond Campbell lowered her voice to a whisper, "She is always bossing me about." Isabelle had no difficulty believing that of the tall, thin, shrewd woman.

"Dain was the next born. He married Fiona over there, she is expecting a happy event soon. Then there's Anne, she married Conall and lives wi' him, then Gill and Finn, twins, ye ken, then Hamish, then me, I'm Cait, I'm eighteen, then there's Effie and Elyne, they are sixteen, more twins, then Gwyn is fourteen, Jyne is thirteen, and then Rabbie. He is the baby."

"A pleasure to meet you." Isabelle paused, trying to recall the name of the girl in front of her. "Cait?"

"Aye, 'tis a pleasure to meet ye too. Then there are the cousins…" Cait prattled on, telling Isabelle the names of all the women in the room. Isabelle hoped she would not be questioned on this later. Listening to Cait list her extended family was like listening to the priest read from the book of Numbers. It was too much for her tired brain.

"Och, but ye can barely keep yer eyes open. Ye must have had a long journey. Let me fetch ye a pillow," said Cait, midway through her genealogy lesson.

"Thank ye kindly," yawned Isabelle. She was tired, though better for having met a friendly face. Isabelle leaned back against the wall and shut her eyes. She needed to rest.

When darkness fell she would try to escape.

❧

"Ow!" Isabelle woke to a sharp kick in the ribs.

"Och, sorry. I dinna recall ye being there," whispered a female voice in the dark.

Isabelle sat up from the straw pallet they had put on the floor for her. She had been given some floor space near the window in a sleeping chamber for some of the younger Campbell sisters.

"I've got so much on my mind, I forgot about ye." The voice moved nearer the window, the curtains were pushed aside, and the shutters opened.

Cait Campbell stood in the moonlight in a white linen chemise, a plaid draped around her, her long, straight, blond hair loose. The Campbells were a handsome lot.

"No harm done," said Isabelle, standing up and rubbing her sore side.

"I like to sit here when I need to think on something. I would like to take the view one more time, if ye dinna mind, before I leave on the morrow." Cait climbed into the large window opening, the thick walls providing room to sit. Isabelle leaned on the window ledge next to her. The view of the moon and stars was spectacular, but the steep drop at least five stories to the moat below would give anyone pause.

"Nasty drop," commented Isabelle, noting that this was one wall she would not like to climb down.

Cait grinned. "Aye. Dinna tell David I'm sitting here or he'll give me a lecture. He is forever yelling at me not to fall off a tower or out a window or some such."

Isabelle sat down beside Cait on the window ledge. "I hear I am to wish you felicitations on your betrothal."

Cait turned toward the inky landscape. "Aye. To Gavin Patrick. They say I've met him, but I dinna recall." Cait wrapped her plaid around her a bit tighter. The night air was cool and damp.

Isabelle stooped and picked up her own blanket from her pallet and wrapped it around herself. She sat gingerly back down on the rough stone ledge trying to find a spot that was not too bumpy on her sore backside, still tender from her long journey.

"'Tis no' the most prestigious o' marriages. Gavin is apparently the nephew o' Graham's son-in-law or some such thing." At Isabelle's blank look Cait added, "Graham is a well-respected clan, ye ken."

Isabelle did not ken, but she nodded obligingly.

"At least Gavin is my age, no' some auld gray-hair," muttered Cait.

"Then you are lucky," said Isabelle. "My husband, Lord Tynsdale, was widowed three times before we were wed."

"Och." Cait scrunched her nose. "Have ye been married long?"

"Since I was sixteen years. 'Tis good to marry a young man. You might be able to prevent him from developing bad habits."

"Does yer husband have bad habits?"

Isabelle sighed and stared at the black water below. "One or two." If you counted a tendency to murder your wife a habit.

"I am sorry for ye. At least David tries to take our feelings into account when he makes a betrothal."

Isabelle grunted in a most unladylike fashion. "The only thing my uncle took into consideration was how much coin he could get to secure my betrothal. I wish I could have had a chance to make my own marriage."

Cait raised an eyebrow in a gesture that was reminiscent of her older brother. "Make yer own marriage?"

"I had a maid who fell in love, or so she told me, with one of the soldiers. He wooed her for months, bringing her flowers, reciting poetry. Does it not seem unfair that our servants are free to marry where they choose but we are not?"

Cait stared at her for a moment, leaning her head back against the stone wall. "I ne'er thought o' it that way."

Isabelle closed her eyes. In the dark it all seemed hopeless. "More than anything I just want to be free."

"Come," said Cait, grabbing her hand. "This is a good view, but I know one better." Isabelle followed her through the dark room and out the door. Isabelle wondered with a splash of hope whether Cait knew some secret escape route from the castle, but instead of going down, Cait took her up the circular stairs.

They emerged onto a tower lookout, the cold night wind teasing their hair. The view was indeed impressive. Loch Awe surrounded the castle island, and reflected the pale blue light of the moon. The black outline of the hills formed a distant wall around them. The night sky was ablaze in stars, a band of white star clusters crossing the sky. Isabelle took a breath, it was indeed something to behold.

Cait gazed up at the stars and spun in a circle, laughing. "I used to come up here a lot." She dropped her wrap and scrambled up on top of the parapets.

"What are you doing?" asked Isabelle, questioning the sanity of her new friend.

"Flying. Watch." Cait stood on the battlements, her arms stretched wide.

"Come down or you'll fall!" exclaimed Isabelle.

"Nay, I used to do this all the time." Cait leaned forward, the wind flapping earnestly at her chemise. She turned to Isabelle and smiled. "You said you wanted to be free."

Isabelle returned a hesitant smile. It was mad, but... Isabelle was pulling herself up on top of the stone wall that protected her from certain death, before she could consider the consequence of one false step. Copying Cait, she stood up on battlements and stretched out her arms. She was afraid to look down, so she closed her eyes.

The wind blew strong and cold against her, waking her senses. Her heart pounded with the excitement of doing something colossally stupid. She leaned ever so slightly into the wind. Cait was right, it was like flying. For one moment, she was free.

"Och! Get down! Get down!"

Startled by Cait's fierce whisper, Isabelle stumbled on the battlement. Her heart stopped and her stomach lurched as she lost her balance, but she caught herself on the stone wall and rolled down onto the top of the tower.

Isabelle lay on the tower floor, her heart beating a rapid chastisement for being so addlepated as to attempt such a feat.

"Whatever did you scare me like that for?" she demanded of Cait, but her friend was not paying any heed. Instead, Cait was lying on her stomach with her head between the stone battlements.

Isabelle crawled forward to see what had so rattled Cait. In the courtyard below a man was leaving a wooden building and walking with purpose to the stone castle. Even in the faint light, Isabelle could tell by the fluid walk and the broad shoulders that this was David Campbell. She stared at him, unable to turn away. Despite being held for ransom by this man, she still enjoyed watching him move. If only things could have been different.

"Dinna let him see ye," Cait whispered. "He caught

me up here once before and was so angry he swore to have me flogged if I e'er came up to the tower again."

Isabelle, who had decided that battlement flying was definitely not the sport for her, was in sympathy with Laird Campbell in this instance. "What is he doing?"

"Leaving the chapel. He often goes to pray after everyone has gone to bed. He is always worrit o'er something."

Isabelle watched the shadowy figure of Campbell enter the tower house and disappear from view. She considered the conversation she overheard between Campbell and the Steward of Scotland. It appeared both the steward and Douglas wished him to marry into their clan. Yet there was more at stake than simply choosing a bride. Neither of them were free.

∽

David Campbell lit a candle in the wood frame chapel. It had been a long day reuniting with family, sharing the latest news. Yet some things he could share with no one. Some burdens he alone must carry. When everyone else took to their beds at night, he came to the chapel. He dropped to one knee before the altar and prayed for guidance.

Stewart, Douglas, Bruce, and Campbell: those were the names of the powerful clans in Scotland. Years ago they had united for a common purpose of defeating the English and maintaining their independence. They were bound by more than just politics, they were united by blood. His mother was a Stewart. His father's dame was a Douglas. Even the current king of Scotland, David Bruce II, was his second cousin. And yet these clans were heading toward war, sure as the morning mist settled on the loch.

He had to choose a side. Yet this rivalry was a mistake, born of allowing the English to manipulate them into fighting amongst themselves. What a waste. He could stand with Douglas, his foster father, and with his king. Yet if Stewart was correct, as he often was, and King David and the Douglas were plotting to gain land and freedom at the expense of the Scottish throne, how could he support such a scheme?

No, he would fight to the death before allowing England to claim the throne of Scotland. However, to stand with Stewart meant treason against his king and war against the Douglas. Not something one entered into without considerable reflection upon one's better judgment.

Campbell shook his head. Neither option was acceptable. He could support neither one. He bowed his head and prayed with earnest pleas for guidance. Opening his mind, he asked the Lord to show him the path that he must tread. He brought to mind both ladies to whom he was informally betrothed. One of them must be his destiny.

He asked for guidance, yet as the night wore on his mind began to wander. Instead of thinking of his future bride, an image of Isabelle came to mind. The more he tried to brush her away, the more his mind wandered back. She was beautiful, and determined, and brave, and amusing, and... another man's wife.

The last fact hurt more than it should. Why had she not told him? Why could she be so devious and yet act so kind? Who was this Lady Tynsdale? His mind wandered back to kissing her, to caressing her. His offer to care for her for the rest of his life had been spontaneous, yet sincere. Despite the unfortunate fact that she was married to an English lord, he still wanted to take her to his bed and finish what they had started last night in the inn.

Campbell stood, disgusted with himself. He had intended to pray for guidance, and instead coveted a married lady in the house of God. He was pathetic. Campbell stalked out of the chapel no closer to the answers he sought. He wished for some easy resolution to this situation, some way he could simply walk away from the growing conflict, but he knew that was impossible. He was the laird of the Campbells and this was the legacy his parents had left him.

He would never be free.

Thirteen

ISABELLE WOKE EARLY AND BEGAN A CAREFUL TOUR OF her prison island to ascertain the potential for escape. The Campbell women had too much to do with the departure of Cait to give Isabelle much mind. Isabelle wished her new friend well and tried not to be embittered that the only person to show her kindness was leaving so soon. It only gave her more reason to escape. Campbell must have been confident in her lack of options since he let her roam free, without so much as a guard to watch her. Still, there must be a way off of this island.

Isabelle grabbed a plaid that one of the Campbell ladies had left on a bench and wrapped it around her head and shoulders. Perhaps she could just walk off the island. The flat barge was ferrying people back and forth and much of the attention was drawn toward Cait's departure. This may be an ideal time to slip away.

Isabelle strolled casually to the dock, but when she tried to step on, she was held back by the ferryman. He was quite polite, quick with an "aye, m'lady" and "nay, m'lady" but he was not going to ferry her across, not without Laird Campbell's say-so.

Thwarted, Isabelle continued her review of the castle grounds and approached the small chapel she had seen Campbell leave the night before. She was not sure what she expected to see. Surely this place could not aid her escape, as her disastrous attempt at prayer yesterday amply proved. Yet Campbell spent time here and her curiosity was raised. The stone chapel was built into the castle wall, using one of the thick stone walls of the inner ward as its back wall. The roof was arched, constructed of timber and thatch.

The chapel had not yet been finished, and workers buzzed around the building busy at their tasks. Outside two young men were painting the stones white, while a very old man trimmed the doorway in blue with a steady hand. No door had yet been hung, so Isabelle stepped lightly around the worker and walked inside.

Inside, the chapel was cool and smelled of new wood and fresh paint. Light streamed through leaded glass windows, forming slanted pillars of light. Isabelle walked toward the light and stood in its glow. She took a deep, slow breath and experienced an odd sense of peace. Maybe this was why Campbell came here.

A new idea began to take shape. Maybe she could appeal directly to the Church. Alnsworth castle and the lands she inherited may prove a powerful inducement. She could ask for sanctuary and request to join a convent, offering Alnsworth to the Church in exchange for a divorce.

Living a cloistered life was not her first choice, but it was far and away preferable to being Lord Tynsdale's wife. Surely the Church would be a kinder master to her people than either Tynsdale or Douglas. It wasn't much of a life, but it was a life… which was more than what awaited her if she did not escape her husband.

Isabelle wandered to the front of the chapel, trying to picture herself living a cloistered life. The front wall had been built up beyond the height of the castle wall and had a large, round opening at the top. Many baskets were strewn about, each containing a different color of glass pieces. A picture was being laid out in glass on the floor. Fascinated, Isabelle moved closer to look at the drops of colored glass, like a treasure of colorful jewels.

"It will be the Lord seeking his lost lambs when it is finished," said Campbell from behind her.

Isabelle spun and her heart lurched to see him. Campbell had clearly bathed and shaved since she last saw him. He was a crisp figure of clean lines from his broad shoulders to his square jaw.

"Beautiful," murmured Isabelle. She caught herself and added, "the window, I mean."

Campbell said nothing, his face unreadable.

"You come here often, I understand," said Isabelle, trying to fill the awkward silence.

"Aye," said Campbell. He gazed at the ribbons of light streaming through the windows. "I have many decisions to make as laird."

"Does coming here help?"

Campbell gave her a grave look. "I've always thought the Good Lord has a greater understanding than I."

"And God shares his plans with you?"

"I woud'na quite say it that way. But often when I pray I feel that one option seems lighter, like the better choice. I have tried to live my life within God's will and under the protection of our Savior."

Isabelle was filled with a frustration she could not quite name. She envied Campbell, his family, the safety they enjoyed. "It must be pleasant to live in a world where God hears your prayers." The bitter comment escaped her lips before she could censor herself.

"God may hear my prayers but he does not always answer. Or perhaps I am too distracted to listen." He took a step away from her as if she carried an infectious disease. "Why are ye wandering about? Should ye no' be wi' the women?"

"I did not realize my movements were restricted. Perhaps you would feel more comfortable if you locked me in the cellar."

"I have a dungeon that would do nicely, come to think o' it."

Isabelle glared at him. "You are a perfectly odious man."

"Me? Ye should be thanking me!" Campbell's stony shell cracked in agitation. "How many times have I saved ye? Do ye ken who had ahold o' ye yesterday? That man is a notorious slaver. Do ye ken what would have happened to ye if I hadna saved ye, *again*?"

"I do appreciate your help, but... but I cannot be returned to my husband."

"That is where ye belong, Isabelle. Ye should ne'er have misled me to think ye were..." David looked away and clenched his jaw, the frown lines carved deep in his face. "Ye lied to me."

Isabelle bit her lip, her own conscience paining her. "I did not know if I could trust you."

"Now I ken I canna trust ye." The chill in Campbell's voice sliced through to her bones. "I shall return ye back where ye belong. I have sent a message to Lord Tynsdale. 'Tis the only thing to do."

"You are not only returning me, you are holding me for ransom!" cried Isabelle.

"And why should I not? Ye have cost me dear. Ye and all yer kind. Do ye ken how much I am expected to pay each year in ransom to buy back our bloody King David that yer king is holding for ransom?"

"You are holding me responsible for the actions of King Edward? Who, by the way, was full within his rights to take your King David hostage since it was Scottish forces that invaded England."

"We had every right to invade," said Campbell, his voice raised.

"And what right might that be?" demanded Isabelle in a similar tone.

"Ye are English!"

"You say English like it is a curse."

"It is!"

"So that is what you truly think of me." Isabelle put her hands on her hips, her fingers clenched into fists.

"What do I think o' ye?" Campbell's face became alive with emotion. "Ye are a wicked woman! Ye trick me into believing ye're available, ye seduce me, and make me dream o' ye. I want ye out o' my head and out o' my life!" Campbell's loud voice rang through the chapel.

"You dream of me?" asked Isabelle softly, her anger deflated.

Campbell flinched. He had revealed too much. In a brief unguarded moment Isabelle saw longing in his eyes. "I must send ye back. I have no choice." Campbell turned abruptly and stalked out the chapel door. Tears pooled in Isabelle's eyes and she wiped them away with an impatient hand. Campbell was never hers to lose so she could not be feeling loss. She took a quick breath and fought against her tears. Campbell was right. She must go.

She must escape.

Fourteen

"Please, Alys. *Please*." Cait Campbell was not above begging. Not when it came to something important like the contents of her breakfast.

"Nay, m'lady. What would yer brother say?" Alys braided Cait's blond hair into a sensible plait for traveling.

"Fie on my brother. 'Tis no concern of his. I promise I'll switch back before we reach Laird Graham at Dundaff. All will look as it should. What could it possibly hurt to switch places for a bit of the journey?"

"'Tis hardly proper, m'lady."

"I'll hardly look proper wearing my last meal. Please, Alys, ye ken how riding in that dreadful litter upsets my stomach." Cait turned to face Alys, her lady-in-waiting.

"And what about the guards? Surely they would note the difference." Alys stood with her hands on her round hips. She was several years older than Cait and had a curvier figure. Her dark brown hair hung in natural ringlets, which frequently escaped her headdress, a considerable contrast to Cait's straight blond tresses.

"Nay, I'll ride wearing yer cloak with the hood drawn over my face. Please, Alys, they will ne'er know the difference."

"Nay, m'lady. It would no' be right. I'll no' be a party to it."

Cait looked at her with wide eyes brimming with tears. It was an art form she had practiced over the years.

"Och, verra well then," conceded Alys. "But dinna blame me if it all goes bad."

❧

Archie McNab leaned against a tree waiting for the messenger at the appointed time. His life was pathetic. Years ago, Archie had decided that he was born under a curse. Whether his sire or dame was to blame was uncertain; one thing he did know was that he was destined to live out his life a failure and general embarrassment. It was a powerful shame, but he was accustomed to it.

It started to rain, filtering through the leaves and hitting him in the face. He could have put up the hood on his cloak, but what was the use? He had long ago stopped trying to avoid misery. His only hope now was that he might contract the plague or a fever and leave this godforsaken world. Or perhaps with any luck, someone would do him a favor and run him through. In his current occupation of mercenary, it seemed likely that his end would be sooner rather than later.

He heard the sound of horses through the dense forest and motioned his men to hide. They disappeared into the brush. It was too many riders, not the lad they were waiting for. A heavily guarded litter was being carried down the road. He considered for a moment if this good gentleman needed to have his purse lightened for their journey. But McNab noted the Campbell banner and thought better of it. This was not a clan to aggravate, best to leave them alone.

Before the party could pass him, they came to a sudden stop and one of the Campbell guards called for someone to quit blocking the road. McNab peeked around a tree. His messenger stood in the road, blocking the path of the caravan. McNab hoped that the lad would have the good sense to move aside.

"Ho there!" shouted the messenger. "Why dinna ye move yerself o'er to the side? I've got important business to attend to." McNab rolled his eyes. What an idiot. Just his luck, he could not get even a simple messenger to do his business without somehow finding a way to make a muck of it.

"Move aside, ye addlepated whelp," came the response of the Campbell guard.

"Nay, I've an urgent message, let me pass," called the messenger with all the false self-importance of youth and whipped out a sealed parchment, brandishing it with a flourish.

McNab groaned softly. The lad must be daft. What did that hothead think he was doing challenging a Campbell guard? McNab kept his eye on the parchment. That little missive must not fall into anyone else's hands but his. If something like that were to be brought before Campbell... McNab shivered.

The lad kept babbling his bravado at the main

guard, oblivious to the soldiers who dismounted and quietly flanked him. The guards were no fools; several had nocked an arrow and were keeping a close eye on the lad and the bushes around them, wary of an ambush. This was going to get ugly. McNab sighed and gave a silent command to the man next to him, knowing it would be passed along. He wrapped a black cloth around his nose and mouth, preparing for the worst.

The Campbell guards snuck up behind his daft messenger and knocked him clean from his horse. He was trussed and the missive placed in the captain's hands before the lad could make a sound. It was nicely done, but now it was McNab's turn. He needed to retrieve that message before anyone did something stupid like read it.

Fortunately, when it came to acting the part of a highwayman, McNab was a master. Not a skill to be proud of, but a skill nonetheless. McNab drew a short sword, a better and more precise weapon for close combat. He wore dark brown breeches, a linen tunic worn gray, and a black cloak, pinned at the shoulder. Lowlander's clothes. Whenever he went out to do mischief he wore the clothes of a Lowlander. He wore those clothes a lot.

He whistled a bird call, counted to ten, then leaped for the litter. His men jumped in concert with him, some falling from the trees on the soldiers with their bows drawn, a prime consideration for bandits. He grabbed the man out of the litter, held him firmly against his body for protection and had his short sword to his throat before anyone could say Holy Saint Andrew.

"Hold or I'll slice his throat," commanded McNab from behind his black mask. It had been his considerable experience that soldiers traveling with people in litters became quite cooperative and docile when said person in litter was threatened.

"Hold!" yelled the captain of the guard. The Campbell soldiers drew back and McNab's men let them. McNab's men stood, weapons in hand, ready for action, which they generally hoped would not be necessary.

It was then that McNab realized two things. First the man he was holding was not a man but most definitely a woman, and second that there was another woman who had dismounted from a horse and was screaming like a banshee for him to release the first.

"If ye please, lass, quit yer screeching," McNab tried to reason with the woman, though experience had taught him that negotiating with the fairer sex was a pointless exercise.

"Get yer bloody sword off o' her," the lass growled at him.

"Madam, please, ye shock me wi' such language. I'd be happy to oblige ye if it were no' for the fact that yer guards would kill me if I did." He smiled, a useless gesture from behind his mask. "Now if ye would be so generous as to make a small contribution to the fund for wayward highwaymen I shall release this lady and be on my way."

The screeching lass drew back her hood, revealing a pretty, young face and a long, blond braid. McNab heard a collective gasp from the Campbell guards. Curious.

"Ye hold the Lady Cait Campbell. Release her at

once or feel the wrath of Campbell," said the fair-headed lass who must be the lady's maid.

McNab appreciated her courage, but he would rob them just the same. He nodded at one of his men who grabbed the disagreeable lass and held a knife to her throat. It succeeded in quieting her into mute compliance. Most of all he needed that missive without revealing how important that parchment was. With any luck, which of course he had none, the soldiers would be so preoccupied by the robbery that they would forget about the missive.

He nodded to his men, and they began to relieve the Campbell soldiers of their tools of the trade. McNab could use the addition to his armory. He would not have chosen to rob Campbell, but he was at it now, and it would hardly do to let opportunity slip through his grasp.

Speaking of, the woman in his arms felt... nice, which was awkward since this was hardly the time to have lustful thoughts. It had been a long time since he held a woman in his arms, and this Cait Campbell was soft and curvy in all the right places. With a quick jerk he removed her linen headdress, revealing a mass of brown curls, falling in ringlets. Very nice.

McNab began to form a rather foolish plan. He was not an idiot, despite what others might say, and he readily identified the scheme as being profoundly stupid. One that would surely end poorly, probably in his own death. But, being cursed from birth, he never met a bad idea he didn't like.

He maneuvered himself and Lady Cait past the soldiers down to the open road, keeping the blade at her throat so as to minimize protest. His messenger was still bound on the ground. He kicked him to the side and left him there. Served him right for starting all this trouble.

"Take the horses." He gave one of his men a look, who grabbed the missive from the captain's hand. The captain had time to look at the seal, which meant he should kill the captain. Truly he should. A wise man would. But, as many would confirm, he was not wise.

"And now I shall take my leave, my fine gentlemen. I thank thee for yer generous contribution to our less-than-worthy cause."

"Ye've got what ye wanted, now release them." The captain spoke in a voice of a man trying to stay calm. The man was worried and scared. McNab must be holding something of value. Something Campbell would pay dearly to retrieve.

McNab continued to back up and waited for his men to mount until the only two still standing were himself and the man holding the maid. Two of his men held the heads of horses ready for a quick departure, so important in any robbery. This was the difficult part, the part that you had to do just right or you ended up dead.

"I'll be taking them for ransom. Good day to ye!" Both women screamed in protest as he sheathed his sword, threw Cait Campbell over his saddle, and jumped up behind her. He dug in his spurs to encourage a hasty retreat. Behind him he could hear the roar of protest from the guards who rushed him. He raced down the road, knowing he would have to ride far and fast to evade the guards behind him.

Even on foot he would not risk underestimating the Campbell guards. Only a fool would do that.

Except that he had just abducted Campbell's sister, so indeed, he was that fool.

Fifteen

MCNAB RODE HARD FOR AN HOUR, THE RUMP OF CAIT Campbell a lovely place to rest his hand. He had to hold the poor lass on the horse after all. Had he been a chivalrous man, he could not have enjoyed it as much as he did, but no one had ever accused him of gallantry. At the point her screams turned into low moans of pain he decided it was time for a brief respite.

He called for his men to pull up by the shores of a small loch. It continued to rain and the air smelled fresh and green. McNab dismounted and pulled Lady Campbell down. She glared at him, but allowed him to assist her to a stone where she could sit. His man did the same for the other. He looked at his prizes with some satisfaction. They should earn him a nice fortune.

"Sir," said the lady, trying to smooth back her wayward curls. "Release my maid. She can have no value to ye."

McNab rubbed his unshaven jaw and considered the idea. He certainly would not get a single coin for a maid. But… his mind devised a plan even less likely to succeed than holding them for ransom. He liked it instantly.

"Nay, my lady, I wish ye to be comfortable, and we poor beggars have little to give ye. Keep yer maid and yer comforts. Ye'll thank me for her later."

"I assure ye, 'twill no' be so," said the lady. Her brown eyes were wide, but her voice was calm. McNab liked it. He felt relaxed with her.

"What the hell do ye think ye're doing?" demanded a familiar voice behind him.

McNab's stomach clenched and his shoulders hunched. He turned to face his sister.

"Have ye gone completely daft?" Morrigan McNab was mad as fire and coming for him.

"Wheesht!" McNab grabbed his sister's arm, and forcibly moved her out of hearing of his two captives.

"Leave them where they are and let's be gone. Bringing them to McNab Hall will only destroy us all."

McNab regarded his sister with resignation. She was dressed in a man's costume, Lowlander's, as were the rest of his men. This irritable lass was McNab's biggest failure. Instead of finding his sister an eligible match, as he should have done, Morrigan had become an outlaw. He had tried to prevent her from joining his men, goodness knows he had tried. She said she would stop when he could best her in the lists. To his eternal shame, she was still here.

It was not that he was inept in the martial arts. No, it was just that, well, not one of his men could best her either, so he was not alone in his failure. Not that a shared defeat was any better. But it was.

"Enough, woman," McNab addressed her as female

because he knew it grated on her. Not the most politic thing to say, but it was his sister. It was his job to be irritating, just as it was hers to aggravate him. They were both well versed in their occupations.

"Dinna speak to me—"

"Listen, Morrigan, have ye thought o' what a ransom she would bring? Or, better yet, if she would consent to marry me or Andrew we could be rich off her dowry."

Morrigan stared at him like he had just claimed to be the Queen of France. "Ye're mad. 'Tis yer only excuse."

"Nay, think on it, she would certainly come with a substantial dowry."

"Have ye no' done this once before, ye addlepated fool?"

McNab winced at the memory of the last time he kidnapped an heiress and tried to force her into marriage. MacLaren had not taken kindly to the abduction of his wife.

"That was different, she had already married MacLaren." McNab tried unsuccessfully not to choke on his name. There was nothing in the world that scared him as much as MacLaren. "This time I'll do it different. I'll woo her, get her to agree to the marriage."

Morrigan rolled her eyes. "Ye're daft."

"Nay, I have a plan. I'll get her to agree to the wedding, then we'll send a message saying I rescued her from horrible bandits and I'll ask for her hand. She will confirm the story and Campbell, being grateful for my assistance, will grant me her hand in marriage."

"Archie, listen to me. This will ne'er work. She'll

ne'er agree to marry ye, and even if she did, Campbell would ne'er agree to the marriage."

"I'll handfast wi' her then. If she bears a child before the year is out, Campbell will have no choice."

"Of course he'll have a choice. He'll put yer head on a stake."

"Nay, no' if I was the one who rescued her."

"This will end badly, mark my words, Brother."

McNab sighed. She may be right, but his whole life he had been waiting to do something big, something unexpected, something that would shatter this curse. He could not afford to be cautious. He must be bold. He must take chances. Maybe meeting Cait Campbell in the forest was fate.

Or maybe his sister was right. He was daft.

❧

"I told ye this was a verra bad idea," hissed Alys.

Cait slumped forward, not looking at Alys. "Ye can hardly blame me for being abducted."

Alys muttered something that did not sound like an agreement.

"Up now," called the bandit.

Cait found herself riding pinion behind a wiry man with weather-beaten skin. He smelled like he avoided water like the plague, and instead rubbed himself with dung for his morning ablutions. Cait tried hard not to fall off the backside of the horse without touching him, and would have held her breath for the entirety of the trip had her lungs not demanded an occasional gasp of air. Her only consolation was the mental image of what her brother would do to these knaves once he caught them.

After spending most of the day on a horse with her aromatic companion, the little band of robbers trotted into the gate of a tower house. The tower was square, about three stories high, and unadorned. Around her was evidence of poverty and disrepair. Even the wooden gate looked like it had been broken at some point and poorly patched back together. The people in the courtyard wore clothes that had seen better days, some no better than rags.

Even the poorest of her brother's men dressed better than these. The people stopped their work and stared at Cait and her maid with suspicion. Cait was uncomfortably conscious of the difference in attire.

The leader of the ragtag band led them into the tower house and up a circular staircase to a solar. It was sparsely appointed and had a small peat fire smoldering in a large fireplace, giving the room an earthy, smoky smell. Perhaps these bandits were squatters in this tower whose original owner had fallen on desperate times.

Another thief entered the room after them, a thin, lanky fellow who ignored Cait and Alys and slumped into a wooden chair by the fire, putting his feet up against the fireplace stone. The thieves had long since removed their masks, revealing dirty, hard, resigned faces.

"Please, make yourself at home, my lady, I wish ye to be at ease," said the leader. He addressed himself to Alys, her lady-in-waiting. Since Alys had been in the litter, he now believed Alys to be Cait. It was a confusing day all around.

The leader's clothes marked him as a Lowlander,

but his speech was that of a Highlander, and far
beyond the class his clothes would suggest. He was
a tall man with black, cropped hair. He removed his
black cloak, revealing dark breeches tucked into black
leather boots and a thick, woolen tunic.

"Ye've had an arduous journey. Here, please sit
down." He looked at his reclining friend and said,
"Morrigan, get up, give yer seat to the lady."

Morrigan glared in return and made no effort to move.

"Well, here now," said the tall leader, dragging a
bench by the fire and motioning Alys to sit. "I hope
ye are feeling comfortable, my lady."

Alys sat cautiously and looked at Cait, questioning.
Cait knew she was waiting to know what to do, not
sure if this thief's mistake was in their favor or not.
Cait was not sure either.

"What is all this, then?" A young man entered the
room. He looked at Alys and Cait and stopped short.
"'Tis true. Ye've abducted a lady?" The lad went pale.

"Aye, let me introduce you," said the leader of the
bandits. "Ladies, may I have the honor of presenting
my brother, Andrew McNab. I am Archibald McNab,
laird o' the McNab clan. I hope you both will have a
pleasant stay."

"Archie, nay, ye must no' do this," said Andrew.

"Dinna worrit yerself, I'll handle everything," said
Archie.

"That's what he is afeared of," snorted the man in
the chair.

Cait did a double take at the lounging figure. The
voice, it wasn't right. Looking again at the face, she
realized the lad was really a woman.

The woman glared at Cait. "Quit yer staring," she snapped. "I dinna take disrespect from anyone, especially no' servants."

Cait gasped at her harsh language. How dare she speak to her like that? Even if she mistook her for Alys, her maid was a lady-in-waiting from a respectable family, not a servant. She opened her mouth to tell her so, but was distracted by McNab's younger brother.

"Nay, we must give them back," said Andrew to his older brother.

"Too late for that now, they know who we are."

Cait's eyes snapped back to McNab. That statement sounded ominous. He was regarding Alys, tapping his fingers together, looking eager to please… and desperate. Desperate enough to do what, she did not know.

"Ye mean to ransom us, then?" Cait asked the leader.

"Aye."

"Well then, I suggest ye provide my lady with suitable accommodations."

"Lady Cait will have every possible comfort."

"Which does not appear to be much," said Cait, rising to the role as her own handmaiden. "Lady Cait requires a chamber now so she can rest. She is not accustomed to this type of treatment and has a weak constitution, ye ken how ladies are. I'm sure her humors have been put out of alignment." Cait sighed dramatically, embracing her performance. "I only hope it will no' be too late."

Andrew McNab turned from pale to green. Even Morrigan eyed her with caution. Cait felt she was on to something.

"She may have my bedchamber immediately," said McNab.

"Nay," said Cait, looking at each McNab with a critical eye. "Give us Andrew's. He's the cleanest o' the lot o' ye. I'll need wine for m'lady and a pallet of fresh straw for myself."

"Ye can take what ye get," said Morrigan with contempt.

"Moldy straw will cause an inflammation o' the lungs in m'lady," said Cait, doing her best to sound imperious and succeeding dramatically. "Unless ye dinna care whether m'lady is still alive when Laird Campbell comes to claim her."

Cait had the satisfaction of seeing her three captors look ill at ease.

❧

Archie McNab leaned against the mantel in the dimly lit solar. After tearing his house apart to find suitable furnishings for his lady captive, he had finally gotten them fed and settled into Andrew's chamber. The maid was right about one thing, it was the cleanest room in the tower.

It was late, the light from a single tallow candle cast flickering shadows into the dark room. McNab took the folded parchment from his tunic. He was finally alone with the missive that had been the start of this tumultuous day. On the parchment was the telltale red seal of two knights riding a single horse, their shields emblazoned with a single cross. Around the edge of the circular seal were the words *Sigillum Militum Xpisti* followed by another cross. *The Seal of the Soldiers of Christ.*

How he had ever gotten himself into so much trouble? He could only hope the Campbell captain had not had time to note the seal and realize it was the symbol of the Templar Knights.

The man who sent him this message was ruthless without end. McNab held the parchment for a moment longer, almost afraid to open it. There must be another way to provide for his clan other than to work for this man. He closed his eyes and sat down in the chair beside the hearth. But his people… McNab sighed and broke the seal. If there was another way to feed his people, he was too dense to figure it out.

McNab opened the parchment and held it up to the light of the single candle. On it was a single command written in the bold hand of the abbot.

Kill the Bishop of Glasgow.

McNab jerked forward in his chair and held the missive closer to the candle. The parchment glowed orange in the flickering light, but the message remained the same.

"Hell and damnation," McNab muttered, his pulse rising. He leaned back in his chair and put his hand over his eyes.

"What are our orders now?" asked Morrigan, entering the room.

McNab bolted forward and held the corner of the parchment to the candle. The missive burst into flame and disappeared into ash.

"There be no orders," said McNab, speaking too quickly. "He says he's pleased wi' our work, 'tis all."

"Dinna speak me false, Brother. 'Tis insulting beyond words."

"How do our guests?" McNab changed the subject. He had done little to protect his sister, but he knew she would be safer if she did not know from whom their orders came.

Morrigan snorted. "What a bonnie lot o' spoiled brats they are. I canna stand to look at them. Why do we no' just let them loose in the marshes and pretend we ne'er saw them?"

"Nay!" McNab stood and rubbed the back of his neck. "They must be made comfortable. If Lady Cait could be persuaded to marry, her dowry could save the clan."

"'Tis ne'er going to happen as ye well ken."

"It must." McNab's voice was ragged. "It must work this time. How does a lady like to be wooed?" He looked over at Morrigan, then shook his head. "Why am I asking ye? I need to find a lass." He quit the room, his eyes glazed, his shoulders hunched forward.

His sister stared after him. "Aye, ye go do that now."

Sixteen

IT WAS ENTIRELY POSSIBLE THAT SNEAKING OUT OF
Innis Chonnel in an old pickle barrel was not among
her wisest decisions. Isabelle's previous attempts to
escape had proven unsuccessful, and she was running
out of time and options. She had attempted to swim
across, reasoning that if fish, not known for their
overall intellectual capacity, could swim, then surely
she could too. Her logic had failed her in a most wet
and embarrassing way.

So she had resorted to a more desperate plan,
which unfortunately involved pickles. Campbell had
proved to be an able jailer, but this morning he had
left on a hunt, so she was free of his watchful eye to
enact her escape.

She had spent the past few days sneaking up to
Cait's tower and watching the comings and goings of
the castle and noted how goods were transported back
and forth in large barrels. The barrel in which she now
sat in had once housed pickles, but was now empty
and being sent back for another shipment.

Not that the lack of pickles lessened the smell. She

had half a mind to struggle out of the barrel for a breath of fresh air, but the recollection of the danger her people faced, should she fail, kept her still. She shifted around a bit, trying to reestablish circulation to her right leg and was determined to be patient. All she needed was to get across the loch.

After some time her patience was rewarded. Her barrel was jolted sharply, and then swayed gently as it was ferried across the water on the raft. Excitement mounted as she was moved again, spun off the barge and presumably onto the dock. It was evening, and she had watched how barrels would be stacked and left overnight to be transported in the morning. All she needed to do now was to wait until dark. Faint light spilled through a small hole she had carved with her table knife in the top of the barrel for light and air. Suddenly, the light went out.

Someone must have stacked a barrel on top of her. She took a slow breath, trying not to panic. She pushed gently on the lid of her prison, nothing happened. She pushed harder, but still, nothing moved. She was stuck in the barrel. Her heart pounded in her chest and the air started to get thin. She shoved hard at the lid with her shoulder. Again, the barrel lid was stuck tight. She took several rapid breaths. The briny stench was not enough to fill her lungs. She was going to suffocate in this barrel. She gasped for air, and wriggled around so she could push with her legs on the lid of the pickle barrel.

Bracing herself, she shoved with all her might. The lid lifted but an inch. She took a stifled breath and screamed, straining against the lid with her last ounce of strength. With a crash she broke free. The barrel above her smashed on the ground, and her own barrel tipped over and rolled until it hit something solid and she spilled out. Men shouted, a horse neighed, and more goods crashed to the ground as her actions caused several other barrels and caskets to go flying.

Isabelle slowly sat up, her head still spinning. She was sitting in the middle of the road, covered in mud. She groaned, how could it get any worse? A black horse walked up and stopped in front of her. Sitting tall in the saddle was none other than David Campbell.

"Lady Tynsdale!" Campbell stared at her like an apparition. Behind him, Dain, Gill, and Finn had equal expressions of disbelief.

Isabelle struggled to extricate herself from the mud and the muck. She regained her feet, but not before she was covered in slimy black filth. Despite being caught, she was relieved to have air once more, but a deep breath made her reconsider.

Something around her reeked. She looked around at the faces of the dockworkers and of Campbell's brothers and clansmen sitting high in their saddles. They all were staring at her with faces of surprise, shock, and repulsion. What was that smell? Confirming suspicion, she took a whiff of herself only to fight her own gag reflex. She stank worse than a month-old mackerel lying in a cesspool.

"Ye certainly have a way wi' the ladies. See how she canna wait to welcome ye home," said Finn, breaking into a mischievous grin.

"Ride on," said Campbell with a scowl.

"If ye require any advice on how to keep a lady at yer side——" said Gill with a sly smile.

"Ride on, I say!" commanded Campbell. The twins laughed but complied, Gill giving her a wink as they passed, of all the cheek.

Isabelle straightened her back, fought the urge to cover her own nose, and said, "Good day Laird Campbell. It seems my plans have gone a bit awry."

Campbell's eyes shone with the twinkle of amusement she had grown to loathe, especially since it set his countenance at its most pleasing. He dismounted and started to come to her, but stopped and blinked his eyes. "Saints above, lass, what have ye done?"

Isabelle's lip trembled, but only for a moment before she regained control of her emotions. It was fortunate she was not prone to large, emotional displays, because this situation called for one, if any did. She was wise enough to realize the only thing more pathetic than a briny lass covered in dung was a sobbing briny lass covered in dung. She was determined to persevere.

"Will you teach me some curses?" Isabelle asked, her words dripping with false sweetness. She had the small satisfaction of seeing his smile fade and confusion fill his eyes.

"I beg yer pardon?"

"I haven't the good fortune to know any curses and this seems an ideal time to express one."

Campbell's mouth twitched and he broke into a genuine smile. He pressed his lips together, but then laughed loud and hard. Isabelle was mesmerized. His joyous laughter radiated warmth and good humor. For a moment, the worries that seemed to press on him vanished and he looked young and carefree. Isabelle had thought him handsome before, but when he laughed, David Campbell was gorgeous.

Campbell stepped toward her and covered his mouth and nose with his hand, though whether to smother a smile or defend his nostrils she could not be sure. He motioned her to march forward and she walked back onto the dock, the workers giving her a wide berth. They stepped onto the ferry barge and found they had the raft all to themselves as none of the Campbell brothers chose to ride with them. Finn and Gill waved to her, laughing hysterically.

When they reached the other side, Campbell took her elbow and steered her toward the castle as his clansmen jumped out of their way. Campbell took her down to a room on the first floor near the kitchens. Buckets of steaming water were being carried in by servants and Mairi approached them from the other end of the corridor.

"Sorry, Mairi," said Campbell, "I fear this be an emergency and we must insist on taking yer bath."

"Nay, Brother," said Mairi with a frown. "I've waited all afternoon for my..." Whatever Mairi was going to say was lost as she froze quite suddenly in an unnatural position, her mouth open. One foot still in the air.

"As I said, a most urgent situation, Sister."

Mairi put both hands over her mouth and nose and scurried back down the hall. "Please take the water with my blessing. And have it dumped in the loch when yer through," she called from a safer distance.

Servants finished their work, or dropped it undone, and hustled out of their way, leaving them in a dimly lit room with the large, wooden, barrel-like tub. It looked suspiciously to Isabelle like a giant pickle barrel, but she could not wait to scrub herself free of all the grime.

"Thank ye, I can take it from here," said Isabelle and watched in dismay as Campbell shut the door with himself still inside.

"Sir, I… you have no need…" Isabelle backed farther into the small room. "This is hardly proper, I can see to myself."

Campbell arched one brow. "Ye smell worse than the time my hunters crossed a skunk. Ye need washing."

"I am perfectly capable—"

"Ye are hardly capable or ye'd ne'er be in this… pickle." Campbell pressed his lips together in a weak effort to avoid smiling at his own pun.

"Ye mock me!"

"Aye. Now let's see ye remove yer gown."

"I'll do naught of the sort." Isabelle was indignant. This day was bad enough without his insensitive puns and barely concealed mirth at her expense.

"Ye need to get that gown off; 'tis ruined. I'll no' leave till I see ye can manage."

Isabelle opened her mouth to protest, but then remembered that while her surcoat was tied in the front, her gown was tied tightly in the back.

"Send a maid to assist."

Campbell shook his head and stepped forward. "They'll no' come and I canna blame them. Let me do this and bathe ye, for yer stench is bringing tears to my eyes."

"Fine then. But I'll only undress to my chemise, then you must leave!"

"With pleasure, I assure ye."

Isabelle struggled with the slick ties of her surcoat and, after close inspection and a bit of a fight, she managed to remove it. Her gown, tied in the back, proved difficult. No matter how she twisted her arms, she was not able to untie the slick knot.

"Come, let me help." Campbell reached out but she backed away from him. In a flash he was upon her. She attempted unsuccessfully to bat him away, but he got his hands around her waist and struggled with the slick ties of her gown. Isabelle tried to wrestle from his grasp, but to little avail. The only thing she managed to accomplish with her struggle was to transfer a large amount of muck from her to him.

When he finally pulled off the gown, leaving her gasping in her chemise, they were both rather filthy. In one easy movement he picked her up into his arms and dumped her into the tub. The warm water engulfed her, feeling achingly good. Her chemise clung to her, wet and protective. Campbell regarded her with deep lines of disapproval etched on his forehead, then pushed her head underwater. For an instant Isabelle thought he meant to drown her, but he let her come up for air soon enough.

"Nay, still dirty." Campbell pushed her under again. This process repeated several times until she was breathless and sputtering. She coughed a bit and pushed her wet hair out of her eyes. Campbell was inspecting his linen shirt and stripped it off with disgust. He dunked the shirt into the tub and started to scrub off the muck.

Later, she would decide the appropriate response

would have been to chastise him for washing his dirty laundry in her bathwater. In the moment, however, all she could do was stare across the steamy tub at his naked chest. She watched with fascination how his muscles moved, smooth as silk, under his skin. She struggled against the desire to put her hand against his muscular chest.

He slowly raised his head and gazed at her, his eyes dark in the dimly lit room. "Are ye always this much trouble?"

Isabelle shook her head in denial, then shrugged her shoulders. "Only with you."

Campbell regarded Isabelle from across the tub, trying to understand her actions. Her eyes were large and black in the dim light. With her black hair slicked back, he noticed a small scar along her hairline he had never seen before. There was much of her in view that he had never seen before. Her white chemise clung to her breasts with transparent protection.

Campbell gave himself a mental shake and walked around the tub to the back wall to hang his sopping shirt on a peg to dry. Water droplets splattered on the stone floor, the only sound in the warm, damp room.

He tried to understand Isabelle's actions with little success. Why would she endanger herself in a barrel of all things? She was not being mistreated. Campbell would see her safely returned to her husband. The thought of the man chilled Campbell. Why had she not been honest with him about being married? Why was she so determined to escape she would risk her life? It was none of his concern, but he could not abide the thought that a lady under his protection was risking her life to escape him.

Campbell reviewed his last interaction with her with some displeasure. He prided himself on his ability to keep a cool head, but with Isabelle he had lost his temper. His reaction to her had surprised him. Perhaps his harsh words had frightened her. He sighed, but he knew he must make amends.

He eased slowly back to the side of the wooden tub next to her. She busied herself with a cake of soap and did not turn around. Despite his chivalrous intentions, he took a good look down her cleavage. His fingers itched to touch her again. She was a passionate woman, one whom he greatly desired to have in his bed, yet the revelation of who she was made that impossible. The realization she was married had hit him hard. She had never been his to lose, so it should not hurt. But it did. He cleared his throat and looked at the ceiling.

"Ye are under my protection, Lady Tynsdale... Isabelle." Somehow the formality did not quite fit the situation. "Ye dinna need to fear me or try to escape. I swear no harm will come to ye."

She stopped scrubbing her arm and turned toward him, her large dark eyes meeting his. "Thank you. I know you have saved me more than once," she said softly.

"Well, as much as I'd like to take credit today, I did naught but save ye from yer own stench."

"As I said." She gave him a wry, half smile.

He smiled back and leaned closer, resting his arms

on the side of the tub. A small voice in his head told him it was time to leave the lady to her bath. He told the voice to shut up.

"Ye have naught to fear from me." Campbell spoke in a low, soft voice. "Ye can stop trying to escape and enjoy yer visit. Yer husband will be along soon enough to collect ye, and this will all be but a memory."

Though she did not move, Isabelle went stiff and tense, as if the soft version of her had been replaced by a stone one. She stared across the black water with vacant eyes.

"Isabelle," he whispered.

Her wide eyes, filled with fear, met his. Where had she gone? What was she thinking? She rubbed the scar along her temple like it pained her. He put his arm around her. It was a fluid, instinctive movement, natural and right. And oh, so wrong.

She sighed, resting a wet cheek against his bare arm. He said nothing, afraid that if he spoke, the spell would be broken, and she would turn to stone once more.

He fought against his growing concern for her. Honestly, whatever her troubles they were not his. Her husband would see to her. And yet... she was quite determined not to return to her husband. Campbell had assumed she was fleeing to some romantic tryst with another man, but what if he was wrong. What if her husband was mistreating her? He exhaled a long breath. Too many sisters had made him weak. He could not stand any female in his care to be frightened.

"Isabelle, what is troubling ye?"

Isabelle turned to face him, searching his face for what, he did not know. He leaned closer, drawn by her full red lips. Those lips needed to be kissed. She tilted her head up. He needed her… now.

He brushed his lips across hers, teasing himself with forbidden fruit. He waited for her to pull back, to voice a protest. Instead, she placed one hand on his chest and reached the other around the back of his neck, warm and wet, drawing him closer. Alarm bells rang in his head, and lightning shot up his spine. He bent down and kissed her softly on the lips. She pressed closer to him and he deepened the kiss, claiming her mouth with his.

Isabelle made a small sound and pulled back, her mouth open, her eyes wide. He waited for the inevitable slap across the face, but contrary to expectation, she cupped his face with both hands and returned his kiss. His heart pounded against his rib cage with such force he wondered if she could hear it. He wrapped his arms around her, lifting her up and pressing her tight against him. He thrilled in the sensation of her wet chest against his, and silently cursed the hard, wooden barrier that remained between them.

She felt wonderful in his arms, like she belonged there. He kissed her lips again and continued down her neck, leaving a trail of kisses. She arched back and he kissed the hollow of her throat. Desire pounded through him, taking control. Tugging at the wet fabric, Campbell pulled at her chemise, even as he pressed her closer. He must have her.

He slid his hand down her chemise, and cupped her ample breasts. She moaned and clung to him, trailing a hand down the back of his neck, sending happy shivers down his spine. Desire coursed through him, growing with every beat of his heart. It was wrong, but he would have her.

"I want ye," he rasped, inarticulate but direct.

If anything, Isabelle grasped him tighter.

"Laird Campbell!" The door banged open with a crash, spilling light into the chamber. Campbell dropped Isabelle and jumped back. Isabelle fell into the tub with a splash.

"Your sister's guard was set upon by robbers," said a page, too excited to notice the goings-on of the tub. "Some have returned, but Cait is no' here. She's been taken!"

Seventeen

CAIT TURNED HERSELF INTO THE MODEL OF A LADY-IN-
waiting. Never had she had more fun.

"Nay, no' cabbage. Pray dinna bring m'lady
cabbage. It makes her bilious." Cait did not care for
cabbage. She had no whether Alys liked it or not.
"M'lady needs wine. Good wine, mind ye. And fresh
bread and roast pork." She gave Archie McNab and
his younger brother a commanding look.

"But we dinna have any pork. Would yer lady care
for fish? We have fresh salmon from the loch," said
Laird McNab. He bent forward, rubbing his hands
together in a pleading manner.

"Nay, m'lady only eats fish on Fridays. 'Tis
Wednesday. She only eats pork on Wednesdays."

"What does she eat on the morrow? Gold leaf
cake?" Morrigan stood in the shadows, leaning one
shoulder against the wall of the dark passageway.

"Wheesht, Morrigan," hushed McNab, and
turned back to Andrew. "Appears we will be hunting
boar today."

"Happy poaching," said Cait brightly, and shut the

door on the face of Archie and Andrew McNab. She smiled to herself and opened the door once more. "Dinna forget the wine and bread before ye leave."

The sister made an audible sound of disgust. Cait could not see her face in the shadows, but she swore she could hear Morrigan's eyes roll.

"Ye shoud'na treat them so harsh," said Alys when the door was safely shut once more.

Cait looked around the room with satisfaction. It had been not much to start with other than clean and functional. Through her demands they now had a roaring fire, bearskins on the floor, and heavy, brocade curtains for the bed. Cait smiled. Every time she wanted something she created a new ailment for "m'lady," and watched the McNab household jump to fulfill her every whim.

"I dinna care if they wear themselves to the bone, it serves them right for kidnapping us. Maybe if we're really a pain they'll just send us back."

"Or maybe they'll bury us in the dungeon. Honestly, Cait, I do wish ye'd curb yer tongue before ye get us into worse trouble."

"Nonsense, they woud'na dare. David will come for us and he will expect to find us in good condition. Even these daft sons of knaves understand that."

Cait sat on a bench by the fire and twisted a golden lock of hair around her finger. "All we have to do now is keep them busy until my brother comes for us."

Campbell armored up and called for his soldiers to follow. He was out of the castle gates and back on the road before the sun had moved far in the sky. He rode hard, following his guards to the scene of the incident. He was going to find this whore's son who dared to touch his sister and tear him limb from limb. And then he was going to do something truly wicked to the bastard who interrupted his tryst with Isabelle.

Campbell blinked at the turn his thoughts had taken. Isabelle... Lady Tynsdale was not his. She was another man's wife. An Englishman at that. He should not have allowed things to get out of hand in the bath. He should never have kissed her... again. Yet she had not pulled away and seemed more than willing, yet woefully inexperienced. Perhaps her English husband had not kissed her as he should. Stupid English sod.

Isabelle's actions confused him greatly. She appeared to fear her husband. Was that Sassenach cruel to her? Campbell shook his head. It was none of his concern. Even if she was being treated poorly in marriage, that was something for her kin to deal with, not him. Just as Cait's abduction was for him to deal with. He focused his thoughts back to the situation at hand; but somewhere back in the corner of his mind, he hoped that Isabelle had kin who would protect her, and he wondered what she would do if she had not.

Andrew and Archie returned from the hunt the next day tired, hot, and successful. The wild boar would be a boon to more than just their finicky ladies, and Andrew hoped it would bring some happiness to the clan. Archie certainly needed something to help dispel his gloomy disposition.

They entered their walls to the cheering of their hungry people. It was good to finally have some success. They dismounted and headed to the tower to give the good news to their captives.

"Andrew, I need ye to get rid o' that moat dragon of a lady's maid for me," said Archie. They paused at the bottom of the stone staircase that led to the quarters now occupied by Lady Cait Campbell.

"Alys?" asked Andrew.

"Aye, wi' her in the way I'll ne'er be able to woo Lady Cait. I must get Cait to agree to this marriage… and agree never to tell her brother it was me who kidnapped her."

"What are ye asking o' me?" His brother took a step away from him and shook his head. "I'll no' be raising my hand against a lass."

"Nay, I dinna mean for ye to harm her. Cait might take offense, and if I wanted it done that way I'd ask Morrigan. Nay, I only want ye to take her off somewhere. Take her for a ride, show her the loch, have a roll in the hay, I dinna care, just get her away from my Cait."

Archie stalked away with long strides. Archie had always been tall, but lately his shoulders had started to stoop, as if he struggled under the weight he carried. Ever since he brought home the Campbell ladies, Archie appeared haunted… even more than usual.

Andrew leaned against the cold stones of the dark staircase. He wished his brother had not brought these two here. It could only bring trouble. He started to walk away. Why should he get involved? Let Archie deal with his own bad decisions. Andrew stopped before he got too far. Whatever bad fortune Archie brought on himself would be shared with the whole clan. Besides, if he did not get Alys away from Cait, Archie might resort to more desperate measures. The thought of what Morrigan might do to her turned Andrew around, and had him hopping up the circular stairs two at a time.

"Good day, ladies, I bring good tidings." Andrew rapped on their door.

The door flew open and Alys stepped out, half-shutting it behind her. "Wheesht, ye fool! M'lady is taking her afternoon rest. Dinna disturb her."

"My apologies. Will she be resting long?"

"She sleeps for at least three hours, for her constitution is verra weak, ye ken."

"Och, well in that case," Andrew reached behind her and pulled the door shut. "Ye have some time to inspect the beast we brought."

"Ye wish me to examine a carcass? Certainly not!"

"Ye may wish to take a tour of the castle."

"Ye have naught here I care to see," said the lady's maid, haughty as a queen.

"We'll take the horses then and ride to the loch. Verra nice vantage." Andrew was slowly ticking off Archie's suggestions, praying that one of them would tempt Alys from her lady. He hoped she would agree to a ride, because he doubted Alys would care for a roll in the hay. Though the idea was not without merit.

Alys was nicely formed, even if she was a sharp-tongued creature. She had bright blue eyes and blond hair she wore with two small braids on either side of her face, wrapped around to the nape of her neck where the two braids met. The rest of her long, straight hair was loose. It would look pretty flowing behind her when she rode. He smiled in spite of himself. Alys hesitated, and Andrew knew he had hit upon something she wanted.

"I canna leave. M'lady may need me." Alys sounded less confident than before.

"Ye just said she would sleep for three hours."

"Aye, but…"

"Ye must be tired o' that same old room, the same old air. Think how nice a ride would be. Lady Cait would ne'er ken ye're gone."

Alys looked up at him, an unbridled look of desire in her eyes. Andrew gulped and something inside him stirred. If she was ever to desire him like that he would march her to the stables without thinking twice.

"Aye then, let's do it."

Andrew bowed and offered her his arm, proud of his accomplishment. He hoped Archie could pull off a miracle in the time he would give him. It would take that to be sure. At least with pretty Alys on his arm, Andrew was sure he would enjoy the afternoon.

❧

Cait filled her lungs with fresh air, filled with the scent of heather, and urged her mount faster. She was having a glorious time, and was having difficulty feeling guilty about it. She knew she shouldn't have left her maid, whom McNab believed to be her, but the offer his brother made was far too tempting. She was tired of staying in that room all day and night and the ride was exhilarating.

Andrew McNab rode beside her, easily matching her stride and comfortable in his saddle.

"Let's stop here." He slowed and stopped his mount and Cait did the same. He dismounted and helped her from her mount. Cait was conscious of his hands on her waist.

"Follow me," he said, with an easy smile and led her up a small rise. Cait followed, thinking that it would be easier if the bad guys were ugly, pockmarked bruisers, not young, tall, and rather braw.

Cait reached the top of the rise and caught her breath. Below her lay Loch Voil, bathed golden in the light of the sun. The green valley stretched before them, the heather flowing like waves in the playful wind.

"'Tis lovely here," Cait murmured.

"Aye, I've always liked coming here," said Andrew.

"Thank ye for bringing me." Cait reveled in the view, until she remembered this man was her captor, not her escort. "'Tis too bad ye have such a brother."

Andrew shrugged. "He may do things I woud'na dream o' doing, but I canna judge him for it. Archie became laird after our father died many years ago when I was only a lad. 'Tis no' been easy for him. Yet he still found a way to send me to the university in Edinburgh, even though he's ne'er been himself."

"If he's so kindly why did he attack my guards and kidnap us?"

"I dinna say he was always bright," said Andrew with another one of his half smiles Cait was beginning to find distracting. "I just said he is no' wholly bad. Often he is trying to do something good."

"Och, what good can come from abducting us?"

"Yer ransom could feed our clan."

"'Tis more likely he'll end up at the end o' my brother's sword."

"Yer brother?"

"My, uh, my…" Cait mentally berated herself for forgetting to be Alys. "My brother is a Campbell warrior."

Andrew nodded and looked out over the sparkling water. "Sometimes I dinna think Archie cares whether he lives or dies."

Cait struggled with mixed emotions toward this man. Andrew was not as tall or lanky as his brother, but was still of goodly stature. His brown hair was cut short and his features were pleasant to look upon. He wore the costume of a Highlander, his plaid belted around his waist to form a kilt and then gathered and thrown over his shoulder, pinned with an iron broach at the shoulder. It was similar to the garb worn by her brothers and all the men in her clan. He turned to her, and she noted that his eyes were hazel, his lips were full and rosy. He smiled and Cait grew warm inside. Without meaning to, she smiled in return.

Cait broke away from his infectious smile and stared out over the shining loch with unseeing eyes. She needed to say something quick to break this spell.

"So while yer brother fumbles to be laird, ye go off to university and let him do what e'er foolish thing he can think o'? I suppose ye feel no responsibility for yer clan."

Andrew's jaw tightened, and he stepped away from her and turned toward the loch. Cait fought the urge to apologize for her comment. Andrew bent down, picked up a stone, and hurled it out toward the distant loch below. Cait watched the arc of the stone as it flew until she saw the water in the distance ripple. Give the lad his due, it was an impressive throw.

He was not as broad-shouldered as many of her brothers, who were generally large, muscular men, but none of her brothers had ever made her feel like this. It was hard to define. She was jumpy and excited, and she wanted to be close to him.

"I'm sorry, Andrew. My words were unfair, unkind." Cait groaned inwardly. Of course her words were unkind; they were intended to be unkind. Why she felt compelled to apologize was beyond her.

Andrew turned back toward her and gave her the half smile she enjoyed rather too much. "Nay, 'tis naught but the truth." He shrugged. "Maybe 'tis time to stand up to him. He has always been so much older than I that I ne'er thought to challenge his leadership. Aye, 'tis time to make my own decisions."

Stepping close, Andrew looked down at her with kind eyes. Cait's heart thumped a confused little beat, and she took a little step forward herself.

"Are ye married, Alys?"

Cait shook her head no. It was strange to hear him call her by another's name, and she struggled against the urge to correct him.

"I'll make ye a deal." Andrew's eyes were shining and he gave her another smile, but this one was far less careless. "I'll release ye on one condition. Ye must give me a kiss."

Cait gasped at him. Of all the things she thought he might say, this was not on the list. Her heart purred with a happy little beat, and the air between them crackled with anticipation. If there was a sensible voice inside her telling her to stay away from this man, it had been stunned into silence.

"What say ye, bonnie Alys?" Andrew moved closer and slowly put his right hand around her waist. With his left he gently took her hand and placed it around his own neck. She tingled with excitement and put her other hand around his neck. He pulled her closer until their bodies were touching, the warmth of his embrace sizzling through her.

"Ye are a lovely, spirited lass," he whispered into her ear and nuzzled her cheek. Andrew drew back slightly and Cait pulled herself up on her tiptoes for his kiss. Andrew leaned forward, until his lips were almost on hers. Cait waited impatiently, but it seemed he was waiting for her to initiate the kiss, which was something she would never do.

She pulled him close and pressed her lips to his.

Eighteen

ANDREW MCNAB WRAPPED HIS ARMS AROUND THE most delightful creature he had ever had the joy to hold. Alys was clearly inexperienced, but when she pressed her body and her lips to his, it was the best kiss he'd ever had. When she finally pulled back, he gave her a smile and then as real a kiss as he knew how to deliver. He was more experienced in these matters than she, but not as much as he would have liked. She seemed surprised at first, then grasped him tighter. She even trembled a bit. He may have too, truth be told.

When their lips finally parted she was wide-eyed, her lips red and swollen, her face flushed. What had his brother said about a roll in the hay? Good man. Best idea ever. But no, he had promised to let her go for a kiss. Bad luck that. Perhaps she would let him renegotiate the terms.

With amazing strength of character, for which Andrew considered he deserved some sort of award, he managed to let go of soft, sweet Alys. For once she said nothing, and they stood simply gazing at each other as the wind swirled around them in friendly gusts.

He did not know why he had demanded a kiss. Perhaps it was an attempt to restore his wounded pride. She had accused him of being a passive accomplice in his brother's crimes. It might have been a careless attack on her part, but her arrow had hit home.

Too long had he let his brother make poor decisions while he did nothing to stop him. It was time to do more than complain; he needed to act. He needed to stand up to Archie, even though he doubted Archie would be affected by reason. The first thing Andrew needed to do was get Lady Cait and Alys back home before Campbell saw them all on the end of a pike. It was time for Andrew to be a man.

"I suppose my only honorable course of action is to let ye go." Andrew's tongue moved slowly over the words as if he had been hitting the whiskey a bit too hard. Alys remained silent. He hoped he had not shocked her into a permanent stupor. "I'll lead ye to the border of our land, or maybe to Kimlet, there be kind folks there ye can stay wi'."

Andrew frowned at the sun, low on the horizon. It was late and would be dark soon. Alys should not be on the road alone at night. "We need to hurry if we are to make it before nightfall."

"Wait, I canna leave…" Alys seemed to choke back her words, and then started again. "I canna leave m'lady."

Andrew took a deep breath of relief. He did not wish to let her go. Also, letting her go meant taking the risk that she would tell Campbell who had abducted them. If Campbell marched in war against them, there would be nothing but the destruction of the McNabs in his wake. Yet keeping the ladies posed an even greater risk. If they were caught with the ladies as captives...

Andrew shook his head. Nothing good would come of that. His brain spun as he tried to think of a plan that would get his clan out of this impossible coil and appease his own wants as well.

"I will make you a new deal." Andrew edged his toe in the dirt, feeling guilty about the plan that sprung forth in his mind. It was similar to one of his brother's ill-fated schemes. Must be the McNab curse. "I will release both ye and Lady Cait, but I need ye both to swear an oath no' to reveal who had captured ye. I ask this on behalf o' my clan who has suffered enough."

"I can and will promise that." Alys nodded.

"And then there is the question of payment," Andrew added. He was a veritable knave, but was unwilling to relinquish the best part of his plan.

"Payment? Ye wish for a ransom too?" Alys frowned, contempt creeping back into her eyes.

"Nay, I dinna want your gold. I want ye. I'll let ye go but ye must agree to... to..." Andrew stuttered over the words. Her innocent blue eyes grew wide and he lost his nerve.

"Ye wish for... more?" Alys whispered.

Andrew nodded vigorously. "Aye."

"How much more?" Her words were breathless, her eyes shining. She did not seem terribly upset by his blackhearted offer.

Andrew paused, wondering how much she would be willing to give. "Ye give me as much as ye ken your freedom be worth."

She blushed and glanced down at her shoes. He cringed. What was he thinking, trying to seduce an innocent? Then she looked up at him through her lashes.

"My freedom is worth quite a lot to me."

Oh hell, was she *flirting* with him? He was a dead man, no doubt. His pulse raced in an unmanly sign of youthful excitement.

"I'd like ye to show me how much." He feared he had a rather goofy grin on his face. It could not be helped. He had not had this much fun in, well, ever.

Alys smiled back at him, a real honest smile that told him he was not the only one enjoying the moment.

Andrew put his arm around her and led her back down to where the horses were tied. The sun was low on the horizon and the sky glowed orange and red. "Tomorrow then, ye'll ride wi' me again?"

"Aye," she said with a grin.

Andrew rode back to McNab tower feeling very pleased with the turn of events. His conscience bothered him a bit for not simply releasing his beguiling captive at the earliest possibility, but the rest of his body thought it was a bonnie plan. It may delay their leaving by a day or two, but otherwise it should make no great difference. Andrew embraced his rationalizations tightly and clicked to urge his horse faster, following the pace set by his lovely lass.

❧

Isabelle sat on a rock on the shore of her island prison. Despite her recent attempt to escape, the Campbells still allowed her to roam freely on the island, even allowing her to exit the postern gate to the shore of the island. The far bank and freedom were tantaliz-ingly close and yet too far to reach. If only she could get to it! Its nearness mocked her.

After yesterday's escapade she had questioned her senses. Why had she allowed Campbell to kiss her? To touch her? Even more perplexing, why had she kissed him back? It was a kiss she had long desired, and it had been delicious. But no, she must not think that way. Campbell was her captor and would give her back to her husband without qualm.

She must find a way to escape. She wished him well on his quest for Cait and hoped she would be found, but Isabelle needed to be long gone before Campbell stepped back on this island. Her best defense against these strange feelings was to never see him again.

She grabbed a rock and stood, hurling it into the water. At least that was what she meant to do, but not having much practice in rock throwing, she released the stone too late and it went sailing behind her instead. She heard a thud and an "ow." Behind her, one of the younger Campbells rubbed his head.

"Oh merciful heavens, what have I done?" She rushed to the boy, who could not be more than ten years old, and grabbed his head, to see if the wound was bleeding. She was relieved to find nothing more than a lump, which would surely grow considerably before the day was out.

The boy gazed at her in bewilderment. "I seen a lot o' folks throw rocks in the loch, m'lady. But I dinna ken how ye threw the rock ahead o' ye and it hit me behind ye."

"Oh, I am so terribly sorry. Does it pain you much?

Here sit down and let me fetch one of your sisters to look after you."

The boy's eyes turned stormy and he removed her hands from his person with the injured pride of the male species. Isabelle caught a glimpse of the man he would someday be.

"I beg ye would no' fetch my sisters," he said most emphatically. "I am no' some weakling that needs coddling. I am *eleven* years old." He puffed out his chest and she could see the boy he still was.

Isabelle repressed a smile. Men and boys were alike in one thing. Their pride was their most sensitive part.

"I beg your pardon, Master Campbell. I did not see you clearly at first. Now I can tell you are quite grown." Isabelle gave him a sweeping curtsy. If she could not repair his head, at least she could restore his pride.

He bowed in return and came up smiling, his wounded head and pride forgot. "What are ye doing here, m'lady? Did ye ken there are beetles under the rocks? And sometimes snakes." His eyes sparkled with mischief.

Isabelle glanced suspiciously at the place she had been sitting. "How... interesting."

"Want to see?" The lad did not wait for an answer, but began lifting up large rocks to see what might be lurking underneath. She wondered if she could escape back to the castle, but he swiftly turned to show her a handful of bugs: three beetles and a spider.

Isabelle put her hand over her mouth to keep from screaming. With all the courage she could muster, she murmured that they were very nice indeed.

He grinned in appreciation and bent over to look under another rock, this time pulling out two worms and a snail for her inspection. This went on for longer than she wished, especially since she considered that things under rocks ought to stay under rocks. But every time she gently suggested that perhaps they might stroll back to the keep, he assured her that even better things were under this next rock and so she stayed, figuring this was penance for having hit him on the head.

The next rock was disappointing for the lad, only two more worms. He shrugged an apology. "There's better stuff on the other side; see those bigger rocks there?" He pointed toward the not-so-distant shore.

Isabelle nodded, giving the far shore and her freedom a longing glance. "Do ye go over there often?" she asked absently.

"Aye. Want to go over there now?"

More than you could ever know.

"That would be very nice, um... I beg your pardon, Master Campbell, but what shall I call you?"

"My name's Rabbie."

"Well, Rabbie, they will never let me on the ferry to the far side, so I suppose I must content myself with the rocks on this island."

"But we can take my boat," Rabbie said proudly.

Isabelle's head snapped around so fast she almost injured herself. "Did you say, I mean, do you have a boat?"

Rabbie smiled. "Aye. Made it myself. But ye must no' tell my sisters or they'll take it from me. They are always worrit about things like me falling in the loch."

"No, I will not tell them, I promise." Never had she spoken words so sincerely. "Where is this boat of yours?" Isabelle tried to remain calm, but was afraid her excitement was plain. Her heart beat faster. Could this young Campbell be her salvation?

"Come, I'll show ye."

Isabelle followed the lad down around some large boulders and up and over some others, making their way behind the main keep. It was not an exercise she would have taken under normal circumstances. Her guide, dressed in a smaller version of the plaid his brothers wore scrambled over the rocks with ease. Isabelle, wearing a nice linen gown, was not nearly as nimble. She feared her gown would look a sight when she was through, but none of that mattered if she could find a way to escape.

"Here!" Rabbie finally came to a stop at a small, sandy space between two larger boulders by the water's edge, forming the world's smallest beach. He pointed proudly at some flotsam lying on the sand. The remnants of several barrels had been lashed together with rope and covered with tar. Sticky black tar.

"Is this your boat?" She hoped he would laugh and produce some other craft that was a bit larger, less sticky, and more... boatlike.

"Aye, ye like it?"

"It's quite something, isn't it?" She was at a loss. Could anyone float in that thing? "But how does it work?"

"Like this, I'll show ye." He proceeded to climb into one of the halved barrels and grabbed a piece of wood that had been carved into a crude oar. He pushed himself out into the water and Isabelle gasped, sure that he would capsize and she would have to rescue him, which would be difficult since she had already proven her inability to float. But he did not sink immediately to the bottom and instead paddled around a bit before coming back to shore.

In the distance came the call to supper.

"Time to eat," said Rabbie enthusiastically and took off back over the rocks without so much as a glance behind.

She followed him as best she could, a plan forming in her mind. If he could do it, so could she. All she needed was a chance. It would have to be tonight, waiting any longer was dangerous. Her husband may be here to claim her at any time. No, it must be tonight.

It had to be better than a pickle barrel.

Nineteen

Tynsdale Castle, England

SIMON GLARED AT THE GIRL COWERING IN THE CORNER and curled his hands into tight fists. "When I tell you to lie on the bed and spread your legs, you'll do it, wench!"

The girl glanced furtively at the door and gritted her teeth. "I tell you, I'm no wench. I'm the daughter of the ironmaster."

"You are what I say you are," growled Simon and lunged for her. She dove out of reach and scrambled up, putting a chair between her and her attacker.

"Have you no respect for the guilds? Even Lord Tynsdale, cruel as he was, honored the guilds." The girl glanced again at the door.

Simon grabbed the wooden chair between them and smashed it to the ground, splinters flying everywhere. "I am the Lord Tynsdale now. You must learn to serve your new master."

"You are naught but his bastard son, not fit to serve as lord," cried the girl, running for the door.

Simon smiled a cruel snarl. "And for that, you will die."

He caught her by the throat and slowly squeezed, enjoying her look of terror, her desperate clawing at his hands. He was in control. None would ever challenge his authority again.

"Simon!"

A page stood in the doorway, his eyes wide. Simon dropped the girl in favor of new prey. In two long strides he reached the door and punched the lad in the side of the head, sending him sprawling to the ground.

"I am the Earl of Tynsdale, when you speak you will address me as such."

"Yes, my lord," said the page meekly, struggling off the floor.

"How dare you interrupt me while I'm taking my pleasure."

The page glanced at the girl, coughing and gasping on the floor. "R-riders approaching from the south. An army of men, they carry the banner of Sir William and... and the king's own."

"No! It cannot be." Simon slapped the page down again and strode from the room. "Lock the door, I'll finish with the whore later."

The young page met the eyes of the girl. She struggled to stand, her hand protectively on her throat. "Run," he mouthed and left the door ajar.

Simon, bastard son of the recently deceased Earl of Tynsdale, stood on the lookout tower, his hands clenched on the rough stones of the battlements. In the distance, a veritable army was on the move. The banners told the tale. It was Sir William, his cousin of sorts. He had been expecting him. Now that his father was dead, Sir William came to claim the title and the seat of the Castle Tynsdale. It was his right, since he was heir, but Simon cared not. He was prepared to fight William. But the other banner gave him pause. It was the king's men. Could he raise his hand against the king?

Simon grabbed the first thing he saw, a quiver of arrows, and threw it over the edge of the battlements where it crashed to the courtyard below. It was a pointless gesture and he did not feel the better for it. Should he make ready for war against the king? And why would the king lend his aid to Sir William?

Simon shook his head. William was no favorite of the king. If King Edward sent his men to Tynsdale, then he wanted to claim it for himself and give the castle to a man more favored. The king must wish his forces present so he could expel William and give these lands to someone more favored. William was a fool. But there was nothing new in that.

Simon watched the approaching hordes, his mind calculating his odds. Having been born the son of a serving wench, he had learned to take when he had the advantage, and to run when the risk was too great. Honor was a flight of fancy for the privileged. It was not for those who had to fight to survive.

"What are your orders? Do we fight?" Simon's battle captain was at his side. He was an excellent warrior and followed Simon's commands without scruple.

Simon ground his teeth, thinking of the repercussions. The king would not care a whit if he destroyed William, but would no doubt take offense if Simon took up arms against his own men. A lengthy battle defending the castle from a siege of the king's own

soldiers was not in his plan. He wanted to be acknowledged as Tynsdale's son and heir, not hung from the
nearest tree as a rebellious peasant.

"A message for Lord Tynsdale," said a page who
joined the men on the tower. "Actually two messages,
they both arrived today."

"Well read them, boy."

Simon would have read it himself if he had ever
bothered to learn to read. He had better things to do,
most of them with a sword in his hand.

The first message was from the captain of the men
he sent to collect Lady Tynsdale.

> *Much regret to inform you that Lady Tynsdale*
> *has either escaped or was carried off by a spooked*
> *horse and we have been unable to locate her. We*
> *have searched these past several days and will*
> *continue. Her men also search for her, but none*
> *have found her.*

"Damn them to blazes! How hard can it be to
bring me one wench?" Simon · shook his head.
Maybe she had gone and got herself killed and saved
him the trouble. He could not be bothered by such
trivial matters.

"Read the next," he commanded.

The next missive began with some vague flatteries
about the beauty of Lady Tynsdale. Simon drummed
his fingers impatiently on the battlements waiting for
the point of the missive.

In order to return the Lady Tynsdale to hearth and
home, the captor demanded a ransom be paid. The

missive ended with promises that no harm would come to her and it was signed *Laird Campbell.*

Simon snarled in response and the page prudently dropped his messages and ran back down the stone staircase.

Someone dared to demand ransom of him? That little whore! All she needed to do was get her sorry arse to him, but no, she somehow managed to get herself kidnapped in the process. She was doing this on purpose to irritate him. She would pay dearly for her impudence. The last time he saw her would be nothing compared to what he was going to do to her now. Simon grabbed the missives, crumpled them, and threw them over the battlements, smashing a large fist into the stone.

"What are your orders?" his battle captain asked again.

Simon thought fast. He had faults enough, but was clever when pressed.

"Lower the drawbridge. Invite in my cousin, damn fool that he is. Tell the men to gear up. We ride at first light tomorrow and will not return."

His captain raised an eyebrow. "With Lady Tynsdale's guard out scouring the countryside…"

"Alnsworth will be ripe for the plucking." Simon smiled at his captain's ready understanding. He had wanted to take Tynsdale Castle, but would content himself with Alnsworth instead. "I do believe I am the Lady Tynsdale's guardian since the death of my poor father. Let us take this prize, but we must be quick. Once Alnsworth is under our control, we must away to the Highlands."

"The Highlands? Why?"

"We must find this Laird Campbell and ransom the Lady Tynsdale."

The battle-hardened captain frowned. "But why? Let her rot with the barbarians, I say."

"I would agree, but I cannot allow her to live and possibly wed another who would come to claim Alnsworth. No, since this missive was addressed to my father it seems she does not yet know she is a widow. I must have her before she finds out."

"And what will you do with her?"

Simon shrugged. "Stab her, beat her, drown her. What does it matter as long as she's dead?"

Beneath the tower, the ironmaster's daughter grabbed the two crumpled missives and slipped out the castle gate.

Isabelle waited in her hiding place until it was dark enough to travel. She had feigned illness and left the evening meal early, saying she needed rest. Instead she bundled up some blankets to look like she was sleeping on her pallet, and left the castle by the postern gate while it was still light and the gate was open. She concealed herself between some large rocks and waited for dark, hoping no one would discover her missing until morn. In the pocket of her cloak were several bread trenchers, wrapped in a linen cloth, which she had been stashing for the past several days. In her other pocket was the precious gold coin. She squeezed it for luck. It had to see her safe.

Darkness fell thick and black in the Highlands. There was just a slip of a moon, giving Isabelle barely enough light to walk without bumping into something. She walked around the dark edge of the castle, hugging the wall to avoid being seen by the sentries. Moving slowly to the back of the castle, she began her climb over the rocks. The trek had been challenging in the daylight with a guide. At night it was nearly impossible.

Her scar ached again and she moved on. She would do this. She had no choice. Somewhere along the shore was a tiny boat she had every intention to steal. She had become a thief in the night. A sobering thought. But not sobering enough to stop.

Isabelle scrambled over a large boulder, hoping she was heading in the right direction, and got caught by the hem of her gown. She twisted and tried to release herself, but it was stuck tight between two rocks. She gave a fierce tug and heard the sound of the gown tearing. Isabelle sighed. Another gown ruined. Slowly she worked her way over and around the rocks, but could not find the little sandy beach with her rescue boat. She struggled through the night until she was exhausted. Finally, she could move no more. She collapsed onto the ground and leaned up against a boulder to rest.

She tried to get comfortable, but there was very little space. She pushed something out of her way with her feet. Whatever it was scraped across the sand and smelled of… tar. She sat up with a start and found herself sitting on the beach next to the makeshift craft. She was so happy she could have hugged it… if it hadn't reeked.

Well, she'd survived pickles, she could survive this.

Isabelle pushed the awkward thing into the water and climbed in carefully. She was not a large woman, but she certainly outweighed young Rabbie. She took the oar from the shore and sat down in the boat carefully. The boat wobbled precariously but somehow remained afloat. She gave a little push and drifted away from the safety of the shore. Too late to change her mind now.

Taking a gentle stroke with the oar she moved forward and she grew more confident. The little craft looked horrendous, but young Master Rabbie knew a little something about building a boat. She paddled a bit stronger and headed for the shore. It took a while to get there, since the boat liked to go around in circles rather than straight, but eventually she convinced it to behave enough to ferry her the short distance across to the other side.

Isabelle reached the shore and unstuck herself from the makeshift craft. The air smelled better, the rocks looked friendlier, the birds sang merrily. Oh no, birds? Isabelle had been so focused on her escape she had not noticed it was now approaching dawn. She climbed up the hill, taking care to stay in the shadows. Once she found the main road, she set a quick pace away from Innis Chonnel. She did not like running away from Campbell. He had treated her kindly and had not taken advantage of her... most of the time.

Memories of his kiss in the bathing tub flooded back. Heat radiated from her core and her lips ached to be kissed once more. He made her feel all sorts of confusing things. She should not have kissed him, but if she saw him again, she would likely seek his lips once more. It was infatuation, it must be. What else could it be?

She wished Marjorie was here to help her sort through these confusing emotions. She would set her to rights. Poor Marjorie, Isabelle wondered what had happened to her after she left. Marjorie must be sick with worry for her. Isabelle quickened her step. She must get home as soon as possible.

The sun shone through the morning haze, and she continued her journey at a fast clip. At least she had put some distance between her and Innis Chonnel. She wondered what the sisters would do when they awoke to find her gone. Would they mount a search? No doubt they would. How long would it take before Rabbie discovered his little boat missing and alerted the rest of the clan that she had likely left the island? And how long after that would they come looking for her? In the daylight there was nowhere to hide.

"Whoa there, wee lass. Where are ye off to?"

Twenty

DAVID CAMPBELL'S FACE WAS DARK, IN CONTRAST TO the beautiful, sunny day around him. His men had taken him back to the scene of the abduction so they could track the captors. At first the task was easy; the bandits had ridden as a group down the road at considerable speed. Then the tracks led in all directions.

Not knowing the correct path, they had to follow each lead until the tracks disappeared. It had taken days of careful searching, trying to find the right trail. On this day, David followed another set of tracks, which ended at a river. He searched up and down the bank looking for exit tracks but could find none.

This was maddening beyond words. Who knew what treatment his sister may be suffering while he ran after shadows? If anyone dared to touch her, he swore he would make his death slow and painful. Campbell mounted to ride back to camp. He would kill the sons of whores when he found them. And he would find them.

Back at camp, Campbell was disappointed to learn that none of his men had experienced any better luck than he. He was itching for action, preferably violent.

"Set up camp for the night. We ride to St. Margaret's Convent tomorrow to meet wi' Cait's betrothed," Campbell said to his men.

"What do ye do tonight?" asked Dain.

"I will continue to search."

"I am wi' ye," said Dain.

"Me too," said Gill.

"And me," said Finn.

"I am no' tired," said Hamish, stifling a yawn.

"Thank ye. We will find her," said Campbell, reassuring himself along with his brothers.

"Ye ken Gavin can help?" asked Dain.

"His kin knows these hills well. I hope they can tell us who may have taken Cait."

Campbell signaled for the men who were coming with him to mount up. His brothers and all of his clansmen joined him. Campbell acknowledged their dedication with a curt nod. Searching in the dark would be difficult, but he would not take his rest until he knew Cait was safe.

Cait Campbell waited impatiently for Andrew McNab to arrive. Over the past few days Andrew had been an attentive host, and she his most willing captive. Her body hummed with excitement, as if for the first time in her life she was really alive. Even Alys had noticed her mood and commented on the smile often seen on Cait's lips.

Cait tried to be more circumspect and guarded with her feelings, but it was a pointless exercise ending in abysmal failure after a few minutes of effort. Today,

Cait expected to be taken off by her captor and forced to do goodness only knows what to win her freedom. Her pulse raced merrily, and heat flushed through her in odd places.

Despite her determination to remain aloof, Cait drummed her fingers on the tablecloth and stared at the door, waiting for her captor's knock. Where was this man? Was it too much to ask for him to be prompt in his threat to ravish her senseless?

"Waiting for someone?" asked Alys.

"What? Nay! I mean, Andrew may call on us, but it is nothing to me." Cait smoothed invisible wrinkles out of the tablecloth.

"I expect Archie will come to call as well."

"Oh! That hideous man!" Cait clutched the formerly smooth tablecloth. "Has he bothered ye? Do ye wish me to stay wi' ye?"

"Nay, he's no bother to me. He is quite gentle-manly. He is handsome, no?"

"Nay!" Cait could not think kindly on the man who had abducted her, though she was relieved not to be obliged to remain with Alys.

Alys frowned. "I think he is simply trying to protect his clan, albeit misguided. He needs someone to take care o' him."

"My brother will take care o' him," snapped Cait.

A knock came to the door and Cait nearly vaulted over the table to open it. Andrew stood in the doorway, his big eyes sad, the corners of his mouth drooped.

"What's wrong?" asked Cait.

"Archie is sending me up north to go fishing."

"What! Why?"

"Ye said m'lady only eats fish on Fridays, particularly haddock. Well, our haddock run has already come and gone, and it being Friday tomorrow, Archie wants me to go up north to see if I can find some."

"Nonsense, ye must have misunderstood me. Honestly, I dinna ken why I talk when nobody listens. What fish do ye have in the loch now?"

"Salmon."

"Well that is what m'lady likes best. Shall we go?"

"I need to tell Archie—"

"We'll tell him together and then go for a ride," commanded Cait and marched out of the room, dragging her captor behind her.

⁂

Isabelle awoke securely within the walls of St. Margaret's Convent. She breathed deeply, relishing her newfound freedom. It was marvelous to have finally succeeded in her plans, even if her pallet was made of rocks, and the homespun wool gown they gave her must have been woven by the weaver's blind, drunk cousin. It fit poorly. And it itched. But she was at St. Margaret's, a feat that pleased her greatly.

When a small band of travelers had caught her on the road from Innis Chonnel, she feared her escape would be short-lived. Remembering her lesson from the common room in Glasgow, she clamped her mouth shut and said not a word. Instead, she clasped her hands together, and looked toward the heavens in a universal sign of piety. Maybe it was her look of innocence, maybe it was the gold coin she offered, but the party agreed to take her on to the convent.

A woman in the party dubbed her a little lost nun and took her up in the wagon as they traveled. It took two days to arrive at St. Margaret's Convent. Two days without speaking and looking pious; it nearly killed her. But it worked, and Isabelle relished her success.

She had arrived late yesterday and had been given hospitality without question. Her kindly traveling companions had continued on their journey, so today she needed to make her plea. Convincing some Church official to give her an annulment or allow her to divorce could hardly be as difficult as escaping from Campbell. She smoothed her rough gown, brushing away her fears. It had to work. She had come too far to fail now.

Isabelle briefly considered simply pretending to be some random peasant girl requesting to enter the convent, and to hide here in this foreign place until her husband died. But what would happen to her people while she hid to protect herself? No, she could not treat them so poorly. They were the only family she had left. She must plead to have her marriage dissolved. Besides, the wool gown was itching something fierce.

Isabelle entered the common room and was invited by the nuns to break her fast with them. She quickly learned she needed to present her case to the Mother Superior, but Mother Enid was out visiting and would not return until the next day. There were a few whispers between the nuns about the number of other guests, but an elder nun waved away the concerns and invited Isabelle to stay as a guest at the convent. Isabelle readily accepted.

After a bland meal of porridge, Isabelle walked outside the hall into the bright sun of a crisp morning. A group of men were entering the hall, most likely the other guests the nuns had discussed. Isabelle stepped to the side and turned her face away from the sun shining directly in her eyes. Shielding her eyes from the sun, she brushed against the large form of a man.

"I beg your pardon," she mumbled without looking up.

"Good morn to ye, Lady Tynsdale," said an all-too-familiar voice.

Isabelle's head shot up and she jumped backward with a small shriek. David Campbell stood before her.

Campbell pressed his lips together, glaring at her with accusing eyes. "My congratulations, madam. Ye have finally made yer escape." Campbell's voice was hard and detached.

"Campbell!" Isabelle stared at the figure before her like an apparition. Beyond the shock of seeing him, his appearance was much altered, dirty and worn from the road, his face had taken a grayish tinge. "You look dreadful."

His shoulders hunched with invisible weight. "Thank ye, my lady."

"Will you… are you going to take me back with you?" asked Isabelle. She forgot for a moment she was trying to escape him.

"Nay. If ye find my hospitality so displeasing, I winna force ye to come back. I canna take ye from the convent, or do ye think so poorly o' me that ye dinna think I would respect the sanctuary o' the Church."

Isabelle said nothing. So many thoughts and

emotions bombarded her mind, she could not decide what to say or how to feel. His face was wan, the lines on his forehead etched deep.

Campbell clenched his jaw and took a deep breath. "I only regret ye had to endure my hateful company as long as ye did. Good-bye to ye, Lady Tynsdale. I will no' force ye to suffer my presence any longer." Campbell stormed past her.

"No, wait, 'tis not that I do not appreciate—please stop!" He did not appear to have any intention to heed her, so she grabbed his arm and spun herself in front of him.

Campbell grabbed her arms as if to physically remove her from his path, but held her in place before him instead. "What do ye want from me?" he asked, his voice barely above a whisper.

"Are you well?" Isabelle asked, putting her hand to his face. His eyes were dull and weary. David Campbell was suffering and all else was forgot.

"I canna find Cait." His voice was rough, and splintered with pain.

Tears sprung to Isabelle's eyes and she held David close. "You will find her. You can do anything."

"I am afraid she has been…"

"No, you must not think that way. I am sure she is fine. She is a smart girl and you are a man of remarkable talents. You always find me, no matter where I go."

Campbell stepped back from Isabelle's embrace and put a hand softly on her cheek. "Unfortunately ye are no' the lass I wish to find."

Something tightened in Isabelle's gut. It was her turn to step back.

"I dinna ken how ye managed to escape but it does'na matter," said Campbell. "Nothing matters but finding Cait."

Isabelle nodded and turned away. "I am certain you will find her soon."

"I wish ye well. Good-bye, Lady Tynsdale."

Campbell walked past her into the building. The finality of his farewell struck deep. She had lost him forever. Yet he had never been hers to lose, so it could not matter to her. Why then did her stomach sink like lead?

"Good-bye."

Twenty-One

ANDREW WALKED BACK TO THE MCNAB TOWER HOUSE holding the hand of bonnie Alys. It was the height of foolishness. The looks of his clansmen should have been enough to release her hand. But it felt so good and she beamed so happily that he continued, knowing he would most certainly be mocked for it later.

He had spent a most delightful afternoon in a secluded glen with the lovely, fair-headed Campbell lass. They had talked about nothing, laughed nervously, and then kissed away the rest of the afternoon. When it was time to return, he said something about expecting more for her release, and she promised to comply with a saucy wink and they kissed a while longer.

Andrew lingered at the door of her chamber. "Thank ye for a lovely time, Miss Alys."

She frowned, but only for a moment and smiled up at him through her lashes in a way that got his blood pumping. "Ye are a wicked man, Andrew McNab. I'll expect to see ye early on the morrow."

She opened the door to reveal Archie and the Lady Cait sitting close together on the window seat. Archie bolted to his feet, and Lady Cait blushed red beneath her brown curls. It seemed Archie was having good luck as well.

"M'lady!" exclaimed Alys. She did not seem pleased with the scene before her. No doubt she felt she must protect her lady from the likes of Archie McNab. Smart lass.

"Until the morrow," said Archie, taking Lady Cait's hand and kissing it, earning him another blush.

Archie strode from the room looking taller than he had earlier in the day. He gave Andrew a playful punch in the shoulder and together they walked to the solar. It was clear Archie was pleased with how things were proceeding with his wooing of Lady Cait. For the first time since the arrival of their female captives, Andrew thought Archie's daft plan might actually work.

"Thank ye, Andrew, for getting that moat dragon out of the way. Lady Cait is coming around."

"She's no' a dragon." Andrew was unable to squelch the need to defend his lady. "She's a beautiful lady and if she dinna care for ye, it only shows her good sense."

Archie flopped into a chair and gave his younger brother a knowing smile. Andrew recognized too late his ardent defense had revealed too much of his feelings.

"Things going well wi' Lady Cait, ye say?" asked Andrew in a nonchalant sort of way. Feelings and tender emotions were for the weak. He needed to get himself together before his older brother lost all respect for him and decided to thrash some toughness into him.

"Aye. She is verra different in person than your dragon Alys would make her out to be."

Andrew sat in another chair in front of the small fire smoldering in the large hearth. He was not going to take the bait again.

"Another few days and I may be able to persuade her no' to see us swing at the end o' a rope. Give me a week and I may be able to convince her to wed." Archie McNab was happy, unusual in itself, but his appearance had also improved. His shoulders were relaxed and the corners of his mouth turned up instead of the perpetual down. He even looked hopeful, and hope was not an expression Andrew had ever seen in his brother's eye. Andrew should mock him in return, but he did not have the heart.

"Ye both are naught but fools."

Andrew shrugged at his sister as she entered the room. Morrigan never shied away from giving her honest opinion at its most critical and pessimistic. Trouble was, she was generally right.

"If ye believe Lady Cait, Campbell's own sister, is e'er going to wed ye, then ye are a bigger fool than I kenned." Morrigan glared at Archie with glittering eyes. "She's pretending to be amused by ye just to bide her time until her brother finds ye. Mark my words, Archie, she will ne'er marry ye."

"She'll agree to no' tell her brother 'twas us who kidnapped her." Archie defended his dream. "We'll say we rescued her from the real abductors, and mayhap Campbell will even give us a reward for our service."

"And how will ye know that she winna turn on

ye once she is back safe with her brother. 'Tis easy to make promises now, prudent even, but I would be surprised indeed if she does'na reveal all to her brother once safely back at home."

Archie's smile waned, and he laid his head back against his chair and closed his eyes. "What would ye have me do then? If I send a note to ransom them, Campbell will come, take the lasses, and annihilate us. I canna simply give them back since they already know who we are."

"And now is when ye get to thinking this through? Ye may have pondered this minor problem in yer daft plan before ye abducted them." Morrigan shook her head, her eyes catching the light of the fire.

"'Tis possible they may choose no' to reveal us to our deaths." Archie folded his arms across his chest and regarded Morrigan with dark, cold eyes. "Though ye ken naught about human affection, it does'na mean these ladies have as black a soul as ye."

Morrigan's jaw clenched and her eyes narrowed. "Ye would risk all our lives on that chance? Ye've left us few options, Brother. The ladies must be eliminated."

"Nay!" Andrew was on his feet before he knew he had spoken.

Morrigan slowly turned her maleficent gaze to him. "And ye're just as big a fool as he, running after that wench."

"Alys is no wench, she's a lady-in—"

"She's the castle whore if she's spending her time snogging the likes o' ye. Listen carefully, ye daft fools. 'Tis only a matter o' time before the Campbell tracks them down. Would ye lead us into war wi' the

Campbells? Have ye no care for the lives o' yer clan? Think on that before ye kill us all."

Morrigan stalked from the room, leaving a cloud of desperation in her wake. All the joy and hope Andrew experienced earlier in the evening shriveled in his hands to dust. Collapsing back into his chair he tried to decipher a way out of this mess. He should just return the ladies, but doing that would risk the wrath of Campbell. Morrigan was right; their clan would hardly survive such an attack.

Andrew sat in the solar next to his brother long into the night. Neither spoke, even as darkness smothered the room, and all that was visible was the faint, red glow of the embers in the hearth. Andrew tried to devise a plan in which this situation could end without anyone being killed. The only course of action was to trust his fate to Alys and Lady Cait.

Alys must be made to love him. Their lives depended on it.

Cait lay in bed, far from sleep. She closed her eyes and smiled, reliving every lovely moment of her day with Andrew.

"Cait." Alys spoke tentatively next to her in the dark.

Cait said nothing, hoping Alys would think her asleep. She did not wish to talk to the real Alys. She enjoyed pretending to be Alys too much to let reality intrude.

"Cait, I ken ye're awake. I wish to speak wi' ye about McNab. Archie proposed marriage to me."

Cait snorted. "He wants to marry me, ye mean. Or rather, my dowry."

"Aye," Alys said slowly. "But can ye judge a man harsh for trying to better his lot in life?"

"He's no' bettering himself, he abducted me. I'm surprised at ye, Alys. One would think ye had gone sweet on him."

Alys said nothing, the silence hanging heavy in the darkness between them. "'Tis the first proposal o' marriage I have e'er received, and I'm no' likely to receive another."

"How can ye talk such nonsense?" Cait sputtered. "He does'na wish to wed ye, he only wishes my fortune."

"And what o' ye?" Alys retorted, her voice raised. "How can ye run off wi' Andrew, making yerself the gossip o' the whole castle. Have ye forgotten yer betrothal to Gavin Patrick?"

"'Tis enough, Alys!" Cait's sparkling dream of happily ever after with Andrew shattered into thousands of pieces. She hated Alys for reminding her of who she was. If only she was the real Alys, she would stay with Andrew forever, not just for now.

Cait turned her back to Alys. Andrew could never be hers. She was betrothed to another. She would enjoy this dream as much as she could, but eventually she would be forced to wake. In the end she would wed Gavin Patrick, and Andrew would be nothing but a fading memory.

But not yet. She was not yet ready to relinquish her dream.

❧

Campbell returned to St. Margaret's after another unsuccessful day's search. He followed the faint torchlight of St. Margaret's like a beacon in an inky black night. Somewhere here was Isabelle. What was she doing now? Where would she go from here? Would he see her tonight?

Campbell shook the treacherous thoughts from his head. Must be lack of sleep breaking down his defenses. Isabelle was not his concern. It was his sister he needed to find. His rage at his sister being abducted had diminished into a gnawing fear for her safety.

With a growing urgency, Campbell quickly stabled his mount with his brothers and strode to the room the nuns had given them to meet. He hoped some of the other men would have good news for him, but one swift look around the table told him different.

Gavin Patrick and his uncle MacLaren sat at a heavy oak table. Neither bothered to look up when he entered. Gavin's stepfather, Chaumont, leaned on the mantel, his usually lively face grim. Campbell's brothers Dain, Gill, Finn, and Hamish filed into the room and sat heavily on benches or chairs. They looked something awful.

"Let us examine the map, and see where we have searched and where we have yet to go," said Campbell.

They spent an hour poring over the map with weary eyes, discussing different theories of what happened to Cait.

"We've followed all the tracks of the whoresons who took Cait, but each led to a dead end," said Campbell, rubbing his aching forehead. "I was hoping ye could tell me where bands of thieves may be hiding."

"We've heard of bands of ruffians roaming these parts, causing mischief of one sort or another," said

MacLaren. "Some attacks have been close to the convent, some to the north. It is not known if it is the same or separate bands."

"There has also been unrest in Stirling," added Chaumont.

"I have also heard that McNab to the north has been hiring himself out as protection from bands of ruffians," said MacLaren. "He could be using the situation to increase his purse, or it could be a plot. I've had dealings with him in the past and I dinna trust the cur."

"What sort o' plot?" asked Campbell.

"He creates fear in the countryside by robbing and pillaging, and then sells 'protection' against his own band of thieves."

"So we could go out toward town or farther north into the Highlands," said Campbell. "What do ye think we should do, Gavin?"

Gavin's head shot up, his wide eyes full of surprise. Campbell sighed. As Cait's betrothed Gavin had the right to take the lead, but he was young yet. Still, it was proper to ask, and Campbell would do all that was right.

After more discussion they developed a plan of attack for the morn and the men retired to sleeping quarters given them by the nuns. His brothers offered to continue searching through half-closed eyes, but Campbell ordered them to bed. Never had one of his commands been more readily obeyed. They had all pushed beyond the point of exhaustion.

Campbell himself, however, slipped away unnoticed and went to the stables. He would continue to search. Cait was his sister and he would see her safe... no matter the cost.

❧

Sleep would not come for Isabelle. She tossed one way, then another. Perhaps it was the simple pallet, or the plain sheets, or the thin blanket. She sat up. It was none of those things. It was Campbell. She was worried about him. Worried he would come find her and drag her back to his castle. Despite the obvious contradiction, she was even more worried she would never see him again, and that fear more than anything kept sleep at bay.

Isabelle got to her feet and paced back and forth in her small cell. So tiny was her room that she could only take a few steps before it was time to turn and go back again, making it a very unsatisfactory place to pace. Perhaps a little fresh night air would do her good. She reluctantly pulled on the torturous wool gown. At least the good sisters had washed and returned her linen chemise so the gown did not itch quite as much. She wrapped a long cloak around her shoulders, and slipped down the narrow, dark corridor and out the heavy oak door into the night.

Isabelle took a deep breath, the cool night air reviving her flagging spirits. Thick mist swirled around her. The moon illuminated the fog, making a half circle in the sky. The pale light reflected in the mist, making it difficult for her to see more than a few feet in front of her.

Isabelle strode off in the direction of the chapel, but soon was engulfed by the mist. After a few minutes of invigorating walking, she began to wonder why she had not found the chapel. She stopped and turned around to get her bearings, but could see nothing but gray blankness. She stopped turning and realized she now had no idea from what direction she had come. Isabelle rolled her eyes. Honestly, getting lost all the time was getting tiresome.

With a shrug of her shoulders, Isabelle was off once more. She knew she was still on the grounds of the convent, so she would simply walk until she found the wall that surrounded them or a building. She had come out for a walk after all, so she should be little concerned by the fact that she was getting one.

Soon she recognized a smell that was decidedly not the chapel. She had instead found the stables. Orange light from a lantern beckoned, so she entered the warm barn, breathing in the inviting smell of fresh hay. Several horses were stabled in stalls down a line. In a far stall was a stable lad bent over a horse. Around a corner were more animals, a cow chewing contentedly, a hutch of bunnies, and a momma cat curled up with eight kittens.

"Oh, kittens!" said Isabelle. She ran to the orange and black cat and picked up a ball of fluff to cuddle. Nothing could revive the spirit better than a kitten. She cuddled and mewled at them, picking up two and cradling them in her arms.

"Excuse me, lass," said the stable hand.

"I am sorry, am I in your way…" Isabelle's voice trailed off.

They recognized each other at the same time.

"Lady Tynsdale."

"Laird Campbell."

A wave of excitement coursed through her at seeing him again. She tried to push it away but she could not deny her attraction to him. He was, after all, a good-looking man, except tonight he looked rather wretched.

He rubbed his weary eyes. "My sister I canna find, but ye I canna escape. Dinna distract me. I need to go. Get out o' my way."

Isabelle opened her mouth for a sharp retort to his rude behavior, but noticed him start to sway on his feet and held her tongue. She quickly put the kittens down with their momma and rushed to his side.

"You are barely standing. Where do you think you are going at this time of night?" Isabelle put her arm around him to steady him, though in truth, if he chose to fall she could no more keep him upright than could one of the kittens.

"Cait is out there, somewhere, held hostage by some bastard. I dinna want to think what could be happening... Nay, I will no' sleep until I find her."

"Do you mean you have not slept since she was captured?"

"Nay."

"But that was days ago! You must be exhausted."

"I must find her."

"You will find her, but now you must sleep. Come, let me take you back to your sleeping quarters. You will do much better after some sleep and you can resume your search in the morning."

"I must find her," he repeated stubbornly, but put his arm around her shoulders and leaned heavily.

Isabelle struggled to remain standing as Campbell shifted some of his weight to her. "You need sleep. Where are your brothers?"

"I sent them to bed."

"Which is where you should be. Please let me help you—"

"Nay!"

"Stubborn Highlander! You can hardly stand on your feet and you are about to take us both down. Look, there is a hayloft; at least lie down for a few hours, rest to regain your strength and some sense."

"One hour. No more," he grumbled.

"Fine, fine. You will be better able to find her after some sleep."

Isabelle pointed Campbell in the right direction and he hauled himself up a short ladder to a raised section of the barn where the hay was kept. He crawled back to the wall far from the edge and collapsed on the fresh hay.

Isabelle followed him up and watched him for a moment. His eyes were already closed and he breathed deep. On impulse she removed her cloak and laid it out over him. She was rewarded with a brief, faint smile.

"Cait was very kind to me. I will pray you find her soon," she whispered.

Campbell opened a tired eye and took her hand in his. "Please do."

Isabelle was slightly surprised at the request, but bowed her head. This was perhaps not the moment to mention that God never heard her prayers, or at least never bothered to answer them. Maybe with Campbell present God would be more receptive.

"Dear Lord, please allow your servant Campbell to find Cait tomorrow and please let her be safe and well. Amen." Isabelle looked up cautiously. The prayers of her priest where always much longer, and she wondered if Campbell would find her simple prayer lacking.

He squeezed her hand. "Thank ye."

"I will ask the sisters to pray for you too, and I can light a candle in the chapel for you." Isabelle wanted to do something to help.

"Thank ye. I would appreciate it if ye would. My brothers and sisters, they are everything to me." He gently squeezed her hand again and closed his eyes. "Everything."

Isabelle reached over with her other hand and touched his stubbled cheek. "You will find her. I believe you can do anything."

A slow smile spread across his lips. "I protest this scandalous treatment of my person."

Isabelle smiled in return, recognizing her own words to him from the inn. She leaned forward and kissed him on the cheek. "Good night, David."

"Good night, Edna." Without opening his eyes David wrapped his arm around her, encouraging her to lie down next to him, and cuddled her close.

Isabelle considered breaking free. His breathing was soon slow and steady, and his arm around her relaxed. She should return to her sleeping cell, but the hay was a more comfortable bed and she was warm, snuggled next to Campbell. It was only for an hour, she reasoned. What harm could it possibly do?

∽

"Day!" Campbell shouted.

"W-what?" said Isabelle, sitting bolt upright.

"'Tis light. Ye were only supposed to let me sleep an hour!" Campbell slung himself down from the hayloft, leaving her cloak strewn across the hay without so much as a thank you.

"Well! A good morn to you too!" Isabelle struggled down the short ladder and smoothed her gown.

"There you are!" Campbell's brother Dain marched into the stable followed by his brothers and several other men. The men looked at Isabelle, then at Campbell, then back at her.

No one said anything, but her cheeks burned in the frosty morning air. With as much dignity as she could muster under the circumstances, Isabelle walked toward the door, but her way was blocked by a tall, handsome knight.

"Laird Campbell, I insist you introduce me to your charming friend," said the man in a slight French accent.

Behind her, Isabelle swore she could hear Campbell's teeth grind.

"Lady Tynsdale, may I present Sir Chaumont," said Campbell tersely.

"Lady Tynsdale, it is indeed a pleasure." The French knight swept her a graceful bow. "I do hope you found the hay comfortable."

"N-no," stammered Isabelle. "I am simply passing through. Now please let me pass."

"A thousand pardons, my lady." He reached toward her and plucked a strand of hay from her hair. "I never will understand English fashion."

The men broke into loud guffaws of laughter. Isabelle pressed her lips together and stormed from the stable, leaving the chortles of the men behind her. Her face burned at being caught in such a compromising situation, though this time she could honestly say they had done nothing but sleep. Despite her embarrassment, she was laughing too before she reached her tiny quarters. What a sight she must have been!

Isabelle silently wished Campbell well on his hunt. She knew he would find Cait. He must. And then he would leave her life forever. Isabelle's smile faded slowly in the stark, cold, morning light.

Twenty-Two

ANDREW LED ALYS ON HORSEBACK TO A PLACE HE knew. It was his favorite place, a place he retreated to when he needed to think, or simply escape the daft schemings or angry musings of his siblings. It was at the southern edge of their land, next to the territory of MacLaren and Graham, but to Andrew it was the most beautiful place in the whole of Scotland, and there was no better spot for what he intended to do.

After several hours in the saddle, Andrew stopped, tied the horses and lifted Alys to the ground. She felt good in his arms and he was in no hurry to let her go.

"Are ye going to show me why we've come all this way or just hold me all day?" Alys smiled up at him and made no attempt to be freed from his embrace.

"Hold ye. Most assuredly I'll be holding onto ye. But I warrant I ought to show ye this place."

Andrew took her willing hand and walked up the hill. At the top were several old trees, with low branches worn smooth over the years from climbing its leafy arms. Below them stretched a green valley, lush and full. The valley was alive and moving, the leaves fluttering in the wind, the sea of heather rippling like waves on an ocean of flowers. The world smelled fresh and alive with possibility. Andrew breathed deeply of lavender, green grass, and rich, dark earth.

"'Tis wondrous," said Alys, turning around in circles. She smiled at him and continued spinning, her eyes bright as a child's.

"I'm glad ye like it," said Andrew softly. Of all the beauty before him, none was more than Alys's. Her blond hair flew around her in the breeze, her arms outstretched as she spun. Laughing, she collapsed in a dizzy heap, her gown billowing out around her. Andrew knelt before her. He had never felt this way before. Never had he wanted anything more than the beautiful lass before him.

"Marry me, Alys." The words tumbled out before he could catch them. He had carefully planned a beautiful speech for this occasion, and he had a lad who was to follow him with a basket meal. They were supposed to eat and then he would propose, but now he had gone and blurted out the ending.

Alys did not look pleased. Her smile faded and her blue eyes stared at him in wide surprise.

"Pardon, I meant to say that better. I ne'er met anyone like ye. I'm so happy when ye are near, I ne'er wish to be parted. I ken I have little to give, and perhaps ye may have no dowry, but I care not. All I want is ye."

❧

Cait's happy world crumbled. Before her was the man she loved. He asked her to marry him. But it was impossible. Reality smashed back into her with a painful slap. She was Lady Caitrina Campbell, not Alys, and she was betrothed to another man.

"Nay, stop, this canna be." Cait stood up fast and backed away from him, but there was nowhere to go. Nowhere to run from the crushing truth. Andrew stood slowly. He stared at her with large, sad eyes. "Dinna look at me that way," she pleaded. Her eyes were starting to burn.

"Alys, I love ye—"

"Nay, dinna say that. Please, ye dinna even know my name."

"What are ye saying, lass? Whatever be yer name, I wish ye to be my wife."

"I wanted to tell ye, honest I did." Cait wiped tears away with an impatient swipe of her hand. "I ne'er meant for it to come to this. But I was afraid if I told ye the truth we could no' be together."

"No matter what yer truth is, I will be wi' ye. What could be so terrible ye would think it would keep me away?"

Cait shook her head and looked down. "Ye dinna even know my name."

Andrew closed the gap between them, catching her elbows and pulling her close. She gasped and looked up at him.

"What is yer name?" Andrew's face had gone hard, his eyes narrow. Cait struggled against him, but he held her fast with ease.

"What is yer name?" he repeated.

"Cait."

"Tell me, Cait, what do ye wish from me? If ye

have been doing naught but deceiving me wi' yer kisses tell me now."

"And what would ye do if I had?"

Andrew's face went dark. "I'd ride ye back to Campbell himself and take my leave o' ye. For I'd rather be damned than to look at yer deceitful face e'er again."

Cait swallowed hard.

"I ask ye again. What do ye wish from me? I have spoken the desires o' my heart, what o' yers?"

"I wish… I would so much like to accept yer offer, Andrew McNab, and be yer wife."

Andrew's face seemed to crack and the frozen mask shattered. He smiled a big, lopsided grin, looking as much a boy as a man. "Then so ye shall. I do love ye, Alys… er… Cait."

Cait smiled though she knew he did not understand the truth. "And I love ye, Andrew, truly I do. I ne'er meant to hurt ye—"

Andrew claimed her mouth and Cait melted into his embrace. He felt so good, so strong. And he kissed so well it was easy to forget the problems that stood between them. Perhaps it was possible?

Cait was jerked back and let out a scream of surprise. Men's voices, loud and cursing, filled her ears drowning out her own screams. She fought the arms around her, screaming for Andrew.

"Cait. Cait!" She froze at the familiar voice and looked up into her brother's eyes. David Campbell had come for her at last.

"David?" How had he found her? Why was he here now?

David Campbell searched her face. "Are ye well? Ye're safe now, no one will harm ye."

"I am well, Brother," she said, or at least she tried to but was muffled by a large bear hug from her brother. When he finally released her she saw Andrew on his knees being held securely by three of her brother's men.

"Cait?" Andrew's eyes were wide.

"Andrew, I wanted to tell ye…"

"*Lady* Cait?" he asked, his face shattered with betrayal.

"Ye'll no' be talking to the lady," said one man and struck Andrew on the jaw.

Andrew looked at Cait for a moment longer, mournful and accusing. He spat blood and closed his eyes.

David Campbell drew his sword with a deathly ring of steel.

"For abducting and molesting the Lady Cait Campbell, I sentence ye to—"

"Nay, wait!" Cait rushed to her brother and held onto his sleeve. "He dinna kidnap me. Dinna hurt him."

"I saw him molest ye, Cait," David said, his voice tight. "Gill! Finn! Take her away, she ought no' see this."

Cait's brothers each grabbed one of her arms and gently, but firmly, pulled her away.

"Nay, wait," she cried as she was dragged back down the hill. "Dinna hurt him. Please listen to me. He's no' the one, David. Dinna kill him!"

"Take her home, lads," commanded Campbell. "Take some men, see her safe to Innis Chonnel."

Cait was loaded most unwillingly onto a mount and

carried away. She screamed until her voice was hoarse, and there was no chance of David hearing her anyway. Silent tears ran tracks down her face as her kinsmen took her home.

∼

Archibald McNab returned home a happy man. His horse clopped down the road at a lazy walk, and McNab felt no desire to quicken the pace. In his arms was the most beautiful lady he had ever beheld. He had done it. Finally, one of his plans had actually worked. He had taken the Lady Cait to a hermit he knew who lived in a cave in the high places. There Cait had done the incredible and consented to be his wife. For a basket of smoked pork, the hermit had performed the ceremony. It wasn't quite as good as a real priest, but it was good enough. And Cait had been more than willing to consummate their union in a secluded hunting cottage. Warm tingles ran up his spine. What a bedding it had been. She was his now, no doubt about that.

McNab breathed easily for the first time in a long while. He would convince Cait to tell her brother he had rescued her, and with her help get Campbell to accept their marriage. Her dowry would provide the means for his clan to struggle back from the depths of poverty. And best of all, he could stop working for the coldhearted abbot. McNab gave an involuntary shudder at the thought of the abbot's last message, causing his mount to sidestep and nicker in disapproval.

McNab patted his mount's neck to calm him. The

McNab tower house was in sight. What a celebration they would have tonight.

"McNab! McNab!" Clansmen were running out to greet him. How nice. It wasn't every day he received this kind of reception. He kicked his mount to gallop the short distance home.

"McNab! Yer brother's been taken!"

McNab trotted through the gate with a broad smile. How they will all celebrate the… what had the anxious-looking man said?

"Andrew, he's been taken!"

"What?" McNab jumped down from his saddle and grabbed Cait to stand by his side.

"I saw it," said a breathless lad. "Andrew said he would be taking Alys to a glen. He said I was to follow them to bring a basket of food. He said it would be romantic."

McNab rolled his eyes. His brother had odd notions sometimes. Must be that university training. "What happened to Andrew, quick now."

"I was coming o'er the hill and I heard screaming, so I took cover. There were a bunch o' men, several had Andrew, a few more was dragging Alys away, and she was screaming something fierce."

"Who was it? Who took them?"

"It was the Campbell, or at least I heard a man call him that."

Despite the cool breeze, McNab broke into a sweat. "And Andrew, what did they do to him?"

"They tied him to a horse and rode him off heading south."

McNab's mind spun. "Saddle a fresh horse, I need to get to Andrew before Campbell kills him."

"That's no' all, my laird. Campbell called Alys the Lady Cait. I dinna ken why."

Andrew froze. He turned to Cait, his wife. She had gone very still and very pale. "Who are ye?"

Silence gripped the courtyard, a tattered banner fluttered in the breeze. His wife, the savior of his clan, stared at him with wide, brown eyes. Her bottom lip trembled.

"I am Alys."

McNab closed his eyes and took a step back to steady himself. His world shattered like glass. He covered his eyes with his hand. They were all dead.

"Why? Why did ye do it?" McNab's plaintive question gripped his soul.

"I wanted to tell ye the truth, but I needed to protect my lady."

"But why agree to be my wife? Why give me hope only to crush me? Ye dinna need to do any o' it."

Alys stood tall, her eyes flashing, her fists balled at her sides. "Nay, I dinna need to, but I wanted to. Ye were so kind to me, and so braw. I wanted ye, Laird McNab. I saw my chance and I took it. I do ask forgiveness, for I ken I have done ye wrong. But I will ne'er regret it."

McNab stared at her as if seeing her for the first time. It had all been some twisted game. He shook his head. Nothing mattered now, except getting Andrew back. "Take her to Campbell, or drop her close enough that she can walk the rest, I dinna want anyone else captured."

"Nay, wait. I know I've played ye false, but ye did kidnap us," said Alys.

"Aye. Who am I to accuse anyone o' sin? Go home wi' my blessing, I hold ye no ill will." The words ground from McNab's mouth like sand.

"Nay, I am yer wife. I'll stay wi' ye." Alys stepped toward him, her arms outstretched. "If… if ye'll still have me."

"I dinna ken what ye're about. Why would ye want me?"

"I could go home and continue serving the Campbells, but though we are a prominent family, my father likes me in my current position and has no desire to see me wed. Ye are my one chance to be married. To have a family. And ye clearly need someone looking after ye." Alys reached tentatively for his hand. "In my heart, I wish to be yer wife."

McNab put his arms around Alys and drew her close. He did not mean to, nor even wish to, but he needed to hold her. "Ye are sure ye wish to be wed to the likes o' me?"

"If ye can promise more beddings like today," whispered Alys, "then, aye, I do."

Warmth returned to McNab, radiating out from his rapidly beating heart. "I warrant I was no' intended to wed a rich wife. If I do return, I expect to find ye waiting for me in my bedchamber."

Alys smiled and pressed against him. "This is all I have to give ye and I do it willingly."

McNab bent down to claim his lady in a kiss. She was indeed warm and willing. It was likely more than he deserved.

"This is my lady wife," McNab announced to the crowd in the courtyard. "She may stay or leave as she pleases. Anyone who discomforts her will deal wi' me." McNab released her and mounted the fresh horse the stable lad had brought.

"Wait, I'm coming wi' ye!" Morrigan ran down the steps to the courtyard.

"Nay, I go alone."

"Andrew is in danger, I will go."

"Nay, Morrigan. I need ye here." He caught his sister's gaze. "Protect them." McNab spurred his mount and raced from the castle walls. He did not look back.

He doubted he would ever see any of them again.

Twenty-Three

CAMPBELL TOOK A DEEP BREATH AND RELEASED THE anxiety, bordering on panic, he had suppressed for the past several days. The midday sun filtered down through the trees in yellow ribbons. He had found her. Cait was alive. It was a moment to cherish.

"What now?" asked Dain.

And the moment was over. Campbell had sent Cait on ahead with Gill, and Finn and half his men to protect her. She needed to get off dangerous McNab land and return home as quick as may be.

Campbell's joy and utter relief at finding Cait alive was tempered by the grim task of having to deal with her abductor. She had pleaded for him, but Campbell had seen with his own eyes this young man take scandalous advantage of his sister. Not to mention being found with two of Campbell's stolen horses. He was definitely one of the men who kidnapped Cait. A McNab no doubt, given their location.

The captured McNab sat slumped against a tree, his head on his knees. Campbell walked over to him and kicked his boot. McNab looked up, revealing a youthful face. Campbell shook his head. It was sad to see a lad so young go bad. The lad had been crying, probably out of fear for his life. He should be afraid.

"What is yer name, lad?" Campbell received no reply. "Tell me true what happened to Lady Cait."

The dejected youth shook his head and remained silent. Campbell wanted answers. He wanted to know who had abducted Cait and why she had begged for this lad's life to be spared. He could no doubt beat out the truth, but that was not Campbell's way.

Campbell turned to answer his brother. "Dain, mount up the men to ride. When we arrive at Innis Chonnel tomorrow, we'll need to gather our forces and march against McNab. This cur did not act alone in abducting Cait. I will not rest until I have the man responsible."

"Nay, wait," said the youth. "Dinna march against the McNab clan; they are innocent in this."

"Then tell me who abducted my sister," growled Campbell.

The lad struggled to his feet and glanced around at Campbell's men who surrounded him. "It was me, Andrew McNab. I did it. I took the Lady Cait and her maid."

"Ye dinna do this alone. Who else was wi' ye?"

"Some ruffians I hired. Not McNab's men. Please, dinna punish my clan for something that was my fault alone."

"Where is the maid, Alys?"

"She is safe, I swear it. She will be returned to ye."

"If ye were the one who captured Cait, why did she say ye did no' take her?"

"I... I made a deal wi' her that I would free her if she dinna tell it was me."

"When I caught ye, ye were not freeing her, ye were molesting her. Do ye care to explain that?"

Andrew looked down at his shoes. "Part of the deal was she would give me a kiss."

Campbell slapped the lad, who crumpled to the ground. "Deceitful knave. Ye were no' going to release her, were ye?"

Andrew shook his bowed head and spoke in a voice barely audible. "I wanted to marry her."

Campbell grunted. "Instead ye will be taken to Innis Chonnel where ye will receive a fair trial. If ye are found guilty of abducting the Lady Cait, which I have little doubt ye will be, I will sentence ye to hang."

Andrew McNab's shoulders slumped further. A more dejected lad Campbell had never seen.

Campbell urged his men to move quickly to get off McNab land before they ran into trouble. He made sure the prisoner was well secured for the journey, with guards ahead and behind him. Campbell was not convinced that he had gotten the whole truth from the young McNab, but at least Cait was safe. That was all that truly mattered. His responsibility now was to make an example of this man, to prevent knaves and thieves from molesting his sisters in the future. It was an unpleasant task, but he would see it done.

"Dain, I want you to go ahead, get this bastard off McNab soil and on the road back home. I need to go to St. Margaret's to let the others know we have found Cait alive."

"Shall we not go with ye to St. Margaret's?"

"Nay. I dinna wish to give the lad an opportunity to claim sanctuary or for his kin to ambush us on the road. Ride hard, make haste. Dinna wait for me."

Dain nodded in response and they soon started their journey back home.

Campbell watched them silently, saying a prayer of protection over his clan until they rounded a turn and disappeared from sight. Campbell spurred his mount and galloped south toward St. Margaret's. He needed to talk to his friends who had joined the search. He also wanted to see Isabelle again.

This time would undoubtedly be the last. He was forced to remind himself that she was a conniving English tart, but even that could not keep his thoughts from curling around her memory and holding her tight against his lonely heart.

⁓

David Campbell reached the sanctuary of St. Margaret's by late afternoon, but thick fog rolled in, banking the convent, shutting out the waning sun of twilight. The gray void surrounding him was oppressive.

Campbell urged his mount forward through the gates, his eyes scanning the mist for the particular person he wished to see. One more time. Once more, he reasoned with himself. To say good-bye, that was all. He tried to give himself a convincing reason, but truly what he wished to do was carry Isabelle back to the hayloft and celebrate his success in a more intimate manner.

Campbell shook off these thoughts and slung

himself off his horse He needed to focus on his task and return to his brothers. He found his friends in the meeting room, the dense fog driving them back to St. Margaret's early. Padyn MacLaren sat with his back to the far wall, his thick arms folded across his chest. Chaumont leaned against the mantel, chatting easily with his stepson Gavin Patrick.

"Lady Cait's been found," announced Campbell. "She is alive but distraught. I have sent her home with most of my men."

The men all made noises of joy, commending Campbell for his good fortune. Even MacLaren stood and clapped him on the shoulder, looking relieved.

"But how did you find her?" asked Chaumont.

"I decided to have a talk with McNab," continued Campbell, "but before we got too far into his territory we came upon Cait being… being molested by a McNab."

"Ye killed him," stated MacLaren.

"That was my plan, but Cait pleaded for his life. She said he was no' the man who abducted her. She was distraught, so I sent her home. I sent the McNab back to Innis Chonnel for trial. Do ye accept this decision?" Campbell asked Gavin the question.

Gavin's eyes grew wide and glanced around the room, confused. Campbell sighed. Gavin was a good lad, but he was a lad. As her legal fiancé he had first rights to dispatch the man who had abducted Cait. Not that Gavin looked anything other than uncomfortable in the situation.

"Ye have the right to choose who sees to the man who stole the Lady Cait," MacLaren explained to Gavin.

"And two o' my best mares," added Campbell.

"Oh, well, I..." stammered Gavin.

"Perhaps you would like Campbell to see to the matter?" suggested Chaumont.

"Aye, that would be verra good," breathed Gavin.

Campbell nodded. "About Cait. I ken Lady Graham wished for her to come to Dundaff Castle soon, but I sent her home after her fright. I would like to give her some time to recover."

"Aye, she should take all the time she needs," said Gavin with earnest eyes. "Please allow her as much time as she would like and even more, to be sure she's recovered."

Campbell gave Gavin a small smile. The lad was clearly in no rush to wed. Not that he could blame the lad for that. "Thank ye, all, for yer help in searching for Cait. I dinna ken what I would do if she were lost forever."

MacLaren clasped his shoulder. "I am much relieved she was found. If e'er ye need help, we are always willing to come to yer aid. Ye have stood by us in trouble and we will ne'er forget it, my friend."

"Thank ye."

"Will you stay the night at the convent?" asked Chaumont.

"Nay, I need to catch up to my clan and make sure no harm comes to them. I will send a missive to McNab to demand the return of Cait's maid and start for home."

"And if McNab does not return this maid?" asked MacLaren.

Campbell smiled. "Then I will have the pleasure o'

returning with a larger force to put an end to McNab's miserable existence."

"Send word and I will gladly join ye," said MacLaren.

"Thank ye. I can always rely on ye, my friend."

Chaumont laughed, a mischievous twinkle in his eye, and put his arms around Campbell's and MacLaren's shoulders. "Ah, what merry mayhem we shall have. We can only hope McNab will not relinquish the girl so we can ride to glorious battle, eh, *mes amis?*" Chaumont laughed again at the dark looks of his more somber comrades.

"I must away," said Campbell.

"Godspeed."

☙

Isabelle spent most of her day trying not to think of David Campbell. He was not her man. Besides, he had his own troubles and she certainly had hers. It was time to forget him and try to solve her own problems, namely, her husband.

Mother Enid was still away from the convent and though the nuns expected her back that day, none could say when. The nuns answered her questions in peaceful tones and glided off to do whatever it was nuns did. She needed to be patient and wait. Unfortunately, Isabelle was adept at neither.

After a simple supper, Isabelle saw a black-robed figure striding across the convent grounds, his large form a stark contrast to the small figures of the nuns around him.

"Who is that?" she asked one of the nuns.

"He is the Abbot Barrick."

"An abbot! He is the one I should speak to."

"Nay, please wait for Mother Enid."

But Isabelle was done with waiting. Who knew what had happened to her people in her absence? She needed to return to England, and she needed help. Isabelle hustled after him, but paused in her approach. Perhaps it had something to do with the large sword he had strapped to his belt, or perhaps it was the menacing scowl on his face, but Abbot Barrick's appearance did not invite intrusion.

Standing tall, she reminded herself that though she had many faults, cowardice was not among them. He was her last hope and she was not about to let a brusque façade scare her away from the chance of ending her disastrous marriage.

The abbot was moving at a fast clip and entered the building before she could reach him. Isabelle hiked up her skirts and ran, unladylike though it was. She burst through the door, breathless. The room was dark but she did not slow her step and ran straight into a solid object. She bounced off and staggered backward, barely retaining her footing, as the injured party bellowed his displeasure. She had run into the abbot.

"What the devil are you about?" roared the abbot.

"I-I wish to speak to you," stammered Isabelle, gasping for breath.

"I have no wish to speak to you. Remove yourself."

"But I must ask you for—"

The abbot did not wait for her to finish and brushed past her into a side chamber. Isabelle was a bit surprised; she had thought men of God to be a bit more polite, but stumbled after him anyway.

"But I need most urgently to ask for sanctuary."

"Denied. Be on your way, English."

"But if I am returned to my husband, he will surely kill me."

"That is no doubt a devious falsehood. The beating he will give you will be most deserved."

Isabelle gasped at his callous response. She flushed hot and her blood turned molten. How dare he speak to her thus. "I am the Lady Tynsdale and you would do well to listen to me."

Abbot Barrick turned on his heel and glared at her. Blood pounded in her ears but she would not back down now.

"I wish to have my marriage dissolved. I have lived at Alnsworth with my uncle and guardian all my life. Unfortunately, my uncle had been in conflict with my lawful husband for many years. Now that my uncle has passed, my husband, the Lord Tynsdale, wishes to affect his revenge against my people. The marriage must be dissolved to prevent Tynsdale from taking Alnsworth."

"And what is this to me?" asked the abbot.

"In return for an annulment I would make a sizable donation to the Church. Or—or join the convent and give all my worldly possessions to the Church."

The abbot regarded her through thin slits of eyes. His face was hard, his eyes were steel. She was wrong in assuming beneath the gruff exterior was a kindly old man. There was no kindness in him, only a bitter, calculating mind.

"And what possessions do you think you own? If you are married it all belongs rightfully to your husband."

"But if my marriage was dissolved, my inheritance—"

"Would no doubt be claimed by your greedy king." Barrick tapped his fingertips together. "Your husband, Lord Tynsdale, he is wealthy?"

"Yes, 'tis true, but I fear he may be out of favor with his king, another reason I wish to end the connection." She cared not for the fickle preference of her king, but considered this would be the type of argument that would make sense to the abbot's cold heart.

"Most understandable. But how did you come to St. Margaret's, Lady Tynsdale?"

"I became separated from my guard and was helped by Laird Campbell. But now he wishes to ransom me back to my husband, something I cannot abide."

"Naturally you cannot return to him," spoke the abbot in smooth tones. Isabelle wondered at how quickly he had reversed course. The abbot looked almost kindly, or would have had it not been for the opportunistic glint in his eye. "How much did he set for your ransom did you say? You can rest assured that I will take this matter under careful consideration."

"Thank you," said Isabelle. She had a suspicion she had said too much to this man, yet he was the only one who could set her free. If joining the convent was the price, at least she would be alive and her people would be safe.

"Yes," said the abbot, rubbing his hands together with a calculating smile. "Yes, you have certainly been brought here to serve our community. Take care not to leave the convent grounds, or you will be in grave peril."

Isabelle recoiled from the abbot's threatening tone.

"For how can I protect you if you leave the grounds," he revised with a sweet smile. "You stay on the grounds and I will see to everything." He pointed toward the door. "Now go."

Isabelle walked outside on shaky legs. A chill wrapped its bony claws around Isabelle's arms. What had she just done?

"Good evening, Lady Tynsdale." Leaning a shoulder against the stone wall of the building was David Campbell.

Twenty-Four

"DAVID!" IN HER EXCITEMENT TO SEE HIM ISABELLE took a step toward him with open arms, but realized what she was doing and stopped, awkwardly hugging herself. "You have returned."

"Why did ye no' tell me?" asked Campbell, nodding his head to the window open to the room where Isabelle had been standing with the abbot.

"I… I tried. Were you able to find Cait?"

David Campbell gave her a rare, broad smile that warmed her to her toes. "Aye. We found her well, or alive at least. I have her captor too."

"I knew you would do it." Isabelle returned his smile. It was good to see him happy.

Campbell took her arm and led her to a quiet place in the convent garden. They found a stone bench and sat down. "Now tell me the truth for once. Why are ye asking the abbot for an annulment?"

"'Tis a long story." Isabelle sighed. "I shall endeavor to give you the brief version. My uncle, the Earl of Alnsworth, became my guardian after my parents and other siblings died. Having no children of his own, I also became his heir, destined to inherit the Alnsworth Castle and all the lands surrounding it. I was married off to Lord Tynsdale after my sixteenth birthday, but things did not go well and a feud developed between our two houses. I returned to live with my uncle and resided there until he died."

Isabelle stood and began pacing before Campbell. "We left shortly after my uncle died to go plead our case before the king. If Tynsdale should take control of Alnsworth, you understand, his revenge against my people would be brutal. Unfortunately, on the road we met Tynsdale's men coming for me. I fled, got lost, and…"

"Found me," supplied Campbell.

"Yes."

"Why did ye no' simply tell me the truth?"

"I did not think you would believe me. And if you did, I thought you would return me to my husband, which you fully intended to do!"

"Aye." Campbell nodded his head and shrugged an apology. "I dinna ken yer circumstances. Had I known…"

"Would you have helped me? Or would you have thought I was fabricating stories to manipulate you?"

Campbell rubbed his forehead and did not answer. "Why all that talk of Bewcastle? I thought ye were running to a man there."

"I told my guard to wait for me there. They must have moved on since then. I hope they are all well, I have been most anxious to return to find them."

"I understand. But why come wi' me into Scotland at all?"

"I had intended to try to make it back to England on my own, but when I climbed that hill I saw Tynsdale's men on the road tracking me. I needed to escape."

"Ah, so that's why ye were twitching wi' nerves." Campbell reached for her hand and drew her back down on the bench beside him. "I hesitate to say this, since ye've had me confused since I met ye, but it is all starting to make sense."

"So you are no longer angry with me?" asked Isabelle.

Campbell shook his head. "Thank ye for telling me."

"So we may part friends."

"Aye." Campbell wrapped his arm around her and drew her close. "There was a time I had wished for more. I hope ye will forgive me for making advances that, in hindsight, were unworthy of ye."

A tingling warmth spread from the weight of his arm around her and filled her core with the heat of remembrance and a longing for more. "Perhaps we did what we should not, but your actions were always worthy of me. I never knew it could be like that." Isabelle bowed her head to hide her blush.

"The truth is I would never have slept wi' ye had I known ye were married, but I canna bring myself to feel one drop of regret. I shall remember ye all my days, Isabelle." David's voice was gentle.

A lump started to form in Isabelle's throat. "That is why I left that morning in the inn. I wanted so much to accept your offer and leave all the problems of my life behind. Being with you was like a glimpse of heaven."

Campbell held her tighter and kissed the top of her head. "'Tis a shame. Ye were meant to be loved."

"Unfortunately my husband disagrees."

"He is a fool."

"That and more. I wish we could—" Isabelle
stopped short. There was no "we" in their future. He
was betrothed to another and she was still married to
one of the most ruthless men in England. She must
return to her people, and he to his.

"Forgive me for wasting the little time we had
together with my foolish anger. I underestimated ye
and judged ye wrongly. I confess I was hurt when ye
ran away." David pulled her closer.

"I am sorry too. I should have trusted you enough
to tell you the truth."

They embraced each other tightly, holding close
against the thick blanket of fog engulfing them.
Cocooned in the silent mist, it was easy to pretend
she and Campbell were alone in the world. Alone
and together.

"I must go," David's voice wavered. "Would that
I could stay." He held her closer and gently massaged
the back of her neck in a manner that made her melt
into him.

Isabelle groaned softly. "Forgive me." Isabelle
pulled back. "That was quite unladylike."

"Ye make it hard on a man to leave ye, Isabelle."

"Sorry."

"I wish we…" David broke off from idle wishing.
He must also have realized the hopelessness of their
situation. "What shall ye do now?"

"Stay here I suppose, and hope the Church can advocate for an annulment for me. Can I trust the abbot?"

"I dinna know him well, but from all accounts he is

no kind man. I warrant he would do what he thought would bring him gold. For a share of inheritance, he should be willing to help."

Isabelle nodded. "So this is good-bye?"

"I have no right, but I would ask for one last boon before I leave. I would ask for one last kiss to say good-bye."

A shiver of excitement coursed through her. "I will accept your request, sir knight." Isabelle leaned close to his inviting lips, but with a pinch of mischief changed course slightly and gave him a chaste peck on the cheek.

"*Edna...*" he growled.

Isabelle laughed and gave him a proper kiss on the lips.

"'Tis a shame I canna stay to further yer education on the art of kissing, for if anyone needs it, 'tis ye," said David.

"I am getting chilled waiting for you to stop whining and start impressing me with your kissing arts."

"Whining? A Highlander never whines."

"Still waiting."

"We grunt and growl and scratch ourselves in inappropriate places, but never, ever whine."

"And I am still waiting."

"Now begging may occasionally occur. But only for the company of a lass, ye ken, never for any trifling thing like mercy from torture."

"*I* am about to start begging."

"Torture means naught to a true Highlander."

"You are torturing me!"

A smile gleamed in David's eye. "I remember the time—"

"Oh, be quiet!" Isabelle reached for his face with both hands and kissed him openmouthed, running her tongue along his lips. His growled response was instantaneous. He swept her up onto his lap and deepened the kiss until everything else around them faded away and Isabelle felt weightless, like she was riding a gust of wind. With a sudden flash of insight, she knew this was the man she would love till the end of her days.

Forever in love, yet forever apart.

Isabelle held on to Campbell, slivers of emotion slicing through her, an intoxicating mixture of joy and pain. She wished the moment would never end, and had it not been for a burning desire to breathe she would never have let go. Isabelle broke the kiss with a gasp for air.

"Have mercy." Campbell held her close, wrapping his large arms around her and leaning his head against hers. "That is one kiss I'll never forget."

"Still wish to teach me kissing lessons?"

"Nay, I wish ye'd teach me some."

Isabelle breathed in his warm scent, all man. "When I am near you I hear bells."

"Me too. But I fear it is the bells of the chapel ringing the hours. I must go."

"No." Isabelle held him tighter.

"I dinna wish to leave ye. Ever. But my clan is on the road wi' my sister and her abductor. I canna tarry any longer." He kissed her forehead.

"I understand," mumbled Isabelle. It was not what she wished to say.

David Campbell stood up with her still in his arms

and slowly lowered her to her feet. She held on to his shoulders until her shaky knees could hold her.

"I will never forget you, Isabelle. In the long winter's night when all is cold and dark, the memory of ye will keep me warm."

Tears sprung to Isabelle's eyes. It was the nicest thing anyone had ever said to her, and she knew Campbell was not one to throw away a compliment. "Thank you," she whispered.

Campbell pressed her hands in his. They stood silent, the gray mist thick around them like a shield. It could not protect them from the world. Campbell, she knew, must go.

"Fare-thee-well." Campbell released her hands and stepped away into the fog.

"And also to you," said Isabelle, but Campbell had disappeared into the thick fog.

"I..." Campbell's voice floated to her from the mist, but he spoke so softly she could not make out exactly what he had said. Isabelle played the muffled sound over in her mind, trying to determine his words. She drew a sharp breath of cool, moist air. Had he said he loved her?

Should she say she loved him too? Isabelle froze, her heart pounding, until she realized the moment was over and he was gone. What had he said? She would never know. Nor would he ever know how she truly felt.

Isabelle slumped back down on the bench, noticing for the first time the cold stones. She stared out into the pale void, surrounded by nothing. She was truly alone now. The only warmth in her life was the streaks of her tears on her face.

Twenty-Five

ISABELLE STARED AT THE PLACE INTO WHICH CAMPBELL had disappeared, forcing herself not to call out for his return. Eventually her tears ran dry, the sharp pain of loss replaced by an aching hole in her heart. Soon, the cold pressed in and she stood up and stepped into the gray abyss of mist, hoping to find the building that housed her small cell. It was time to find her bed.

After wandering aimlessly for a while, the fog looked a little rosier to her left and she turned her course to that direction. Drawing nearer, the faint outline of a building and the warm flicker of a candle through an open window became visible.

"Please, ye must help me save my brother," said a male voice she did not recognize.

"And why should I trouble myself with your concerns? You who have refused to follow my simple instructions," said a voice Isabelle recognized as the abbot.

"What ye ask o' me is hardly simple."

"But of course it is. Really, McNab, must I do everything by myself? What exactly do I pay you for, I wonder? Why, did you know that a wealthy English countess is wandering about? Campbell tried to ransom her, and I had to take possession of her myself. This is something you should be doing for me."

"An English countess?" asked McNab.

"Yes, wife of the Earl of Tynsdale. She wanted me to appeal for an annulment from her husband or some such nonsense. In the morn I will send word to Tynsdale to demand a contribution to the building fund for the return of his wandering wife."

Isabelle gasped and clamped her own hand over her mouth. Why that double-crossing priest! There was silence for a few agonizing moments, and Isabelle fretted that she had been heard.

"Please, I need yer support," begged the man called McNab. "I found tracks from where Andrew was taken that led me here. Is Andrew here now? Refuse to let Campbell take him, or tell me where Andrew is being held, I'll do the rest."

Isabelle backed away slowly on tip toe. She must get away.

"Your brother is not here. Campbell will no doubt take him back to his land for a fair trial before having him hung." The abbot made a laughing sort of sound, which sounded too cold and cynical to have any resemblance to true laughter. "Now do not despair, my ill-fated one. I may yet be able to intervene, but you know what you must do first."

The voices of the men trailed off into the night and Isabelle walked more swiftly away. Tears stung her eyes for the second time that night. How could she have been so stupid to have thought any man would wish to help her? No, that wretched abbot only considered how much money he could glean from her predicament. At least Campbell had never lied to her or pretended to offer assistance while secretly plotting her demise. If only he was still here.

She wrapped her arms around herself against the cold and damp. She was very much alone. And once again she needed to escape.

⁓

"But why do ye want him dead?" McNab asked Abbot Barrick, almost pleading.

"'Tis not for you to question me! Who do you think you are?" Barrick glared at him like he was filth. "I remind you that you are nothing. With the merest word I can have all your land revoked and your people removed from their homes. Though you have so little, perhaps you consider this no big loss."

"Forgive me, ye ken how much I appreciate yer support." McNab was not beyond groveling if it would get the abbot to help him. All that mattered now was saving Andrew.

"And if I ask you to do things from time to time, what is it to you?"

"But… but, I canna kill him." Archie had done many a rotten thing in his life, but to take the life of a bishop? Nay, that was going too far.

"'Tis a fine time for you to grow moralistic now, with your brother's life hanging in the balance. How many men have you killed, McNab? Why worry yourself over one more?"

"I've killed in battle aye, but no' like this. He is the bishop!"

"And what of it?" The abbot's voice was steely and cold. "He will bleed and die just like anyone else, I guarantee it."

"But I canna murder a bishop. I'd be no better than the murderers of Becket. I'd doom myself to hell eternal."

"Afraid of hell, are you? Well, of course you are going to hell, you have damned yourself a hundred times over. Very little I can do for you at this point. Do not shirk this little task I've given you for thinking that you will somehow avoid perdition. You are quite well damned, I promise you that."

An eerie silence fell. The dense fog hung still and silent, even the crickets and the frogs held their lively song. Something inside McNab broke. It was his last vestige of hope, his last remaining shred of belief that he could do something to win back prosperity for the clan and the favor of God. Archie put his hand over his eyes. He was damned. Nothing could help him now. Nothing mattered but saving Andrew.

"Will ye guarantee ye will save my brother?"

"I cannot. But I will intercede in your behalf if I am pleased with your work. I would not waste time. I warrant your brother has very few breaths left on this Earth."

"But ye will act as soon as…"

"As soon as I get word the bishop is dead I will go directly to Campbell to intercede. Now go, and take your foul stench with you."

❧

Isabelle scurried through the thick mist, trying to find her way back to the stables. She needed to escape, but couldn't find her way around. She knew she must still be on the convent grounds, but all she could see was the mist surrounding her.

"Now what am I to do?" she muttered.

"Come and pray," said an elderly female voice.

"Who's there?" Isabelle spun around, searching the dark gray mist.

"'Tis Mother Enid, my child." An elderly nun with sparkling blue eyes appeared before her. "Come, help me to the chapel." Mother Enid reached out a gnarled hand and Isabelle took it. She helped Mother Enid, who had considerable difficulty walking, until they reached the chapel.

Isabelle glanced around, not wanting to escort the nun farther. She needed to escape, yet Isabelle was not sure if this nun would raise an alarm to the abbot if she should run off, so Isabelle sighed and continued to help the nun into the chapel and down the main aisle.

Mother Enid reached the front pew and sat down with a soft grunt. "What do you pray for this eve?"

Silence crept through the chapel on padded feet. Isabelle's mind spun, trying to decipher what kind of threat Mother Enid posed. Isabelle had trusted the abbot with the truth and that had brought her nothing but more trouble. No, she would not trust this nun.

"Forgive me, but it seems my prayers have left me," said Isabelle, eyeing the door.

"Come then and sit beside me and we can pray together." Mother Enid gave her a warm smile that crinkled the corners of her bright blue eyes. "Now tell me what burdens you."

Isabelle gave another furtive glance at the door, yet

she did not wish to give the nun reason to fear she was running away. So Isabelle sat, hoping to quickly appease the old woman and be on her way.

"I am well. I thank you for your concern."

"You are having difficulty praying?" Mother Enid continued to smile, though Isabelle had the distinct impression she was not fooled by her denials.

"I do not know. I do not pray as I should, I suppose."

"And why is that, do you think?"

Isabelle took a deep breath against the rising irritation. Could this nun not see she had no interest in a discussion? "Truth is, I have never seen much point in praying. What will happen, will happen. What is the point of prayer?"

"Sometimes God does not always answer our prayers the way we wish."

"Forgive me, sister, but if a person prays and it comes to pass, they say God answered the prayer. If it does not come to pass, they say God had some other plan. Either way, God wins. What is the difference between that and simple fate?"

"You do not believe God answers prayers."

"I have been told to have faith that God will protect me, but how can I believe that? Bad things happen to people all the time." Isabelle's heart beat faster and she spoke with feeling. "My family died in the plague, but I did not. Did God protect me and not my family? To my mind things happen by chance, sometimes good, sometimes bad. Having faith will not protect you from being hurt or killed or *betrayed*... so what is the purpose?"

"The Bible does warn us that we will suffer."

"So we suffer. God must be pleased." Isabelle's words sounded bitter, even to her ears.

Mother Enid leaned back against the wooden pew. Three candles flickered on the altar, casting orange, dancing circles. "You remind me of myself, when I was your age," she murmured.

"Forgive me, Mother Enid, but rarely in my life have I been mistaken for a nun." It was time to go. Isabelle cast another glance backward toward the door and sat forward on the edge of the wooden pew.

"I hardly resembled a nun either back when I was a wealthy man's mistress."

Isabelle's head snapped back to the nun. "You were what?"

"You would not know it now, for time has delivered me from the burden of beauty, but there was a day when my company was much sought. In due course, though, I was called upon to pay my wages of sin, and I found the price to be more than I could bear."

The smile that had played on Mother Enid's lips faded, leaving a pair of gleaming eyes. "I became with child and was in ill health. I was taken in by a holy community and received care until my time had come. I was very scared of childbirth, and though I brought a living babe into the world I became dreadfully ill afterward. I felt my soul slipping away; I knew I would die. It wasn't until I had nothing left to lose that I started to pray. I begged the Lord to save me, promising to become a nun if I should recover."

"You survived."

"Yes. Now I ask you, did God save me, or would I have recovered on my own anyway?"

Isabelle said nothing. How could she answer?

"I choose to believe my prayer did move the Lord to spare my life," continued Mother Enid. "But you may choose to look at it differently. Whether or not you believe that God answers prayer, I know one thing for certain. Prayer changed me. Whether it saved my life, I'll leave for you to answer. But I am not the same woman. Prayer changed *me*." The smile returned to Mother Enid. "Pour out your complaint to God, but be aware that whether or not God changes your circumstances, he will almost certainly change you."

Isabelle leaned back in the pew, a new way of thinking turning in her mind. "Thank you for telling me."

"Godspeed, Lady Tynsdale."

"Where am I going?"

"You are leaving the convent, no? Let me tell you how to reach the stables."

Isabelle followed the directions Mother Enid had given her to return to the stables. It was almost as if Mother Enid knew exactly what she must do. Perhaps… perhaps, she had found a friend.

Directly ahead of her were the stables. Isabelle smiled. She might survive after all. She ran inside and stopped short at the sight of another man in the stables. There certainly were a lot of men around here for a convent.

"Who are ye?" demanded the man. It was the one called McNab who had been speaking to the abbot. "Ye dinna look like a nun to me."

"I am Lady Tynsdale," Isabelle answered without

thinking and internally cringed. When would she learn to keep her mouth shut?

"Ye should no' be wandering off, my lady. Ye could come to harm."

"I just went for a walk and got lost in the fog." Isabelle edged toward the door of the stable. She had no idea if he was friend of foe.

McNab nodded and went back to work saddling a horse. Isabelle backed out of the stables.

"Wait, Lady Tynsdale." McNab called after her and strode to the door of the stable. "I am no' sure why I tell ye this, but ye should know the abbot plans to trade ye to Lord Tynsdale for a donation to his building fund."

Isabelle froze and stared at him. Was he trying to help her? "Thank you for telling me. I fear the abbot lied to me."

"I fear 'tis no' his greatest sin, m'lady."

"Do you know where I can go that will be safe?"

McNab shook his head. "Ye're asking the wrong man. I canna keep anyone safe."

"Will you help me escape the convent?" asked Isabelle. She hated to press this man, but he had shown himself to be a friend, and she had precious few of those at this point.

"Nay, I have my own worries. Campbell has my brother. No doubt he plans to execute him."

"Why would he do that?" Isabelle gasped.

"Because he got caught wi' Cait Campbell."

"He abducted her?"

"Nay, Andrew is innocent. I need to rescue him before it's too late."

"'Tis a shame you did not see Campbell when he was here."

"Campbell was here?" McNab took a step toward her, his eyes gleaming with intensity.

"Yes, about an hour ago."

"An hour ago! Are ye sure?"

Isabelle nodded.

McNab rubbed his chin and studied Isabelle. "Perhaps there is a way we can help each other. I am going to the Bishop of Glasgow, care to join me?"

"Oh, yes, very much." Isabelle's heart soared. Finally someone was going to help her. At least it was a chance. More than what she would get if she stayed here.

"I need to talk to the bishop about intervening in Andrew's behalf. Perhaps ye could tell him how I helped ye?"

"Yes, I can do that." Get her to the bishop and Isabelle would swear he was a prince.

McNab nodded, his mouth a tight line. "Let us move quickly. The abbot will no' be pleased to find ye gone."

McNab finished saddling his horse and soon they were on their way.

"I have few talents, my lady, but I know these woods, and I know all the short cuts. Our road will be rough tonight, but we will get where we are going fast."

"Fast is good for me." Isabelle rode behind him, holding on tight, McNab rode like his life depended on it, down winding paths and across open fields. Finally, in the early dawn the horse was blown and Isabelle wanted nothing more than to stop and rest.

They came to a spot in the road where there were large boulders, one on each side. McNab pushed Isabelle down and hid behind the large rock formation. Isabelle tried to ask what he was doing but a strong hand covered her mouth. This was not right at all. Was she being abducted once again? Truly these men needed to find a better occupation.

Soon a galloping horse approached. The sound grew closer and closer until McNab jumped up in front of the horse and rider, pulling Isabelle with him.

"Halt!" commanded McNab. "Give me my brother and I will return the Lady Tynsdale."

Isabelle looked up at the rider and gasped.

It was Campbell.

Twenty-Six

"YOU LYING PIECE OF—" ISABELLE'S WORDS STOPPED short when she felt the sharp prick of a blade at her throat.

Campbell regarded them with cold eyes. His face was expressionless. "Good morn to ye, McNab."

The world went silent. Even her heart refused to beat.

"I have sent my prisoner on ahead to Innis Chonnel. He is not here," continued Campbell in no apparent hurry. "I'm afraid I am unable to make such a trade as you suggest."

"Get Andrew. Now," demanded McNab. His grasp on her arm slackened and he began to tremble. She doubted he anticipated Andrew would not be with Campbell.

"Nay, I dinna think so. The lady ye hold is more aggravating than any lass has a right to be and has a verra bad habit of finding trouble where'er she goes." He looked directly at Isabelle when he said this.

Isabelle gasped. Did he not even care that her throat might be sliced at any second? He hardly looked concerned that someone was threatening her life. Well that was enough of that.

Isabelle stomped down hard on McNab's foot and gave him an elbow under his rib cage. McNab stumbled in surprise and Isabelle broke free. She ran but stumbled on her gown and went down. A loud cry shattered her ears and Campbell charged forward, his sword in hand, his face twisted into something from the gates of hell.

McNab was quick and flew to his mount and galloped away down the road. Campbell rushed back past Isabelle, grabbed the reins of his horse and jumped up even as the horse started to run. He galloped past her in close pursuit of the fleeing McNab.

Isabelle stared at the swirling mist where the two men had galloped away. She put a hand to her chest to see if her heart still beat. With such a fearsome battle cry, she was sure Campbell's opponents must die of fright before he even reached them.

All around her was a white blanket of fog. It must be close to dawn since the mist had taken on a lighter gray hue, but she could still see nothing. She wondered what she should do now.

"Laird Campbell?" she called into the misty abyss, but received no answer. The air was cold and moist, the chill creeping through her cloak like a bony hand. She shivered, both from the cold and from being left alone in the night on the road.

Isabelle set off down the road in the direction the men had gone, hoping to find Campbell. The longer she walked the more she considered his words. She thought they had become friends, more than friends, perhaps, if fate had allowed it. And yet he had chided her like an errant child. Perhaps it would be better to try to find the Bishop of Glasgow on her own.

Presently, she came to a fork in the road. Isabelle sighed. Where to now? She looked at the road, trying to find tracks, but the muddy road was full of hoof prints going either direction.

"Campbell?" she called again. She folded her arms across her chest. Rather unkind of him to leave her alone in the near dark with no provisions or clue as to her whereabouts. Would he even come back for her?

Doubt and uncertainty crept in her mind. His last words had been intentionally cruel. Perhaps he was angry with her once more and had abandoned her. She could see no more than a few feet before her in the oppressive fog surrounding her, and yet impossible to touch. She had a sudden, sweeping desire to escape the ethereal blanket around her and find someplace more tangible.

She picked the road to her right, hoping it was indeed the right road, and walked along, to where she could not say. She trudged on and hoped for the best. It was simply impossible to have nothing but bad luck. Everyone had ups and downs. It must certainly be her turn for an up moment. Yes, she was certainly due for good luck.

The fog rolled in thicker, making it impossible to see more than a few feet in front of her. She walked through the gray nothingness. The longer she walked, the more she felt as if she was staying in one place. There were no landmarks, nothing to show that she had moved. She was alone in the misty abyss. Could she have stepped into a fairy ring by mistake? Had she been transported into some distant land of nothing? An icy wind blew on the back of her neck, making her shudder.

Isabelle stopped for a moment and shook her head. It was just the dense fog playing tricks on her. She needed to think about something else, something comforting. She continued trudging in an upward direction and considered the words of Mother Enid. It was calming to believe that even if she had no idea where she was, there was one who could see her, who knew who she was, and who cared for her. Isabelle was not convinced Mother Enid was correct, but alone in the mist, she wanted to believe.

Gradually, the mist took on a different sort of feeling. Instead of cold and spooky, it began to feel close and comforting. It was as if the presence of God was in the cloud and the cloud was walking with her, guiding her path. Isabelle felt a peace that was as unfamiliar as it was soothing.

Isabelle walked along for hours, not seeing anything but a few feet of road before her, but was relaxed and at ease. She had been steadily climbing up and as she rounded a bend, the mist took on a rosy hue. A few steps more and bright sunlight broke through the top of the mist. Isabelle blinked at the brightness. She had walked above the clouds. Around her and below her was a puffy, white blanket. Isabelle smiled in delight. She was on top of the world.

Isabelle sat on a large, flat rock to enjoy her accomplishment and to rest. Fatigue of the hard night and the long walk finally seeped into her bones, and she curled up on the rock and fell asleep, a smile still on her face.

Campbell raced after McNab with murderous intent. He was going to hack that kidnapping whoreson into bloody pieces. For abducting Cait, for threatening Isabelle, and for the good of society, that bastard needed to die. Campbell followed the man's desperate ride through the woods with determination, but McNab was wily and quick. Several times he veered out of sight and disappeared into the mist and Campbell had to backtrack to find his trail. Campbell had no doubt in his ability to track McNab, but since he had not been able to catch him in the early sprint, it was going to take some time.

Campbell considered Isabelle alone on the road and wondered what type of mischief she could find. It was a lonely road, rarely traveled, particularly in this fog and this early in the morn. Yet Isabelle had an amazing penchant for making trouble where none should be. Still, Campbell pressed after McNab. He would not let that bastard escape. Never.

Soon, however, it was clear he needed to make a choice. Either he could track McNab and enjoy the infinite pleasure of killing him and hanging his body out for the birds to eat, or he could go back and make sure Isabelle had not come to harm.

With a mouthful of curses, Campbell turned around and headed back to where he had left Isabelle. If she had any sense at all she would have remained there, waiting for his return. He was not at all surprised to

find her not where he left her. Indeed, the lass had no
sense whatsoever. Campbell dismounted and looked
for her tracks. The memory of her being held by
McNab, a knife to her throat, flooded back.

Campbell rubbed his forehead in an attempt to
dispel the image. It had twisted his insides to see her
so. And it should not have been. He had left her safe
at the convent. How had she fallen in with McNab?
When he found her, he was going to beat some sense
into her. Again, for the good of society. He was
nothing if not a dutiful servant of the higher good.

Campbell found her tracks and followed them up
and into a mountain pass. The early morning mist
dissipated, leaving bright sunny skies and a clear view
of his surroundings. None of which included the
figure of Lady Tynsdale. She had climbed far, and
Campbell became concerned that she might have
fallen off of the side of the path. The trail narrowed in
places and was precarious, with steep falls if one should
lose his footing.

Campbell hugged the side of the mountain. Once
he looked over the edge to make sure he did not see
her broken body. A rush of dizziness staggered him
back to the relative safety of the cliff wall. Despite it
being a cool morning, he broke into a sweat. Damn,
but he hated traveling over the pass. This is why he
always chose to go the water route back home.

Campbell continued up the winding path, keeping
his eyes focused ahead of him, not daring to look to
the side where the void threatened to suck him down.
He took a deep breath and gritted his teeth. He would
do this. He had to do this. And if Isabelle wasn't

already dead when he found her, he was going to kill her for making him do this.

He held the reins of his horse with a death grip and walked up the path, his right shoulder hugging the side of the cliff. He rounded a bend and found himself close to the top, which meant leaving the safety of having at least one solid wall. He breathed hard and wiped the sweat from his face. He forced his legs to move him forward, up to the top of the mountain pass. He grabbed the halter of the horse and walked close to his beast, feeling better to have at least something in hand.

Moving with slow caution, Campbell reached the peak of the mountain pass. The wind was brisk but the sun was bright. Had he looked, he could have seen around him for miles, but he kept his eyes on the trail ahead. He did not wish to think of how far up he had climbed. The drop if one stepped off the path would be bone-crushingly, brain-splatteringly fatal. Campbell focused on the path before him, hoping it would lead him off of this mountain and down somewhere safe.

A patch of odd color to his left caught his eye—it was Lady Tynsdale! Campbell gasped and froze in his tracks. She lay unconscious on a rocky ledge, balanced precariously on the edge of the cliff. One slight movement and she would fall to her death.

"Isabelle," he whispered, unable to move.

She moved not. Campbell closed his eyes and bowed his head. He was too late. She was already dead.

Twenty-Seven

CAMPBELL STARED AT THE LIFELESS BODY OF ISABELLE. She was so close to the edge. There was nothing he could do for her now. He considered for a moment just leaving her, but that would be the act of a coward. He straightened his shoulders. He would have to drag the body off the rocks, without falling to his own death. He was loath to step toward the rocky overhang, but he could not leave her body as carrion for the vultures.

He took the reins, wrapped one end around his left hand, and edged toward her, reaching out with his right hand. It was no use, he could not reach. His heart pounded in his ears, his vision became hazy around the edges, but he slowly unwound his left hand. Dropping his lifeline with a shudder, Campbell inched his way toward Isabelle. If he could grab her hand, he could drag her back to the safety of the trail.

Campbell's boots scuffed across the loose rocks, sending pebbles over the edge of the cliff. Every instinct in his body screamed for him to get off the ledge, but he kept inching forward. He was almost close enough to touch her hand. He reached forward, stretching out to her.

Dirt and pebbles rushed under his feet, rocks ground on each other, making a wrenching sound. The ledge was starting to collapse!

Campbell launched forward, grabbed her hand and flung himself back to the path, scrambling up the loose, falling rocks and debris. He kept his grip on Isabelle; he would not drop her. The large rock she had lain on slid off the ledge and smashed below, taking trees and other boulders with it.

Campbell struggled forward, dragging Isabelle's body behind him and landed on the solid surface of the trail. Campbell lay with his face in the dirt, breathing in the wondrous, earthy smell of solid ground. His body shook uncontrollably and he gasped for breath.

When his heart slowed down and the blood stopped pounding in his ears, he became aware of another sound. Something like a woman screaming. He opened his eyes and saw Isabelle yelling at him and rubbing the back of her head.

She was alive!

Campbell stood up and hauled her up too. She looked to be in reasonably good shape. Nothing looked broken, and she was not bleeding anywhere that looked life-threatening. Her gown was ripped and she was covered in small cuts and scratches, but those would heal soon enough. He hugged her tight in relief. Finally, her words began to float into his consciousness.

"Let me go, you big oaf! What are you trying to do? Kill me? Go bedevil someone else and leave me alone!"

The shock of his near-fatal fall from the cliff snapped

away, and bubbling up in its place was hot, seething anger. Isabelle had caused all this trouble and now she was complaining about him saving her life. Campbell, not generally a man who lost his temper, swore at her in his native tongue, then a bit more in English just to make sure she understood.

Isabelle glared at him with eyes blazing, hands on her hips, flushed and angry as a harpy. Probably because he had just referred to her mother in the most unflattering of terms. He felt a twinge of guilt; going after another person's mother was beneath him. She brought him to this; it was all her fault.

"Thank you, sir knight, for fulfilling my request to teach me how to swear." Isabelle's eyes flashed. "I fully understand your low opinion of me. You need not elaborate further on that account. And you needn't drag me across the rocks just to show your displeasure."

"I was no' dragging ye for my own amusement, I was saving yer life," Campbell yelled in return.

"Saving me from what? A life-threatening nap?"

"Look!" Campbell pointed to the ledge where she had been sleeping.

Isabelle was quiet for a moment. "The view is lovely," she said in an awed voice. "I could not see it when I first climbed up here." She admired the vantage a little longer, then frowned. "What happened to the rock I was sleeping on?"

Isabelle glared at the back of Campbell's head as she followed him down the path. It had been a trying day. Campbell had dragged her down the other side of the mountain, never letting go of her for a moment. When they finally got beneath the tree line he seemed to relax a little, but that just made him vocal.

Campbell had explained in a calm voice that did little to hide his irritation how little he thought of her for running away from the convent, for taking up with the likes of McNab, and for leaving where he left her on the road. He blamed her for letting McNab get away. Worse yet, he had not wanted to hear anything she had to say. Finally, she stopped trying to defend herself and he stopped talking altogether. Whatever connection they had shared now appeared to be irrevocably shattered. The loss of his affection pained Isabelle the most.

Campbell stopped and turned back to her. "The trail is safe enough for us to ride now."

Isabelle narrowed her eyes to intensify her menacing glare, determined he should not know how much she wanted to cry at his hateful words. If Campbell noticed, he did a good impression of someone who did not care. Isabelle scowled harder at the man, but only succeeded in giving herself a headache. Isabelle gave up and rubbed her forehead.

"Ye done wi' glaring at me then?" asked Campbell.

"Yes," replied Isabelle as haughtily as she could manage. "I've moved on to visualizing your demise."

"Ah, I hope it brings ye great amusement."

"You have no idea."

"I have some, the way ye've been giving me the evil eye," muttered Campbell.

So he had noticed! Isabelle smiled in triumph. Campbell caught her eye and smiled tentatively in return. Isabelle scowled at him and his smile faded.

"I need to ask for yer pardon, Isabelle. I said some things I regret. I spoke out o' anger, which is ne'er wise." Campbell sighed and rubbed his forehead with his hand. "Ye have no idea how I felt… how scared I was seeing ye wi' McNab's knife at yer throat. Why, for the love o' the saints, did ye leave St. Margaret's wi' McNab?"

"I overheard the abbot saying he was going to ransom me back to my husband. I needed to escape, and McNab offered to help. I did not know he was the one who abducted Cait. I thought you said you caught the man."

"Aye, but I doubt he acted alone."

"How was I to know that?"

"Ye… well… everyone knows no' to trust a McNab."

"Yes, thank you ever so much for all your warnings in that regard. Quite helpful." Isabelle let the sarcasm drip from her voice in a manner that would have won her sharp disapproval from her nurse.

"Why did ye run off after I went after McNab? Ye should o' stayed where I left ye like a sensible lass."

"Stay on an unknown road in the dark by myself without having the slightest notion whether you would return? I was trying to follow you at least."

"Ye took a wrong turn. Why did ye go up through the pass?"

"I came to the fork in the road and guessed."

"Why no' follow the tracks?"

"Many tracks were on the ground leading both directions."

"Can ye no' tell the difference between old and fresh tracks?"

Isabelle put her hands in the air. "I shall have to inform my tutor that he wasted his time teaching me Latin and philosophy. I should have been learning the science of the hunt."

It was Campbell's turn to glare at her. "I thought someone had attacked ye and left ye for dead, lying on that rock like that."

"I was sleeping," said Isabelle with indignation. "I did not realize how close to a cliff I was. Why did you drag me off the rock if you thought I was dead?"

"I could no' leave yer body for the birds."

Isabelle shuddered. Not a pleasant thought. And yet, it was kind of him to put himself at risk to retrieve her body. Isabelle sighed. She did not wish to give up her anger so easily, especially with how he treated her, and yet he had prevented her from falling to her death.

"Thank you for saving my life," mumbled Isabelle begrudgingly.

"Will ye forgive my words?"

Isabelle bit her lip to keep it from trembling. "After all we shared, your words were so cruel. I understand you being upset, but I do not understand how, how mean you were to me."

Campbell avoided her eyes. "I was scared. I dinna like being scared. I was furious at ye for making me feel such fear."

"Oh." Isabelle exhaled, and with it drained her anger and hurt. He did not make the confession easily. "I am sorry to scare you," said Isabelle, though inside she was cheering that her situation had affected him so deeply.

"And I am sorry for my words."

They stood silently in the forest in the early morning. Birds chirped a merry song, melting away the last of Isabelle's anger. She wanted to reach out to him, but somehow was unable to bridge the distance.

"We should go," said Campbell. "I must get back and check to make sure my kin traveled safely home."

"I need to get to a place where I can ask for sanctuary. McNab had agreed to take me to the Bishop of Glasgow."

"Now ye ought no' be trusting any man that comes around promising ye this or that."

"Certainly not one of those Highlanders," agreed Isabelle.

Campbell narrowed his eyes. "*Especially* one of those Highlanders."

"I hear they are barbarians."

"True every word."

"Shall I scream and run away?"

"I would only track ye down and drag ye back to my castle by yer hair," said Campbell with a faint smile.

"Then I suggest we get going," said Isabelle with a smile. It was good to jest with him again.

"Good," said Campbell. "To be frank I have little time for a merry chase today."

"Only, I must know this." Isabelle's smile faded. "Will you help me to claim sanctuary with the Church or will you give me back in ransom to my husband?"

Campbell paused a moment and took a great breath, letting it out slowly. "I ne'er thought I'd step between a man and his wife, but I'll help ye. At least I can see ye safe to Glasgow after I settle some matters at home."

"Thank you! Oh, thank you so much. You are the only one I can trust." Isabelle threw her arms around his neck and squeezed him in a tight embrace. "Thank you. Thank you on behalf of myself and my people."

"Damn it, Isabelle," cursed Campbell. "'Twas hard enough to say good-bye to ye the first time, now I am going to have to do it again." Campbell pressed her close and claimed her mouth with his.

Isabelle was momentarily shocked by the suddenness of his kiss. He was not slow or gentle, no, this time she feared he might devour her. Her body responded with a powerful rush of pure, animal lust. Memories of their time together in the inn rushed back, and she wanted more. And she wanted it now.

Emboldened by his kiss, Isabelle ran one hand through his hair, pressing his face closer to hers, as if such a thing were possible. With the other she cupped his backside.

Campbell growled in response, kissing along her neckline and pulling down the rough fabric to kiss some more. Isabelle gasped and arched toward him, offering herself to him fully. Her knees gave way and she would have fallen had he not caught her.

Campbell held her close and panted for breath. "This canna be right... Whatever am I to do wi' ye?"

It felt mighty right to Isabelle, but her head was spinning too fast for intelligible speech.

"I need to get back to Innis Chonnel. I canna tarry, no matter how much... how desperately I would rather stay."

Isabelle nodded and turned away to straighten her gown.

"I'd like to get back inside the castle walls before dark. Wolves, ye ken."

"Wolves?" Isabelle eyes snapped to his. "I am glad I did not know about that when I was creeping through the forest trying to escape the castle."

Campbell shook his head and looked to the heavens. "Ask Mairi to give ye the lecture on wolves. Ye require so much scolding, I have none left for ye."

Campbell swung himself into the saddle and reached down to pull her up behind him. She held on tight as he spurred the horse to a gallop. Despite her circumstances, she felt she was back where she belonged.

His kiss had claimed her. Whether it would be for good or ill, she did not know, but she would be forever his.

Twenty-Eight

CAMPBELL RODE HARD BACK TO INNIS CHONNEL. HE could not risk spending a night alone with Isabelle. He knew what he would do. He knew what he had almost done. She was no help at all, the little vixen. She had wanted all he had given her, and more. It was true she wanted to be released from her husband, but that didn't make her any less married. Or him any less betrothed. He needed to get her back to Innis Chonnel and put her into Mairi's care. If anyone could chill ardor into ice, it was his sister.

Finding Isabelle again made his life complicated at a time when it was bloody well tangled enough as it was. He had shared too much when he thought it was farewell forever. How could he go back to being acquaintances now? He tried to block her from his mind. But how could he with her arms wrapped around his chest and her thighs pressed against his? She should have stayed in the convent, not come back to bedevil him with her bright eyes, smooth skin, and silky, black hair. It was too maddening for words!

Campbell chose a challenging route home, overland,

high in the hills. The terrain was rocky and there were treacherous bogs that could swallow a horse whole. No road went through these parts, only the smallest trail, but Campbell found it and raced along as fast as he dared. The benefits to this route were to arrive home before dark and, more importantly, use the risk of certain death to keep his mind focused on the trail ahead, not the lady clinging behind. By midday he had descended north of Loch Fyne. The terrain became less steep and dangerous and soon he met the main road to Innis Chonnel.

Two miles from home, the faint sound of singing floated through the trees. He rode forward cautiously, and found the minstrel he had met in Glasgow, walking down the road before him, playing his lyre and singing a jaunty tune.

"Why it's Jacques le Chanteur!" exclaimed Isabelle behind him.

The minstrel stopped playing and turned to face them. He was dressed in a yellow tunic, red surcoat, and bright blue trews. A dark brown, tattered traveling cloak and red cap protected him from the elements, and on his back was slung a leather bag and his lyre. Campbell dismounted and Jacques swept him a polished bow.

"Greetings to you, my lord, my lady," said the minstrel in a smooth, French accent. "This is indeed a pleasant surprise to meet you on the road."

"You are well met," said Campbell. "What brings you to the Highlands?"

"Your kind invitation to Innis Chonnel has tempted me to brave the journey."

"Ye are indeed most welcome. My sisters especially will be well pleased if I return home with a minstrel."

Jacques gave him a wide smile. "I shall do everything I can to please your family, my lord."

Campbell nodded but wondered what the minstrel meant by pleasing his family. He had heard rumors of philandering musicians, and he would tolerate none of that nonsense in his household.

"Indeed, it will be delightful to have a musician of your talent to play for us," said Isabelle. Her eyes shone at the minstrel in a manner that displeased Campbell.

Campbell helped Isabelle off the horse, standing between her and Jacques. She hardly gave him a glance before walking around him to be near the traveling musician. They exchanged a warm greeting and the minstrel gave her another one of his courtly bows and dazzling smiles.

Campbell was beginning to take a dislike to the itinerant minstrel. The musician was a poor-looking character, scrawny and ill-favored. Isabelle laughed. Campbell's mouth tightened into a thin line. Apparently Isabelle found him pleasing enough.

"Such a delightful surprise to see you here. I am all anticipation to hear you play," said Isabelle with animation.

"Come now," said Campbell, walking between them. "We are not far from Innis Chonnel. If we step lively, we should make it to the castle by the evening meal."

"Ah, for that I am grateful," said Jacques. "My stomach has been complaining this age that I have not fed it as well as it would have liked."

"Ah, you poor dear. Let us make haste to the castle and see you tended to," said Isabelle with warmth in her eyes and a smile on her lips.

Campbell ground his teeth and wondered how fast he could get rid of the minstrel.

❧

Isabelle was thrilled to have met Jacques on the road. He had been her rescuer in the Glasgow inn and was a pleasant, charming fellow, unlike her taciturn, brooding Highlander. The minstrel was a tall, lanky lad, with trim black hair and bright blue eyes. A smile often played on his lips as if he was laughing at some secret joke, yet his eyes were kind and his manners pleasing.

The minstrel's countenance was well favored, though in truth she preferred Campbell's more rugged features, especially when he smiled. A glance at Campbell told her she would not be seeing an elusive smile any time soon. He was brooding silently again over goodness knows what. Jacques, however, was charming and talkative, a welcome change.

Isabelle chatted with the minstrel as they walked along, straining to see around Campbell, who walked like a brick wall between them. The company of the minstrel had done nothing to lift Campbell's mood, and instead he looked even more irritable than before, if such a thing was possible. She swore she even heard his teeth grind. What was wrong with this man?

They walked on at a fast clip set by Campbell. Several times, Isabelle found she needed to run a few steps to catch up. She considered asking him to ease the pace, but remembering the minstrel's hunger, she silenced her complaint and trotted along. On a hill above them were the remains of an old motte and bailey castle, probably several hundred years old. It had obviously been abandoned for many years; the original stone wall had fallen down and many of its stones had been pilfered for other building projects. Part of a wall of the inner ward stood attached to a partially crumbled tower.

"Campbell!" called a young voice across the wind. "Hey, David, look at me!"

Rabbie was perched high on the tower wall. Isabelle gasped.

"Rabbie!" shouted Campbell, his eyes wide. "Get down from there. Now!" He sprinted up the hill to the remains of the castle, Isabelle and Jacques following behind.

"There's Lady Tynsdale. Did ye take my boat? I canna find it, so I thought I'd go looking for ye to ask. Do ye have my boat?"

"Yes, yes, Rabbie," Isabelle answered. "Just come down carefully, and I'll show you where."

Rabbie seemed oblivious to the danger he was in. "I told myself if I climbed the tower, maybe I would see where the boat was at. And I did and I found ye!" Rabbie's delight was evident.

Campbell ran into the tower and Isabelle hoped he could make it to Rabbie before something terrible happened.

"Please, Rabbie, climb down," cried Isabelle, straining her neck to look up to him. He was quite high.

Rabbie smiled. "I'll come down now, dinna worrit

yerself." The lad scrambled over some of the castle wall, then turned and began to lower himself down on the other side of the wall inside the tower.

Suddenly the rock wall crumbled under the weight and Rabbie pitched forward with several large pieces of the rock wall.

Isabelle screamed.

The minstrel rushed forward and collapsed to the ground as Rabbie and debris fell on top of him.

"Rabbie! Jacques!" Isabelle rushed forward and began pulling away rocks and debris. The minstrel stirred and slowly sat up. He was bleeding from his lip and held a limp Rabbie in his arms.

"Rabbie?" said Isabelle softly. Rabbie did not move. For once he was quiet and still. Blood ran from a cut on the back of his head, onto Jacques's arm, and dripped to the ground.

The minstrel laid him gently on the ground, his eyes wide. Isabelle's chest was heavy. It was hard to breathe, hard to swallow.

"Rabbie?" It was Campbell, kneeling beside them. He spoke words of an unknown language, but Isabelle knew it to be a desperate prayer.

"I'll get Mairi, she is a healer." Campbell put a hand on Isabelle's shoulder, his green eyes blazing with intensity. "Watch over him. Dinna leave him."

Isabelle put her hand over his. "I will care for him. Go, bring Mairi."

Campbell ran to his horse and was gone, nothing but dust in his wake. Isabelle hoped Mairi was not only a healer but a miracle worker. The wound was bad. Very bad.

The pool of blood under Rabbie's head was growing. Isabelle hiked up her gown and tore off a strip of her linen chemise. She folded it into a compress and held it against the cut to try to stop the flow of blood. The compress was soon soaked in blood so she ripped a larger piece. The blood slowed its rate but continued to flow. Isabelle knew it must be stopped.

The minstrel sat beside her, gray-faced and grim. "Hold this to the wound," said Isabelle. "I am going to try to find a plant I know of that may help stop the bleeding."

The minstrel nodded and took her place holding the compress to Rabbie's head.

Isabelle ran down the hill and toward a grove of trees. She searched the forest floor for a particular plant her nurse had shown her. She did not even know if it grew in the Highlands, or where to begin to look. It was hopeless. Remembering the words of Mother Enid, Isabelle said a silent prayer that she could quickly find this plant. She was not sure she believed all of what Mother Enid had said, but she could use all the help she could get.

Isabelle took three more steps and found it. She stared at it for a moment, unbelieving. Had God actually answered her prayer? She grabbed what she needed of the little, green-leafed plant and breathed a word of thanks in case something divine had led her to where she needed to be.

Isabelle struggled back up the steep hill to the ruined castle. When she reached the top, the minstrel knelt over the child's body and made the sign of the cross. Isabelle froze, icy fingers of fear running down her back. The minstrel was softly chanting in Latin.

Despite her limited knowledge of Latin, this chant was familiar to her. Last rites.

"Is he...?" asked Isabelle.

The minstrel started at the sound of her voice and turned to face her. "No, he lives still, but barely."

Isabelle found two flat rocks and pounded the leaves between them. She added whiskey from a flask the minstrel carried and created a paste. It was not how she had been shown to make it, but it was all she had and it would have to do. She ripped more from her chemise and made another compress, this time adding the paste. She held it firmly to the child's head and prayed again. Perhaps if God answered her prayer before, he would answer this one too. Isabelle had told Mother Enid that she did not believe in prayer or that God cared enough to save people. Never before had she wished more fervently to be proven wrong.

Isabelle knelt by Rabbie and kept the bandage to his head. The boy was limp and white. She prayed he would wake, but he remained deathly still. Jacques sat on the other side of Rabbie, his eyes closed. He was either praying or taking a nap. Isabelle preferred to think he was praying since her prayers did not appear to have made much effect.

Why would such a terrible thing happen to such a sweet little boy? He was looking for his boat. The boat she stole. Guilt punched her in the stomach. Rabbie would never have climbed the crumbling tower if she had not run away with his toy. It was all her fault.

Below her she heard horses and a shout. Campbell

had returned. Isabelle kept her eyes on the still form of Rabbie. She could not look at Campbell. What must he think of her now?

"Rabbie!" It was Mairi.

Isabelle gave way to Mairi who knelt beside Rabbie. She felt him over, making a quick assessment of his injuries. The minstrel stood and backed out of the way, his head bowed, the cut on his lip beginning to swell.

"What is this?" Mairi asked, pointing to the compress, which itself was soaked in blood, yet Isabelle was pleased to see that the wound had stopped bleeding.

"I made a paste with this." Isabelle showed her the plant she used. Mairi's eyes bore into her like nails, her lips a thin, tight line. Isabelle held her breath. Would Mairi find fault with her ministrations?

Mairi nodded, "Verra good. There is no' much more I can do. Let us bring him to Innis Chonnel, but verra careful now. I wonder what that boy was thinking climbing this crumbling heap."

Isabelle glanced at Campbell, but he said nothing. He directed the minstrel to help him gather wood to make a stretcher. More of Campbell's brothers arrived, Dain driving a cart with Hamish, Gill, and Finn. They quickly wove together a stretcher, and under Mairi's careful direction, moved him gently to the stretcher and onto the cart. The family gathered around the cart and held him still as Dain slowly drove down the road. The minstrel ran ahead, kicking away rocks or anything that might jar the cart. Isabelle followed along behind.

They entered the gates of Innis Chonnel a bedraggled little troupe. Not wanting to take him up the stairs to the living quarters, Mairi directed a small storeroom be emptied and a bed be brought down for him. The brothers jumped to her commands, happy to be given a task they could do.

Isabelle held the compress to Rabbie's head as his siblings prepared his room. Isabelle willed him to wake, but he did not. She walked with him as they slowly moved him into the makeshift sickroom. The news of his fall spread fast and they were soon joined by the sisters and many other family members. The room began to shrink in size and Isabelle struggled for breath in the stiflingly hot room.

"Out!" commanded Mairi. With a look she emptied the room. Mairi closed the door after the rest of the clan was in the hall, her eyes blazing. Isabelle felt relieved to be hustled out into the cooler air of the castle passageway, and knew Mairi would make sure Rabbie got the best care. She was a formidable woman and Isabelle had an idea that even unconscious, Rabbie would not risk her disfavor by disobeying her command to wake up. He was in good hands. He was surely going to be well. The alternative was too awful to contemplate.

"Go on now," said Campbell to his siblings. His face was gray. "Dain, Will, Finn, Hamish, get back to the lists, ye shoud'na be standing here like this. Fiona, take the ladies back to the solar. Ye will be told if there is any change." Several of Campbell's siblings eyed Isabelle and shifted slowly as if waiting for an explanation as to her disappearance and return. They received none from the stoic Campbell. They moved away with reluctance until there was only Campbell and Isabelle left in the hall.

Isabelle glanced up at Campbell. She wanted to say how sorry she was. She wanted to give him comfort. Campbell's eyes bore into hers like arrows of accusation. Isabelle opened her mouth to speak, but the words died in her throat.

Campbell's jaw was clenched and a large vein stuck out at his temple. "Ye took his little boat?"

Isabelle nodded and took a step back.

"He was up there because o' what ye did," said Campbell, his voice low almost a growl. "He fell because of ye."

"I am sorry, truly, I am," whispered Isabelle.

"Sorry will ne'er be good enough," spat Campbell, even as his face crumpled.

"You blame me for his... accident?" She had almost said death. She closed her eyes, wishing she could take back the unspoken word that hung in silence between them.

"Why did ye do it? Mayhap yer husband would no' be as cruel as ye believe. Maybe his feud wi' yer uncle would have died wi' him."

"He means to kill me! He waited until my uncle died and I inherited Alnsworth. Now that I have inherited, I am of no further use."

The anger drained from Campbell's face leaving him pale. He rubbed his forehead and his shoulders slumped. "Ye truly think he means to kill ye?"

Isabelle nodded. "I am his fourth wife. His two previous wives lived only a few months into the marriage."

Campbell shook his head. "There are many reasons why people die."

Isabelle opened her mouth to argue, but fatigue

seeped into her bones and weighed her down. She had struggled for so long to try to save herself and her people and look what it had gotten her. She had not meant it to happen, but Rabbie would never have been up on that tower if she had not taken his boat. Perhaps it was time to give up and let Tynsdale take her. She knew her life would be rather unpleasant and quite short, but perhaps this was of no consequence.

"I will return to my quarters. Please inform me when my husband arrives."

Isabelle tried to walk past Campbell, but he blocked her, stepping in her path. They stood close, not touching, not moving.

"I canna lose him." Campbell leaned closer to Isabelle. He stared beyond her at the rough stone wall, his eyes brimming with tears.

Isabelle reached up and wrapped her arms around Campbell's neck and pressed herself to him. For a moment, it was as if she was hugging a cold marble statue, then he wrapped his arms around her and pressed her close. Her own anger slipped away as she recognized his harsh words were born in fear. He was large and warm and holding her uncomfortably tight, but she would not stop him for anything.

Twenty-Nine

"DAVID!" CAIT CAMPBELL'S VOICE CHARGED DOWN the hall.

David Campbell jumped away from Isabelle like she was a hot poker.

"David, where are ye? David!" Cait rushed down the stairs into sight. "Is Rabbie hurt? I heard he hit his head?" Tiny worry lines appeared on Cait's forehead, like a miniature version of David's deeper ones.

"Aye, he fell and cut his head. He's resting now. Mairi is wi' him."

Cait took a breath. "Good, Mairi will see to him. I need to speak wi' ye, David." Campbell shook his head and opened his mouth to protest, but Cait cut him off saying, "I need to speak wi' ye most urgently on a matter o' life and death."

Campbell trudged up the stairs followed by Cait and Isabelle. Campbell and Cait entered a solar Isabelle had never seen before. She guessed it was Campbell's own.

"I will retire and see ye in the morn," said Isabelle.

A weariness clung to her, weighing her down. All she wanted was to sleep.

"Nay." Campbell spoke with authority, his hands on his hips. "Nay, ye canna be free to roam the castle, no telling what ye might do."

"I swear the only thing I will do now is find a pallet for sleep."

"Nay, ye be trouble and I'll no' be having ye hurt anyone else." Campbell's face was stone.

"What are you going to do? Lock me in the dungeon?" Isabelle hoped he would laugh. He did not.

"Aye, that is one option." Campbell raised one eyebrow. "I'll give ye one other."

∽

Isabelle stood outside the solar door feeling awkward. Voices were raised, and it was impossible not to hear what was being said. Good breeding demanded she walk away, but she could not; she had taken Campbell's second option. At the time it seemed better than the dungeon. She thought Campbell might be joking, but the look in his eye... she did not want to put it to the test.

Isabelle felt a tremendous tug and was flattened against the door. The price of option two. A rope was tied around her wrist and led from her hand, under the door, to the belt of her Highlander. The rope started to move from side to side of the oak door. He was pacing, the beast.

"Please, Andrew is innocent, can ye no' see?" wailed Cait. Isabelle felt for her, she sounded distraught.

"I caught him wi' ye in his arms, Cait. How do ye explain that?" roared Campbell.

"It wasna what it looked like."

"I know what I saw, Cait. And Andrew himself admitted to me that he abducted ye."

"He did? Why would he say that?"

"Mayhap he decided to tell the truth."

"Nay, it wasna him. It was…"

"It was…? Tell me who else abducted ye and I'll make sure they will swing as well."

"I dinna ken. They wore masks. But Andrew wasna there. He rescued me from them. Aye, he rescued me from a band o' vicious thieves, single-handed."

"Dinna tell falsehoods to me, Cait. 'Tis insulting."

"He was verra kind," said Cait in a smaller voice. "Why will ye no' believe me?"

"What I see is that he took advantage o' ye and made ye believe he was yer friend. But he dinna return ye nor my horses, and I dinna find he had any intention of doing so. Whate'er he said to ye was lies, Cait."

"Nay!"

Isabelle could plainly hear Cait crying. Poor girl.

"What will ye do to him?" asked Cait, her voice wavering.

"There will be a trial o' the elders. He will have a chance to say his piece."

"And then? What will ye do then?"

"Ye must prepare yerself, Cait. If he is found guilty of the charges before him he will be sentenced to death."

"Nay! Please, ye canna do this."

"I'm sorry this displeases ye, but I must see justice served."

"I hate ye. I hate ye!" screamed Cait and the door flung open.

Cait bolted out the door and ran down the passageway, tears marring her beautiful face. Isabelle was embarrassed for having overheard such a contentious exchange between brother and sister and hoped Cait had not seen her.

Campbell leaned on the doorpost and sighed. "I suspect ye may have overheard some o' that."

"I did not mean to intrude on your privacy. But…" Isabelle held up her tied wrist.

Campbell motioned for her to come inside his solar.

"Forgive my intrusion." Isabelle settled herself on a bench in his solar. "Since I could not help but overhear, why is it that you would sentence the lad to death? Is that not a severe sentence for his crimes?"

"For holding my sister captive and stealing my horses? It is a just punishment."

"But she seems to be undeniably attached to him."

"That is what concerns me. If I find he compromised her in any way, his death will be from my hands around his neck, forget the noose."

"You don't think that she and he…"

"She denied he molested her, but…" Campbell collapsed into a chair next to her. He rubbed his eyes, the worry lines on his forehead growing deeper on his tired face. "I'm only her brother. I know nothing."

"Might there be a way justice could be served without ending his life?"

Campbell shook his head and looked up with sad eyes. "I have seven sisters to me. If word spreads that I let Cait's abductor go free, none o' my sisters will e'er travel safe again. I need to make a statement here, now, or my family will ne'er be safe. Understand?"

"Yes, but did you not abduct me? Are you not as guilty as he?"

"Abduct ye? Lady, I saved ye from yer own suicidal tendencies. If it were no' for me ye'd be dead several times over."

"True." It was a forced admission, one that Isabelle wished she could deny.

"David." Mairi's pale face appeared at the door. "Rabbie. He's no' breathing well."

Campbell stood. "What can I do?"

Mairi shook her head. "Ye need to be prepared for the worst."

❧

Campbell stormed out of the castle with Isabelle trailing along behind. Not that she had much choice in the matter since she was still tethered to the man. Campbell needed some time alone, particularly time without her within reach. Yet the rope around her wrist forced her to run after him to avoid being dragged behind.

They were heading to the chapel, a place she knew he would go even before they turned in that direction. Just as she knew he would pray until he lapsed into unconsciousness or he got the word that Rabbie was awake or dead.

The chapel was deserted when they entered and Campbell stalked to the front, crossed himself and lay prostrate on the floor. A wave of compassion washed over her, and Isabelle wished she could make things better. She had a sudden urge to touch him and comfort him, but pushed it aside. The last thing he wanted was to be reminded of her presence.

She slid into a pew next to him and bowed her head. Was this all her fault? She had stolen Rabbie's boat. Stolen. The truth was undeniable. She had been so concerned with saving her people she had not considered the result of her actions. The wages of sin is death. The verse came floating back to her from one of the many sermons she generally ignored. She had always thought that the wages of sin would be her own demise, not someone else's. Not Rabbie. He was innocent.

She was praying before she knew what she was doing. She prayed for Rabbie to be well and for him not to suffer because of what she did. Tears welled up in her eyes. She was not sure God would listen to her pleas, especially since she had espoused a lack of faith in the whole prayer process. And yet, she prayed anyway. It was the only thing she could do.

Campbell groaned and pulled himself off the stone floor. He sat next to her on the pew, and covered his face with his hands.

"'Tis all my fault," he whispered.

Isabelle put her hand on his shoulder. "No, 'tis my fault."

Campbell wiped his eyes with his hands. "Nay, I could have reached him in time but I... I faltered. I hesitated when I reached the top and he..." Campbell put his face back in his hands.

Isabelle rubbed his shoulder. "If you had rushed over to where he was you would have both fallen. Truly, you are too hard on yourself. There was naught you could have done. If there is fault to place, it is mine for stealing his little boat. And for that I will be forever sorry."

Campbell looked at her, his eyes red. In one sudden movement she was in his arms. He was warm and smelled of leather and sweat. She breathed deep and held him close.

"'Tis no' yer fault, Isabelle. I apologize for saying so. I was just so… scared." He broke away from her and looked at the floor. "'Tis shameful, but I am powerful afeared o' heights."

Isabelle was surprised by his admission. It seemed impossible for this big man to be afraid of anything. The implication of his words hit her and his actions started to make more sense. "So that is why you were so angry at me on the top of the cliff."

"Ye have no idea my feelings at that moment."

"And yet you climbed up after me, though you were scared to do so. Why?"

Campbell looked up, his face tired and lined. He carried much on his shoulders. "Ye might have been in danger. I coud'na leave ye to yer fate."

"So you climbed up after me and saved me from falling off a cliff, even though you were afraid?"

"It had to be done."

"Yes, and you did it. You saved me. It did not matter that you were scared, you still acted to save me. Do you not see? You would have done the same for Rabbie. You did not stop because you were scared, you stopped because it was not safe. The ledge would not have held your weight, you would have brought both of you down. Your only hope was to talk Rabbie back to safety, but he fell before you could do it."

Campbell's green eyes flickered with intensity. "Ye ken?"

"Yes. Only a fool feels no fear. You show courage because you feel fear, but it does not control you. Remember how you saved me on the cliff? You would have done the same for Rabbie if it was possible, but unfortunately it was not to be. I only regret that you saved me and not Rabbie."

"Do no' regret it, for I have no regrets in saving ye." Campbell stared up at the unfinished stained glass window in the front of the chapel. "Thank ye, Isabelle, my mind is much more at ease." He put his arm around her and she leaned her head on his shoulder. For the first time in a long while Isabelle felt at home. She took a deep breath and closed her eyes. This was nice. Very nice.

"Laird Campbell, if ye please!" Someone called from the back of the chapel.

"Aye?" Campbell stood up.

"'Tis Rabbie. He's awake!"

Thirty

CAMPBELL RAN FOR THE CASTLE COMPLETELY FORGET-ting that he had tied Isabelle to him. He swung open the main door and raced through only to be stopped by a sudden yank on his belt. Confused, he saw he was being held back by the rope tied to his belt leading straight to the closed door behind him. Isabelle!

He opened the door and found Isabelle standing there, holding her nose.

"Ow," she said.

"I beg yer pardon, my lady. Will ye please keep up!" Campbell grabbed Isabelle's hand and took off running again, pulling her behind him.

When they reached the room it was crowded with Campbell's family, packed with siblings. They spoke in hushed tones, all eyes on the spare boy in the bed. Campbell pushed his way through, dragging Isabelle behind.

"Rabbie, Rabbie lad," he spoke softly to his youngest brother and knelt beside the bed.

Rabbie's eyes fluttered and then opened. He blinked several times as if trying to focus, then smiled.

"Lady Tynsdale," said Rabbie in a soft voice.

Isabelle felt all eyes in the room turn to her. "Rabbie. Are ye well?" Isabelle asked.

"'Course I am. Do ye know where my boat is?"

"Yes, 'tis on the other side of the loch, in some rushes."

"Did ye take it o'er the loch? Mairi winna let me do that. Did she sail well?"

Isabelle kept her focus on Rabbie, but it was getting unbearably hot in this tiny little room with all these silent, hostile Campbells staring at her. She smiled at Rabbie's innocent face, so happy he was awake, so wishing he would be quiet.

"Yes, very well. Laird Campbell has been worried about you. Do you not wish to speak to him?"

"Hullo, David. Sorry I fell off the tower. I suppose ye'll be making me cut ye a switch."

"Nay, lad. Ye've been punished enough."

"Thanks, David, that's right nice o' ye. Isabelle, did she take on water? Did ye have to bail?"

Isabelle felt the eyes turn back on her again. Would he please stop talking about how she stole his little boat? "No, no, it was quite well made."

"I wish I could o' seen it," said Rabbie more slowly, his eyelids heavy.

"Time to sleep now," said Mairi.

"Aw, Mairi, I'm no' tired." But Rabbie's eyes were already closed. "Isabelle?" He held out his hand, and she kneeled beside his bed and took it. His breathing became slow and steady, a peaceful sleep.

Campbell bowed his head and led the group in a quiet prayer of thanks for Rabbie's recovery.

"Out now, all o' ye," whispered Mairi and hustled her siblings out of the sickroom. Isabelle started to stand, but Mairi waved her back down. "Nay, Rabbie wants ye, and ye're staying till he says otherwise."

Isabelle went back to her knees and continued to hold the boy's hand. He was a sweet lad. When he woke, she hoped they would be alone so she could ask him not to prattle on about her taking his boat. She wondered if these Highlanders would ever forget it. Probably not.

&

Isabelle woke hours later, still kneeling by the bed. Rabbie had let go of her hand and rolled over in sleep. At some point in the night, Campbell had unbound her hand, so she was no longer tethered to him. She tried to stand but her legs were asleep and stiff. She sat back and slowly unbent her knees, wincing at the effort. She rubbed her legs, a thousand pinpricks stabbing her as feeling gradually and painfully returned. Trying to stand, she pulled herself up the bed and then tried to put her weight on one of her legs.

Pain shot up her leg like a cursed dagger. She cried out and stumbled back to the floor. Two hands grabbed her around her waist and she was lifted off her feet.

"Good morn to ye, Laird Campbell," Isabelle said wearily.

"Good morn to ye, Lady Tynsdale. Let's get ye to bed."

She nodded her head against his shoulder. He sat her briefly on the bed and shook Mairi, who was sleeping on a pallet on the floor. Mairi nodded and got up, taking his place in the chair beside Rabbie's bed. Campbell reached back for Isabelle and put his hand around her waist, pinning her to his body and half carrying her from the room.

"Ow, this hurts," whimpered Isabelle halfway down the hall.

"I imagine it does. Perhaps I should have brought ye a chair, but I warrant I was still a wee bit angry at ye for stealing Rabbie's little boat."

Isabelle sighed. She wished Rabbie had not chatted on about that boat. Rabbie may not hold a grudge, but the rest of the clan did. "Are ye still angry wi' me then?"

"Nay. Ye stayed wi' him. Ye dinna complain. I ken ye dinna mean to harm him. Mairi says the compress ye made stopped the flow o' blood. Ye may have saved his life, Isabelle, and for that I thank ye."

Isabelle exhaled in relief. "Thank, ow, you. Ow, ow, ow."

Campbell let her bear more of her own weight and it hurt something fierce. "Sorry, Isabelle, but ye need to get the feeling back." Campbell half supported her as they walked down the corridor and out into the courtyard of the inner ward. It was in the wee hours of night and not another soul was awake in the pale light of the moon.

"I recall once I got stuck in a tight place and both my legs went numb," said Campbell. "When I tried to walk again it hurt like blazes. 'Course it was my own fault for hiding there."

"This was your fault for not bringing me a chair," Isabelle blurted. The comment was woefully impolite, but pain had turned all her words sharp, so she had limited options from which to choose. She gritted her teeth. "I beg your pardon. Please, go on. Why were you hiding?"

"I hid in a small cupboard in my father's chambers. He was having a meeting with the Douglas, and I verra much wanted to hear what was said."

"You fit in a cupboard?" Isabelle could not get beyond that statement without astonishment.

Campbell laughed. "Aye, at twelve I was a scrawny thing. Dinna look too promising to tell ye the truth. My father was talking to the Douglas about my fostering with him. I supposed he hoped it would make a man o' me."

"So you hid in a cupboard for that?"

"Nay. I hid because they were also going to negotiate the betrothal between me and one of Douglas's daughters. I was verra interested, or perhaps I should say terrified, wi' the prospect of getting married."

"Seems you have done an admirable job of avoiding the married state. So you are betrothed to Douglas's daughter?"

"Aye and nay," said Campbell. Isabelle waited to see if he would explain. She took another step with an involuntary whimper.

"My sire was always close with Douglas. Fought wi' him against the English bastards, forgive the phrase." Campbell added. "I fostered wi' him for several years as a lad. He taught me to fight as a knight. Taught me to fight to win too. The two being no' always the same, ye ken. My father wanted me to form an alliance wi' the Douglas clan, but my mother had other plans.

She wanted me to form an alliance wi' her kin, the Stewarts. Ye ken that Stewart is currently the Steward of Scotland in the absence of King David who was captured by your king?"

Isabelle nodded.

"Well, because my parents could not agree, the betrothal was ne'er formalized wi' the Church. It remains a more informal agreement between my sire and the Douglas."

"And you are also pledged to the granddaughter of the steward."

Campbell looked down at her with a sharp eye. "How do ye ken that?"

Isabelle swallowed hard. "Ye told me just now."

"Nay, I dinna speak of his granddaughter. How do ye ken about the steward?" Campbell stopped and released her waist, forcing her to stand on her own legs.

Isabelle cried out and reached to him for support. "I... I..."

Even in the dim light, Isabelle could identify the moment of realization on his face.

"Ye were on the ledge long. Ye heard my conversation wi' the steward in Glasgow." It was not a question.

"Aye, ow!" said Isabelle, wondering at the strange word coming out of her mouth. She was even starting to sound like one of them. She grabbed his arm and he put it around her once more, supporting her legs, drawing her close.

"'Twas not a conversation meant for anyone else's ears." His voice was low with warning.

"I did not intend to overhear anything. I just wanted to get away."

"And instead ye landed in my bed."

Isabelle inhaled sharply. Pressed against him, her skin turned hot.

He continued on. "We discussed things which could prove dangerous to yer health were ye ever to reveal them, ye ken?"

"I will be discreet as always." Isabelle attempted to change the subject. "Tell me, how did you come to be so entangled with two ladies?"

"My father arranged an informal betrothal with Douglas, everyone knows that. Trouble is, my mother secretly made arrangements with the steward for me to wed his granddaughter, leaving me wi' two brides."

"That is awkward," said Isabelle. It was all starting to make more sense. "Should not your father's wishes take precedence?"

Campbell snorted and began to stroll around the courtyard with Isabelle once more. "Ye clearly ne'er met my mother. Aye, perhaps my father's wishes should be considered first, but both the Douglas and Stewart clans are powerful and both expect me to form an alliance with their clan."

"So you need to choose a side."

"Aye, but how to do so without starting a clan war? With King David captured, both the Douglas and Stewart fight for control of Scotland. Whoever I choose may tip the balance in their favor."

"Is one cause more just?"

"I fostered wi' Douglas. I would stand wi' him in any battle. Yet I fear he has become greedy for power, and may be tempted to make an unholy alliance wi' the English king in order to gain power and land. Yet

Stewart also seeks power, and I ken he has verra little desire to see our King David return."

"What will you do?"

Campbell looked up at the stars that covered the sky. A dense cluster of stars formed a gleaming path across the black night sky. "It would be easier if the correct choice was laid out before me so I could discern the right path, but I dinna ken which clan to choose, and I sorely wish I did."

"I'm sure you'll make the right choice when the time comes," said Isabelle with true conviction. She was confident he would always do the right thing.

"Thank ye. I would ask for yer discretion, the choice before me is no' widely known."

Isabelle nodded.

"How are yer legs feeling?"

At that moment Isabelle realized she was walking on her own, her arm linked with his. He had distracted her through the process and she was able to walk without pain. She also realized that he had shared something personal, something which left him vulnerable. It was a gift. Something in return for the pain he had caused her. She smiled at him.

"Thank you, Laird Campbell. I am well again."

He wrapped his arm around her waist and held her closer than he needed to, and walked back into the keep.

Isabelle was at peace. Rabbie had recovered. Campbell had forgiven her. All would be well. Her stomach rumbled a loud protest that all was not entirely well.

"How long has it been since we last ate?" asked Campbell. He led her quietly into the great hall, the servants still sleeping on their makeshift pallets on the floor and tables.

Isabelle honestly could not remember. "We have fasted long."

Campbell's stomach rumbled in reply. "Aye, time to break our fast, and get some rest."

Isabelle smiled as he led her to the kitchens. She was ravenous. Sitting at a long, wooden table in the kitchen, worn smooth from use over the years, Isabelle was eager for whatever Campbell could find.

He dropped some day-old wheat trenchers and a jug of ale on the table. Isabelle grabbed the bread and stuffed it into her mouth. Never had an old trencher tasted so good. Campbell followed and ate much. Neither spoke as they filled their empty bellies.

Isabelle sighed with contentment. "I should like to get some sleep now, unless you feel you must bind me to a post for the safety of your clan."

Campbell averted his eyes and had the decency to look sheepish. "I confess my reasons for binding ye were no' entirely to protect the clan."

"No?"

Campbell sighed and rubbed his forehead. "I wanted ye near." His eyes met hers. "I needed ye near."

Something warm melted through Isabelle, taking all rational thought with her. She should be furious. She chose to be flattered. "'Twas very wrong of you." Her chastisement might have carried more weight had the smile not gave away her truer feelings.

"I most humbly apologize."

"Will you agree to help plead my case to the bishop as a sign of contrition?"

"Aye, when I have settled things here."

Isabelle lunged across the table and hugged Campbell around the neck. "Thank you! Thank you so much! Now I do not have to try to escape again."

"Escape *again?*" Campbell disentangled himself and walked around the table toward her, pulling her up by her shoulders and holding her at arm's length. "Now dinna ye be causing any more trouble here."

"Me? Trouble?" Isabelle slowly wrapped her arms around Campbell again and sighed with contentment as he wrapped his large arms around her. She breathed in deep and laid her head against his chest. He smelled of wood smoke and a musky scent that was all his own. It was intoxicating. She breathed deep again and closed her eyes, fatigue claiming her.

Campbell patted her gently on the back. "Naught but trouble. I knew it the instant I realized ye were English."

He picked up the sleeping form of Lady Tynsdale in his arms and took her upstairs. He paused at the door that led to the ladies' sleeping quarters. He should put her in there somewhere. Except, he rationalized, if he did he would wake all the ladies and they certainly must need their sleep. Surely it would be best to take her upstairs to bed.

His bed.

Thirty-One

ISABELLE DRIFTED SOMEWHERE BETWEEN DREAMING
and waking. A sense of comfort she had never before
experienced wrapped her with its warmth, seeping
into her very bones. Every muscle relaxed, leaving her
like jelly. Happy, warm jelly.

"Isabelle," whispered a familiar voice.

Isabelle's eyes flew open. Where was she? She
brushed aside some soft fur blankets and propped
herself up on one elbow. David Campbell murmured,
snuggled closer to her, and continued to sleep.

"David?" She was in bed with David Campbell?
She sat upright. Pale sunlight filtered through linen
drapes, revealing the undeniable truth. On one wall
of the bedchamber was the large family crest. On the
opposite wall was an impressive arsenal of weapons
hanging from brackets. His large claymore was there,
along with many other sharp implements, all looking
more deadly than the next. Charming. She sat farther
up in the bed, piled high with soft fur pelts. She was
in bed with David Campbell!

What had happened? How had she got here? She

remembered nothing. Did they... ? Surely they had not... It was not possible to sleep through *that*, was it? Was it?

"David?" she whispered.

His breathing was slow and steady. His face, for once, was relaxed, no frown lines marring his appearance. He was simply beautiful in the morning light, a promise of a smile on his inviting lips.

"David." She gave him a little nudge. Nothing happened so she gave him a proper shake.

David grunted, rolled over, and began to snore. Isabelle rolled her eyes. So much for romantic.

What should she do now? Should she stay? Memories of their night in the inn rushed through her with a hot wave of desire. He snored louder. She waited for him to wake. He started to drool.

He was certainly exhausted. Had they...? Isabelle jumped from the bed and fanned herself with her hand, trying to cool down a sudden hot flash. She found she was still fully dressed. So they probably had not... except skirts are rather easy to lift... but surely she would remember...

"Bother!" She still didn't have the right words for the occasion. She found her shoes on the floor and stomped to the door, half expecting to find herself locked in. She was not. She opened the door, walked through and slammed it shut behind her. She made herself jump at the sound. He must be awake now. He must. Should she run?

Slowly, her heart pounding in her chest, she opened the heavy oak door and peeked inside the room. He still slept. She took a deep breath and closed the door, placing her hand on the cool stones on the castle wall, then placed her hand on her fore-head, trying to cool down.

He was an impossible man. He had her all hot and flustered and he was not even awake! She was pathetic.

Isabelle slunk down to the women's quarters. No one was in the room except Cait, who sat on the window seat, her head bent over her embroidery. She was different from the last time Isabelle had seen her, smaller, her shoulders more rounded, her eyes swollen and red.

"Ye have returned," said Cait, without looking up.

"Er… I was… Rabbie and the chapel and…"

"We thought ye had gone back to England."

"Oh, yes! I did try. My plans went a bit awry."

Cait gave her a half smile that did not reach her eyes. "Me too."

"Are you… well, Cait?" Isabelle took a few tentative steps toward her.

Cait shook her head. "David is holding Andrew and he winna listen to me. Andrew dinna abduct me. He is innocent and David is going to kill him." Fresh tears spilled down well-worn tracks on Cait's face.

"Oh, Cait." Isabelle sat next to her on the window seat. "I am so sorry, but who is Andrew to you?"

"He is… he is… my friend."

Isabelle took Cait's hand. "Tell me what happened. Maybe I can help."

Cait told Isabelle about being kidnapped by Archie McNab and then meeting Andrew. Cait described her relationship with Andrew as a friendship, but her occasional breathy sighs and surreptitious tears were not fooling Isabelle.

"So Andrew McNab would take you riding?"

"Aye," said Cait with a smile that lit her face. "He took me to the nicest places. One place had a remarkable vantage, a lovely view." Her face fell and she looked at the floor. "That is where they found us," she added softly.

"Sounds like you did not wish to be found," suggested Isabelle softly.

Cait continued to look at the floor. "He was... verra kind. I looked forward to his visits."

"He touched your heart."

Cait looked up at Isabelle with searching eyes. "He asked me to marry him."

"Oh," said Isabelle, trying to stifle a gasp.

Cait was instantly wary. "No one believes me, I dinna ken why I bother talking at all. I can see ye disapprove too."

"No, well, have you thought that he might have wooed you to try to get your dowry. Sometimes people can be less than sincere if it would mean their own enrichment."

"But that's the thing no one understands. I switched places with my lady's maid and everyone, including Andrew, thought I was Alys." Cait frowned, causing tiny worry lines to appear on her forehead. "Poor Alys, she is still a prisoner."

"Poor Alys, indeed."

"David will get her back."

"I am certain of it." Isabelle nodded, that much she knew of David Campbell.

"The point is, Andrew wanted to wed me when he believed me to be nothing more than a lady-in-waiting. He truly loves me!"

Isabelle pondered for a moment. "And you? How do you feel about him?"

Cait looked at her with large, liquid eyes. "I love him. Indeed, I do."

"And Campbell is going to try him for the crime of abducting you?"

Cait's bottom lip trembled. "Which he did not do. He is innocent."

"Forgive me, but I could not help but overhear. Did Campbell not say that Andrew had confessed to the crime?"

"I dinna ken why he would say that. It wasna him. It was his brother, Archie."

"Well then," said Isabelle thinking fast. "We should try to find him and ask him."

Cait's face brightened and she smiled a big grin, even as the tears continued to fall. "Would ye? Would ye help me?"

"I would be honored to help you," said Isabelle and gave Cait's hand a squeeze. Even as she did so, she had a pang of guilt that this was exactly the type of behavior Campbell had considered locking her in the dungeon to prevent. Isabelle shook her head to dispel the notion. She had told him she would not try to escape. She had never mentioned anything about not helping Cait.

"Thank ye, Isabelle. I kenned ye were a true friend the moment I met ye. Except... why are ye wearing that ugly thing?"

❧

Isabelle followed Cait to the entrance of the prison, which was carved into the rock below the storeroom

304 AMANDA FORESTER

on the western wall of the castle. Cait had helped her
dress in one of her old gowns. Despite its age, it was
a relief to be back in a silk. Compared to the wool
kirtle, it was heaven. Isabelle was also careful about her
headdress, making sure all her hair was swept up under
the lace snood. She may not be respectable anymore,
but at least she wanted to look the part.

"Do ye think Andrew is well? What if he hates
me now that he knows who I am?" Cait's eyes
opened wide and she clutched her hands to her
breast. "What if he blames me for what David did to
him? Why do ye suppose he took the blame for my
abduction? But how will we get into the prison? Do
ye think he is well?"

Noting the circular and repetitive course of Cait's
speech, Isabelle stopped listening and focused her
attention on the one relevant question Cait had asked.
How were they going to get into the dungeon to see
Andrew McNab?

The door to the storeroom was open a crack,
allowing the ladies an opportunity to peek into the
room. Besides the stacks of barrels and other stores one
would expect to find, there was a young guard sitting
on a barrel, humming a jaunty tune.

"How do we get past him?" whispered Cait.

"Just follow my lead," Isabelle whispered back,
hoping she could devise a plan in the five seconds it
would take them to cross the room to where the lad
was sitting. Isabelle opened the door.

"Halt! Who goes there?" called the guard before
either of them could set a foot in the room. Isabelle
rolled her eyes. Not even five seconds! So unfair.

"My, but you are assiduous in your duty," said Isabelle, entering the room.

The guard blinked and gave her a blank look.

"Ye do yer job verra well," said Cait with a winning smile. Her pale blond hair was loose, a simple gauzy veil framing her face. Even with her eyes swollen and red, she still was a lovely creature.

The guard snapped his focus to Cait and gave her a slow, warm smile and a low bow.

"Has your prisoner given you any trouble?" asked Isabelle.

"Nay, no' him. He's been quiet enough. Want me to rough him up a bit, Lady Cait? He deserves nothing less after what he's done to ye."

Cait grabbed Isabelle's hand so hard Isabelle had to grit her teeth to avoid screaming.

"I need to see him," said Cait, the desperation clear in her voice.

The guard looked taken aback and Isabelle squeezed Cait's hand to remind her to keep better control of her emotions.

"Is the prisoner secure?" asked Isabelle.

"Aye, shackled to the wall. He will no' be going anywhere."

"You are sure he is secure? There is no chance of his escape?"

"None. Ye may sleep well, m'lady."

"In that case, Lady Cait needs to confront the man who abducted her to speak the words she needs to say."

"Nay, I canna allow that."

"By whose authority do you deny the Lady Cait access?"

"Uhhh," the guard stammered.

"Unless Laird Campbell has ordered ye to block my path, then stand aside," commanded Cait.

Without waiting for a response, Cait whisked past the guard and down the stone steps.

"W-wait—"

"Best to let her be," said Isabelle. "She needs to confront him, to speak her mind. Surely you can understand why she would wish to do so without others hearing."

The guard looked unsure.

"I'm certain Campbell would be very pleased with how you are standing guard. Tell me, have you been in his service long?" Isabelle smiled, determined to keep the lad in conversation until Cait returned. The guard eyed the stone staircase. Cait best be quick.

Andrew Campbell sat on a stone bench shackled to the wall. It was cool and damp in the prison, but at least they had provided him with a serviceable blanket and there was no standing water. Overall his cell was clean and he was fed at least once a day. Not too bad, considering the crime with which he was charged. Not that he had experienced prison before. This was his first. And considering the charges, most likely his last.

Andrew leaned his head back on the rough, stone wall and tried to keep his mind blank. There was not a single topic that did not cause him pain. Though he rarely drank in excess, he wished they would bring him some whiskey. If any circumstance warranted inebriation, waiting for one's execution certainly qualified.

The swish of silk brought his attention back to his surroundings. Andrew froze as Cait Campbell walked down the stone staircase and into sight. Cait Campbell, the reason he was in shackles. Cait Campbell, who only a few days ago he had desired to wed. She was wearing blue silk with gold embroidery. Even his limited knowledge of fashion informed him that the gown alone was worth more than the entire contents of McNab Castle. Her blond hair was loose, with a gauzy veil framing her face. She was beautiful, and the reason he would die.

"Andrew?" Her voice was soft, her eyes were large.

"Aye." He should insult her, say something cutting to make her regret her deception. He should hurt her the way she hurt him. He looked away, her perfect face too painful to look upon. Even though she deceived him, he still could not hate her.

"I feared my brother would kill ye." Her voice was strained.

"Ne'er fear, there is still time. I warrant he brought me back for a proper trial before he has me executed."

"Nay, dinna say that. I'll speak to him. I'll tell him it was no' ye who abducted us."

"With all due respect, my lady, but why do ye care? Ye have deceived me well. I was completely taken in. Whatever ye hoped to achieve was accomplished. Ye are home. I am in shackles. What more is there?"

"I ken it was wrong o' me to deceive ye—"

"Nay, m'lady. 'Twas verra clever. I am impressed, truly I am. Please forgive me, but the sight o' ye pains me. I have spent the past several days trying to forget ye. Ye standing there is hardly helping my resolve."

"But this is no' yer fault."

"Nay, I am to blame. These past several days I have been forced to take responsibility for myself, and I canna be pleased wi' the man I see. I have let my brother talk me into many ill-conceived plans or simply watched and let things unfold wi'out making a stand. I may no' have kidnapped ye, but I helped to hold ye prisoner. I did no' release ye as I should have." Andrew bowed his head. "I was enjoying myself too much," he added in a voice that was barely audible.

Andrew held up his shackled wrist. "This is my fault. I might wish for a second chance to make things right, but I deserve none."

"But why tell David ye were the one to abduct me?"

"To prevent him going back to destroy my clan. 'Tis too late for me now. I will pay for my crime, but my clan, ye ken how little they have. If Campbell marches against them, how many would die, the guilty and the innocent alike? If I am to die, at least I wish to be the only McNab to suffer for this crime."

The prison was silent. Andrew regarded Cait with sad eyes.

Cait clasped her hands in front of her. "I need to know one thing, Andrew. I want an honest answer. I deserve that much, ye ken?"

"Ask anything and I will tell ye true."

"When ye said… when ye said what ye said on the hill. The part about how ye felt." Cait shifted from one foot to the other. "The part about love. Was that a description o' how you truly felt, or were ye simply after my dowry?"

Andrew looked her in the eye. "Everything I told ye that day was the truth, Lady Cait. Everything."

"Then I need to provide ye wi' an answer to yer question." Cait stepped closer to Andrew, her eyes wide and black in the dim light. "Yes, Andrew. I will marry ye."

"Lady Cait!" yelled down the guard. "Are ye well?"

"Aye," said Cait, and flounced up the stairs.

Thirty-Two

ARCHIE McNAB SLUNK INTO GLASGOW WITH A DARK purpose. He left his horse tied in a secluded glen. It had taken him days of riding and slogging through rivers and hiding in caves before he had convinced himself Campbell was no longer a threat. At least for today.

His last attempt at freeing his brother without resorting to the abbot's heinous request had failed. He had hoped to trade Lady Tynsdale for Andrew, but his brother was not there. No one was there, just the bastard Campbell. The last person he wanted to confront.

McNab crept around an inn, keeping to the shadows. The cold, hard truth of his life was that everything he did was wrong. He could not get ahead for anything. Every instinct he had was wrong. Every natural inclination was wrong. He was born a horrible mistake, ought to have been drowned at birth. Considering all the harm he had caused, he wished he had been stillborn.

If there was any justice in the world it would have been a dark and stormy night. The previous night, he waded through a bog with rain pouring down on him so thick he thought he'd drown simply by taking a breath. But now, when he could have used the dark night and the inhospitable weather, it was a warm night with a moon so bright you could see your shadow. He tried to be inconspicuous as he neared the bishop's castle, but he was quite sure he had been spotted by several people along the way. Mostly couples gazing longingly in each other's eyes. Truly, there was no justice at all.

McNab reached the bishop's residence, and slipped through the open gate and in the front door. It should have been barred. Why didn't God warn his own bishop to keep thugs like him from entering their homes? He muttered curses and grasped his knife. He must do this. He had to follow the abbot's demand to have any chance of saving his brother. He had to save Andrew. Nothing else, not his life, not the bishop's mattered anymore, if they ever did.

McNab crept down the hall and up a steep set of stairs. He guessed the bishop's rooms would be at the top. At the top of the stairs another hallway filled with closed doors greeted him. McNab sighed. Would nothing be easy tonight? There was only one way to do this.

He drew his blade.

He put his hand on the latch of the first door when suddenly it swung into him smacking him hard on the nose.

"Arrgh!" he said. It was the involuntary sound a person makes when their nose has been broken.

"Dear me, I beg your pardon, I did not see ye there. Please come in, sit down. Let me see how I can help."

McNab allowed himself to be ushered into the room and sat down by a small fire. Through the tears that filled his eyes he could see the white-haired bishop hover over him, the picture of concern.

"Here now, take my handkerchief for yer nose. Gracious, but ye are bleeding like a fountain."

McNab took the handkerchief and pressed it to his nose. This was all going wrong. He needed to complete his errand and be away. He reached for his knife but realized he had dropped it on the floor when he was hit. It was somewhere on the hallway floor. He leaned back in his chair and groaned.

"Whiskey?" asked the bishop.

"Aye," mumbled McNab. "By the barrelful."

A mug was offered and he used his right hand to drink and the left to press the bishop's cloth to his nose. Neither spoke for a while, until the whiskey warmed his insides and dulled the pain. McNab took the linen cloth from his nose. It had been a fine piece, embroidered with lace around the edges. Now it was a bright red rag.

"Sorry for ruining this."

"'Tis I who should be sorry for injuring ye, my friend. Usually I'd be asleep in my bed at this hour, but 'twas such a fine night I thought to have a little walk in the moonlight."

Archie nodded. God was protecting the bishop after all. And in a way that caused Archie pain. Aye, his luck was holding as well as ever. Which meant, of course, he had none.

"I fear I may have broken your nose," said the bishop.

"Would'na be the first time," McNab mumbled.

"What brings ye here at this hour, my friend?"

McNab figured it would come to that. He needed to come up with some plausible reason, and quick.

"I was sent to kill ye." McNab's shoulders slumped and he put his head in his hands, which caused the blood to start flowing again. That was the *truth*; he was supposed to *lie*. He was an idiot. Maybe he had been injured worse than he realized. He had heard if you hit a man's nose hard enough, a piece of skull could get lodged in the brain, causing death. He could only hope.

"I beg your pardon?"

"I think I have a piece o' skull lodged in my brain."

"What's that?"

"But I canna die right now 'cause I must save Andrew or they will hang him for sure."

"Who?"

"My brother. Which is why I have to kill you. I am terrible sorry about it. Ye seem nice and all."

"Perhaps I could convince ye to lean yer head back, ye're pooling blood on my floor."

"Sorry." McNab tilted his head back up. "Can I speak wi' ye?" He desperately wanted to talk, the words spilling from his mouth. And since he was going to kill the bishop anyway it seemed he might as well speak the truth.

"Aye, my son. Tell me what is troubling ye."

McNab told the bishop of the poverty of his clan, his failed attempts at improving his fortune, and his dealings with the abbot. He talked about trying to give Andrew a better life by sending him to university, of failing to protect his sister, of wishing he was never born. He spoke of abducting Lady Cait and her maid, and being tricked into thinking the maid was Cait. He told the bishop of how Andrew had been taken by Campbell and would most likely be killed. Last of all, he spoke of how killing the bishop was the only way he had left to try to save Andrew and how it didn't matter anyway because he was already damned.

If the bishop was surprised or concerned by any of McNab's words, it did not show on his face. A man accustomed to hearing the confessions of many, the bishop hid his feelings well.

When he was done, McNab laid his head on the table. He was so tired. He wished to sleep and never wake.

"Abbot Barrick, ye ken he be a man o' God?" asked the bishop.

"He be the devil incarnate," groaned McNab.

"Strange then, ye would go to him for spiritual advice. How can ye account for it?"

"I ne'er went to him for no spiritual advice."

"Get yer story straight, lad. Ye just told me it made no difference whether ye committed murder because the abbot said ye are damned."

"Aye... am I no' then? Speak yer mind clear for me. 'Tis too late and I've drunk too much whiskey for riddles."

"Yer abbot has been a boil on my backside for the past score years. Truth is he lied to ye. Ye are no more damned than the rest o' us. That is why God sent a savior. All sinners, even grievous sinners, can be forgiven if they come before God with a repentant and contrite heart."

McNab tried to make sense of what the bishop said, his wits dull with whiskey and pain. "Ye're saying I can be forgiven."

"Aye, lad."

"That's good. But 'tis no' me I wish to save, but my brother."

"What if I went to talk to Campbell for ye?"

McNab's eyes opened wide. "Would ye do that? I would gladly trade myself and take my brother's place. 'Tis me who is to blame."

"I will speak to him, but I will no' trade ye. There is something I need from ye. I need ye to bear witness against the abbot. I am going to appeal to the archbishop or to Rome itself to have him defrocked. I need yer testimony."

McNab rubbed the back of his neck. "I want to help ye, but who would believe me against the word o' the abbot? And I am no' partial to displeasing him. He has more than me working for him and he woud'na care if my crops were burnt or my clan was killed."

"I canna protect ye from him. I can only say that wi' him gone, fewer people will be hurt. Yer clan included."

"Ye'll go to Campbell and get Andrew?"

"I will try. That is all I can say."

McNab slowly nodded his head. "Aye, bishop. I'll serve ye as I have served him. I ken ye to be a better master."

"I am and no mistake."

The bishop stood and motioned to the door. "Let us retire for the night. This is much too much excitement for these old bones." The bishop led McNab down the hallway to an empty chamber. "I think ye will be comfortable here for the night."

McNab entered the clean, serviceable room and turned back to offer his hand to the bishop. "Thank ye, yer grace. Ye have given me hope. 'Tis no' a common thing for me."

The bishop shook the hand offered, saying, "Sleep well, my son. Tomorrow I will ride for Campbell."

The bishop closed the door to the bedroom, locked the door, and pocketed the key. He may be a trusting soul, but he was no fool.

Thirty-Three

ISABELLE WALKED THROUGH A SEA OF MIST. WHERE was she? A dark figure loomed in the distance and she walked toward it. As she drew nearer, she could see he was the figure of a knight, concealed in armor.

"Who are you?" she asked.

"Do you not know your own husband?" The knight removed his helm revealing the withered face of her husband. "I am master of Alnsworth now."

"No!" The mist dissipated and she was in the courtyard of Alnsworth, her people standing in chains around her. "No! You cannot do this!"

"If only you had returned," said her nurse, her eyes dark and sorrowful. "None of this would have happened. But now it is too late."

"You cannot do this!" Isabelle shouted to Tynsdale.

"There is none to stop me. I am coming for you, Isabelle."

Isabelle woke with a small scream.

"What's wrong?" asked Cait, opening a sleepy eye.

Isabelle sat bolt upright. She was on her pallet on

the floor next to Cait's bed in the room that served as the sleeping quarters for the unwed Campbell sisters.

"I-I had a nightmare. I must go home, now!"

"Now?" Cait stifled a yawn. "'Tis early, no?"

"But I must. Oh, I have been away too long. They must think me dead or that I have abandoned them."

"Who?"

"My people. At Alnsworth! I must speak to David, uh, Campbell—Laird Campbell," Isabelle corrected herself. She was so spun around she could not keep her innocent façade in place.

Isabelle had worried herself sick all yesterday about what to say to Campbell when she saw him, but she never did. He never sought her out and sent his apologies to the supper table that he was much too engaged making "arrangements" to join the family for the meal.

Cait closed her red, swollen eyes. "What good is it to ask David anything? He is too busy preparing to kill Andrew."

Isabelle drew up her knees and rested her chin on them. Cait was right about one thing, Campbell was much too engaged at present to arrange travel for her. Isabelle thought fast, her mind considering, turning around, and discarding many bits of plans. There must be a way. She could not abandon her people. She could not.

"Cait!" Isabelle moved closer to Cait and glanced around the room, but all the ladies continued to sleep. "I have a plan to save Andrew," Isabelle whispered.

"Oh! Tell me!" Cait sat up, her blue eyes sparkling, her golden hair falling around her.

"Shhhh!" Isabelle admonished and they leaned their heads in closer. "Remember you said your lady-in-waiting was still being held by McNab? What if you asked Campbell to trade Andrew to get her back?"

Cait clutched Isabelle's hands. "Aye. That's perfect. We can trade Andrew for Alys. Thank you, Isabelle!" Cait grabbed Isabelle into a quick, tight embrace. "Quick, let us dress, we will speak to David directly."

"Good," said Isabelle. When Campbell sent Andrew she meant to be one of the party at least to Glasgow. She must get help for her people. Time may have already run out.

❧

Campbell nodded to his elders as they left. He walked back into his solar and eyed the bottle of whiskey. Tempting, but it was yet too early for drink. He had spent the morning arranging a trial for Andrew McNab. It was an unwanted responsibility and one he would gladly give up, as Gavin had been fortunate enough to do. But Andrew must have a fair trial, and Campbell would see it done. It was a grim business, for unless something dramatic happened to sway the evidence, Andrew would most surely be sentenced to death.

It was a difficult time, made worse by his rambling mind that would not stay a steady course. Isabelle. She haunted his thoughts. He had awoken yesterday at midday, well rested but alone. What had she thought when she woke up in his bed? Why had she not even woken him to say good-bye? She must be furious with him.

It may be cowardice, but he had avoided her all day yesterday. He was truly busy, so it was not difficult to do. He must see her sometime, but how could he explain? He had no right to take her to his bed. Worst part was, if he had the chance to do it over again, he would do the same thing.

Campbell pushed thoughts of Isabelle aside. He must focus on the situation at hand. He may be marching in war against McNab soon to get Alys back and punish him for his compliance in Cait's abduction. He would punish the bastards who dared to abduct his sister.

"David!" Cait rushed into the room, flushed from running. "David, I ken what we must do to save Alys. We must arrange a trade wi' McNab. We will exchange Andrew for Alys. Is it no' a perfect solution?"

"Nay, Cait. I winna bargain wi' McNab." He was about to admonish Cait about bestowing her affections on inappropriate people, but Isabelle glided into the room after Cait. She wore an emerald silk gown and her long hair was pulled back under a modest wimple. She was a queen. Campbell poured himself a whiskey and sat down hard on a bench by the empty, black fireplace.

"But ye canna leave Alys to him. Ye must do this!" Cait ran to him and sat beside him, clutching his sleeve. "Please, David."

"Ah, Cait." Campbell shook his bowed head. He could not meet Isabelle's eyes. "I am sorry for ye, I am." Campbell stood for a moment and retrieved a missive from the mantel. "This arrived this morning. I already sent word to McNab demanding he return Alys or face war. This is the reply."

Cait took the missive and opened it, Isabelle

stepping by her side to read it too. Scrawled in a poor hand was a message from Alys.

> Dear Laird Campbell,
>   Thank you for caring for my rescue. However, I have wed Laird McNab and choose to stay with him of my own free will. To prove what I say is the truth, I offer this knowledge of Lady Caitrina. If you look between her two middle fingers of her left hand you will find a small scar she received when she tried to rip out a seam with her table knife. I told her not to do it.
>
>   Respectfully,
>   Alys McNab

"Is this message in Alys's hand?" asked Isabelle.

Cait nodded, staring blankly into the black fireplace.

"Is it true about the scar?" asked Campbell.

Cait held up her left hand and both Campbell and Isabelle bent down to inspect the small, white scar between her fingers.

"I dinna ken ye had a scar there," said David.

"Few do," answered Cait.

"So Alys has truly wed McNab? Why?" asked Isabelle.

"She spoke of him favorably, that he needed her. But I ne'er·thought she would do something like this." Cait shook her head, her eyes dull beneath red, swollen lids.

"Do ye think she will be mistreated?" asked Campbell.

"Nay, we were treated wi' kindness while we were there." Cait's shoulders slumped. "So we canna exchange Andrew for her."

David put his arm around Cait and gave her a brotherly squeeze. "I'm sorry, Cait. I dinna like to see ye so sad." He was concerned by her frank devotion to Andrew and her distress at having him imprisoned. Unfortunately, it was likely going to get a lot worse for Andrew McNab.

Cait nodded mutely and walked out the door.

"Lady Tynsdale, I would speak to ye," said Campbell, gathering his courage.

"Yes, I would like to speak with you too," said Isabelle.

"Ye would? Aye, well, I feel I need to apologize for the other night. I dinna intend to... that is to say I did intend, but I..." Campbell rubbed his forehead with one hand and gestured in the air with the other. "It just happened."

"It?" Isabelle's eyes grew wide. "*It?* How could you?"

"I was tired. Ye dinna seem to mind at the time."

"I was asleep!"

"True..."

"You should at least have woken me up and asked me if I would like to."

"Ye are verra right." Campbell's heart sank. He was right, she was angry at him. He had thought... but no, her feelings did not match his. "I apologize. I thought that since we had before and... forgive me, I mistook yer feelings on the matter."

"We did *before* too? I remember some things, but I do not recall doing... doing..." Isabelle flushed prettily. "Was I asleep?"

Now it was Campbell's turn to be confused. "Aye. People do sleep when they are asleep."

"What are you talking about?" Isabelle tilted her head slightly to the side.

"Sleeping. Together. In my bed. What do ye speak of?"

"Sleeping? As in actual sleep?"

"Aye." Campbell drew out the word, speaking slowly. He had strong suspicions he knew what she was thinking, and it was not about sleep. He tried unsuccessfully to suppress a grin. "Ye speak of sex."

"Campbell, please!" Isabelle glanced into the corridor and shut the door. "Someone might hear you."

"So ye dinna mind speaking o' it, but ye dinna wish anyone to know." Campbell's heart began to beat quite merrily. She did like him. Her blush gave her away.

"We should not."

"Did ye think I had made love to ye while ye slept?" Now that was plain insulting.

Isabelle looked off at a tapestry hanging from the wall. "But for a moment. Is this not a nice tapestry?"

"Isabelle." He stepped close and softly brushed her cheek. Her breathing increased, and he shamelessly enjoyed the view of the top of her breasts straining against the fabric of her gown when she breathed. Damn, but he wanted her. "If I should ever take ye to my bed to love instead of sleep, I will promise ye two things. First, ye will wish for it as much as I. And second, I dinna wish to brag, but there is no possible way ye will sleep through my lovemaking."

Campbell had the satisfaction of watching Isabelle's blush deepen to the color of a fine wine.

"Campbell." A page knocked on the door. "Riders approaching."

"Be there in a moment," called Campbell.

"I-I need to speak to you," Isabelle shook her head like she was trying to collect her thoughts.

"Later, I must go see who approaches."

"Wait!" Isabelle put her hand against his chest. The gentle weight of her single hand held him in place. "I must ask for your help."

"What can I do for ye, my lady?"

"I must return home to Alnsworth. I cannot tarry any longer. I fear Tynsdale has taken Alnsworth."

"How do ye know?"

"I had a dream—"

"A dream?" Campbell was skeptical. He needed to go. Who knew who approached his walls, be it friend or foe?

"Yes, a dream." She placed her other hand against his chest, her warmth seeping through his linen shirt. He could not move now had he wanted to. "I must return to Alnsworth."

"And what would ye do there?"

Isabelle's shoulders slumped. "Probably die at the hand of my husband."

"Die?" Not on his watch.

"Now that he has Alnsworth, he does not need me alive."

"Nay. Ye will no' return."

"But I must do something!" Isabelle dropped her hand from his chest and gestured into the air.

"I will help ye go to the bishop in Glasgow, but not now. I have to settle things with the prisoner first and with Cait."

"I cannot wait any longer!"

"Forgive me, Isabelle, but I winna allow ye to give yerself back to a man who is going to kill ye! Now try no' to worrit yerself, 'twas only a dream. I must see who arrives at my door!"

Campbell strode from the room. He needed to see who approached. He almost hoped for a foe; he could use a little swordplay to work off the heat she raised in him.

Campbell shook his head as he walked up the stone staircase to the wall walk. Battles he could fight and win, but when it came to affairs of the heart, he was outside his depth. He stood on the battlements of the outer wall and turned his focus to the party advancing on Innis Chonnel. The banner waved defiantly in the wind. It was the Douglas.

Campbell inwardly groaned and gripped the stone battlements wondering what ploy he could use to avoid his impending nuptials. He considered for a moment having his steward tell Douglas that he was away hunting... on an extended trip. But that was pure cowardice. He counted the men Douglas brought with him and wondered how much he valued his courage. Sometimes being a knight was a pure pain.

Campbell heard light footsteps behind him and assumed the page had followed him up. "Tell Mairi to prepare for our guests and that the lads will have to double-up."

"We're already double-upped," protested Rabbie.

Campbell turned and saw his errant youngest brother. "Should ye no' be in bed?"

"Nay," said Rabbie defensively.

"Did Mairi let you out?"

Rabbie's eyes widened and he paused considering his answer.

"Dinna answer if ye're going to lie to me," said Campbell, turning back to his approaching houseguests.

"Who's coming?" asked Rabbie.

"See for yerself. 'Tis the banner o' the Douglas."

"Which one is he?"

"Fourth one back. He has the fanciest cape and the tallest horse. Oh, nay, it canna be." Campbell shielded his eyes against the sun, straining to get a better look and hoping that he did not see what he thought he saw. He cursed softly under his breath.

"What did ye say?" asked Rabbie.

Not softly enough. "I said behind him rides the Lady Eileen, daughter to the Douglas."

"Is that the one ye're supposed to marry?"

"Aye," said Campbell, but it came out as more of a grunt.

Campbell leaned against the battlements and scowled into the sun at the approaching line of unwanted visitors. What was he going to do? Douglas clearly felt it was time for him to wed and was pressing the issue. But choosing a bride meant choosing a side in a struggle for power that may soon turn bloody.

"They sure have brought a lot of stuff," said Rabbie.

He was right, wagons of supplies followed the Douglas. "Some nobles travel with their own furniture, beds and such, so they will be comfortable where'er they go." And Lady Eileen no doubt expected to be the Lady Campbell soon.

Campbell groaned and rubbed the back of his neck.

Was it too late to use that hunting excuse? Trouble was he was on an island and they would notice if he took the ferry over. Perhaps Isabelle could figure a way off the island. She was always creative in a devious sort of way.

Campbell shook his head at himself. Sheer cowardice. Besides, he doubted he would even fit in a pickle barrel.

"Go find Mairi and help wi' the preparations. Tell her I'll await the Douglas in my solar."

Rabbie went pale. "I have to find Mairi?"

Campbell smiled at his brother. "So that's the way it is. Ne'er ye mind, go to bed wi' ye and I'll find Mairi."

Campbell dispatched his errands in a timely manner, finding Mairi had things well in hand. He walked to his solar, meeting Jacques, the minstrel, on the stair. Jacques was dressed in his colorful attire, a satisfied grin on his face. It irked Campbell beyond reason.

"Jacques, I wish to speak to ye about yer musical selection," said Campbell.

"You are displeased, my lord?"

"Aye." Campbell had the satisfaction of seeing the grin fade from the minstrel's face. "Ye play well, I grant ye, but all yer songs are about glorious battles with England or tragic tales of English brutality."

"You have a love of England?"

"Nay, I hate the bastards, but Lady Tynsdale is English and yer songs are inciting the hatred o' England. I should be verra displeased if she is discomforted."

"I apologize, my lord. I do not wish to make her uncomfortable." The minstrel bowed his head, and

Campbell nodded his dismissal of the troubadour. If this was the minstrel's regular selection of songs it was little wonder Harry had reacted violently to Isabelle in the tavern at Glasgow.

Campbell entered his solar to wait for Douglas. He eyed a bottle of whiskey on the table but refrained. If he was to emerge from this audience alive he needed to be stone-cold sober. Which, considering the shrew that was about to invade his solar, was truly a pity.

Thirty-Four

DAVID CAMPBELL WAS NOT A MAN WHO GAVE MUCH thought to fashion. He followed the Highland form of dress, as his father before him, which did not require fancy silks or ornate stitching. If he did consider garments, it was only in respect to outfitting his sisters, who had more refined tastes in their apparel than he. Considering he was their banker, he had learned, through great expense, to identify the cheap cloth from the dear. So when Lady Eileen Douglas swept into the room, Campbell nearly choked calculating the cost of her raiment. It was silk, embroidered, and plenty of it.

Campbell forced a tight smile on his lips, but he could not stop his brain from ticking up the expense as he noted the gold thread and the elaborate jewels. "Lady Eileen, 'tis a pleasure to see ye again so soon." Campbell bowed over her hand. Merciful heavens, did she have rings on every finger? Look at the size of that stone!

"Laird Campbell," she replied, her smile just as false as his.

Laird Douglas entered the room and gave Campbell a firm hug and a quick slap on the back that was more akin to a wrestling move or an opening attack. This was how the man showed affection and Campbell responded in kind. "Campbell, my lad. Ye are well met." His affection at least was sincere.

"Aye and ye. To what do I owe this surprise visit?"

"Do I need a reason to visit my old foster? I've trained ye from a lad, so I thought to take a look at how ye have been improving this castle o' yers. Quite something, no? I ken Eileen will be quite comfortable here."

Danger, think fast. "I hope ye both will have a comfortable visit. I only wish ye had given me more time to prepare rooms for ye both and prepare a meal fit for the company."

"And give ye a chance to run off hunting or some such? I think not," muttered Eileen.

Now how did she know that? Campbell forced the smile back on his face.

"No need, no need. We will be comfortable where'er we are. Any small, out-of-the-way room will do," said Douglas jovially.

Campbell chuckled in return. That was sheer nonsense and Douglas could only have meant it as a joke. "Whiskey? Ye must be parched after yer long ride."

"Now that is something I can use. Pour a tall one, lad, I've traveled far."

"Forgive me, Father, I beg to be excused. We have traveled long, and I need to wash off the dirt of the road," said Eileen in clipped tones.

"Go on wi' ye then," returned Douglas.

Campbell walked Eileen to the door of the ladies' solar and instructed a gillie to see to her needs.

"Did ye meet wi' difficulty on the road?" Campbell asked Douglas when he returned.

"Nay, my daughter is unaccustomed to the discomfort of the road. The journey was long for her."

Campbell nodded and sat down in a chair across from Douglas. He pictured Eileen complaining throughout a long journey. He remembered traveling with Isabelle and her happy chatter. Even when she was angry and the chatter stopped, she never complained.

Douglas took another long draft and drained his glass. He held it up and Campbell refilled it. Campbell knew better than to hope that Douglas would lose his senses to drink. He was a man with a lamentably iron constitution.

"Ah, there now, that's better. Ye were always a good lad, David."

"Thank ye, sir." Campbell had fostered with Douglas for four years, and even now, he felt twelve years old when he spoke to Douglas. He respected and admired the man, which was only a slight slip from the sheer adoration of his youth. He should be proud to marry Douglas's daughter, but there were concerns here that went beyond his own personal feelings on the matter.

"Have ye collected yer share o' the ransom for that useless King David?" asked Douglas.

So it starts. "Aye, though I admit it was a scrape."

Douglas grunted in agreement. "I tell ye the truth, between that ransom demand and outfitting my daughters I'll be beggared afore the harvest."

Campbell smiled, secure in the knowledge that Douglas was nowhere near poverty.

"Truly though, the English seek to bring us to heel wi' this impossible ransom demand. What they could'na do on the field o' battle, they will achieve through bleeding every last mark out o' Scotland. And for what? A young king who's spent more time outside our borders than within them? We waited while he grew up in France. He comes of age, and has no' taken his throne for more than a year when he marches us into the hands o' York, and gets himself captured."

Douglas leaned forward in his chair, his eyes glittering with intensity. "There must be another way. We must negotiate wi' England for better terms, or we Scots will starve to death. We fought too hard to let it all go to perdition now." Douglas's voice rose. Gone was the jovial man who entered the solar. This was the warrior with the heart of stone who would kill anyone who challenged him with deadly efficiency.

"What kind of deal would ye propose?" asked Campbell, the hairs on the back of his neck pricking up.

Douglas glanced around to make sure they were alone and lowered his voice even more. "I have been in contact wi' King David. He wearies o' his imprisonment and is willing to barter anything for his freedom. In fact, the little worm is willing to sign away his future heir's rights to the throne, if England would release him. Think on that. We would be free o' this ransom, which will surely be our demise."

"And who sits on the throne o' Scotland?" Campbell asked, wary.

"Our King David would reign until his death, then the son o' the king of England would be elevated."

"Never!"

"Wheesht! I understand yer feelings. I, too, would rather die than see an English monarch on our throne, but I intend no' to let that happen. In this deal, my land will be increased and I will be able to raise the kind of army I need."

"Army for what?"

Douglas sat back in his chair and watched Campbell closely, noting every movement, every expression. "I would rather die than see an English monarch on our throne," repeated Douglas.

Campbell exhaled quickly as if someone had smacked him in the gut. "Ye mean to take the throne."

Douglas smiled and raised his glass. "Ye always were a smart lad."

&

Isabelle and Cait sat in the back of the solar having a secret conversation while trying to appear like they were not having a secret conversation. The solar was packed that afternoon with Campbell ladies. Sisters, wives, and cousins were in abundance, with Mairi at its center. Isabelle and Cait sat on a bench in the corner, their heads bent over a piece of embroidery that neither cared a whit about.

Isabelle had learned much of Cait's audience with Andrew. Cait's emotional state vacillated like a clock pendulum, one minute in raptures over her newfound love, the next minute in the throes of despair considering the danger he faced.

"What are we to do?" asked Cait in a mournful whisper. "David is meeting with the elders today. What if they sentence him to death?"

"Let's hope it does not come to that," said Isabelle.

"At least I know he still loves me. He loves me, Isabelle, truly he does." Cait stared dreamily off into the distance.

"Forgive me, Cait, but could it be possible that he declared his love to you to get your support in being freed?" Isabelle hated to bring up the obvious, but the stakes were high now. Cait needed to look at the truth.

"Nay! I know his feelings for me are true. He wants to marry me, and I him!"

"Hush now, not so loud," whispered Isabelle, randomly stabbing the piece of embroidery. "But, Cait, even if his affections are honest and true, the best we can hope for is that Campbell will release him. You must know that your brother would never consent to your marriage, especially when you are betrothed to another."

"'Tis so unfair." Cait bent down over the embroidery and wiped away a surreptitious tear. "Please, Isabelle. Please help me. I need to escape with Andrew."

"Cait, there is no way…"

"Please, Isabelle. Ye escaped from here before."

"And I am right back here as you can see."

"Did ye no' once tell me we should be free to choose our own marriage partners?"

"Did I?" It was ironic her previous conversation with Cait now seemed like it had occurred during a simpler time.

"Isabelle." Something in the way Cait said her

name caught her attention. Cait took her hand and
gently squeezed it. "I canna bear to be another man's
wife. No' when I love Andrew. To be taken to
another man's bed, to be forced to…" Cait swallowed
hard in an attempt to control her emotions. "I canna
do it. Ye dinna understand. I canna do it."

But Isabelle did understand. Memories she had
meticulously shoved away came flooding back. Her
wedding night. Lord Tynsdale came to her that night,
his round, watery eyes gleaming. Isabelle closed her
eyes and could almost smell his fetid breath hot on
her neck, his icy hands crawling over her body, the
shock of intimacy that had made her cry out. He had
laughed and told her to get used to it. She had thought
she had survived the worst of it, but later that night
he returned like a fiend from hell. Isabelle rubbed
her forehead, her fingers tracing along the scar she
would forever carry to remind her of her husband's
murderous rage.

"Please help me," whispered Cait.

Isabelle doubted Andrew McNab was an eligible
marriage prospect. She could do little to change the
situation, but she nodded. "Yes, I'll try to help."
Isabelle could not let Cait suffer as she had on her
wedding night.

Cait hugged her tight, the smile returning to her
face. "Thank you, Isabelle!"

The door of the solar flew open, and in swept the
Lady Eileen Douglas. She cast a critical eye across the
inhabitants of the ladies' solar. Isabelle nearly gasped.
Lady Eileen's gown was fine silk, and the gold embroidery of her deep red surcoat was exquisite. Eileen's

headpiece was ornate, her dark brown hair swept up
into a veil, which showed off her fashionably high
forehead. Her figure was attractive and she held herself
like royalty. Two ladies-in-waiting followed her into
the room. Isabelle was impressed.

"Lady Eileen," said Mairi, rising and walking
toward her. "Let me welcome ye to our home. Ye
are verra welcome here and we hope yer stay will be
comfortable and to yer liking." Campbell's sisters all
stood and gave their curtsies. Isabelle did too, though
she was not sure she was required. Still, it was the least
she could do to acknowledge such fine craft as what
Lady Eileen wore. Perhaps if Isabelle was kind, Eileen
might let her know how she could commission such
fine work for herself.

Lady Eileen nodded her head in return. "'Tis as I
thought, no' much here is there?" Eileen strode over
to the fireplace where the rather pregnant Fiona was
standing beside the chair she just vacated. Lady Eileen
sat down in it. "Yer brother must no' give much
thought to yer comfort. I'll change that when I am
mistress here."

Isabelle blinked. How could anyone wearing such
beautiful embroidery be so ill tempered?

"We are quite comfortable, I assure ye," said Mairi
in an even voice. She was too experienced to rise to
easy bait. "If ye require anything for yer comfort after
such a long journey I will request it at once."

"Nay, I shall request what I need when I need it.
The servants must understand who will be their new
mistress. Who has been serving as chatelaine in the
absence of a proper lady of the castle?"

"That would be me, Lady Eileen," said Mairi in the same smooth voice.

"And what is yer name?"

"I am Mairi, Laird Campbell's eldest sister."

"Ah yes, there are so many sisters it is difficult to keep track. Why are ye all here anyway? Should ye no' be married? Campbell has neglected ye. I shall have ye all married and gone. Fewer names to remember that way." Eileen laughed as though she had said a joke. Her ladies-in-waiting joined the merriment.

Eileen's maids carried bundles in their arms and got to work in the area in front of the fireplace that Eileen had chosen. The women worked quickly, throwing colorful throws over Eileen's chair and rolling out a bright tapestry at her feet. A table was taken from another part of the room, and an ornate cloth was draped over it and placed next to Eileen. A golden pitcher and goblet were placed on the table and Eileen took a few sips of the wine her maids poured. None was offered to the Campbell sisters.

Isabelle squeezed her eyes shut to prevent them from rolling back into her head. It was a throne room with Lady Eileen sitting as their queen.

"Several of my sisters are married and their husbands serve with Campbell. I assure ye, he has no' neglected us," said Mairi.

"And ye, Mairi? Are ye married?"

"Nay, my husband died," said Mairi softly, a subtle warning ringing in her voice. But Eileen was not one to notice subtle cues.

"Well, ye must have another husband. But ye must no' leave before ye give me yer full report o' the castle.

Mind ye, I will be checking to make sure the accounts are in order. And I winna tolerate any o' ye helping yerselves to the castle goods when ye leave. I'll be making sure everything stays where it should, so dinna even bother trying to sneak anything out."

Isabelle gasped and her jaw dropped.

"And who are ye to stare at me in such rude a fashion?" Eileen turned her critical eye on Isabelle.

Isabelle shut her mouth and cringed inwardly. She had not meant to call attention to herself. "I am Lady Tynsdale." Isabelle gave the lady no curtsy. She deserved none for speaking with disrespect to Campbell's sisters.

Eileen looked at Isabelle as if she was something she had scraped off her shoe. "Aye, the English hostage. Should she no' be locked in a tower or a pit somewhere? I assure ye, there will be many changes when I am the Lady Campbell." Eileen turned to speak to one of her maids, though she did not bother to lower her voice. "I suppose I canna blame them. They can hardly ken better being raised in the Highlands." The maids twittered in response.

"Mairi!" Eileen called out her name as if she would beckon a servant. "After I wed Campbell, I think it best for ye to live elsewhere. I dinna wish for the servants to feel mixed in their loyalties. Ye can understand that, I'm sure. If we canna find ye some man to marry, I'm sure Campbell has someplace else ye can live." Eileen gave her a broad, false smile. "I'm sure ye can understand the necessity for a fresh start."

Mairi remained silent, her face giving nothing away. Eileen went back to speaking with her own maids, utterly ignoring the other women in the room.

The rest of the room was silent, watching them. Mairi's face was passive, but in her eyes was a glint that Isabelle had seen on Campbell before.

Lady Eileen was in grave danger.

❧

Isabelle had been pondering the question of how to help free Andrew. Of course, she had not had the best luck in trying to escape Campbell herself. She also had some doubts whether Andrew McNab made a particularly wise marriage alliance. But she had promised to help Cait. Besides, Cait was in raptures over him, so he could not be all bad.

"Do not fear, Cait, I've got a plan," said Isabelle. They walked behind the group of women heading to the great hall for supper.

Cait walked slower, her eyes filled with the trusting anticipation of a puppy.

"I was taught a few things about herbs," said Isabelle. "There is one that, when swallowed, gives the victim the appearance of death. Andrew could take this drug and then the guards will think he is expired and take him out for burial. You could also take this medicine and then when he wakes in the crypt, you will be there too."

Cait stared at her in disbelief. "That's the worst plan I've ever heard of in my life! Where'er did ye get such a terrible idea?"

"Well," said Isabelle, feeling rather unappreciated. "It was only a thought."

A gillie brushed past them with a hasty bow on his way to give Mairi a message.

Mairi bore the report that Lady Eileen was indisposed, and too ill to come to the table, with equanimity. It was whispered by some of Campbell's younger sisters that Eileen was not able to be parted from her chamber pot at present.

"I shall see what I can do to help," said Mairi, and went back down the corridor toward Isabelle.

"Go to the table, Cait, I'll see if I can help Mairi," said Isabelle and followed Mairi to a small room of drying herbs.

"Can I help you minister to the Lady Eileen?" asked Isabelle, skirting around what she really wanted to say.

"Nay, thank ye, Lady Tynsdale."

"I am surprised you did not kill her."

Mairi looked up sharply and studied Isabelle with grave eyes. "She is the daughter o' the Douglas. I feared in death she would prove more irksome than in life."

"Hardly seems possible," said Isabelle.

"She is also betrothed to my brother."

"You are all charity."

Mairi gave a wicked smile. "I doubt Lady Eileen would agree wi' ye." Mairi swept out of the room, the picture of serenity.

Thirty-Five

"NAY," SAID CAMPBELL WITHOUT LOOKING UP. HE swept the sharpening stone over his blade with an easy, fluid movement, the early morning sun glinting off the blade.

"I promise you I will not run away." Isabelle flashed her prettiest smile. It was getting her nowhere, especially since Campbell refused to look at her. The Campbell sisters were planning an excursion to the small village across the loch from Innis Chonnel that morning, to visit with a group of traveling merchants. Though Isabelle had not yet figured a way to free Andrew, she wished to be among the party. Even Cait was planning to go, the arrival of merchants this far in the Highlands being reason for some excitement.

"Again," said Campbell.

"Pardon?"

"You promise not to run away again."

"Well, yes, except that I never promised not to run away before, so this would be the first time."

"How many times have you run on me? Four? Five?"

"That you know of," muttered Isabelle.

"What's that?" Campbell finally glanced up at her.

Isabelle gave him a winning smile. One she hoped conveyed how trustworthy and delightful she could be.

"Nay," Campbell repeated.

So much for the smile. "But we are only going to the village, in sight of the castle. I'll be with your sisters the whole time. And I promise not to run away."

"Nay."

"I just want to see the beautiful sights of the far bank." This was not true.

He raised an eyebrow.

"Cait says there are traveling silk merchants, and I want to convince your sisters to beggar you by buying more than they ought."

Campbell smiled. "The truth at last."

"So I can go?"

"Nay."

"You are a cruel man, David Campbell."

"Aye." He did not appear at all displeased with the prospect.

"David, David!" Rabbie raced up to him.

Campbell's body tensed and he stood, ready for battle. "What be the matter? Are ye well?"

"Fine, I'm fine. The sisters are forever asking me that. Dinna ye be all worrit too."

Campbell relaxed. "What do ye want? Ye're disturbing me." But Isabelle could see the lad had his brother's full attention.

"We're going to the village and I'm going to show Isa—Lady Tynsdale the specimens I found."

"She is no' going anywhere," said Campbell.

"Specimens?" asked Isabelle.

"Why can she no' come wi' us? 'Tis only to the village."

"She canna be trusted outside the gates wi'out a guard," said Campbell.

"I will guard her," said Rabbie proudly. He stood tall and jutted out his chin.

"I dinna ken…"

"Ye said I was better. Ye said I was a man now," said Rabbie accusingly.

Campbell glared at Rabbie, then Isabelle, with weary eyes. He made a sick, growling sound and Isabelle knew she had won. "Verra well. But keep a close eye on her. She's a slippery eel and no mistake."

"I can do it. Just wait until ye see the huge insects I've found." Rabbie flashed Isabelle a smile and ran across the courtyard to the keep. Isabelle waited to shudder until he was out of sight.

"Ye've made yerself a friend for life if ye take an interest in those vermin o' his."

"Perhaps you are right. I should stay here."

Campbell smiled. "Thank ye for yer kindness to Rabbie. He is fond o' ye. Dinna make me regret this."

Isabelle saw both the sincerity and the warning in his eyes. He took her hand and kissed it. Before she could think of something clever to say in response, he turned and disappeared around the side of the building.

Isabelle slowly followed his path and peered around the building. It opened onto the lists, where men trained to be warriors. Isabelle put a hand to the rough stones and kept herself mostly hidden behind the corner of the wall as she watched Campbell. He walked forward toward his men with an easy confidence and was greeted with good-natured enthusiasm.

Many of his brothers were there and they insulted him for his lateness. Isabelle was shocked for a moment, but Campbell insulted them in return and drew his sword. Three attacked him at once, which was rather unfair, but soon she could see that this was his younger brothers' only chance. Campbell not only held his own but took the time to be instructional as they fought.

"Parry quick, Hamish. Nay, too slow!" Campbell struck down and knocked the sword from Hamish's hands, he swore and lunged to retrieve it. Other Campbell men took up the fight, but Campbell only laughed. Isabelle smiled, watching him. He was enjoying himself, laughing and goading his men while they whacked at each other with giant, deadly swords. This was not a safe game, but he played it well.

"He is a verra braw man, my brother," said a female voice behind Isabelle.

Isabelle nearly jumped out of her shoes. She turned to see Mairi regarding her carefully, her arms folded across her chest. Isabelle blushed down to her toes. She tried to think of some legitimate reason to be hovering around corners watching the men at the lists, but her mind went treacherously blank. Stupid brain. It always abandoned her when she needed it most.

"I was..." Isabelle hoped something clever would pop into her mouth if she just got started. Nothing came to mind.

"Ye were gawking at my brother like a starving man staring at a side o' beef."

Well, there was that. Denials were pointless, so

Isabelle just closed her mouth and waited for Mairi to get to the point.

"Do ye have no respect for yer husband?"

"No," answered Isabelle quickly. That, at least, was an easy question.

"No love for him."

"None." Another easy one.

"And what then do ye feel for my brother?"

Isabelle drew a sharp breath. This was not such an easy question.

"I will no' mince words wi' ye." Mairi gave her a withering stare. "I see the way he looks at ye and ye at him. But take care to recall that his betrothed is here within these walls."

Isabelle raised an eyebrow. "You support Lady Eileen?" Surely Mairi would not defend the woman who insulted everyone she met, and whom Mairi poisoned last night in revenge. Though Eileen had indeed recovered and was as irritable as ever this morn.

"I expect David to marry her, and shortly. He has called for a priest to do the last rites and to perform a wedding. If ye were unwed it may be different, but ye are married to our enemy. David must marry the Douglas harpy and ye must return to your husband, though it pleases few, it must be." Mairi gave her a clear look of warning. "I will prevent anyone from interfering with this marriage. Do we have a clear understanding on this?"

Isabelle nodded. She did not wish to be the object of Mairi's displeasure.

"Who is dying?" Isabelle called after Mairi, recalling that she mentioned something about last rites.

"The prisoner has been tried and found guilty. He will hang." Mairi strode off toward the keep.

Isabelle sighed and shook her head. Cait would not take this well. She expected Isabelle to save Andrew... but how? Isabelle walked slowly back to the keep to meet with the other sisters for their excursion to see the traveling merchants.

She must devise a plan, and soon.

❧

Isabelle accompanied the Campbell sisters to the village, but the joy of the escapade had been drained. Mairi's words washed over her like a bucket of ice-cold loch water. The priest would be here soon no doubt, and that would mean the end of young Andrew McNab, and David's marriage to the most venomous snake womanhood had ever boasted as its member. This was not going well at all.

Cait linked arms with her and even smiled with enjoyment. Isabelle had not the heart to tell her Andrew had been sentenced to death. She noted that Mairi also did not volunteer the information.

"I wish to find some cloth to make a wedding dress," whispered Cait, her golden hair flowing in the soft breeze. "I hope David will release him soon. Then we need only to convince him to allow me to wed Andrew."

There was so little hope for that sentiment, Isabelle did not know how to begin. "This looks a pleasant village," she said instead.

The village was indeed pleasant, and the traders had set out wagons of wares. Whoever had given the report that they had silk had been correct. Isabelle brushed her hands over a soft silk the color of a light blue sky. It would look very nice trimmed in silver, particularly with Cait's coloring. She was thinking again of Cait's wedding to the doomed man. Isabelle sighed. Unhappy topic. How was she ever going to save Andrew?

Isabelle brushed her hands over a scarlet bundle of damask. She had a bundle not unlike this at home. She doubted she would ever see it again. Another sigh escaped her lips.

"I can see m'lady is no' pleased wi' the wares. But I have more, here in the wagon. Come, let me show ye our finer weaves."

Isabelle absently let herself be taken to the back of the wagon. She was well within sight of the Campbell sisters.

"My lady," whispered the man when they could no longer be heard. Isabelle started at the familiarity of his voice. She stared at his face, recognition hitting her with a physical force.

The captain of her guard grabbed her hand to keep her from falling.

"Nay, I can see ye are still no' pleased. But wait; I have something here ye will like," said her guard in a loud voice and drew her farther to the back of the wagon.

"My lady, are you well?" asked Captain Corbett in a cautious whisper.

"Yes, yes, but this is incredible!"

"What's incredible, Isabelle?" asked Cait behind her.

"Why… why these prices. Are they not remarkable?" said Isabelle.

Cait frowned. "I woud'na say so." Cait gave her a look that said she thought Isabelle was a poor negotiator and wandered off to shop some more.

"Why are you here?" Isabelle's brain was whirling in a dizzy attempt to comprehend the meaning of the man before her.

"I have sworn to protect you. We obtained the ransom demand Laird Campbell sent to Tynsdale and came to rescue you."

"Captain Corbett, you are truly remarkable, but how did you travel through Scotland?" Isabelle was incredulous.

"I am merely a humble merchant."

"You posed as a merchant to pass through Scot territory? Oh, that was my damask I saw there! But how are you able to blend in? You sounded very much the Scot."

"My mother was a Scot, but this is not important. We must free you. It is Campbell who is holding you for ransom?"

"Yes, he sent word to Lord Tynsdale demanding ransom for my release, though he has changed his mind about that now."

"He will receive no ransom, for Lord Tynsdale is—"

"Isabelle, come look at this," called Cait.

"We must get you out of here, m'lady," Corbett said in a low voice.

"I cannot leave now," Isabelle whispered back.

"My men can cause a distraction and we can run."

"No, I gave my word. I cannot go now." Isabelle thought fast, looking at the cart of wares. "Is there some reason you could come to the castle? You could sneak a person out in your cart when you leave."

Her guard thought a moment. "I have ten men with me. I'm not sure why they would ask us to go into the castle."

Isabelle remembered the troubadour who seemed to go anywhere he wished. "Is there any act you could do? Can you sing?"

"Nay," said her guard, looking affronted, but then he thought for a moment. "Some of my men like to tumble, a few quite good at it."

"Could you make it into some kind of acrobatic performance?"

"I suppose I—"

"Mairi!" called Isabelle. "This man says his brothers are acrobats. Do let's invite them in to perform tonight." Isabelle clasped her hands in excitement and smiled. It was no act, she was excited.

Mairi frowned as if weighing her options.

"And they juggle," added Isabelle, sweetening the deal.

"Ooooh, Mairi, let's invite them in. I love jugglers," said Fiona.

Mairi shrugged and gave her consent to the plan.

"I don't know how to juggle," whispered her captain.

Isabelle smiled at him. "You have till supper to learn."

Isabelle went to find Rabbie with a bounce in her step. He promised to show her his favorite insects by the bank of the loch and the hills above, and she would not miss it for anything. Isabelle smiled. She would save Andrew and her people. She had a plan.

Thirty-Six

EVERYTHING WAS GOING ACCORDING TO PLAN. Isabelle's guard, along with their wagon of wares, was brought over the ferry to the castle island. She was thrilled to have them so close, but noted that they were grim and stone-faced. She acknowledged that walking into the castle gates of their enemy must not be their first choice of things to do with their evening. They did it because she asked it of them. A humbling thought, but she shook it off. It would all work out in the end. It must.

Isabelle found a quiet place to tell Cait of Andrew's death sentence and Isabelle's plan for rescuing him. As Isabelle expected, Cait's tears flowed freely at the news, until Isabelle could redirect her thoughts on her escape plans. Cait was overjoyed, yet she found something missing in the scheme.

"I must be wed," said Cait, the authority in her voice ringing like a female version of David Campbell.

"Wed?"

"To Andrew. We must be married before he leaves. We must."

"Cait." Isabelle shook her head. "How do you plan to do that?"

"I dinna ken, but it is the only hope I have of avoiding marriage with Gavin Patrick. If I am already wed, David canna force me."

"I find it very likely that he would refuse to acknowledge——"

"Please, Isabelle. I need this. I need a reason, some rationale for refusing the man David chose for me. Without it, I have nothing."

Isabelle opened her mouth to say it was impossible, then stopped, a flash of insight striking her. "I will try, Cait. That is all I can say." Isabelle hustled away. She needed to find the minstrel.

Isabelle looked through the castle, but could not find him laughing in the great room with the men or strumming a romantic tune in the solar. She wandered through the courtyard and around the grounds and finally found him wrapped in a long cloak.

"Where do you go, sir?" she asked.

The minstrel smiled. "You have new entertainment, 'tis time for me to move on."

Isabelle glanced around to make sure she was not overheard. They were standing inside the inner gate of the castle, but no one was near or taking particular notice.

"I need your help tonight," she said in a low voice.

The minstrel gave her a suspicious half smile. "I think it is most definitely time for me to go."

"I need you to perform a wedding," Isabelle whispered.

The minstrel raised his eyebrows and said nothing.

"I know you can do it. I heard you give the last rites to Rabbie. Are you a priest or do you just know the words?"

The minstrel's face turned ashen. He continued to stare at her in silence.

"'Tis for Lady Cait and Andrew McNab."

"The man who is condemned to die?"

"Yes. Can you not do this little thing? It would mean so much to Cait and Andrew."

"'Tis not a little thing you ask of me. Even if I spoke the words, this marriage would not be sanctioned by the Church. It would not be recognized."

"I understand, but it would mean a lot to them, and you said yourself that the man is condemned to die. Could you think of it as a last request?"

"If I do this," the minstrel's eyes blazed into hers, "I would ask for your discretion and that you not reveal what you have heard or seen of me."

"Who have I to tell? You can rely on my discretion, I promise you."

The minstrel looked less than pleased, but folded his arms across himself and asked, "What would you have me do?"

❦

Campbell sat at the high table, the Douglas on one side of him, Lady Eileen on the other. He feared looking at either of them so he watched Isabelle take her place at the table. She was looking bonnie tonight, stunning actually. Not that he noticed. Eileen at his elbow exhaled sharply. She had noted his gaze. He could feel her anger seep from her pores. What a lovely couple they would make. He should say something to her, but frankly, the woman scared him.

He could not bring himself to marry her. Not just because she was a viper of the first order, but by aligning himself with Douglas he would be expected to support his scheme to turn over the monarchy to England, then try to steal it back by putting Douglas on the throne. As much as he loved the man sitting at his left, this sort of treason could not sit well with him, and would plunge the country deep into civil war.

And yet his alternative was to align with Stewart the steward, who asked him to stand against his monarch and leave king David with his English captors indefinitely, while Stewart became the default King of Scotland. It was not a happy choice.

Isabelle's smile caught his attention. She was talking to one of his brothers, lucky bastard. What was going to happen to her? He noted Douglas failed to mention exactly how large a settlement he would gain from England when he agreed to the unholy alliance. Tynsdale's estate. Isabelle's home. Campbell could arrange for her to avoid going back to her husband for now, but unless her king decided to champion her, she would be sent back to her husband. Were her lands to be given to Douglas too? What would happen to her if Tynsdale lost everything and her plea for a divorce was denied?

A page tapped his shoulder, and Campbell turned to receive his message.

"Another party approaches, Laird. 'Tis Lord Stewart the steward."

Oh. My. Hell.

Campbell gripped the table to keep from a telling emotional outburst. When would this nightmare end? "Are ye sure?" he finally managed.

"Aye, sir. 'Tis the Steward o' Scotland and no mistake."

"Here? Now?" asked Douglas. He eyed Campbell suspiciously. "Ye dinna tell me ye expected Stewart."

"'Tis no' expected. Though he is always welcome," Campbell hastened to add.

"How cozy we shall all be," said Douglas, his voice cold.

"Aye, well, Innis Chonnel is always happy to welcome visitors." Campbell tried for forced cheerfulness and fell well short of the mark. "If ye will excuse me, I will invite them in for supper." He left the great hall, the eyes of Douglas burning into his back. What on Earth would bring Stewart here? Douglas, that had to be it. He would not be surprised if Stewart had his own spies on that powerful laird. He must have learned of his journey to Innis Chonnel and decided to come himself.

Campbell's fears were confirmed when he met Stewart in the outer gate. He had arrived with his own long line of conveniences and his granddaughter in tow. The Steward of Scotland would not sit back and let Campbell be wed to a Douglas without a fight.

"Greetings, my lord." Campbell bowed to Stewart.

"Greetings, lad, I daresay ye dinna expect me, did ye?"

"Not at all, but ye are always welcome. Please join us in the hall for supper, ye must be famished from your journey."

"Any other visitors here, lad?" Clearly, Stewart did not feel the need to play coy.

"Aye, Douglas awaits yer pleasure in the hall."

"And he's brought that daughter wi' him, no doubt. That's no wife for ye, lad. She'll see ye to an early grave and no mistake."

Campbell gave him a tight smile. The man was right of course, but Campbell's goal was to avoid all mention of matrimony with either of his houseguests. This was going to end poorly. There was no way to pick a bride without picking a side of war and mortally offending one of his allies. This was going to end very poorly indeed.

Moments later, Stewart was seated on the chair of honor at the high table and Campbell found himself wedged between the fuming Lady Eileen and Miss Beatrice, a wisp of a girl barely out of the nursery. Stewart proclaimed her to be twelve years old, but Campbell sincerely doubted the truth of that statement. She looked around the room with big, watery eyes, her bottom lip trembling. He turned to speak to her but she started to shake so he merely smiled and tried not to notice her fear. He wished he could hand her back to her mother for clearly she was not fully grown.

Lady Eileen stabbed at her meat with her knife and glared at him. He smiled in return, a false, please don't kill me, sort of smile. He glanced over at Isabelle who was watching him with some interest. He had to fit in a pickle barrel. He just had to. Anything would be preferable to this.

Stewart stood and raised his goblet to get everyone's attention. Campbell forced his face into something he hoped was neutral interest. Whatever Stewart was going to say, Campbell was certain he did not want to hear it.

"Please raise your cups to drink to the sovereignty of Scotland," announced Stewart. People stood, cups in hand. "To Scotland, may we defend her freedom from the English oppressors with our hearts, our minds, and our very lives."

"To Scotland!" the people responded cheerfully and drank.

Campbell glanced at Douglas, hoping that somehow he might have missed that indirect jab at him. No such luck. Douglas glowered in his whiskey.

"Aye, let us drink to Scotland." Douglas rose and addressed the crowd. Campbell silently willed him to be civil, hoping to avoid a brawl in his hall. "To all her faithful servants. Let us cast away those who do not love her truly, and raise those who will serve her unto death." Campbell cringed at the veiled reference to Scotland's long-absent King David, but Campbell's clan cheered and drank again, unaware of the battle between the two great men that was taking place at the head table.

It was Stewart's turn to glare at his wine. He pushed back his chair as if he was going to stand up to make another toast. Campbell was desperate. How could he get the men to cease hostilities? He glanced across to Isabelle, sending her a silent plea for help. She took an apple from her plate and tossed it from hand to hand.

Stewart began to stand but Campbell shot up and exclaimed, "Entertainment! We have a great treat for our esteemed guests. Please bring in our jugglers at once. Hurry men, dinna keep us waiting." Corbett and his men were hustled out and began to perform their acrobatic routine around the central hearth of the great hall. Campbell collapsed back in his chair. He looked again for Isabelle. What a blessing she was there.

Except, when he looked for her, she was gone.

Thirty-Seven

CAIT AND ISABELLE SLIPPED OUT OF THE HALL WHILE everyone was watching the performance, then dashed down the side stairs toward the dungeon. Outside the door, Isabelle dumped the crushed herbs she had picked while appreciating insect life with Rabbie into the goblet of wine.

"Are ye sure this will work?" asked Cait. Her eyes were wide and she chewed on her lower lip.

"Certainly," replied Isabelle, hoping she sounded more confident than she was. "I nursed my uncle for many years, and this never failed to put him to sleep." She stirred the mixture with her finger, wishing she had been able to grind the herb a bit smaller. Little green flecks were now spinning around in the glass.

"Here," said Isabelle, handing the goblet to Cait. "Get the guard to drink this without looking at it too close."

"What if Andrew does'na wish to marry me?"

"I doubt that will happen."

"But what if it does?"

"Then we can send him to perdition with the knowledge that we attempted to save his ungrateful neck."

"Nay! We canna do that. Even if he does'na wish to wed, we still must save him."

"Fine, fine. Hurry now, we have not much time."

Isabelle gave Cait a bracing smile and set off to find the minstrel.

❧

Andrew sat in the gray gloom of the dungeon waiting for a miracle he knew would not come. He was a McNab after all. He had taken responsibility for the abduction of Cait in order to prevent Campbell from destroying what was left of his clan. Yet he had hoped Cait would convince Campbell to spare his life, or his brother would arrive to save Andrew from the need to die bravely.

When the priest came in the morning for confession, his hopes disappeared into the dark corner of his room. It was hard to sit alone with the knowledge of his fate. His only comfort was that he probably would not have to wait much longer.

Andrew sat back on his bench and closed his eyes. His thoughts turned to Cait once again. He had decided that if he was to die for it, those few days with her were enough. Though, if he had known he would be condemned to die, he would have taken her to his bed. It was a shame to die a virgin, but nothing could be done about it now.

He pictured Cait on the grassy hill, her blond hair blowing around her. He remembered their sweet kiss. He could almost feel her soft lips on his. He

pictured going down on one knee, asking her to be
his wife, and in his dream she did not refuse him.
This time she said yes and hugged him tight. He
wrapped his arms around her and gently laid her
down on the soft grass of the hill. She kissed his neck
and pulled him closer. And this time there was no
burly brother to ruin the moment.

Andrew sunk back on the stone bench. His senses
must be starting to go for he could hear the swish of
her skirts, smell the lavender soap she used. It was
wonderful and torturous. He opened his eyes feeling
more alone than ever.

Before him stood Lady Cait. He wondered
at what point his mind had abandoned him for
madness. He stood, but the vision remained. She was
an angel of perfection, her silver gown shimmering
in the light of the single candle she held. She looked
so real he stepped forward until he reached the end
of his chain.

"Cait," he rasped, his voice rough from lack of use.

"Andrew?" The apparition spoke. He was hearing
voices now too. Oh well, at least his madness gave him
a vision of her.

"Andrew, are ye well?" She ran to him and
wrapped her arms around him.

"Och, but ye're real, my dearest, sweetest Cait."
Andrew crushed Cait with his embrace.

"Canna... breathe..."

Andrew released her. "Sorry, but how is it... oh, ye
are here. I love ye, I love ye."

"Andrew, I feared ye would be angry wi' me for
no' telling ye the truth."

"I could ne'er be angry wi' ye. Only, can ye stay a while? I would so much like to have ye here for a while, if ye could."

"Aye, we have a plan. A plan for ye to escape." Cait took the key she'd swiped from the guard's belt and unlocked Andrew's chains.

Andrew stared at her. Could this be true? He wondered for a moment if the honorable thing to do would be to refuse and accept his sentence. He quickly rejected the notion as sheer foolishness. "Sweet Cait, I knew ye would help me. But I dinna want to put ye in danger."

"Dinna worry yerself over me. I am not the one they want to hang."

"True."

"I winna let them kill you. I winna let ye die for something ye dinna do."

"Yer brother is a fair man, Cait. He is no' executing me for abducting ye."

"Then why has he sentenced ye to die?"

"Stealing the horses."

"The horses?!" Isabelle put her hands on her hips. "Why should he care for that?"

"'Tis a hanging offence," Andrew said apologetically. "And truth be told, I wasna going to return them."

A faint glow of a candle grew brighter. Someone was coming.

"Hide," hissed Andrew, and pushed Cait under his stone bench.

"Cait?" said a female voice.

"'Tis safe, 'tis my friend, Isabelle," said Cait in relief.

Isabelle emerged with a single candle and a man

cloaked in a cape and hood. "This is the man I spoke of," said Isabelle. "He can marry you if it be your wish."

"I can perform the service, but it will no' be recognized by Campbell," said the cloaked man.

Isabelle looked at the minstrel. He didn't look like himself. He didn't sound like himself. Interesting. She set out to find the minstrel when he had approached her cloaked, his face obscured, saying he was ready to perform the service.

"We understand, we wish to be wed," said Andrew. He looked nervously at Cait. "At least I do, if it be yer wish."

"Aye," said Cait with a bright smile. "I wish nothing more than to be yer wife."

Isabelle raised an eyebrow. She wished nothing more? Isabelle shivered in the dank surroundings. The ambiance was somewhat lacking, but Cait was beaming at Andrew as if standing in a field of flowers.

"I understand ye confessed to the abduction of Lady Cait," said the minstrel in an odd Scottish accent. Cait and Andrew would never know who he was.

"Nay, it wasna him, it was his older brother Archie," said Cait.

"Wheesht, Cait," hushed Andrew. "I dinna wish to bring trouble to my clan, sir."

"So ye accept blame for a crime ye dinna commit. Admirable. Please take the hand o' yer betrothed," The minstrel priest performed the Latin service well. At least he did as well as Isabelle's understanding of Latin allowed her to judge. He switched to English for the vows, which the couple repeated with breathless anticipation.

Isabelle fluctuated between happiness in seeing her plan come together and irritation at the dewy-eyed couple before her who were oblivious to the barriers before them. If Andrew could escape from the castle, he would have to stay one step ahead of Campbell. And how could Cait ever hope that Campbell would allow her to be with Andrew? The happy couple did not seem to appreciate the kind of danger that surrounded them. Or perhaps they were just savoring what might be their last moments together.

The minstrel spoke a blessing and prayed for the couple. He prayed for eternal salvation and peace in the arms of Mother Mary which, considering Andrew's death sentence, seemed appropriate. "Ye both understand this marriage will no' save ye in Campbell's eyes."

"Aye, I understand," said Andrew. "It was verra kind o' ye to provide a service. May I ken the name o' our benefactor?"

The robed minstrel stood silent for a moment, then made the sign of the cross. "Be at peace. Go wi' God."

The robed man walked slowly up the stairs, as if he carried many more years than he did. Truly, Isabelle began to wonder herself if this was truly the minstrel or if he had sent some other Scottish priest to do the job. Shaking her head at the puzzle, she turned back to Andrew and Cait who were ignoring her in their embrace.

"Wait until dark, then make your escape," said Isabelle, getting back to the essentials. "I have told the silk peddler to expect you to hide in his wagon. You will leave when he does at first light."

"Are you sure he can be trusted?" asked Andrew.

"Yes, I would bet my life on it. And since you have few alternatives I would say this is your best chance at regaining your freedom."

"But what of the guard when we emerge?" asked Cait. "Surely there will be a new guard to take the place o' the sleeping one. Can ye get him to drink the sleeping draft too?"

Isabelle's shoulders slumped. She had not thought of that. "No, I used all I had on this potion."

"I can overpower the guard," said Andrew. "Especially if ye put the key back on his belt, no one will know I've been unchained."

Isabelle took the offered key, unease creeping down her spine. "You will not do serious harm, will you? I do not want the blood of Campbell's guards on my hands."

"Nay, I swear to ye on my life I shall overpower him and leave him tied up, but alive."

"O' course Andrew winna hurt anyone," gasped a shocked Cait. "And I'll be here to help."

"No," said Isabelle. "You must go back to the ladies' solar. You can meet Andrew to say good-bye in the wagon, but you will be missed if you are gone any longer."

"Nay," said Cait, folding her arms across her chest. "I'm no' going to say good-bye to Andrew, I'm going wi' him. I'm his wife now and I shall stand by him." Cait's chin started to tremble. "I winna leave now. This is my only chance to be wi' him."

"Cait," Isabelle ground out. This was getting out of hand. Her plan was to free Andrew and perform a mock wedding to make Cait happy. It was not her plan to enable Cait to escape. Campbell's response would be... oh she didn't even want to think about it.

"Listen to me," said Isabelle. "Andrew will have a better chance of getting away if you are not with him. If Campbell thinks he has kidnapped you again he will never stop searching until he finds you."

"As long as he finds us after our firstborn enters the world, there will be very little he can do but accept us. Please, Isabelle, this is my only chance. I know I am the sister of the laird, but shoud'na I have a chance at happiness? If I stay, David will force me to wed Gavin Patrick, and I will be miserable all my days." Tears streamed down Cait's face.

Isabelle sighed. "What am I supposed to say when you are missed?"

"Ye'll think of something. Ye're smart that way."

Isabelle trudged back up the stairs to place the key to the shackles back on the belt of the sleeping guard. She had certainly gotten herself into a muddle now. Good thing she planned to be on that wagon herself. She did not want to be around when Campbell found out they all were gone. And yet, she understood wanting to be with the man she loved.

Even for just one night.

Thirty-Eight

ISABELLE SLIPPED BACK UP TO THE SLEEPING QUARTERS and bundled some pillows under the blanket on Cait's bed. She hoped Mairi would not check on her. Then she went into the ladies' solar. It was empty, since the entertainment was just ending. She would have but a moment to do this. She took a quill and found a parchment. She would not leave again without an explanation.

Isabelle hoped that if Campbell knew she was safe with her own guard, he would let her go without pursuing her. The need for secrecy might not even be warranted. He might allow her to leave with her guard, without complaint. He had, after all, said he would give her to the bishop instead. Yet he was still a wanted man in England, and her soldiers were Englishmen. Captain Corbett had trusted her by coming into Campbell's gates. She could not betray him, not knowing what Campbell or his illustrious houseguests might do. No, she needed to sneak away quietly.

She stared at the blank page, wondering what to

write. How could she express her feelings toward Campbell? Her conscience bothered her. She had promised Campbell not to escape. She argued with herself that if she left a note, it wasn't truly running away. It was a poor excuse, but it was all she had.

Footsteps and happy female chatter could be heard from down the hall. Isabelle scratched a few lines of inadequate explanation and rolled the parchment, stuffing it in the pocket of her skirts.

"Lady Tynsdale," said Mairi, entering the solar. "Where is Cait?"

"She is over-tired from lack of sleep. I had her lie down to rest."

"Poor Cait. Ye missed a fine performance," said Fiona, her folded arms resting on her large belly.

"Aye, 'twas amazing," said young Gwyneth.

"'Twas a paltry attempt at best," said Lady Eileen, and all the heat left the room.

The Campbell ladies gave Eileen a wide berth and talked softly amongst themselves.

"Did ye see Gavin Patrick arrive wi' his uncle, Laird MacLaren, and his stepfather, Chaumont?" asked Fiona.

"Is Gavin the one Cait is going to wed?" asked Effie.

"Aye, he is a handsome one," said Elyne. "But why are they here now?"

"They come to witness the execution," said Fiona, her voice low. Isabelle strained to hear the conversation.

"Poor Cait, she winna be pleased," said Effie.

Isabelle rolled her eyes at the understatement. Yes, Cait would be quite displeased indeed, and possibly homicidal. Isabelle was glad Andrew would escape that night. She doubted he had many mornings left him.

Isabelle tarried in the solar only as long as she deemed necessary, then made a great show of yawning and telling the company she needed to get some rest. In her sleeping quarters, Isabelle stuffed some pillows under the blanket on her pallet and slipped in the note for Campbell. She hoped he would understand.

Isabelle crept to the courtyard toward the wagons. Darkness had fallen fast, the thick clouds shutting out the moon. If she was wise, she would crawl into the wagons and wait for her men to leave at first light. No more pickle barrels or tar-filled boats. This time she would escape on a bed of silk. A faint light shone in the window of the chapel.

Campbell.

❧

Campbell knelt before the altar in the chapel and prayed for guidance. Had he not always sought to follow the will of God? How could God abandon him now? What was he to do? He had carefully managed to keep Douglas and Stewart apart after supper and ushered them to bed rather early. It was all he could do. Cait's betrothed, Gavin Patrick, along with MacLaren and Chaumont, had come to witness the execution.

Campbell put his head in his hands. He did not like this responsibility. He actually found Andrew McNab to be a likable lad, and Campbell guessed he took more on his shoulders than was his due to protect his clan. Campbell admired that, yet the lad had been caught with Cait. He had to die. No member of his family could travel safely again if he did not make an example of him.

Campbell shook his head. Being laird meant he had to do some unpleasant things. But he was laird, and he would see them done.

"Why do you pray so long, my lord?"

Campbell knew her voice without looking. Isabelle had come for him. She sat in the pew next to him, her silken black hair covered by a simple, gauzy veil and flowing loose down her back. Her brown eyes shimmered in the candlelight, bringing warmth to the cold night.

His Isabelle was here. Everything was right once more. "Ye left before the entertainment," said Campbell.

"I was helping Cait," answered Isabelle. It was true, if vague.

"Thank ye for yer kindness to her."

Isabelle frowned and pursed her lips together, trying to block the stab of guilt. "I have only wanted to help her. I hope you know that."

"Aye, and I thank ye for yer help tonight. I dinna ken what to do wi' Douglas and Stewart. That is why I pray. I pray long because I have not received an answer to my question."

"And what is your question? Maybe I can help."

"I doubt it." David Campbell put his head in his hands and his elbows on his knees. "I pray for guidance in marriage."

"After speaking with both Douglas and Stewart have you been swayed to one side or the other?"

"Nay. They both have plans for power. Plans they

wish me to support. They will be at war soon I fear, and I will be forced to take a stand."

"Well then, in absence of a clear choice, you are free to choose whichever bride you find more palatable."

Campbell snorted. "That rules out Lady Eileen."

Isabelle laughed. Campbell joked so rarely it always surprised her when he did. "I tell you, there is no love for her in the ladies' solar. What is Miss Stewart like? Surely she is a better match for you."

"Ye saw her at the banquet."

"Did I?"

"Aye, she arrived wi' Stewart. She was seated to my left."

"The child?" Isabelle was incredulous.

"Stewart says she is twelve years."

"No! She is no more twelve years than I am. Why, you would become an old man before she reached her maturity."

"Thank ye verra much."

"'Tis true and you know it. How old are you? You could be her father I feel sure."

"I am thirty-three and until this moment I had thought I had a few years before my dotage. I so appreciate yer correction of my false pride."

Isabelle smiled. "I did not mean to suggest you would be singing with the angels soon."

"Thank ye for that at least."

"I mean a man of your stature could have two or three years left in him at least."

David Campbell's eyes gleamed in the candlelight and the corners of his mouth twitched up. "Two or three years. How generous."

Isabelle smiled and patted his hand consolingly. "At the very least."

David Campbell laughed out loud. Isabelle reveled in the sound, loud and throaty and very much alive. David slid a little closer and put his arm around her shoulders. Isabelle liked the feel of his arm, solid and warm. Isabelle closed her eyes for a moment and listened to the faint sound of crickets floating through the night into the chapel. The chapel was dark, lit by a single, flickering candle, throwing faint dancing shadows onto the walls.

"I was married at sixteen," Isabelle began, a lump forming in her throat. She had never spoken of it before. She had wished to forget, to pretend it never happened. Somehow, though, she wanted to tell Campbell. She needed him to understand. "Tynsdale was in his fifties at that time. I was to be his fourth wife."

Campbell said nothing but gently rubbed her shoulder.

"After the plague took my parents and siblings, I was left the heir of Alnsworth. I understand Tynsdale well compensated my uncle for the marriage contract with me." Isabelle spoke a little fast not wishing to dwell on the sad facts. "I was married at Tynsdale Castle. I met him for the first time in front of the priest. I was terrified. After the feast, they took me to his chamber." Isabelle's voice trailed off. She stood and took a step toward the altar. She could not look at Campbell when she told him.

"I was put in his bed. Tynsdale came for me. It was... unpleasant. Afterward, he laughed and told me to cry if I needed to, but to accustom myself to it. He left, and I did cry. I thought my life could not get any worse, but I was wrong. A few hours later, Tynsdale stormed back into the room. He dragged me from the bed and screamed that I was a whore. He struck me across the face. I was so shocked I didn't even feel it. He hit me several times I think, I… I do not like to… 'tis difficult to remember."

Isabelle took a breath, her scar throbbed in pain. "He threw me across the room, then bashed my head into a table. There was so much blood…" Isabelle's voice abandoned her.

Warm arms engulfed her, and Isabelle melted into David's embrace. He gently touched her hand where she had been rubbing the scar along her hairline. Isabelle rested her head on his shoulder and listened to the crickets' faint lullaby until she felt surer of her voice.

"Simon ran into the room, he must have heard the commotion."

"Who is Simon?" asked Campbell.

"He is the son of Tynsdale's mistress, grown to manhood. Tynsdale has no other children, you understand. He wanted me to breed him a legitimate heir."

Campbell nodded and continued to hold her.

"Simon pulled me from the room and took me back to my maid. He told me that Tynsdale had killed his two previous wives. Indeed, I had heard that each of them only lived a few months into the marriage. Simon helped me escape with my maid that night and warned me never to return or Tynsdale would kill me too."

Campbell pulled her closer and stroked her hair, murmuring something in Gaelic. Isabelle closed her eyes, comforted by his strength and warmth. Her muscles relaxed and she breathed in his familiar scent.

"I have wondered what I did wrong," said Isabelle. I must have done something wrong to enrage my husband."

"I have seven sisters to me. As their brother and laird I have the right and the responsibility to discipline them. And trust me when I tell ye that they have enraged me beyond speech on more than one occasion. But, Isabelle—" Campbell gently tipped her face up to look him directly in the eye. "Only a rat-bastard coward would ever strike a woman."

Isabelle closed her eyes and laid her head back down on his chest. She smiled faintly, experiencing an emotion that was new to her. She felt safe.

"Trust me, Isabelle, I will not give ye back to him. After I deal with our current guests, I will take you to the Bishop of Glasgow. He can get you back to England safely. Since yer husband has fallen out of favor, your king may well support your annulment."

"And give me and Alnsworth to another man," Isabelle finished.

"Aye, 'tis likely," said Campbell softly. Neither spoke, the murmur of the crickets the only sound.

Campbell wrapped his arm around her waist and strode with her out of the chapel into the cool darkness of the night. It felt natural and right.

"I wish… I wish…" Isabelle took a breath. "If I did not have to protect my people from Tynsdale, I would be content to remain here with you."

Campbell held her tighter. "I wish I could keep ye, but I must choose a wife and soon. It would be…

distracting to have ye here and no' fair to whichever
bride I choose."

"I suppose you must choose one of them."

Campbell nodded, his jaw set.

"Do you yet know your mind?"

Campbell gave her a wry smile. "Aye, I ken what
I want."

"Which would you choose?"

David stopped by the castle wall and drew her into
the shadows. Wrapping his arms around her, he kissed
her slowly and without apology. "I want what I canna
have... Isabelle." His green eyes smoldered. There
could be no mistaking his meaning.

They entered the stone keep and walked up the
spiral staircase to the third floor where the sisters slept.
At the doorway he hesitated, then pulled her back into
the stairwell.

"Stay wi' me tonight." Campbell held both her
hands, his eyes reflecting the dancing torchlight.
Isabelle's heart skipped a beat. "I winna force ye but...
I must choose a bride from two unappealing options.
I will do my duty, yet I would wish for one night to
be wi' the lady I want, the lady I choose. I would ask
for one night wi' ye."

Isabelle caught her breath. She opened her mouth,
but no words came out.

"Just one night," he repeated. "Just one night I can
look back on after I wed."

Isabelle nodded. It was all she could manage. Her
body hummed to his tune. She would follow him
anywhere. They continued up the spiral staircase.

David stopped when he got to his door. "Ye dinna

have to do this." He leaned back against the doorpost. "Truly at this point ye could ask for anything and I'd give it to ye. Ye dinna need to sleep wi' me." Campbell looked up at the ceiling and folded his arms across his chest.

Isabelle reached up and twined her hands around his neck. "I would like nothing more than to spend my last hours at Innis Chonnel with you."

David exhaled as if he had been holding his breath. "Good. Because I was going to have a hard time letting you go." He slowly embraced her in his large arms, one hand moving up through her hair, the other cupping her backside. "Ye dinna ken how long I've wanted to do this."

Isabelle pressed herself closer, her heart dancing a happy little beat. He was warm and solid. She was safe. She sighed in contentment and her shoulders relaxed. Campbell opened the door and led them inside. Her heart beat even faster at the sight of his large bed, covered in furs. She was not sure she was ready for this, but the only other option was to leave, and she would not, could not leave his side tonight.

The window was open, providing a cool breeze, which was a welcome relief to Isabelle's burning skin. Campbell undressed. Slowly. She had seen him undress before, but this time his eyes never left hers, as if he was afraid if he moved too quickly or looked away, she might scamper off. Isabelle closed her eyes for a moment and forced herself to take a deep breath. Her body responded in an odd fashion, she was trembling and her heart pounded. She feared she would have an apoplectic fit and miss the promise of what was to come.

"Isabelle."

She opened her eyes to David standing before her. His plaid was gone. His shirt was gone. She looked at his bare chest and then up at his face. Would it be rude to look down?

David looked at her carefully, then sighed and turned around. He strode back toward the bed, giving Isabelle a clear view of his backside.

"Forget it. I'll take ye back to bed," he said.

"What?" Isabelle was confused. "Why? Have I done something wrong?"

"Ye look scared. Ye look like ye dinna want to be here. I dinna want that."

"No. I do want to be here. I do. 'Tis only…"

Campbell pulled on his shirt. "Only what."

"I have never seen a man… undress."

Campbell sat down on the bed with a thump. "Aye, I forgot. I always thought of ye as more experienced."

Isabelle slowly walked across the room to where David was sitting. It was her turn to feel that any sudden movement would cause him to bolt. He looked at her as if she were pointing a loaded crossbow at him. Not exactly the most romantic of expressions. "I do not understand you, David. At one time you wished me to be your mistress."

"That is before I knew ye were married. And aye, it makes a difference."

"I'm not leaving you," said Isabelle. He turned to face her and she looked into his eyes. "I will leave soon and never see you again. I'm not leaving you tonight."

Isabelle's voice wavered, but her determination was strong. This was her last chance. Assuming she was successful in her request for an annulment, she would either give Alnsworth to the Church and take up the veil, or her king would wed her off to some other knight who could benefit from her holdings. Either way, she would never again have a chance to be with this man who made her feel alive. She took his hand. This was her last chance to be with the man she loved.

Isabelle looked away and blinked back tears at the sudden recognition of what David meant to her and what she would be losing soon. They only had the remaining hours until dawn.

David reached his arm around her and pulled her closer onto his lap. She laid her head against his chest and he rested his chin on the top of her head, wrapping his other arm around her. They sat there for a moment, Isabelle enjoying his strong arms around her. But the image of David Campbell naked was emblazoned in her mind. Cuddling was nice, but she wanted more.

David sighed and disentangled himself from her, standing up and taking a step away. "I dinna ken what to do. I shoud'na take ye to my bed. Ye are married. 'Tis wrong, and yet…" David began to pace. Isabelle watched the edge of his shirt as it flapped along, hoping for a glimpse of something interesting. "I want to do the right thing. And I want that right thing to be ye."

Isabelle opened her mouth to say something and voiced the first thing that came to mind.

"What did you say to me when you left that night at St. Margaret's?"

Campbell stopped pacing and stared at her. "I thought I would never see ye again."

"I could not quite hear you and I would like to know."

Campbell shook his head. "My feelings for ye... Some words should not be spoken."

"This is our one chance. I understand we both must do our duty come the dawn, but for tonight..." Isabelle stood and reached out her arms. He closed the gap between them in a flash and wrapped her in his embrace. He began kissing her temple and down her cheek while he worked her gown open in the back. Isabelle wrapped her arms around his neck to keep her knees from buckling. She stood on the tips of her toes to return his kisses.

Isabelle heard a growling sound that was not like anything Campbell would say. She leaned back to see what was the matter and her gown fell to the floor. Campbell slid his hand up her spine to her neck and claimed her mouth with his. This time her knees did buckle and he held her tight to his body to keep her from hitting the floor along with the gown. When he finally gave her reprieve for a breath, her head was spinning. She made a decision to forgo the nun option.

Isabelle felt the heat rising from his body, even through her chemise and his linen shirt. Her skin was hot and she was flushed like she was feverish. Truly, she needed to get some air and cool down. She pressed herself closer. He made a strange, groaning sound again, which this time she interpreted as enjoyment, and tried to squeeze herself even closer.

He broke apart for a moment, stripped off his shirt and divested her of her chemise. He reached for her again, and she could feel everything: his soft chest hairs, the rippling of his abdominal muscles, the hard thing that was poking her accusingly in the stomach. Just as she was trying to figure it out, he stepped back and she got an educational eyeful.

David steered her to the bed and pulled back the furs. Isabelle climbed up into the large bed, and David slid in beside her. He rolled over on his side facing her and put his arm around her. Every place he touched, her skin burned.

"Isabelle, I've wanted ye so much," David murmured and claimed her mouth once more. Isabelle melted into his kiss. She wrapped her arms around him and made some strange guttural sound of her own. David deepened the kiss and she learned new ways a tongue could be used. She forgot all else but the sensations he was building in her.

David reached down to cup her breast and she gasped at the sensation.

"Sorry," he said, jerking his hand away like it had been bit.

"No, do not stop. I was startled. I did not know it would be like this."

Campbell rolled back. "I shoud'na be doing this."

"Yes, yes you should. You are doing very well. Please, do continue." Isabelle felt a trembling need for him to return. He made no move so she rolled over onto him and ran her hand up his side to his chest as he had done to her.

A bit of encouragement was all he needed, and he rolled her back over and settled on top of her. She held on to him with arms and legs, wanting, needing him closer. He rubbed against her, building tension until she could take it no longer. Yet the one thing she wanted he was not giving her. Was something wrong? Confirming her fears, David began to curse.

David rolled back with a groan. "Sorry, love. It seems I canna…" David sighed again, he sounded almost ill. "I canna do it. I want to, but I… I canna take another man's wife. It goes against everything I know to be right in this world."

Don't stop! Isabelle grabbed the sheets in frustration until the demanding throbbing slowly ebbed. She rolled toward him and put her head on his chest.

"Your morals do you credit," she said, not really feeling the sentiment.

"My morals are a pain in the arse," he muttered.

Take me now!

Isabelle pursed her lips together to keep from blurting it out. She would not beg this man for sex. She would not. She could not. But oh, David felt so nice and smelled so good. How could she resist him?

"I love you." Isabelle froze. Had she truly said that? By the saints, why had she just said that? Isabelle cringed. She was so focused on not revealing one thing that another secret slipped past. Campbell was very still, not even breathing. Surely that was not a good response to her declaration. He brought his other arm around her and gently held her close.

"I wish ye were mine to love in return, my lady." He reached up and slowly threaded his fingers through her hair, holding her head to his chest. "I wish ye were mine, my love."

Isabelle felt her eyes sting and shut them tight to keep from dropping tears on his perfect chest.

She was his love.

Thirty-Nine

ISABELLE WOKE BEFORE DAWN ALONE IN CAMPBELL'S bed. She reached over to where he had slept. The sheets were cold. A chill seeped into her bones. She would never see him again.

Never.

She sat up abruptly and rubbed her eyes. She had no time for tears. She needed to get on that wagon before the rest of the castle awoke. Isabelle searched the dark room for her clothes and dressed herself as best she could in the gloom. She wrapped her cloak around herself and hoped it would conceal her less than perfect results.

Isabelle slipped out the door into the dark hallway, softly pulling the door closed.

"Are ye leaving David's room?" hissed a voice.

Isabelle jumped a foot and spun to see who had caught her. It was Cait, holding a single candle and looking disheveled.

"Ah, Cait. I was… it was… nothing happened." Her words rushed out in a damning display of defensiveness.

Cait grabbed her arm. "Ne'er mind that. They

came for poor Andrew. They've taken him away! Where is David?"

"What? David is not here. Why is Andrew not on the wagon by now? Tell me what happened."

"We had to wait till dark anyway and since we were just married, well... we..." Though the light was dim, Isabelle was sure Cait was blushing. "We are married at least, which is more than I can say for ye and David," Cait added with defensiveness of her own.

"Nothing happened," Isabelle repeated with more emotion than was required. "Wait, are ye saying the two o' you... in the dungeon?" Cait opened her mouth for what would no doubt be a defensive tirade, but Isabelle held up her hand to stop her. "Nay, that does not matter now. Just tell me how they got Andrew."

"Well, we were, that is, afterward it was so tiring we fell asleep. We dinna wake again until we heard steps on the stairs, and Andrew shoved me under his bench. And they took him—"

"You fell asleep?" Isabelle was incredulous.

"We were so exhausted—"

"You *fell asleep*?" Isabelle's voice rose. "After all I did to arrange this escape for ye? All ye had to do was get in the damn wagon!" In all her adventures, Isabelle had finally managed to learn how to curse.

Tears pooled in Cait's eyes. "I'm verra sorry. But do ye ken where they would take him?"

Isabelle looked into Cait's worried eyes with a sense of dread. Andrew could only be taken for one reason. "I warrant they have taken him to commence with the hanging. David is probably doing it early to reduce the chance of you becoming upset. Where are sentences carried out?"

Cait gasped and put her hands over her mouth. Her eyes went wide. "The far shore, I suppose. I have ne'er been a party to it."

"I should think not."

"Isabelle, please help me. We must stop this." Cait grabbed her hands, the tears that had been threatening spilling down her face.

"Cait, I have tried to help you, but your situation is beyond what I can repair. I would help you if I could."

"Just get me to the shore. I know ye can. We can take Rabbie's boat."

Isabelle firmly shook her head. "If I steal Rabbie's boat again, your brother might decide to have a double hanging with me as the other victim."

"How can ye no' help me? What if it was someone ye loved? Ye dinna understand. Ye've ne'er truly loved someone. Ye dinna ken what it is to have yer heart break." Cait wept openly.

A freezing jolt hit Isabelle at her core. She wrapped her arms around herself. She was so cold she feared she would never get warm again. "I understand," said Isabelle softly.

"Nay, ye've ne'er been in love," Cait sobbed accusingly.

Isabelle closed her eyes and balled her fists at her side. "Just because I do not express my feelings as freely as you, it does not mean I do not love."

Cait blinked and stopped crying.

"I know what it is to love. What it is to lose

someone forever. To never be able to see him again." Isabelle squeezed her eyes shut. She would not cry. She would not.

"Ye love David," said Cait. It was a statement, not a question.

"Yes." Isabelle opened her eyes to find Cait looking at her with sympathy.

"I've seen how he looks at ye. He's ne'er looked at anyone like that. I think he shares yer feeling."

The tears Isabelle had been fighting chose that moment to win the battle. They ran unchecked down her face.

"Help me, Isabelle," Cait whispered.

Isabelle nodded. "I will take ye to Rabbie's boat." She hoped Campbell liked her well enough not to kill her.

David Campbell was having one of the worst days of his life. He had to remove himself from the bed of the woman he loved, after his damnable conscience prevented him from showing her the full extent of his affection. To make his day worse, he now stood on the shores of Loch Awe with the hangman and a group of sober witnesses to put to death the lad his sister claimed to love. She was not likely to soon forgive him.

It was a cool morning, a feisty breeze whipping off the lake and cutting into his skin. He pulled his plaid around himself to protect from the biting wind. The sky was gray, and the sun had not yet emerged from behind the hills. Before him, Andrew McNab stood tall and shivering. He had not been given a cloak. He would not need one for long. Though Campbell wondered if it was only the cold making the man shake. It was an unpleasant thing to face one's death.

MacLaren, Chaumont, and Gavin stood a ways apart. The older warriors were grim. Gavin had taken a greenish hue. It was a sad business.

"Do ye have anything ye wish to say?" Campbell asked Andrew.

"I apologize for no' returning your horses, and I apologize for being a party to the abduction o' your sister. But I am no' sorry to have met the Lady Cait. Wi' my last breath I declare that I love her wi' all of my worthless being. Please care for her. I fear she will take this hard."

Campbell was surprised by the declaration of love by this man. It had been his firm belief that Andrew had misled Cait in his affections to try to seduce her or win her dowry. Andrew's declaration of love on the verge of standing before Judgment spoke to his sincerity.

Campbell nodded to the hangman to continue. It didn't change anything, but it made it more regrettable. A rope was tossed over a high limb of the tree they stood under and a noose was put around Andrew's neck.

"I'm glad my mother is no' alive to see this," said Andrew, his voice wavering.

A lump formed in Campbell's throat. He did not want to think of this lad having a grieving mother. He did not want to think of him falling in love with Cait. He did not want to think of him at all. He just wanted to get it over with. Andrew had committed a crime.

None of his family would be safe if he let the lad live. This was the law of the Highlands. Everyone knew it. He had been found guilty by the council and sentence had been passed. It was Campbell's responsibility to see it done.

"God have mercy on ye, Andrew McNab. I bear ye no ill will and hope ye will find mercy in the Judgment."

"Thank ye," Andrew said in a voice barely above a whisper. "I forgive ye this. Take care o' Cait for me, will ye?"

"I always have," said Campbell gruffly, but added more gently, "I will care for her. I will tell her ye met death as a man, and yer last thoughts were o' her."

Andrew nodded and closed his eyes. Campbell hesitated, dreading very much what he had to do next.

Campbell gave the signal and the hangman pulled Andrew McNab off the ground.

"Nay!" A screeching voice rose up from the loch like an avenging banshee, so inhuman was the sound. The hangman dropped the rope to cross himself, sending Andrew back to the ground.

Campbell stared into the mist, his hand on his sword hilt. Out of the fog two figures emerged.

"Dinna hurt him, David," screamed Cait in a voice he had never heard from her before. "Dinna hurt him or I swear I shall make ye regret this day."

"Cait!" coughed Andrew.

"Isabelle!" growled Campbell at the other shadowy figure. It could only be her. Meddling, defiant, impossible lass.

"Let him go now!" shrieked Cait.

"Dinna let her see this," begged Andrew.

"Isabelle, come here where I can see ye. How did ye get here? Dinna tell me ye took poor Rabbie's boat again," shouted Campbell.

Isabelle shrugged. "How else could we cross?"

"Ye are no' paying heed to the important issue here," yelled Cait. "I want ye to let my husband go!"

Campbell continued to direct his attention to Isabelle. "I canna believe ye would steal his boat again, especially after all the pain ye caused the last time."

"But I'll put it back straightaway," explained Isabelle. "Yer sister can be most persuasive."

"Cait is no' at issue here, she…" Campbell stopped midsentence as if suddenly coming to a realization. He looked down at Cait. "Did ye say husband?"

"Aye!" declared Cait triumphantly, glad to have Campbell's attention at last. "We were wed last night. He is yer kin now. Ye canna kill him."

Isabelle wished Cait would stop talking. With every word Isabelle felt herself slipping in Campbell's estimation. He glared at her now.

"Did ye know o' this?" he asked Isabelle, his voice deceptively soft.

Isabelle could not bring herself to lie directly to him so she chose the next best thing and pretended she could not hear him. She stared at her feet as if something very interesting was occurring near her toes. She could feel the heat from Campbell's glare.

"Ye do no' have my approval to wed this man," said Campbell to Cait. "Ye will marry Gavin Patrick here." Campbell gestured to a young lad hardly older than Cait. Was this the monstrous Gavin from whom she helped Cait to escape?

"Approval or no', we have wed just the same," said Cait.

"Then ye shall soon be a widow," said Campbell. He signaled the hangman who tied the rope to a tree branch. Andrew was fine as long as he maintained good posture. Campbell motioned to a few of the guards. "Take Lady Tynsdale and Lady Cait back to the castle."

"Ye canna kill him. He may be the father o' my unborn child," declared Cait with vengeance.

"Cait, wheesht!" exclaimed Andrew, looking even more pale, if such a thing was possible.

"Cait," said Isabelle in an undertone. "I do not think you are improving Andrew's odds of seeing tomorrow."

Campbell grabbed Cait by the shoulders. "Did this bastard get ye wi' child? Answer me!"

"I... I dinna ken... yet. But I could be. We... after the wedding last night, ye understand."

Isabelle could tell by the murderous look of death in Campbell's eye that he did understand. He understood all too well. Campbell let Cait go and gripped the hilt of his sword with white knuckles. He took a step toward Andrew, and Isabelle wondered if they now needed to advocate for him to hang Andrew, as opposed to hacking him to death in some slow and torturous manner.

"Riders approaching!"

Whatever Campbell was going to do was halted with the arrival of several men on horseback. Four horsemen stayed on the hillside, their identities cloaked in the mist. A fifth rode forward to meet them. The sound of many hooves echoed off through the hills, but how many more horsemen remained unseen in the mist, Isabelle could not tell.

"State yer name and yer business," cried one of Campbell's soldiers.

"I am a messenger from Lord Tynsdale for Laird Campbell."

Isabelle's heart lurched and sank. Tynsdale had come to ransom her? No, no it could not be. She was so close to escaping him.

Campbell exhaled loudly. "I am the Campbell. I am attending to business as ye see. Please step back, I will see ye when I have completed my task."

Another rider rode forward until Isabelle could make out the form of Simon, Tynsdale's bastard son.

"You bring the Lady Tynsdale to watch a hanging, do you?" asked Simon. "Curious habits you barbarian Highlanders have. Come now, this business will take but a trifle of your time. We have your ransom, the Lady Tynsdale comes with us."

"And ye are?"

Simon dismounted along with the other riders that were visible and bowed with a flourish. "Sir Simon, sent by Tynsdale to return his beloved wife."

Isabelle's blood turned to ice, chilling her with every beat of her heart. "No," Isabelle's voice was no louder than a whisper. "No, I will not go back with him."

"Take the ladies back to the castle," Campbell commanded one of his solders. His face was gray and without emotion. He did not look at her.

Simon stepped forward. "I would rather you not do that. Here is your demand in full." He nodded to a man who brought a velvet pouch and opened it. It was full of gold coins. "You have been paid. Hand over the Lady Tynsdale. There is very little else to discuss."

"There is much to discuss. Ye will wait."

Simon motioned with his hand, and more dark gray figures emerged from the mist on the hillside above. Many appeared to be holding crossbows. Isabelle stepped nearer to Campbell.

"Cait," Isabelle said hoarsely, "get back to the boat. Go back to the castle."

"I will no' leave wi'out Andrew."

"What trouble is this?" said a low voice behind them. Isabelle spun around to see James Douglas stroll up the bank dressed for battle. "We heard the screaming."

"What goes here?" said Stewart, also stepping out of the shadows. They were followed by Campbell's brothers and several of their retinue.

It was becoming a full house, and the bank by the loch was getting crowded. Isabelle glanced back and forth between the English and the Scots. She had the unhappy realization she was standing at the center of what may be their next battle.

"Now 'tis truly a party," said Simon in a mocking tone. "Tynsdale has done what you have asked. The ransom has been paid. The return of his wife is all that is required of you. Come, Lady Tynsdale. Let us return to your husband."

"No," said Isabelle, stepping even closer to Campbell. She could not return to Tynsdale, but if she did not go... the English had the high ground. Campbell, his brothers, and Cait stood below them. If there was a fight, the Campbells would be caught in the crossfire. Isabelle turned to Simon, she must find a way out of this. "Simon, why do you wish me to return? Was it not you who warned me never to return to Tynsdale?"

Simon's eyes never left Campbell. "What a fancy imagination my lady has."

"'Twas not my imaginings and you know it, Simon," said Isabelle with the indignation of surprise. All these years she had thought of Simon as a sort of savior. What was he doing now?

"And if the lady does not wish to return to her husband?" asked Campbell.

"What does her ladyship's opinion have to do with her return? She is his wife. Her wishes can have no bearing on this matter."

Behind her, Isabelle heard the slosh of the ferry raft going back to the island. They were bringing out more troops. Campbell was stalling for time.

"As a knight, I canna return a lady to anyone who may do her harm."

"As a man you cannot stand in between what God has joined together. She is his wife. You have already shown yourself to be opportunistic in the advancement of your own coffers. Take your coin and be done with it. The lady belongs to her husband, and to him she shall now return or you be no knight." Simon stepped closer to Isabelle and she moved closer to Campbell.

"Be that as it may, ye shall no' take her against her will."

"'Tis her husband's will that matters. Or have you thought to put yourself in that role? Do you think to steal another man's wife? You shall be excommunicated from the fellowship of the Church, and

Tynsdale will raise an army like you have never seen to wreak havoc on the Scots in vengeance for the defilement of his wife." Simon lowered his voice and stepped closer to Campbell. "Come now, my friend. No wench is worth that. Let the harlot return to her husband and you can buy a hundred comely wenches to keep you company."

"Dinna disrespect the Lady Tynsdale," Campbell growled.

"No disrespect intended," said Simon, the words somehow emerging from his lips pressed together in a tight, fake smile.

"What seems to be the trouble here?" asked Douglas. "If she be ransomed, give the English lass back so we can be rid o' her."

"Aye. We can ill afford the ill will o' the king o' England. Give the lady back to her kin," said the Steward of Scotland in a voice that sounded more like a royal decree than a friendly suggestion.

"No!" shouted a voice from the fog. "The Lady Tynsdale will not go with Simon, for he is a thief and a liar."

Captain Corbett emerged out of the mist, walking up the shore to the hangman's tree. Isabelle shook her head, trying to prevent him from revealing himself, but he would not be thwarted.

"And what business is this o' yers, peddler?" Campbell's voice growled with irritation.

"I am Corbett, the Captain of the Guard for the Lady Tynsdale. The Earl of Tynsdale is dead. It is not her husband who ransoms her."

"Dead!" gasped Isabelle.

"I know you not, and I declare your words false," said Simon to Corbett. "Tynsdale is alive and concerned to retrieve back what is his. Give me the lady, Campbell. You have no right to keep her."

"Hold now," said MacLaren. He turned to Corbett asking, "how do ye ken Tynsdale is dead?"

"After we lost the Lady Tynsdale, we searched for her long, but she could not be found. I sent some of my men to spy on Tynsdale. From those with cause to hate Simon, we learned Tynsdale was dead, and that Campbell was holding Isabelle for ransom. Soon it was all the talk in the town of how King Edward waited less than a fortnight after Tynsdale's death before seizing his castle and lands since he had no issue."

"He does have a son!" shouted Simon. "I am Tynsdale's heir. It should all go to me."

"So ye admit that Tynsdale is dead," said Campbell in a low voice, steady and calm.

"My husband is dead?" Isabelle's gaze drifted between Simon and Captain Corbett. Could it be true? Could she really be free?

"Aye, m'lady, Tynsdale is dead. But when Simon was ousted from Tynsdale castle, his army took Alnsworth by force," continued Corbett.

Isabelle inhaled a sharp breath. "Simon attacked Alnsworth?"

"I'm sorry, m'lady. Most of my men were out looking for you and he caught us unawares."

"Marjorie! Is she safe?" Isabelle asked Corbett, her heart frozen between beats.

"Yes, she escaped the castle before he took possession," reassured Corbett.

Relief melted into molten anger, which rushed up Isabelle's spine, making her bolder than she ought. She turned a malevolent glare on Simon. "And all these years I thought you were my friend. But no, Simon, you have been trying to get all that you could for yourself." A sudden realization struck her. "It was you! It was you who turned my husband against me. What did you say to him? Did you accuse me of being a whore as you just did to Laird Campbell? You did not wish to save me, you wanted to get rid of me."

Isabelle stepped even closer to Simon as if to see him better, to look through his hauberk into the darkness of his soul. "I see it all so clearly now. You wished to inherit, but to do so you could not let your father have any other children, any *legitimate* children. So you chased me away. And it was you who killed his other two wives."

"Yes, of course it was me," jeered Simon. "It was hardly difficult and no great loss. Just as no one will mourn your sorry life." With the quickness of a man who lived his life by cunning and violence, Simon leapt forward and grabbed Isabelle, twisting her around and holding a knife to her throat.

"Now I am going to take this piece of baggage back to England and you are going to get back to your hanging." Simon backed away slowly, dragging Isabelle with him.

Campbell drew his sword with a sharp, metallic ring that sliced through the gray morning mist. "Let her go and I may let you live." It was his best offer to Simon.

On the hillside above them, more gray shapes became visible, holding bows at the ready. "I think not," said Simon, his voice tight with excitement. "Call back your men or you all will die."

Forty

ISABELLE WENT RIGID. HER HEART STOPPED BEATING. Unlike when McNab threatened her, the knife at her throat was cold and sure. It would take but a quick flick of his wrist to leave her dead.

Campbell growled and her heart sprang back to life. He held his sword at the ready. If Simon slit her throat, she had the grim satisfaction of knowing that Campbell would see Simon dead before she hit the ground. Simon knew it too, and it was the only thing keeping her alive.

Simon dragged Isabelle back away from Campbell and his brothers. Isabelle kept her eyes on Campbell. As long as she could see him, she knew she would be safe. Though how he was going to rescue her she did not know. She was not one to pray often, but she did so now, praying for a way out, for safety for Campbell, his clan, and for her.

A fierce battle cry sliced through the mist and was suddenly strangled into silence. Simon's arm jerked up and the knife flew away. Isabelle broke free and spun to face her attacker. She gasped at the sight. Andrew was hanging by his neck from the tree, his legs wrapped around Simon, pulling him away from her.

"Attack!" someone called and everything became a blur of motion. Simon threw off Andrew as arrows began to rain down from the hillside.

"Get down," shouted Campbell and pushed her to the ground. "Stay down," he said, giving her shoulder a squeeze and jumped up to run after Simon.

"Cut him down," screeched Cait, running to Andrew's side.

Isabelle started to get up to do so, but Captain Corbett pushed her back down. Gavin Patrick raced to Andrew, slicing through the hangman's rope, and Andrew collapsed on the ground.

Simon's men shot bolts down from the hillside, while others ran into the fray. Campbell's men rushed out with shields to protect them from a barrage of arrows. Douglas, Stewart, and their men created a shield barrier and charged up the hill at Simon's men. Isabelle's own guard had not shields, so they ducked behind some rocks and fought any who came near.

Arrows rained down on them with a crisp slice through the air as they passed. Close, very close. More gray figures joined the others on the hill. We're all dead, thought Isabelle. Simon's army had caught them on low ground with nowhere to go but the loch. Yet the bolts came at a slower pace, and Isabelle realized with a rush of joy that the new figures on the hill were Campbell's own men who had flanked Simon's archers.

In the thick, gray mist, figures disappeared and reemerged into her vision without warning. Around her were the sounds of battle. Steel and iron bashed together with a ring and crunch. Men yelled, cursed, and shouted a barrage of commands. The smell of blood was in the air.

"Get her. Kill the bitch!" yelled the voice of Simon. Isabelle knew it was her he was trying to kill. He appeared above her, slicing through her guards. He raised his sword for a death blow, but suddenly Campbell was there, his sword blocking Simon's steel with a tremendous clang.

Simon held a broadsword in his right hand, a mace in the other. Isabelle scrambled out of the way of the fighting men. With a brief sneer in her direction, Simon charged Campbell who ducked, the mace swinging perilously close to his head. Campbell swung his claymore in a great arc, coming down upon Simon, but the Englishman proved quick and dodged the blow, parrying with a jab at Campbell's shoulder. Campbell slouched and spun out of reach of Simon, reaching up to touch his shoulder.

He has no armor. Isabelle noticed it now. Campbell had not anticipated the fight so he wore no armor; Simon's men wore mail or plate.

Simon allowed Campbell no respite and attacked with a fury of sword and mace. Campbell fought him off, defending himself against the blows, backing up on the uneven hillside. Campbell took one more step backward, hitting a loose stone, which rolled out from underneath his foot. Isabelle stood in horror as Campbell went down.

"No!" shouted Isabelle.

Simon pointed at her. "Kill her!" He swung his

mace down at Campbell for the death blow but Campbell rolled and jabbed up with a knife he pulled from his boot. Simon was quick and deflected the attack with his sword, but the movement put him off balance and he stepped backward. Campbell was up and on the attack. Campbell swung his blade against Simon's mace, slicing the weapon in two, the iron-spiked ball flying through the air and hitting Simon's messenger in the side of the head.

Simon's men rushed at Isabelle, but she was defended by Corbett and her guards. She wondered how long her line could hold. Campbell attacked without expression, his face stone, his actions precise and meticulous.

"You defend the wrong woman," sneered Simon. "She is naught but a whore. A favorite at court for an easy roll between the sheets. My father found out only too late what she truly was."

"Ye do yerself no favors by insulting the Lady Tynsdale," growled Campbell.

"By all means, I have no complaints from my poke with her. She was a most eager bed partner."

Campbell attacked in anger, powerful but careless. Simon easily evaded and sliced back with his sword in a move Campbell was barely able to deflect. Campbell stumbled back a few steps before finding his footing.

"All I want is to return the lady to her country," Simon continued in his slick voice. "Our king will wish her back and take it poorly that she be taken. Do you risk war with England over this one wench? Is an easy lay worth the death of your family? Because make no mistake, King Edward will come after you, leaving your kin slaughtered."

"You vile creature," screamed Isabelle. "You speak nothing but lies. King Edward has not a care for me. And I have never even been to court, you lying dog."

MacLaren and Chaumont joined Isabelle's guard to fight against Simon's men. Their considerable skill turned the tide and Simon's men fell back. The din of battle lessened, and an eerie quiet hung in the air. Simon's men on the hillside had been flanked and defeated. The men he had with him were either dead or taken. He alone stood against Campbell.

Simon glanced around with narrow eyes and took a step back. "All I ask is for the Lady Tynsdale to be returned. King Edward will certainly take offense if the lady is not returned after the ransom has been paid."

"Campbell," said the Steward of Scotland. "This man is right. We cannot refuse to return the Lady Tynsdale without condemning Scotland to another invasion from the English."

Campbell and Simon continued to circle each other, the weapons at the ready.

"If I give her to this man, he will kill her, you ken that to be truth," said Campbell.

"'Tis not our concern," said the steward. "She belongs to the king of her country, to their damnable King Edward. If he canna protect her, 'tis not our job to do so."

"Listen and hear me well," growled Campbell. "I will no' give up the Lady Tynsdale to a fiend who only wishes her harm. *I will not give her up!*"

Isabelle clasped her hands together and held them

over her lips to refrain from cheering. To claim her before his friends and enemies alike, he must truly care for her.

"Even if it means open war wi' England?" asked Douglas. "Think, lad. Is one Sassenach lass worth the blood o' yer countrymen?"

"She is worth all to me. My actions are on me alone."

"The king will not see it in such a light, I fear," said the steward. "It is often the innocent who suffer for the misstep of another."

"And what would you have me do? Give her back to this bastard?"

"She must be returned, lad," said Douglas. One lass canna possibly be worth the destruction o' yer clan. Think on yer brothers and sisters. Where will this leave them?"

"I will take her back to England," said Captain Corbett. "I will keep her safe."

Isabelle closed her eyes for a moment and breathed the morning air. She could smell the dirt that had been kicked up in the fight and clung to her gown. She breathed in the scent of loch and the tang of blood of the wounded. Campbell risked his family, his kin, his very brothers and sisters to protect her. The power of this fact struck deep, but she could not let him or his family be harmed.

"I will go with my captain," Isabelle said in a voice that didn't quite sound her own. She met Campbell's eyes. She hoped he understood. "I will go back to my king." It was an acceptable solution, considering her options. She would probably be given in marriage to another English baron who would make war against the Scots. The thought filled her stomach with gall, but there was nothing else to do.

Simon's attack was swift and decisive. He lunged at Campbell who, though still holding his claymore, was distracted by the negotiations. Simon stabbed forward with his sword, but Campbell was not as inattentive as Simon thought. Campbell spun to the side, deflecting the thrust with his sword and rolling around to the side of his enemy. With a cry he jumped up and plunged a knife into the gap of armor at Simon's neck.

Simon gasped and fell to the ground. Isabelle stared in silence at his crumbled body until she was sure Simon was dead.

It was over. Isabelle gasped and her legs swayed beneath her. Since girlhood she had feared her husband, living in dread of being put back into his power. Now her husband, Lord Tynsdale, was dead. And the true monster, the one who planned her murder, was dead too. She was free.

"Riders approaching!"

More riders? She glanced around at the people before her. Who could possibly be missing from this assembly?

"'Tis the minstrel returning."

Out of the mist the minstrel returned on horseback. His same wool cloak was pinned at the shoulder, but underneath chain mail glinted beneath his bright blue surcoat. A sword was belted around his waist. What on Earth was this about?

"Isabelle?" growled Campbell.

Isabelle shrugged. For once, a strange occurrence was not of her doing. Why Campbell was always blaming her was beyond her.

"Welcome, minstrel. What brings ye back to us dressed for battle?" asked Campbell, his sword still drawn.

The minstrel opened his mouth to speak but paused a moment looking around him. It must have seemed an odd sight to him too. "I come to bring you news and to make you an offer in the name of my lord, but I seem to have arrived late for the party. What goes here?"

"I will ask the questions, minstrel," growled Campbell. "Who are ye and whom do ye serve?"

"I am Sir Dragonet. I serve the Duke of Argitaine, the Golden Knight."

Silence descended on the group as everyone took a moment to comprehend his statement.

"Another spy in yer midst, Campbell?" asked Stewart. "Ye should have a better watch on whom ye invite to entertain yer guests."

Campbell raised one eyebrow at Stewart, and turned back to the minstrel turned Sir Dragonet. "Ye have deceived me once, and I have little time to be fooled by yer words again. Get to your own business and let me to mine." Campbell wiped his blade clean and sheathed his sword.

"Forgive the ruse, my friend," said a shadowy man. His horse clopped slowly out of the mist. Isabelle stared at the figure, her mouth open wide. The man on horseback was dressed in golden armor. His helm and gauntlets were golden. The plates on his legs and arms were golden. Over this he wore a red and blue surcoat trimmed lavishly in gold thread. The cost of his harness alone would be enough to cover her ransom fiftyfold.

"I am the Duke of Argitaine," said the Golden Knight in a smooth, easy voice. "I sent my trusted knight, Sir Dragonet, to seek the will of the Scots to determine if they would continue to respect the Auld Alliance with France. I am pleased to know that Scotland still maintains her freedom against English aggression and domination."

"I am the Steward of Scotland," said Stewart, stepping forward. "May I ask what has driven ye to travel so far from yer home to visit us today?"

"Only the most desperate of circumstances, and the desire to help my brother Scots in their struggle against the English oppressors. Behold, I bring a token of France's support of Scotland against the English devils."

The Golden Knight motioned, and four soldiers rolled forward a cart carrying a large, wooden trunk. They took a moment to open a large lock and opened the lid. Isabelle was not the only one to gasp. It was full of gold.

"And what would ye have us do to earn such a boon?" asked Douglas, ever suspicious, his arms folded across his chest.

"Join me in arms against the English. Together we will stand victorious where divided we will fall alone."

"Join ye in arms?" asked the steward. "Ye mean for us to go to war wi' England?"

"Yes. We fight the English in France. If Scotland invades from the north, we shall surround our mutual enemy and drink to her defeat."

"Or we could be slaughtered like the last time we invaded England. I saw what was done at Neville's

Cross. I know how many o' our men died that day," put in MacLaren.

"MacLaren!" The French duke raised his hand in greeting. "You are well met."

"And ye have bought yerself a new set of armor since the last time we met," replied MacLaren with a glint in his eye.

A slow smile crept over the duke's face, and he inclined his head. "I do ask you to join with us against our common English enemy, but this time we not only request your help but pledge our support to raise your armies. And we will send French troops to march alongside you."

"'Tis a fair offer, to be sure," said Douglas, his eyes on the chest of gold.

"I would hear more," agreed Stewart.

The Duke of Argitaine dismounted, and the lairds met with him, discussing details of the proposed French plan.

Isabelle's heart sank. Her holdings were on the border so her King Edward would no doubt use her castle to reinforce the line against Scotland. She would be married off to some warrior who could promise security. Would Alnsworth be home to battle? Would she see Campbell again from the other side of her castle wall?

A low moan caught her attention. It was Cait, weeping over the body of Andrew McNab.

"Cait!" cried Isabelle, rushing to her side. "Is he... is it too late?"

Andrew McNab made a raspy noise that gave Isabelle hope. "Look, he lives still. Oh, stop that crying and see what you can do to help."

"Does he live?" asked Gavin, taking a keen interest.

"Dinna hurt him!" cried Cait, trying to cover Andrew with her body.

"By the saints, I'm no' going to hurt him," replied Gavin, irritated. "Give him some room to breathe now."

Cait sat back up, and Gavin gave Andrew some drops from his flask. Andrew's eyes opened wide and then blinked at the faces around him.

"Am I dead?" rasped Andrew.

"No' yet," said Gavin, helping the lad to sit up and giving him a healthy swig from the flask. "Are ye well, lad?"

"My throat pains me, but all things considered, I am glad to feel it." Andrew took the flask from Gavin's hand and drank until his color returned. He offered it back to Gavin who shook his head.

"Keep it," said Gavin, a smile brightening his face. "Consider it a wedding present."

"So ye will no' press yer right to wed me?" Cait asked, eyes wide, her blond hair falling down around her.

"I would ne'er press anyone into marriage," responded Gavin gallantly.

Isabelle noted that Gavin was a broad-shouldered, attractive lad. Had she known Cait's betrothed to be such a handsome young man, she doubted she would have assisted her escape. Isabelle wondered why she had doubted Campbell's plan for his sister. Surely he would care to make a match for Cait better than the one that had been made for her.

"He lives?" asked Campbell, not sounding particularly enthusiastic.

Andrew struggled to his feet and stood before

Campbell, his arm around Cait, more for support than affection.

"Since he saved my life," Isabelle caught Campbell's eye. "I would ask that you grant me this one boon and let the lad live."

"I also advocate for the life and freedom of this lad," said an elderly voice, new to the conversation. Isabelle turned to see a man in white robes with an equally white beard walk up to Campbell.

"Bishop!" stated Campbell, clearly surprised. "What do ye do here?"

"I come to ask for Andrew McNab's life. He is important for the Church."

"How could Andrew be important for the Church?" asked Campbell. Even Andrew's eyebrows rose in surprise.

"Andrew McNab," said the bishop. "Are ye prepared to make a new life for yourself? To walk the path of righteousness and not follow the path yer brother was on?"

"Aye, yer grace."

"And will ye convince yer brother by any means necessary to serve me."

"Aye, yer grace."

"There's a good lad. Now introduce me to your lovely bride." The bishop was all smiles.

Campbell sighed and rubbed the back of his neck. "Andrew McNab, for acts of heroism in saving the life of Lady Tynsdale from the hands of a madman, I pardon ye from the sentence of death by hanging. Now take yer arm off my sister and get the hell off my land."

"Thank ye, Brother," said Cait with a brilliant smile that immediately turned mulish. "But I will leave wi' my husband."

"Ye will marry Gavin Patrick as ye are betrothed to do," growled Campbell.

"I canna marry him when I am wed to another," cried Cait.

"Forgive me, sir," broke in Gavin. "I am conscious of the honor ye do me to accept a betrothal between yer sister and myself, but I feel I must break the engagement, for the reasons of..." Gavin stumbled over his words and gestured in Andrew's general vicinity. "I mean no disrespect, but I would like to find a bride o' my own choosing."

Campbell sighed again, but nodded saying, "I understand and hold naught against ye."

Campbell glared at Andrew, then Cait, then Isabelle. "How is it ye were wed?" Campbell's voice was deceptively soft.

Andrew swallowed and put a hand to his throat. "Last night an old man came to my cell and performed the wedding rites."

"Ye were there, Cait?"

She nodded.

"And how did a priest come to be in your cell, or Cait for that matter?"

Andrew grew pale once more and paused, the silence loud and painful. "That I canna say."

"Isabelle!" Campbell barked. "This was yer doing, dinna deny it."

"I have no desire to deny it," said Isabelle, holding herself up a little taller.

"And what concern is it to ye that ye be meddling in it?"

"She came to me for help and why should I not assist her? People talk of love and sing of love, but so few people actually experience it for themselves. True love is found so rarely. I wanted someone to have it." Isabelle's words came out in a jumble, and she felt perilously close to spilling tears.

"The Church accepts the marriage of Andrew McNab to Lady Caitrina Campbell." The bishop spoke with religious authority. It was done. They were wed.

Isabelle glanced at Campbell expecting to see his anger, but he was staring at her, his eyes dark and mournful.

"Gavin!" shouted MacLaren and Gavin immediately returned to his uncle's side. The men had huddled around the Duke of Argitaine and were speaking in low, fervent voices. MacLaren gave Isabelle a hard stare.

The steward stepped forward. "This is a fortunate day for ye, Lady Tynsdale. The man who wished ye dead is now himself a corpse. 'Tis time to return to England with yer guard. I wish ye well and I advise ye not to dawdle long in Scotland, but return home by the shortest route possible."

Campbell's face returned to stone, expressionless in the gray mist. He had protected her, killed for her, and now he said nothing. He was letting her go.

"Good-bye then, my lords." Isabelle curtsied to the men. "Your Grace." She inclined her head to the bishop.

Captain Corbett motioned for his men to move

out. It was past time to go. At least Cait was going to be able to keep her lover. Campbell would have to pick between two poor choices for a bride and Isabelle would be given to another man.

"Farewell, Lady Tynsdale." Campbell stepped toward her.

"Farewell to you, Laird Campbell."

"Godspeed."

Isabelle nodded and bit back tears.

"Hold there," said MacLaren. "The lady and her guard know too much. She should no' be allowed to return and give the news to her king o' this meeting wi' Argitaine."

Isabelle glared at MacLaren, then at Campbell. Would he dare to make her a captive again? Her anger wilted the moment she looked into his eyes. Campbell's expressionless mask cracked, revealing raw hope. He wanted her.

Though others stood around, Campbell was the only one she saw. If they were speaking, she heard nothing. Wind played with her hair, clearing the mist so the castle was once again in sight. It had never been far away.

Isabelle. Campbell spoke her name without saying a word. *Isabelle.*

With a flash of insight, Isabelle realized something that changed everything. *I'm not married.* A smile crept over her face. *I'm not married.* She mouthed the words to Campbell. His eyes flashed with sudden comprehension.

"MacLaren is right," said Campbell. "Lady Tynsdale canna be allowed to return to warn King Edward. Alnsworth, the fortress she inherited, is too vital to the success of this mission. It must be taken."

Isabelle's guards clustered around her and stood at the ready. "I will not let you hold the Lady Tynsdale prisoner," said Captain Corbett.

"Nor will I," added Isabelle.

"Then I will marry the Lady Tynsdale," stated Campbell with a look of satisfaction that even his disciplined control couldn't remove from his face.

Isabelle's heart leapt and happy tingles flashed through her. "I accept your offer, Laird Campbell."

"Nay," interjected Douglas. "David is betrothed to my daughter."

"He is not formally betrothed and you know it. He will wed my granddaughter," said the steward.

"I will do neither." Campbell's voice rang with authority. "Ye are both my allies, my friends, and my kin. Let us keep it that way. I will wed the English countess and hold Alnsworth for yer invasion."

Douglas scowled. Stewart looked regally displeased.

"You will hold Alnsworth against the English?" asked Douglas.

"Aye," said Campbell.

"We can use Alnsworth to push forward into England?" asked Stewart.

"Aye," said Campbell.

Douglas and Stewart seemed appeased, or perhaps the amount of gold offered by the Duke of Argitaine was enough to make them forget old rivalries in the pursuit of new wealth. Isabelle smiled at the men. The Scots were a practical sort.

"Captain Corbett, I give ye this choice," said Campbell. "Swear allegiance to me and continue to serve your lady or—"

"Please, Captain Corbett," interrupted Isabelle. She did not wish to hear the alternative. "Please stay with me and swear allegiance to Campbell. You have served me with honor and I would not have you harmed for coming all this way to rescue me."

Corbett nodded. "Thank you, m'lady. I would be pleased to serve you and your new lord. My men also. My mother was a Scot. Alnsworth has changed masters often, and many of us who live there have mixed blood. You will need to take it back from Simon's men, and I would dearly love to help you do so."

"Come, let us retire to Innis Chonnel," said Campbell, a smile still on his face. "We can discuss our plans in further detail and I can begin plans for the wedding. Bishop, would ye do the honors for us?"

"I need to be back to Glasgow soon."

"Then we will wed tonight."

A chill went down Isabelle's back at the announcement. People started to move down the shore to the location of the ferry back to Innis Chonnel. Isabelle was vaguely aware that Campbell's brothers were clapping him on the shoulders as they left. She was reasonably certain Cait tearfully said something kind before she also made her way to the ferry on Andrew's arm. Isabelle only had eyes for Campbell.

"Isabelle." Campbell's voice broke with emotion. He held out his arms and Isabelle ran to him. "I ne'er thought ye could be mine. All this time I've prayed for guidance in marriage and all I saw was ye. I thought ye were a distraction, but nay, ye are God's answered prayer."

Happy tears streamed down her face. She was home.

Forty-One

THE BREEZE OFF OF LOCH AWE PLAYED WITH ISABELLE'S hair and swirled her gown. The sun broke through the mist and sparkled off the green-blue water. David Campbell held her tight. Everything was right with the world.

Pulling back with a smile, David wrapped his arm around her waist and they walked slowly to the dock. The birds chirped happily, the air was fresh and… actually it smelled of fish, but never mind that, it was still lovely. Isabelle smiled and closed her eyes, breathing in the romance of it all. Her problems were solved, the crisis had passed, all was well.

She opened her eyes to the leering grins of David's brothers. Dain raised one eyebrow at her, Hamish smirked, and Gill and Finn grinned maliciously.

"Damn, but I may have to kill them." David released Isabelle and stormed off to his brothers with the same scowl he had given his enemies.

❧

Isabelle hovered in the doorway of the chapel. She had

been there before, but never alone. Campbell was busy preparing for the wedding. The Campbell ladies had taken her measurements and promised to alter a gown to make her look stunning, then shooed her out the door. Isabelle, the bride, found herself with nothing to do but wait for a few hours until the ceremony.

Isabelle leaned her head against the smooth, oak door frame. Campbell certainly was not delaying their nuptials. She, too, wished to be wed at once before anything could disrupt their plans. She stepped forward with hesitation. The chapel was empty, but she still feared someone would ask her what business she had here. She wasn't sure why she had come, but still, she walked forward to the altar and sat in the first pew.

Colored shafts of light shone through the finished stained-glass window above the altar. It was a beautiful sight, but not why she came. She had not been one to pray, she had not believed it would do her any good. But now... now she wasn't so sure what she believed. She had prayed for help and had received it. Was it divine intervention, or just dumb luck going her way for once?

Isabelle sighed and leaned her head back against the pew. She no longer knew what was true, but she felt more at peace with this lack of knowledge than she ever did when she was certain of her lack of faith. But would that be enough? Could God accept her humble prayers since she had so little faith?

Isabelle looked up at the stained glass window. It depicted the parable of the lost sheep and showed a shepherd reaching over some rocks to find a little lost lamb. A lost sheep. A chill ran up her spine. The good shepherd searching for his lost lamb.

"Thank you," she prayed. "Thank you."

Isabelle smiled and stood, crossing herself before the altar. Colored shafts of light shown on her through the stained glass and she believed. She believed the Good Shepherd had found her. Mother Enid was right. Isabelle had changed. The hurt of losing her family was still there, but the bitterness was gone. It was time to become part of a new family… if they would ever accept an Englishwoman as Lady Campbell.

Isabelle turned and walked to the door. Mairi stood in the doorway, frowning.

"So here ye are, we've been looking for ye." Mairi crossed her arms in front of her. "We need to get ye fitted, go on wi' ye." Mairi inclined her head for Isabelle to leave, but Isabelle paused by the door.

"Mairi, I wish you to understand that I would not presume to take your place here at Innis Chonnel." Isabelle wished to make peace with Mairi. She would have a difficult life in the castle if Mairi took a disliking to her.

"Ye will take yer place as chatelaine as is proper for ye to do."

"Certainly, I will fulfill my role to the best of my ability. It's only that I understand you wished David to wed Lady Eileen and I would hope we could still work together."

Mairi put her hand on Isabelle's arm. "Ye ken I wished Eileen to be mistress here?" Mairi burst into uncharacteristic laughter. "Nay, dinna worrit yerself on that account. I was resigned to the marriage when

I thought we had no other choice, but I am quite happy to be given an alternative. In truth, I come to the chapel to give my thanks and ask forgiveness for something I said to Lady Eileen."

"What did you say?"

Mairi grinned, her eyes sparkling. "I had the immeasurable joy of telling Eileen exactly what I thought o' her. The look on her face is something I will cherish forever." Mairi hugged Isabelle lightly and kissed both cheeks. "Welcome to the family, Isabelle. Now stop dawdling and get to the fitting."

True to his word, Isabelle and David Campbell were married that afternoon. It was everything Isabelle wanted, namely David as groom. Later she would not be able to recall the color of her gown or if she held flowers, all she knew was she was marrying David Campbell. Even Eileen's ferocious glare appeared, if not cheerful, at least humorous. Isabelle smiled at her from her seat of honor beside David at the feast.

"We have a problem." David Campbell eyed his grinning brothers with a wary glance.

"I am not sure I understand your concern. What do you fear your brothers are going to do?" Isabelle asked, taking another helping of roast pork. The cook had no more than five hours to prepare for the wedding feast but he had acquitted himself well. She savored the flavors.

"Are ye familiar wi' the customs for the bride and groom on their wedding night?"

Isabelle paused a moment to give the question some thought. She had lived isolated for many years with precious few weddings, but hazy recollections slowly returned.

"Is that when they strip you—"

"Aye."

"And then they make you—"

"Aye. And ye can be sure they will make us do every humiliating custom and make up a few o' their own."

"Your brothers are not so bad, once you get accustomed to them. How do you know they will do that?"

"Because I did it to Dain when he was wed. 'Tis a grudge match now."

"That was a mite shortsighted of you."

"Yer wisdom astounds me."

"Sarcasm will hardly help your cause. I suppose you wish me to fix this for you? Very well, enjoy your meal, I will be back shortly." Isabelle wiped her mouth and stood from the table. David's brothers indeed took notice, and she could feel their eyes upon her, plotting and devious.

"Where are ye going?" hissed David.

"To defend the honor and dignity of my person."

Isabelle strolled around the great hall, speaking to a few people, happy and laughing. David wished to go to her, but dared not stand lest his brothers take it to mean he had finished his meal and decided to march them up to his bedchamber.

Presently, Isabelle returned with a knowing smile.

"Ye've done something," Campbell whispered to Isabelle from the side of his mouth.

Isabelle nodded and smiled.

"Some daft thing, no doubt." Campbell put his arm around her shoulders. "I am glad ye are on my side."

Sir Dragonet, the former minstrel, stood from his place at the high table next to the Duke of Argitaine. "I would be glad to play for the happy couple and wish them many prosperous years to come." The French knight walked around the tables to the center of the hall with his lyre.

"Nay, 'tis right for her kinsman to entertain the bride first." Captain Corbett and Isabelle's guards stood and also strode to the center.

"I'm sure you are a very entertaining diversion, but we are in the presence of his grace, the duke. He prefers more accomplished talents." The minstrel's voice rang through the hall and people quieted to hear the growing confrontation in the middle of the room.

"'Tis so like the French to arrive unannounced, uninvited, and expect preferential treatment. Well, not tonight, Frenchie."

The minstrel knight laid his lyre on the table behind him, out of harm's way. "You insult me! I demand satisfaction."

"I'm right here, if you are man enough." Isabelle's guard stood with five of his mates, giving him an unfair advantage, or so it must have seemed to the French soldiers accompanying Argitaine who now stood and jumped over tables to join the fray. The minstrel knight ran forward, throwing the first punch and was soon swallowed up in a sea of bodies. The French joined in, followed by the Scots who picked their own sides. David's brothers, not ones to avoid a fight, jumped from their table and joined in the chaos.

"Come now," whispered Isabelle to David.

"What? What is happening here?"

"A diversion, make haste."

Isabelle and David slipped from the hall and ran up the circular stairs toward his chamber.

"Merciful heavens, ye arranged a brawl so we could escape?"

"I did not hear any better ideas from your quarter," retorted Isabelle.

"I'm no' angry. I'm impressed." They reached David's room and dashed in, closing the door behind them. David caught Isabelle around the waist and drew her close. "Ye're a devious wench, but ye're mine."

"How long before they note we are gone?"

"Soon, I warrant. I've trained my brothers no' to start fights, but they ken how to end one."

"We must go somewhere they won't find us."

"My chamber is the first place they'll look."

"Yes, yes, I know that much. Where can we hide that they won't find us?"

"I'm certain ye'll think o' something. Ye always do." David's eyes danced. "Only not a pickle barrel."

Isabelle glared at her new husband. "Pray tell, when are you going to let me forget that?"

"Ne'er." David tried unsuccessfully to squelch a grin. "When we reach the end o' our days, I will lie on my deathbed and gently take yer hand and whisper, *pickle barrel.*"

"Your deathbed may be sooner than you realize." Isabelle drummed her fingers on his shoulder, a slow, malicious smile creeping across her face. "I know just the place we can go. A place they will never find us."

~~~

"I apologize most humbly and sincerely. I regret my words and anything else that may have caused ye pain or embarrassment."

"Too late for that now," said Isabelle, dragging her husband forward with one hand, holding some blankets with the other.

"I beg your pardon a thousand times over. I swear I'll never mention pickles ever again, or even eat a pickle. Pickles will be banished from my domain. Anyone found wi' a pickle will be flogged. Please, can we go back now?"

"You are not considering the consequences. Would you rather go here or face your brothers?"

"Brothers. Most definitely I choose my brothers. They at least, winna kill me."

"I am not going to kill you." Isabelle tugged him up one more step.

"So ye say, and yet ye keep pulling me higher."

"We are almost there."

"Nay, no' one more step. Ye ken how I feel about heights."

Isabelle stopped a few steps away from the top of the tower. "Yes, and so do your brothers. They will never search for you here."

"That's because they know I'd rather die than go up here."

"Would you rather they find me and strip me—"

"Come on then, up ye go." David stomped past her and pulled her up to the top of the tower. The waxing moon was nearly full, and the sky twinkled with stars. Atop the highest tower, they could see all around, the black water of the loch, the torches in the courtyard below, small and flickering like a mirror of the stars.

David swayed and fell to his knees, one hand on his head, the other on the stone floor.

"Swooning for me, my love?" asked Isabelle, blinking three times.

"Aye, I'm fainting for ye, I am." David closed his eyes and lay down on his back. "I must be a fool in love wi' ye to come up here."

Isabelle said nothing. The breeze whipped her hair around her face. She laid out the blankets, making a cozy nest.

"Why are ye so quiet?" asked David.

"Is that wrong?"

"Nay, but for ye 'tis a wee bit peculiar." David propped himself up on his elbow. "Did I say something to upset ye?"

"I still do not know your feelings for me."

"I should think they were readily obvious," said David with a smile.

"Not to me."

David took her hand in his. "I love you. It is what I said that night in the mist, and what I declare to ye now that I have the right to speak the words."

"Truly?" Isabelle's voice was small, she focused on spreading out the blankets before sitting on them.

"Truly. I love ye, Isabelle. Now and forever."

Isabelle met his gaze, her eyes wet with tears. "I love you too."

"There now, no need to cry." David sat up and slid over to sit with her on the blankets. He wrapped her in his arms and smoothed her hair with his hand. "Ye are what I've been wanting all my life. Ye are the wife I thought I would never have. I am so blessed to have ye. By the saints…" David released her and lay back down, his hand over his eyes.

"What is wrong?"

"I can see over the wall when I sit up. Please let us go back down," David's voice was tight.

Isabelle lay next to him and put her hand on his chest. His heart pounded and he had broken into a sweat. "Do not fear, it will be all right."

"That's what a man is supposed to say to his wife on their wedding night," complained David. "Are ye nervous at all?"

"Should I be?"

"Nay."

"Then I'm not." Isabelle rested her head on his shoulder, keeping her hand on his chest.

"I wish it was that easy for me."

Isabelle unpinned the broach that held David's plaid to his shoulder and slowly unwrapped it. She paused a minute at his belt, then unbuckled it.

"What are ye doing, lass?"

"When my legs were paining me, you distracted me until I felt better. I thought I would do the same for you." She pulled up his linen shirt and slipped her hand under to feel his muscular chest. "Is this helping?"

"A-aye. Dinna stop."

Isabelle ran her hand over his chest and down to his taut stomach. Tension was building inside her and buzzed in her ears. She let her hand travel lower. David inhaled sharply. Her hand went lower still, until her heart was beating as wildly as his. Tentatively at first, then bolder and more daring, Isabelle answered the age-old question of what Highlanders wear under their kilts.

David groaned, long and slow. With a growl, he sat up and tugged at the ties holding on her gown. In a quick movement, he pulled her gown and chemise up over her head, the sound of ripping cloth an indication of his haste. David removed the remainder of the plaid from around him and spread it over them. He rolled onto his side taking Isabelle in his arms. He held her close, and Isabelle pressed her face into the softness of his neck. He smelled of wood smoke and wine and sweat. Their legs intertwined.

David slowly caressed up her back, and threaded his fingers into her hair at the nape of her neck. He snuggled down until his lips claimed hers. He moved with slow, purposeful movements, deepening the kiss. Isabelle held on and pressed him tighter, wanting more.

The buzzing in her ears grew louder and her whole body hummed along with it. Vibrations coursed through her, tingling her skin, curling her toes. A thrumming tension was building deep inside her. She ran her hand up and down his back, pressing him to her, rolling him on top of her. She needed him closer. She needed him. Husband and wife, joined forever.

He responded with slow determination, ignoring her urgency, caressing her body with long, smooth strokes. Isabelle's head fell back and she grabbed him tighter, he was driving her mad. Cruel man. The humming became a throbbing, a tension coiling within her, demanding release. She feared she might be torn asunder by the force of what was building inside her. She cared not, she wanted more.

Isabelle arched upward with her hips, and this time David's response was not measured. He growled low and hungry and quickened his pace and power. David's muscles flexed and rippled under her fingers, his skin slick with sweat. The throbbing became pounding, tense, reaching, stretching, until shock waves radiated through her and she shattered into slivers of light. Weightless and floating, she was one with the stars. She was in heaven... until her husband collapsed on top of her.

"David... can't breathe," gasped Isabelle.

"Och, sorry, lass." David rolled off her and wrapped his arm around her, pulling her to him. "I apologize to ye. I so much wanted to make this good for ye... different than, well, but I lost control. I've ne'er wanted anything the way I wanted ye. Next time I'll try harder not to let my base nature get the best o' me."

"David Campbell, you take that back or I'll never let you in my bed again!"

David blinked and stared at her. "So ye were no' displeased?"

"Foolish man, ye rarely get anything right... except that."

"Well... well then." David closed his eyes, a happy smile on his lips.

"You are mine. Now and forever," said Isabelle.

"Ye keep stealing my lines," complained David, without opening his eyes.

Isabelle smiled a warm, sleepy grin. "I beg your pardon, sir. Do continue."

"Ye are mine. Now and e'er."

"You are right. I like it even better when you say it." Isabelle snuggled into her husband, laying her head on his chest. She closed her eyes, unable to hold them open.

"Aye, I'm *right*. Now ye're sounding like a proper wife." David braced himself for her retort, but Isabelle was already asleep. "My wife," he murmured and breathed deep.

&

Isabelle jerked awake to the loudest howl she had ever heard.

"Arrrgghhh!"

What was that? Isabelle sat up. Before her was an unexpected sight. David Campbell stood stark naked in the middle of the tower. His eyes bulged from his head, his face was frozen in fear. He started screaming again.

"Hush!" Isabelle stood, but realizing she was in much the same attire as he, dropped back down to grab a blanket. "Hush now, you're fine. You'll be waking the dead now."

"W-what. Why am I here?" Campbell started howling again.

"Oh hush now!" Isabelle just got his plaid around him when his brothers rushed up the stairs and burst onto the tower. "Help me get him down."

"Why is he up here?" asked Dain, his mouth open wide.

"We were desirous of our privacy; could you help him down?"

"I canna believe ye got him up here," said Gill.

"Truly amazing," said Finn.

His brothers surrounded him, and gradually edged him down the tower stairs and into his chamber. David spent much of the journey with his hands over his eyes.

"Thank you for your assistance," Isabelle told his brothers as they moved to leave.

"How did ye do it, m'lady? How did ye get him on the tower?" asked Hamish.

"As I said, we wished for our privacy."

"He must feel for ye something fierce to go up to the tower." Dain shook his head. The brothers stood staring at her.

Isabelle felt herself blush under the scrutiny of David's brothers, becoming painfully conscious that she wore nothing under the blanket wrapped around her.

"I'm glad ye decided to be on our side, m'lady." Dain bowed low.

"M'lady." Gill and Finn bowed as one. Hamish too, paying his respect.

Isabelle smiled. They had accepted her. Life was good.

Epilogue

Alnsworth Castle
Two months later…

"WELL," SAID ISABELLE. "'TIS A SHAME, TO BE SURE."

"What's that, my love?" asked Campbell, reclining near the hearth, his feet propped up on a stool by the dancing flames.

"I've been banished from England." Isabelle stared at the parchment as if to make the words change their meaning.

"Good news to ye! I always knew ye was a Scot."

"I am in earnest, the king has taken a severe dislike to me and this marriage."

"Your once and former king does'na dislike ye, 'tis me he despises, which is only fair since I return his regard in full."

"But I find it very likely that he will mount an attack against us, to win Alnsworth back to the English crown."

"Aye, he may at that. But soon he will be fighting on many fronts when the Scots attack in the north and the French continue to harass him from the south. He may have better things to do wi' his troops, but if he comes, the harvest is in. We are ready."

It had been one month since Campbell and a small force had taken Alnsworth. Despite the loss of Simon, Alnsworth Castle was well-defended. It would have been a long siege had Isabelle not shown them the secret entrance. It was over in less than a few hours with very little effort or bloodshed. Campbell stretched back in his chair. His duty now was to maintain the keep and see to his wife. It was important that she bring a child soon, so as to seal their marriage. He was a man devoted to his duty.

"There is another message from the courier, this one from Cait."

"How much does she want?" Though Campbell had insisted that Cait and Andrew stay at Innis Chonnel where his clan could keep an eye on them, Cait was in frequent communication with Alys regarding the state of the McNab clan and had fully embraced her status in that clan, taking their cause as her own.

"Cait is doing well. She writes that Andrew is training with your brothers and he plans to join the French in their war against the English. Many other clans are joining in their cause. Swayed by French coin, I warrant."

Campbell gave her a lopsided grin. "The Scots have ne'er needed much excuse to go to war wi' the English."

Isabelle shrugged, a habit she had picked up from Campbell. "True enough."

"What does Cait want now?"

"Are you not concerned with her welfare? What makes you think she only writes to ask for something?"

"Isabelle, how much is it this time?"

Isabelle scowled. "Thirty chickens and forty head sheep."

"Thirty chickens! Forty sheep! Is she daft? I dinna ken what's possessed the lass."

Isabelle smiled, knowing Campbell would loudly deny and bemoan the request, and then quietly comply with much of what Cait asked and send the goods to help the McNabs. "You're a good man, David Campbell."

David paused in midcomplaint and took a deep breath. He rose and walked to Isabelle, taking her hand. "'Tis nice o' ye to finally notice the truth o' it. Time for bed, my love."

Isabelle yawned.

"Hardly the response I was hoping for," Campbell said dryly.

"I beg your pardon, I do not know why I am so tired. I am sleepy all the time."

"Tired or not," Campbell said with a grin, "'tis our duty to get ye breeding. And I am no' a man who shirks his responsibilities."

"Ah, if that's all you want, you can let me rest. Your task is completed."

Campbell raised an eyebrow. "I dinna ken."

Isabelle smiled at his befuddled face and took both his hands in hers. "You have completed your responsibilities to me. I am with child."

Campbell's face broke into a look of wonder. "Truly? We are going to have a wee bairn?"

"I'm not sure about a 'bairn,' but I hope to give you a baby."

"Isabelle!" Campbell grabbed her and twirled her

around, laughing. "Och, nay, I forget myself." He put her back down awkwardly and held her gently. "I love ye so, my Isabelle."

"I love you too, David." Isabelle rested her head against his shoulder, feeling his warmth.

"I am afraid I lied to ye," said Campbell.

Isabelle jerked her head up. "About what?"

"I dinna bed ye just to get ye wi' child."

Isabelle lay her head back down. "Oh, that."

"I'm sorry to say I enjoyed every minute."

"I guessed as much."

Campbell kept one arm around her waist as he guided Isabelle to the door leading to their bedchamber. "So how tired are ye?"

"Verra tired," said Isabelle in an exaggerated Scottish brogue.

"Now ye're talking like a Scot, and we are known for our endurance."

"Are you now?"

"Aye, and our pathetic begging if our wives deny us. But ye woud'na let it come to that, would ye, lass?"

"That does sound tragic."

"Verra tragic. Dinna worrit yerself, just lay back and get some sleep, I promise to wake ye for the good part."

Isabelle giggled. "You are charity itself."

Campbell leaned down and kissed her, his lips moving gently over hers. Gradually, he deepened the kiss, until she clung to him for balance, all thoughts of sleep forgotten.

"Are ye still tired, my love?"

"Nay, not at all."

David drew her closer and kicked the door closed.

Author's Note

One thing I enjoy about writing historical fiction is doing the research. *The Highlander's Heart* is set nine years after Scotland's King David was taken prisoner by England after the disastrous Battle of Neville's Cross. After years of captivity, King David was ready to make a deal to secure his release, even if it meant naming the English monarch as heir to the Scottish throne. Not surprisingly, the nobles of Scotland did not support such a plan.

On the eve of a settlement, France entered the picture with a tempting offer. If you have now read *The Highlander's Heart*, you perhaps thought I let my imagination run wild by placing French troops in Scotland—but it is all true! The French were currently at war with England (in what was later known as the Hundred Years' War), and had no interest in seeing peace on the British Isles. So a legion of French knights sailed off to Scotland and offered 40,000 moutons of gold if Scotland would agree to go to war with England.

The Scots accepted their offer, and in 1355 Scot

and French forces invaded northern England. The result was later known as the Burnt Candlemas. I'll give you a hint—it did not go so well for the Scots. Find out more about this war in my next book, *True Highland Spirit*, where we discover if feisty Morrigan McNab can ever find true love. Happy reading!

Read on for a preview
of Amanda Forester's

True Highland Spirit

Coming March 2012
From Sourcebooks Casablanca

∽

Scotland, 1355

MORRIGAN MCNAB SILENTLY DREW HER SHORT SWORD, careful to remain hidden from the road. She checked to ensure her black head-scarf was in place, concealing her nose and mouth. The target of today's villainy clopped toward them through the thick mud. Twelve men were in the mounted party, their rich robes identifying them as wealthy, above the common concerns of daily sustenance… in other words, a perfect mark.

Concealed by the tree and thick foliage, Morrigan scanned the party for weapons. It appeared to be a hunting party, since all had bows slung across their backs and long knifes at their sides. The dead boar they carried strung between two riders was also a clear sign of a hunt. Despite their alarming arsenal, most looked complacent, paying more attention to the flask they were passing around as they laughed and joked amongst themselves. One man, the one carrying a metal-tipped pike, scanned the woods around him as if he sensed danger.

Morrigan glanced at her brother Archie, only his

eyes visible over the mask he wore. He pointed to her then to the man with the pike. Morrigan narrowed her eyes at her brother. He always gave her the hard ones. Morrigan gave a curt nod and turned her focus back to the pikeman. He looked fit and vigilant. She preferred fat and careless. The war horse was a fine specimen too, tall and strong, trained to stand his ground in battle. It would not be easy to take him down.

The hunting party clomped closer, and a man walking behind the riders came into view. Morrigan wondered why he was left to slog through the mud behind the hunting party. Many of the horses would carry two men with ease. The walking man was dressed in a worn traveling cloak and a brightly colored tunic with a lyre strapped to his back. He must be a minstrel. Those wealthy hunters must not consider him worthy of a ride. Damn rich bastards.

Archie gave a bird call, the signal. Morrigan tensed in anticipation, coiled, ready to strike, and counted. The men jumped at twenty; she always leaped at nineteen.

Morrigan sprung onto the road and charged the man with the pike, screeching like a fey creature from hell. Archie and the men surged into the fray, the men's shouts blending with the surprised cries of the beset hunting party. The pikeman lowered his weapon toward her with a snarl, but Morrigan dropped to the ground and rolled under the nicely trained war horse, which was obliging enough not to move.

Regaining her feet on the other side of the horse, she pounded the hilt of her sword into his elbow holding the pike, now fortunately pointed the wrong direction. The man howled in pain, his black teeth showing, and swung to hit her. She anticipated the move, ducked out of the way, grabbed the pike and flipped it out of his hand. She had her sword tip stuck under the edge of his hauberk before the pike sunk into the mud. She applied just enough pressure to give him pause.

Her fellow bandits had likewise subdued the rest of the party. It was quiet for a moment, an odd silence after the explosion of sounds a moment before that had terrified both man and beast into mute submission.

"Good afternoon, my fellow travelers." Archie McNab stood before the hunting party, a scarf covering his nose and mouth. He gave a practiced bow with an added flourish. Morrigan rolled her eyes. Her brother liked to think of himself as a gentleman thief. True, he was laird of his clan, but Morrigan had little tolerance for petty niceties. They were there to rob them. What was the point of being genteel about it?

"I see ye are burdened wi' the evils o' worldly possessions. But ne'er fear, my brethren, we have come to relieve ye o' yer burdens."

Morrigan held out her free hand, hoping the man would readily hand over his pouch of coins like the other wide-eyed members of his party. He did not comply and instead nudged his horse, causing it to step sideways.

"Grab the reins," Morrigan commanded a young accomplice. The lad took up the reins of the war horse and holding the animal's head while Morrigan kept her eyes and her sword on the black-toothed man. He snarled at the lad, who balked and stepped back.

"Hold its head!" Morrigan snapped. The last thing she needed was this man making trouble.

"Now if ye fine gentlemen will make a small donation to the fund for wayward highwaymen, we shall set ye on yer way in a trifle," said Archie.

On foot, Morrigan mentally added. The warhorse Black-tooth sat upon was a fine specimen. She reckoned she would look better than he on such a fine animal. The rest of the hunting party readily handed over their money pouches and weapons easily, but not Black-tooth. He glared a silent challenge. Morrigan sighed. For once, just for the novelty of it all, she'd like things to be easy. It was not to be on this day. Not any day, truth be told.

Morrigan stabbed her mark harder but other than a scowl, he made no move to comply. She could kill the man, but Archie was firm in his orders not to kill unless necessary, and Morrigan had to acknowledge the wisdom of it. Robbing folks was one thing, murder was another. The last thing they needed was a band of Highlanders come to rid the forest of murderous thieves.

The man still refused to hand over his money bag so Morrigan grabbed the pommel of his saddle with her free hand and put her foot on his in the stirrup and hoisted herself up. It should have been a quick move. She grabbed his purse and pulled it free. Suddenly he shouted and kicked the horse. The lad dropped the reins and the horse lunged forward, throwing Morrigan off balance. One punch from Black-tooth and Morrigan fell back into the mud.

The black toothed terror charged the horse in front of him, causing the mount to spook and rear. The result was chaos, as the remaining horses broke free, urged on by the hunting party who sensed a chance to break free.

"Grab the horses, ye fools!" Morrigan jumped up shouting. "They be unarmed, get them ye bastards!"

But more than one thief, having secured the desired reward, melted back into the shrubbery rather than face the angry hunters. The hunting party broke free and galloped away down the path they had come.

"Damnation!" Morrigan yelled at her thieving brethren. "What is wrong w' ye cowardly knaves?"

"We got the coin," grumbled one man in response.

"But not the horses, ye fool! Now they can ride for their friends and come back for us. And ye," Morrigan turned on the spindly-legged lad who had dropped the leads of the warhorse she had coveted. "Ye ought to be more afeared o' me than any bastard on a horse." Morrigan strode toward the boy with the intent of teaching a lesson that would be long remembered, but her brother caught her arm.

"Let him be, he's only a lad."

"I was younger than that when I joined this game," Morrigan shot back.

"Aye," Archie leaned to whisper in her ear. "But we all canna be heartless bitches like ye." With teasing eyes he straightened and said in a louder voice. "Besides we have a guest."

Standing in the middle of the muddy road was the colorfully dressed man with a lyre slung on his back. Damn hunters had left him with a bunch of thieves. Morrigan cursed them once again along with their offspring and their poor mothers for general completeness. She was nothing if not thorough.

Despite being surrounded by thieves, the man appeared surprisingly calm, though perhaps after their pathetic display of incompetence he rightly felt he had nothing to fear.

"Allow me to introduce myself," the stranger said with a seductive French accent and an equally appealing smile. "I am Jacques, poor traveling minstrel, at your service." He gave a polished bow that put Archie's attempts at gallantry to shame. Morrigan caught her brother's eye to make sure he knew she had noted it.

"And what brings ye to be traveling with such cowardly companions that they would leave ye at the first sight of trouble?" Morrigan asked.

"The hunters I met on the road, and they invited me that I may walk behind them to their hunting lodge." Jacques gave an impish grin. "I can only assume my services are no longer required."

"Ah, then they are doubly fools, for a minstrel is a rare prize indeed," said Archie.

"You mean for me to be ransomed?"

"Nay, nay, ye are our guest. We are but humble thieves, but we shall take ye to…" Archie swallowed what he was going to say and coughed. "We shall take ye to the doorstep o' the great Laird McNab. We dare no' cross the border o' his domain for he has no tolerance for our kind, but I am assured he will welcome ye. And he can pay for yer services," said Archie McNab jingling his ill-gotten gains.

"Archie," hissed Morrigan drawing him aside. "What are ye doing? We canna bring him back to our Hall."

"Nay, we will drop him close and let him walk the

rest," whispered Archie in response. "Then we will ride ahead and wait for his arrival. We are still masked, so he canna identify us as McNabs."

"But he has certainly heard us, Brother. Do ye no' ken he will recognize our voices?"

"Nay, nay, ye worrit yerself. Think, Morrigan. When was the last time we had a minstrel?" Archie's eyes gleamed above his mask.

Morrigan shook her head. It had been a long, long time. And for good reason. What minstrel in his right mind would travel into the Highlands to sing for the poorest clan west of Edinburgh? It was a tempting opportunity, and Morrigan knew all too well the devious gleam in Archie's eyes. They would soon be hosting the clan's first minstrel in twenty years.

Archie gave some quick commands. The men, quick to see a potential reward, eagerly complied, gathering the weapons, money, and the dead boar. The minstrel appeared to be a pleasant sort of man, making no complaints and readily agreeing to the plan of taking him near the "great Laird McNab." Morrigan wondered at the shocking hubris that would lead to that bold lie. Her brother always dreamed big, and generally settled for much less.

Morrigan jumped up on her own mount. They needed to make haste before their hunting friends returned in greater numbers looking for the return of their property and a hanging for their supper amusement. Perhaps the hunters would have the minstrel play a lively tune while Morrigan and her fellow thieves danced at the end of a rope. Aye, it was most assuredly time to leave.

"Here, my friend," said Archie leading the minstrel toward Morrigan. "Allow us to give ye a ride."

"Nay," said Morrigan, easily seeing Archie's intent. "Let him ride wi' someone else."

"But ye are the lightest among us."

"Nay, Toby over there is hardly seven stone."

Archie walked quickly toward her and hissed, "Toby is a young fool. Ye take the minstrel and dinna let him get away." Archie turned back to the minstrel saying, "So pleased ye could join us."

The minstrel smiled at Morrigan. "I am causing you inconvenience? I must apologize." His voice was smooth as velvet with his polished French accent. His eyes were a shocking bright blue in contrast to his black hair, and even Morrigan had to admit he was nice to look upon.

"No inconvenience, I assure ye," Morrigan found herself saying. Maybe inviting a minstrel back with them was not such a bad idea.

She reached out her hand to help him onto the horse and he took it, swinging himself up easily with very little assistance. He positioned himself behind her, the thighs of his long legs touching hers. Suddenly Morrigan felt quite hot in her hauberk and she took a deep breath. Damn, but he smelled nice too.

Morrigan revised her opinion of the minstrel. He was trouble. Like most of Archie's plans, this was no doubt doomed to go horribly wrong.

Acknowledgments

My dream of seeing my books published would not be possible without the encouragement, motivation, and support I have received from my local RWA chapter, the Greater Seattle Romance Writers of America. You folks are simply the best! I especially wish to thank the incomparable Cherry Adair and her "Write the Damn Book Challenge," and Gerri Russell for her encouragement and insight. Many thanks to my "beta" readers, Laurie Maus and Skye Sellars, who kindly read my first drafts. Thanks to my editor, Deb Werksman, who has taught me much, and to my agent, Barbara Poelle, who always has my back. And thanks to my parents for simply being Mom and Dad. I never realized how hard you worked until I had kids of my own—being a parent is one tough job. Thank you!

About the Author

Amanda Forester holds a PhD in psychology and worked for many years in academia before discovering that writing historical romance novels was way more fun. She lives in the Pacific Northwest with her husband and two energetic children. *The Highlander's Heart* is the second novel in her Highlander series. The first, *The Highlander's Sword*, was published March of 2010, and the third in the series, *True Highland Spirit* will be released spring of 2012. You can visit her at www.amandaforester.com.